THE MINNESOTA KINGSTONS | BOOK ONE

JACK

THE MINNESOTA KINGSTONS | BOOK ONE

JACK

SUSAN MAY WARREN

Jack
The Minnesota Kingstons, Book 1

For Your glory, Lord

ONE

THIS TIME, FAILURE WASN'T AN OPTION.
According to his witness, the girl had gone missing twelve hours ago.

"Where did you last see Misty?" Jack Kingston crouched in front of the little blonde girl, age five, named Pearl, who clutched a small plastic piggy bank to her chest.

Around him, the living room had been tossed, blankets and pillows and stuffed animals cluttering the floor. Most of it due to last night's movie marathon of *Moana* and *Frozen*.

In the kitchen, the smell of bacon had woken the beast inside him, the aroma wafting through the small bungalow in a city just outside Des Moines, Iowa.

"We were outside, playing. I went to get frosted crackers that Mommy made, and when I came back, she was gone." She held out her piggy bank. "Please, Unca Jack, you have to find her."

He suppressed a smile and glanced up at her mother, Natalie, dressed in baggy sweats and a T-shirt, who held baby Amber on her hip. The four-month-old, her dark hair spiked and wispy, sucked on a passie, leaning into her mother. Natalie tried to hide a smile at Pearl's plea and raised an eyebrow.

Jack sighed. "I can't take your money, Pearl."

"It's a reward." She held it out. "Please?"

He nodded, his expression turning serious to match Pearl's. "Okay. But I have three rules." He held up his fingers.

"What?" She was so solemn he had to glance at Natalie not to smile.

"One. I don't make promises."

"You'll find her, Unca Jack. I know it."

He held up two fingers. "I don't break the law."

She rolled her eyes.

"And I work alone."

She stuck out her lower lip.

"Except this time." He winked. She grinned, then put the piggy bank on the counter.

"Okay, I'm on the hunt. Let's track Misty down. Can you give me a description?"

"Red hair. She's wearing a blue dress. One of her feet was chewed off by Snowy."

"Got it. So she's got a limp. Shouldn't have gotten far." He then scooped up the little white dog sniffing at his feet. "Snowy, I think you're a prime suspect here."

The little Havanese poodle licked his chin.

Pearl laughed.

He spotted West in the kitchen behind her, also in sweats and a T-shirt, holding a cup of coffee, shaking his head.

So maybe this overnight hadn't been a terrible idea. West and his family always managed to ground him.

And it wasn't a terrible fortification before the Big Reunion.

Darkness, fireworks, and drama awaited four hours north. But it wasn't like he could phone in his role as a groomsman at the Epic Family Wedding.

"Okay, let's try this. Does Snowy like to hide things? Bones, or slippers, or toys—"

"Yeah!" Pearl fisted her little hands, her golden curls bobbing. "She tries to bury them in the sofa!" She scampered over to the saggy green sofa and started to tear off the cushions.

He caught them, set them down, and leaned over her. Spotted a couple uneaten doggie treats, a round chew toy and . . . *wait*—"Is that my sock?" He picked up a wool sock—the one that had gone missing last night by his bed.

"Misty!" Pearl grabbed up her Barbie doll, its red hair a tuft of tangles. Indeed, the remaining foot bore the mauling of canine teeth, and now—"Snowy chewed off her arm!" She held out the mangled appendage. "Oh, she was my favorite."

Jack crouched next to her. "She can still be your favorite. Just because someone is hurt doesn't mean that you can't still love them. Maybe you love her more because she survived the Great Snowy Attack of '25."

Pearl nodded, wiped her cheek. "Okay. Thank you, Unca Jack."

Aw. He pulled her tight against him, met West's smile. See, maybe this was still what it was about—the happy endings.

He let her go, and West came in, handed him a cup of coffee. "I'm not sure she can afford the reward. I think there's nothing but a few buttons in that jar."

Jack laughed. "Let's call this one a pro bono. You can pay me in breakfast. It smells amazing."

"Bacon and eggs. We're fancy around here." West headed back into the kitchen, and Jack slid onto a counter stool at a long island in their newly remodeled home. They'd taken out the wall from the galley kitchen, added an island, opened up the dining area.

Natalie had put baby Amber down in a swing, strapped her in, and now slid onto a stool beside him.

"So, Nat, you have good news for me?"

"If you mean another gig, I'm also on the hunt." Nat shook

her head. "But I did manage to talk Sheriff Wade out of pressing charges for obstruction—"

"Seriously—if they'd listened to me, no one would have gotten hurt."

"I pointed that out. He's just grumpy. It's an election year."

"Yeah, that's why he sent SWAT in—sheesh, talk about overkill. I was already in the house, already talking the guy out—"

"Which brings me to the next point. The family is making noises about suing."

West set a plate of eggs and bacon in front of him. "More coffee?"

"Could you add some whiskey to it?"

West laughed. "Sorry. Dry house, and since when did you start drinking?"

"Haven't yet. But I'm considering . . ." He shook his head. "This is why I never got my PI license. There was no binding contract, just me, following leads—"

"That led to the police raiding a farmhouse thinking the family's daughter had been kidnapped, only to have her shot, in a coma, her kidnapper dead," West said, handing Nat a plate too.

"I still believe it was a lovers' tryst. But the cops took one look at the guy—the much older felon out on parole—and said he'd kidnapped her." Jack salted his eggs. "Although, for a while, I thought the same thing, so . . ."

Nat took the salt from him. "The sheriff had a press conference talking about the dangers of letting unlicensed, rogue reward seekers try to home in on an investigation. You made social media. Congratulations, Jack, you're famous again."

There went his appetite. "Probably a good time to leave Florida."

Nat gave him a grim nod.

He sighed, his throat tight. "Tansy's still in a coma?"

"Yeah," West said. "The family says it's medically induced, to keep the brain swelling down, but . . ." His hazel-green eyes softened. "You weren't to blame, Jack."

"You've said that before."

"I meant it before. And I mean it now."

Jack looked past him, out the window to where Aggie, his schoolie, sat on the driveway. On her last legs—or wheels, in this case. He'd heard some ticking in the engine on his way through Georgia. Maybe they both were ticking, ready for something different.

Although, Minnesota might not be the *right* different.

He looked back at West. "I've been thinking that it's time I hang this gig up. Maybe retake the bar."

West glanced at his wife, back at Jack. "Don't do that to us, bro. We live vicariously through you and your epic hunts." He stopped the swing and reached for the baby as she spat her pacifier from her mouth. "Not a lot of excitement here in Iowa."

Behind him, the dog barked, and Jack glanced over to see Pearl playing tug with him and his chew toy. Baby Amber resucked her passie, watching them with big blue eyes.

Seemed like enough excitement to him.

"Maybe what you need is a partner, though. A Watson to your Sherlock."

He shook his head. "The last thing I need is to babysit some sidekick." He glanced at Nat. "So, you hear from Austen? Is she coming to the wedding?"

"She's your sister. You have to ask *me*?"

"Please. I know you two still talk. You have that roomies-forever bond."

Nat grinned. "Fine. Yes. Last I heard, she was planning on being there. And Steinbeck too."

"Really? I thought he was on some Caribbean island."

"It wouldn't hurt for you to pick up the phone and call your siblings."

"We talk. We all Zoomed in for Christmas."

"Your poor mother."

"She's busy with the inn. And for the record, I talk to her and Dad once a week."

Nat held up a hand. "It's just that the Kingston family dinners are hard to forget."

"Times change."

She lifted a shoulder. "I guess."

The words sank in like arrows, into his soul.

"So just Doyle and Conrad home this year for Christmas?" West said.

"Not even Conrad—the Blue Ox had a game in Toronto."

A pause, and West glanced at Nat, back at Jack. "So Brontë's big event will be the first time you've all seen each other since—"

"Yes." Jack's mouth tightened.

West nodded.

"And Brontë's okay with you showing up for her big day?" This from Nat, who'd gotten up to grab Amber from the swing.

"Dad called. It wasn't optional. I'm in the wedding. And apparently she goes by Boo now."

"Right, from the TV show."

He nodded, but he could agree that the entire thing felt weird. Who knew what was going through Brontë's head? And nobody needed to know about the fist in his gut, tightening with each mile north. "It's going to be fine. I'm going home, lying low, no drama, no questions, and in five days, I'm gone." He pointed to West. "And you'd better have a gig for me."

West pointed at his wife. "She's the one with instincts."

"And the Crime Stoppers connection," Nat said. She stopped the swing and unstrapped the baby. "Mommy's going to have to scour the reward boards." She handed the baby to her husband.

"Or maybe some of those cold-case podcasts—they often have rewards for 'information leading to.' I was listening to *Penny for*

Your Thoughts on my drive up. She's still trying to find the 'masked man' in the Sarah Livingston case." He finger quoted the words *masked man*. So much drama.

That's probably what hooked him.

"I like that podcast. She's supposedly going to name her strongest suspect in this week's drop. She spent the last four months covering the Mike Grizz murder attempt last year. Think he'll be at the wedding?"

"Mike Grizz? Maybe. He's a friend of the groom." He finished his eggs. "I hope this thing isn't a circus. With all of Oaken's superstar music buddies . . ." He shook his head.

"You're really in the wedding?" Nat pulled out a bottle from the fridge, took off the top, and set it in a bottle warmer on the counter. "Wow."

"I know, right? But it's why I have to get there early. Apparently, Brontë has a bunch of events lined up for the bridal party. I might have to learn a dance."

"Please, please, get a video of that," Nat said.

"I don't dance."

"I know." She laughed. "Except—didn't you go to prom with one of Brontë's friends? I thought I remembered West telling me—"

"No. I definitely *did not*." He shook his head. "Harper Malone."

"Didn't she ask you to the dance?"

"No. She did *not*. That was a comment made by my stupid brother Doyle."

"I'll never forget the story." West was laughing.

"Please forget. It's a chapter I'd like to erase."

"Why? What was—"

"She was six years younger than me, that's what."

Nat glanced at West. "Clearly, there's a story."

"Oh, and it's good," her husband said.

"Thanks for that, West." Jack turned to Nat. "I think I need to hit the road. Thanks for breakfast."

Nat was laughing. "Don't be a coward."

West turned to Nat. "This girl, Harper, showed up at spring break, and Romeo here fell for her completely, not realizing she was—"

"Still in high school," Jack said.

"Really?" Nat's eyes widened.

"Yeah. She was eighteen, but . . ." Jack looked at Nat. "For the record, I didn't recognize her as Boo's friend. And I thought she was in college. At least twenty-one."

"Why didn't she tell you she was in high school?" Nat asked, checking the bottle. She put it back into the warmer. "What was she thinking?"

"I don't know. I should have asked, maybe. But the moment I figured it out, I realized she was Pigtails, my little sister's best friend, and it was . . . bad. So, lesson learned. She's some big magazine reporter in Nashville now, according to Brontë. Probably, hopefully, she's forgotten about me."

"Right." Nat shook her head. "Nobody forgets Big Jack."

He gave her a look.

She laughed. "Is she going to be at the wedding?"

He stilled. He hadn't thought about *that* possibility.

"Oh, she's going to be there," West said. "With your luck."

"Hey. I found my sock. My luck is still holding."

Nat walked over, took the baby from West, and handed her to Jack. "Hold a baby. You'll feel better."

Maybe. He looked at Amber, who still sucked her passie, her eyes widening. *Uh-oh.*

She opened her mouth, the passie dropped out, and she wailed. *Right.*

Nat laughed. "Okay. Not quite ready for Unca Jack." She took her back. "It's okay, sweetheart. I had the same reaction the first time I met him."

"Hey—"

Nat turned to him. "Really? You're the only law student who took cold showers and did interval training between study sessions. Not to mention the fasting."

"It's supposed to help with mental clarity."

"As his roommate, I still have PTSD from the lucky socks," West said.

"Lucky socks are a thing."

"I did like the Memory Palace trick," West said. "It helped me hold on to the black-letter law for the bar."

"See? It's all about strategy." Jack got up and grabbed his plate. "Thanks, Nat, for untangling me from the fiasco down in Gainesville."

She nodded. "Keep your head down. With luck, it'll be gone by the next news cycle."

West glanced at him. "You leave the hunt to us. Go home, connect with your family. Try not to blow up Brontë's wedding."

Jack rolled his eyes, but his soul burned a little. *Right.* "Pearl, c'mere and say goodbye to your sad Unca Jack before he faces the firing squad."

Pearl ran toward him, her arms out. He scooped her up.

"What's a firing squad?" she asked.

"Nice, Jack," Nat said, shaking her head.

He made a wry face. Then, "It's a guy named Steinbeck." He tousled her hair and grabbed his other sock from Snowy's mouth. *Seriously.* He glanced at West, Nat, baby Amber, and Pearl, now climbing onto the stool. "Thanks for the last meal, guys."

"Try not to die, Jack," West said. "That would wreck all our fun."

She could do this. She. Could. *Do this.*

All Harper had to do was stay focused and ignore *He Who Shall Not Be Remembered.*

Harper turned off the highway, toward the road that led to the town of Duck Lake, her gut tightening with each mile. Her manager's voice, on speakerphone, didn't help.

"Oaken's team will never agree. You've let your wishes do the talking here, Harper. You need to face reality. You're not going to land the exclusive on the wedding."

Maybe. Wishes—or maybe just blind hope—had always gotten her in over her head.

But not this time.

This time, she had an inside edge.

"Trust me. Boo will say yes."

Harper turned up the heat in her cute little Chevy Sonic. She should have packed better for her drive north. Hopefully her mother hadn't gotten rid of her winter clothing.

Then again, her mother made her living helping people let go of the past.

"It's not Boo Kingston I'm worried about," Clarice said. "It's her fiancé's manager, Goldie. You don't know her like I do."

Outside, the wind cast snow across ice-crusted fields and into the late-afternoon shadows. Now and again, a red silo pierced the horizon, the rumpled cornfields cordoned off by stands of oak or pine.

Serene. She'd forgotten that, maybe.

She took a sip of her hot cocoa, cooling in the paper cup from Caribou Coffee. "Listen. Boo's an old friend. We went to all twelve grades together. I'm practically family. She'll say yes and talk Oaken into it."

"It won't matter. Goldie's probably fielding all the exclusive of-fers, including *People* magazine."

"Boo is not interested in fame, believe me. The last thing she wants is for her wedding to be splashed across a national magazine—"

"Excuse me, but isn't that what you're asking of her? To get the nitty-gritty details of Brontë Kingston and Oaken Fox's fairy-tale wedding and sell it to *Inside Nashvegas* or *PopMuse*?"

Harper imagined Clarice sitting in her home in Franklin, outside Nashville, in the cute office above her three-car garage, with its vaulted ceilings and pictures of her clients—artists, photographers, and the occasional freelance writer who got in over her head.

"Yes, but . . . I'll make it . . . *authentic*. Talk about how they came together during the reality show and how she supported Oaken during the Mike Grizz case, and maybe talk to the family members."

She drew in a breath at her words. *Some* of the family members. *Please, please let Jack be off chasing a missing person . . .*

"*Let the past be a stepping stone, not a stumbling block.*" Yeah, thanks, Doctor Malone.

"Fine. I'll put out feelers and see who bites. But Goldie is still pretty angry about the tell-all piece you did on her client, that singer-actress-whatever-she-is superstar, Bliss."

"I sent Bliss the copy before I published it. Got the okay."

"She claims she never read it. That she had no idea you'd gone digging into the death of her mom, and her dad's history—"

"That's what made people love it! It was one of *PopMuse*'s best-selling issues last year. Especially after *Main Street Blues* won the Oscar for best picture."

"And that's the only reason that Bliss isn't pursuing a lawsuit. Goldie negotiated for higher residuals on the article—but we're back to our roadblock. Goldie. She's going to be a tiger for Oaken's privacy."

"I got this. Trust me. It's going to be amazing."

"It better be, because your career might be over if it isn't. You'll be writing for the *Duck Lake Gazette*."

"It's the *Duck Lake Currents.*"

"Clever."

"It's a weekly. And it's where I started. I'm sure they'd take me back."

Kidding. The last place she wanted to live was Duck Lake. Too close to the Doc and, well, memories.

"It'll give you plenty of time to write that novel you've been talking about. Maybe fiction is your gig anyway."

"I don't write fiction. I write ... *vivid nonfiction.* It's why people love my stories. I bring them into the world I'm describing." But the idea of writing fiction had lived in her head since *PopMuse* fired her from their regular staff roster six months ago. Frankly, she'd been working on a romance for years.

Just not one that could ever be published.

"Vivid nonfiction. That's one way of putting it." Clarice sighed. "I'd call it overuse of your imagination. One of these days you're going to go too far, dig too deep, and I'm not going to be able to rescue you."

"Some people just can't handle the truth."

"Funny. How about some people just don't think every truth needs to be told."

Harper braked as she hit the outskirts of Duck Lake where the road veered north, toward the lakeside homes.

Here, the forest had thickened, created a whimsical corridor of wintry pine laden with heavy snow. Banks of white piled either side of the road, and as she drove along the shoreline, the scantily clad trees revealed stately homes, most of them standing on the foundations of former cabins and cottages, the getaways of the wealthy from Minneapolis, only an hour to the east.

"Listen," Clarice said now, maybe realizing defeat. "I know that if anyone can do this, it's you. You have good instincts, you're intuitive, and I've never met anyone more tenacious. If you want something, you get it."

Well, not always . . .

"Just don't get sued."

"Thanks for that. But yes, we don't need any high drama. Boo's had enough scandal. This will be a quiet, poignant piece."

"Perfect. By the way, is your friend Penelope going to be there? After the ratings on her murder podcast about the attempt on Mike Grizz's life, I wouldn't mind talking to her—"

"I promise to give her your info."

"I love *Penny for Your Thoughts.* Do you think she's going to solve the latest case?"

Harper caught a view of 458 Whispering Pines Drive, the 1960s cottage painted a fresh yellow, probably her mother's last-summer project. Smoke curled from the stone chimney along the backside of the house.

Beyond the house, the lake stretched out in a pristine, beautiful blanket of white. Of course, near the Duck Lake landing in the distance, the shapes of icehouses created a small city.

But here, near the northern end of the lake, it was all lazy forest, towering birch creaking in the wind, fires in the hearth, and the sense of escape.

If, she supposed, one didn't look up shore at the King's Inn.

Escape might be overstated.

"I'm a listener, just like you," Harper said as she turned into the long drive. "Penny keeps her investigations pretty close. But she's always wanted to work a cold case, so I think she's really loving it. And maybe finding closure after Bryce's death."

"So sad. How's her sister?"

"I don't know. Listen, watch for my email."

"Have fun dancing at the wedding."

"Oh, I hope not. I don't dance."

"Everybody dances, Harper."

"Not this girl." She'd learned *that* lesson.

Clarice clicked off, laughing.

Harper sat in the cleared driveway in front of the cottage, next to her mother's green Subaru, her gaze on the cleared path to the house, then on the trail into the forest, still an opening in the trees, between the King's Inn and the 458 cottage.

She played with her bracelet, running the charm over the chain. Okay. She could do this.

Harper turned off the car, then wrapped her scarf around her neck, grabbed her gloves, and got out.

The wind sheared off the lake and stole her breath, pinched her nose. Who got married in Minnesota in January? *Crazy.*

But Boo always did like to push the edge. And maybe, with Oaken's recording and touring schedule, this was the only time they could squeeze in the nuptials.

Harper took a breath, then tromped to the lavender entry door.

Funny that her mother hadn't repainted it when she'd made over the house. She knocked, then realized that might be silly and pushed open the door. "Mom? It's me!"

"Up here, Bee!"

She walked into the small entryway, where her mother's thick orange puffer jacket hung from a hook, along with a bulky knitted scarf and her white SORELs. Shucking off her jacket, Harper hung hers next to it, slid off her UGGs, then padded into the main room.

Stopped. *Holy cats*—"You gutted the place. Again."

Instead of a small kitchen with a pass-through to the main area stood a gray granite island and, along the wall, a contrasting new black granite counter with white cabinets. The wood flooring— maybe original, but sanded and re-stained—stretched out to cover the entire room, with the stone fireplace cleaned and rechinked. Orange leather furniture, a number of brightly patterned floor rugs, all overlapping, and new contemporary art hung gallery style on the walls.

Not that Harper really expected her father's oils to be hanging there, but the massive Picasso-style watercolor moose in turquoise and orange seemed a unique choice.

The stairs leading to the second-floor bedrooms had been opened up, with a hand-turned wood railing and fresh black risers.

"You've been holding out on me, Mom. When you said remodel, I thought paint and new carpet. Who knew you were such a DIYer?"

She came up the stairs, expecting to find Dr. Phillipa Malone in her expansive bedroom, maybe sitting at her writing desk or in a lounge chair reading one of the books from the wall-length shelf that held her expansive library on psychology and other mental-health-related topics.

Nope. The master bedroom was empty, and recently redone too. No carpet save the plush white rug, a new king-sized bed, and a small secretary, with a roll top and an antique chair.

"Where are your books?" Harper just stood in the room, wordless.

"I got a Kindle."

The voice came from behind her, and she turned, found her mother, her messy shoulder-length blonde hair tied back, wearing a pair of—"Are those my track pants from high school?"

Her mother looked down at the paint-stained orange-and-green pants. "They make great paint pants. And I found this shirt in your throwaway pile." She picked at the white T-shirt—Duck Lake Storm, regional track champions—now dotted with light-blue paint.

"That wasn't in my throwaway pile."

Her mother made an O with her mouth. "Sorry."

Harper held up a hand. *Let go and grow.* She could almost read the mantra in her mother's hazel eyes. "It's fine. But what—wait . . ." She stepped past her, into *her* room.

Not her room.

No furniture. No pink carpet. The once stenciled walls, some of them inscribed with her poetry quotes, repainted in a gray-blue. "Where's my desk?"

"Oh—I'm having it stripped and restained."

She turned. "Mom. That was Dad's desk. I wrote . . . I mean . . ." She took a breath. "I was hoping to give it to my daughter someday."

Her mother had put down the painting rag and now came over to her. "Oh, darling. Of course. If you get married and have a daughter, you can definitely have it." She reached in for a quick hug.

"But . . ." *Aw, never mind.*

Her mother let her go, smiled at her. "It's so nice that you stopped by on your way to the inn. What time do the festivities start?"

It took a second for the words to click in. *Wait*—"Mom. I'm staying *here.*"

Again, the O. "But I'm having the floors sanded and stained this week. I need to get the painting done first, and the new furniture won't be here for at least a month." She made a face. "I suppose you could sleep on the sofa, but I'm taking clients here now, so . . ."

Harper forced a smile. "Okay. I get it. I . . ."

"Can't you ask Emily if you can stay with them? I mean, you practically lived with them, especially in high school."

Harper glanced at the inn, visible, of course, from her window, along with the trail. *Shoot.* "Yeah, I'll drive over and ask."

"It is very nice to see you." Her mother took her hand. "I'll look at my calendar—I'm sure I can rearrange and we can find a time for lunch. Oh, wait . . . I have that conference this weekend." She forced a smile and gave Harper's hand a squeeze. "I'll text you."

Right. "Okay, so . . . I'll pop down to the Kingstons' and see if they have a room . . ."

Her mother let her hand go. "Say hi to Grover and Emily for me. And of course, Brontë. I can't believe she's marrying a celebrity."

"She goes by Boo now, and she is a celebrity herself, Mom."

Her mother had gone back to the paint trough, grabbing some rubber gloves. "Oh, please. She's a reality television persona. That's vastly different than using your talents, like Oaken Fox. And even he only got there because of his dead sister's reputation."

Oh boy. "Okay, Mom. Yes, text me." She walked over, leaned in, gave her mother a whisper of a kiss, then managed a smile and escaped.

Or maybe . . . *escape* wasn't the right word.

She could do this.

She just had to stop wishing for happy endings.

TWO

MAYBE FATE HAD DECIDED TO WARN HIM OFF, because fifty miles out of Duck Lake and a hundred miles over the Iowa border, steam poured through the hood of good old Aggie, like her entire engine might be on fire.

The white smoke curled out in the brisk, pale-blue sky. It dissipated quickly, the frigid air gobbling it into the ether.

Just another sign that this trip home was a no good, very bad idea.

Jack grabbed a wool hat and his gloves as he opened the door and climbed out onto the shoulder.

Not a soul in sight on this lonely stretch of country road. The sun cast a few shadows over the scarred and rumpled cornfields, blanketed with a fresh layer of white after an early-January blizzard.

Maybe this was punishment for missing Christmas. And the Christmas before. In fact, he had a lot of making up to do.

He blew out a breath as his feet crunched against the shoulder snow and ice. He reached in to unlatch the hood and then wrenched it up.

The radiator cap bubbled, hot and angry, the steam pouring forth like Vesuvius.

He reached out a gloved hand to unscrew the top, then yanked it back, the heat seeping through the leather.

Perfect.

He grabbed his hat for padding, added it to his grip, and managed to pry off the top.

Water spurted out like a geyser. He stepped back, away from the steam and boil.

Way to go, Jack. This was what happened when a guy lived in Florida and fed his radiator hose with water instead of coolant.

So much for his brilliant idea to stop over at West and Nat's place. Apparently, the frigid Iowa temps had done a doozy on his hose.

Which meant he'd either have to hitch the rest of the way and ask for a tow or . . .

Well, he could wait until his engine cooled and turn around, head south.

They probably wouldn't even miss him at tonight's prewedding soiree.

Aw. Then his father would really murder him.

No, he'd wait for the boil to die, fill 'er up, and limp the rest of the way to Duck Lake.

Twenty minutes later, after scrolling through the Crime Stoppers board on his phone, he found a water bottle and went back out to his now cold engine. The water had stopped bubbling, the smoke dissipated.

Here went nothing. He poured the water into his radiator and capped it.

Got back into his schoolie. "C'mon, Aggie, give me some love." Then he closed his eyes and started up the bus. It rumbled to life, the 1995 GMC Vandura 3500HD shaking a little, like she might be tired. Exhausted, actually.

Him too. "You can do it, sweetheart. Just fifty more miles."

He pulled out, watched the heat, and kept it under sixty as the sun sank into the snowy hills, turning the blanket of snow to fire. The landscape merged into forest as he drove through river country, the maple and oak stripped, brightened with snow, the tall paper birch white against the green fir.

Aggie coughed and he eased up even as he started to roll into the outskirts of Duck Lake. The facelift after the great tornado of '18 had revitalized the town. New storefronts, updated to look like a Hallmark movie scape, with tall lampposts flanking Main Street like the Gates of Argonath. (Maybe he'd watched the *Lord of the Rings* trilogy too much as a child). Still, the town seemed buzzing, even at the height of January, and maybe Brontë and Oaken's wedding had brought in a few gawkers.

He braked for a couple of women who ran out between cars, wearing UGGS and pom-pom hats and holding pink bags from, if he could read right, Elle's Secret Garden Boutique.

So much for the Ben Franklin.

He spotted other newer joints—a gift shop called Maple Treasures, and Frost and Feather Outdoor Gear, the Tipsy Canoe—a craft brewery—as well as an upscale restaurant called the Paddle House. At least the Lumberjack's Table still sat at the end of the street, but losing the attached bowling alley had upscaled the establishment—no more neon lights in the windows.

Jack hardly recognized the place, really.

A Sip and Paint place, Serenity Spa, and a coffee shop caught his eye—Echoes Vinyl Café.

Okay, maybe it wasn't a terrible overhaul. Thankfully, the King's Inn hadn't been hit by the tornado. He couldn't wait to climb into his old bed, listen to the wind off the lake, smell his mother's cinnamon rolls.

Apparently, he was eighteen again.

No. If he were eighteen, that would make Harper Malone

twelve, and that was just Not. Right. At best, maybe he could be twenty-four again, but even then . . .

Please, let her not be at the wedding.

Aggie crept all the way to the parking lot of the Duck Lake Market, two blocks off Main, then settled there as if she might be an old dog, finding its final resting place.

He got out to a pillow of steam and didn't bother opening the hood. Instead, he headed inside the market, looking for the manager.

A woman sat at the desk.

Huh. He walked to the counter. The woman, in her midtwenties, sat on a stool, wore a blue smock, her name—Anna—pinned to her shirt. "I need to speak to the manager."

"He's out."

"I just need to ask if I can leave my bus here while I get a tow." She shrugged.

Great. He grabbed one of the nearby community cards—this one for a late-night transportation for parties, weddings, etc.—and wrote his name and number on the back. Held it out to Anna.

She looked at it. Then picked up a card and handed it to him. "Call him yourself."

Oh. He pocketed his card and took hers. "Gordo Martin. Thanks."

He turned to leave—

"Jack Kingston."

He found the source of the caller and smiled. Okay, so maybe coming home didn't have to be a failure. "Hey, Mr. Harrison."

His former history teacher leaned hard on a cane, wearing black galoshes, an oversized canvas jacket, and a plaid wool hat, and held warmth in his eyes. "You're back for the wedding."

He shouldn't be surprised. When your sister was marrying an international country-music star, your little town, population 1,200, might know about it. "Yep."

Mr. Harrison held a basket, and Jack wanted to carry it for him, but Harrison had always been a tough old codger, so he held back the urge. "You okay?" the man asked then, glanced outside, maybe at the old bus.

"Yeah."

"Tan."

"I live in Florida. Most of the time."

"Mmm." Harrison looked him over. "Keeping out of trouble?" He smiled.

Jack smiled back. "Not much."

"I read your book."

Jack raised an eyebrow.

"Riveting. As was the interview on *Nightline*."

Even after all these years, a burn swept through him. "Thanks."

The man patted his shoulder. "Always knew you'd amount to something." He winked. "Once a Boy Scout, always a Boy Scout."

Oh. He swallowed. "Yeah. I guess."

Harrison laughed, familiar and kind, and then gave Jack's arm a frail squeeze. "Nice to see you home." He shuffled past.

So maybe this hadn't been such a terrible decision.

Jack headed back outside, undid the hitch to his old Geo Tracker, keyed the engine on to warm, then packed some gear into a bag, locked up the bus, and gave Aggie a pat on her worn white exterior. "I'll be back."

Then he got into the Geo he'd towed behind him and headed home.

He expected something quiet, maybe a couple family cars pulled into the cleared lot of the King's Inn—surely his mother would have blocked out this weekend from guests.

Instead, as he neared the inn, the lot seemed almost full. He counted upward of ten cars. *Perfect.* The celebrity wedding gala had already begun.

He wedged his tiny SUV into a spot between an Escalade and a snowbank, then got out and headed toward the door.

"Seriously?"

The voice stopped him and he looked up.

Brontë stood on the porch, her parka open to the wind, her dark hair under a hat, wearing a pair of furry UGGs, holding a pair of keys.

"Hey—"

And then, just like that, she rushed him. He got his arms out just as her arms flung around his neck, holding tight. "You made it!"

Oh. *Oh.*

He didn't know what to do with the rush of heat to his chest, to his throat, to his eyes. Talk about *seriously.*

She broke away, held his arms, staring up at him, her pretty brown eyes watery. "You showed up."

Wow, had he misread . . . maybe everything? "Of course I showed up. Can't let my kid sister get married without checking out the guy."

She smiled.

He shrugged.

Maybe, just like that, it could be over. His words, her hurt, four years of regrets.

She wiped her cheek. "You'll like him. He sings songs."

"So I've heard."

She wrinkled her nose. "I gotta go over to Doyle's. Penelope Pepper is there and I'm checking her in."

"Really? The podcaster?"

"Yeah. She did the podcast on the Grizz case. We got kind of close, and I needed an extra, so she's in the wedding. Besides, she and Harper used to be roomies, so we thought that would be fun."

She said it just like that, dropping Harper's name as if the woman hadn't made him run from Duck Lake for the better part of a decade.

No big deal.

"Harper?" He managed, somehow, to say it like a bomb wasn't exploding in his chest.

"I know you remember her."

He swallowed. "Um . . ."

"Oh please. My best friend? Blonde hair? Lived down the trail?" She pointed to a trail in the woods that connected the King's Inn property to the cottage on 458 Whispering Pines Drive. "We called her Bee."

Yeah, and he'd called her *Pigtails*. Which only brought to mind the fact that for most of his life, he'd seen her as one of his kid sister's friends.

Never as a woman he'd consider kissing.

"Yes, I think so." He shoved his hands into his pockets. Shrugged.

"I *hope* so." She shook her head. "Anyway, you two are walking down the aisle together." She squeezed his arm. "And by the way, you're bunking at Doyle's too, so giddy up after you say hi to Mom. I'll get you settled."

Oh. Great.

He'd never needed Aggie more than right now.

Because clearly, the trouble was just beginning.

———————•———————

Please, God, if you're listening, don't let Jack be here.

Harper sat in her car for a long moment, letting the vehicle warm up, fighting a shiver. She could do this. She could . . .

Her breath made a fog spot on the windshield, so she finally put her car into reverse and backed out of the driveway, then headed down the road toward King's Inn Drive.

Something about seeing the old place, however, loosened the tightness in her chest. Even if Jack did show up, maybe he'd forgotten the . . . well, the horror.

Mortification.

Right. As if.

She pulled up next to a smattering of vehicles and got out. Left her bag in the car just to take in the changes.

Maybe none. The old Victorian seemed to have weathered time. The apron porch circled the house, bumping out around the turret, swept clean of snow, and now twinkle lights hung from pillar to pillar, glinting in the fading sunlight. Pine trees decorated in white and blue ribbons—probably wedding decorations—sat at the base of each pillar.

Inside would be three stories of gleaming parquet floors, stamped-metal ceiling tiles, leaded bay windows, a fireplace in every room, and facing the lake, a turret bedroom that a princess might live in .

Five second-story bedrooms, two with sitting areas that overlooked the lake, a couple third-story rooms with an adjoining bath, and of course the turret bedroom meant they specialized in family reunions and other cozy events.

Harper had received the digital invitation: the ceremony taking place at Heritage Church, the reception in the third-story ballroom that could easily seat eighty or more.

Probably, the majority of the guests would stay in Duck Lake at the rebuilt Duck Lake Motor Lodge on the south end of town, but hopefully the family had room for Harper somewhere. She would sleep in a closet if she had to.

Or maybe at the carriage house, where the Kingston siblings had grown up. It sat away from the main inn, a two-story home with another five bedrooms, remodeled over the years by her father. Three more homes, built at the turn of the twentieth century by the original owner, Bing Kingston, newspaperman turned Gilded Age millionaire, sat farther on the north end of the property, with their own set of multiple bedrooms, gleaming mahogany trims, multiple chimneys. Palaces of their time.

Grover and Emily Kingston ran them all with their son Doyle, who occupied one of the smaller homes.

Smoke drifted from the largest chimney in the main home, and Harper took a breath and climbed the stairs to the porch. It creaked as she walked up to the main entrance with the Welcome to King's Inn sign.

She opened it.

The smell of baking cookies nearly made her moan. *Yes.* This was home, really. When she stepped inside, to the warmth of the foyer, the laughter from the kitchen, deeper in the house, swept her back to dreams and hopes and the family she'd longed for.

Before, of course, she'd blown all that up.

She could do this.

A lemony verbena scent emanated off the gleaming woodwork. To her left, a small fire flickered in the heart of the parlor slash turret, and to her right, the dining-room table held cookies and cupcakes and chocolates all under glass domes for guests.

Ahead arched the rotunda that held the circular stairs leading to the second and third floors. The antique table in the center held a massive bouquet of holly leaves and pine boughs, velvety amaryllis, pristine white roses, and deep red peonies.

Harper, can you arrange the flowers? Make sure to use plenty of blue thistle and lavender.

She swallowed back the memory, pulled off her jacket, and hung it on a tree rack. Stamped off her boots then and followed the carpet through the rotunda to the massive sitting room that overlooked the lake.

A fire blazed in the tall stone hearth with the walnut mantel. A couple rounded sofas faced each other—a private chatting area.

Another grouping of overstuffed cigar chairs, all in a circle, sat near an alcove, and in the center of the room, two long tufted-leather sofas flanked a massive oak-slab coffee table, hauled from California that one summer.

A couple groupings of wingback chairs anchored the corners of the room.

Guests sat in the overstuffed leather chairs, and an older woman and a man in jeans stared out the massive picture windows overlooking the lake, talking.

She ducked into the kitchen.

Two women stood at the expansive stainless-steel island.

The room went silent, just for a second. Then Emily Kingston put down a bowl of batter, wiped her hands, and held out her arms. "Look what the wind blew in!"

Harper didn't care about the flour or the fact that she would probably get batter on her cashmere sweater. "Mama Em."

"You look amazing." Mama Em held her by the shoulder. "That haircut—oh so cute."

"You think? I took it off above the ear this time—"

"I'm telling you—I always loved your summer cut. This is darling. Austen, don't you agree?"

Austen came over, her dark chestnut hair long enough now to be tied back, wearing a hairnet and an apron, lean and tanned and gorgeous—oh, Harper had longed for one ounce of the older Kingston sister's beauty.

"Girl, you look like you belong on a beach." Austen gave Harper a hug. "Have you seen Brontë yet?"

"No. I uh—"

"I think she's getting your friend Penelope settled over at Doyle's place." Mama Em had returned to her batter. She wore her own short blonde hair tied back in a handkerchief, her King's Inn apron cinched around her tiny waist. Not the picture of an award-winning baker, but the woman knew her cakes, breads, and cookies.

And she possessed the gift of hospitality like she'd written the book. "We had to double up on the accommodations with all of Oaken's people staying on-site. They're over at Grover House."

Oh. "Um . . . do you . . . I mean . . . so, my mom is remodeling my bedroom—"

Emily looked up at her. Blinked.

Oh. "Forget it—" Maybe she could find a room at the Duck Lake Motor Lodge. They usually had vacancies this time of year.

"What? Do you think we'd let you stay anywhere other than with us?" Mama Em added a little oomph to her words, the batter taking the brunt. "Brontë has you bunking with Penelope. I really like her, by the way." She put the bowl down. "Brontë has gotten really close to her this past year with Penelope doing that murder podcast."

"I heard she's in the wedding."

"Yes. Well, head down to the house—Brontë will get you checked in. And then"—she used the spatula to stir—"dinner is out at the Moonlight Supperclub."

Austen waved as Harper left the kitchen.

Harper got in her car and headed down the road to Doyle's place, Mama Em's greeting sitting sweetly in her mind.

See? Maybe she would survive all of this.

Doyle's place was a smaller version of the big house, with an apron porch, parquet flooring, a stone hearth, and three bedrooms upstairs. So much room for Doyle, but he had his reasons for wanting space, probably, after the tragedy.

She got out, left her bag in the car, and walked up the front porch. Knocked, then opened the door. "Boo?"

Footsteps sounded upstairs, and she shut the door. Stood there, listening for Boo's voice, hearing her laughter upstairs.

Yes, she was going to be—

"Harper."

She turned, stilled, and of course, he looked . . .

Devastating.

Dark hair curling past his ears, wearing a denim shirt that outlined his shoulders, his muscled arms. A skim of dark whiskers, and worst of all, those crazy blue eyes the color of a stormy sky, cutting off her breathing, stripping words from her brain.

Jack.

She may have mouthed his name, because he arched a dark eyebrow.

He even smelled good, something of the woods and the sky and the sense of adventure radiating off him.

So. Not. Fair.

Footsteps thumped on the stairs, and she nearly collapsed into a heap when Boo called out, "Harper! Oh good, you made it."

She nodded, her eyes still on Jack. *Run. Or breathe. Something.*

Boo grabbed her into a hug, and it did the job of tearing her gaze off Jack.

Beautiful, horrible Big Jack, the oldest of the Kingston clan—the charmer, the hockey captain, the Eagle Scout, her first and enduring childhood crush, who clearly still had a knee-wobbling effect on her.

Sheesh.

Boo let her go and looked at her, then Jack. "Perfect. You're both in time for dance lessons."

Dance . . . what . . . "Dance—wait—*what*?" Harper said.

Boo laughed then, her beautiful eyes lighting up. "Yeah. You're walking down the aisle together, so guess what—you're partners!"

Clearly, he already knew because his mouth tightened, a look of pain on his face. Yeah, well, her too.

Like, what was Boo thinking?

Did she have amnesia? Because certainly Boo knew . . . or maybe not. Harper fished back through her memories and found herself stuck.

"I know things were a little awkward between you too after—" Boo made a face and turned to Jack. "Well, we all know it was just a big misunderstanding, and so many years ago, and we've already paired up all the other bridesmaids—Austen with Steinbeck, and my current roommate, London, is walking down with our friend Shep, and Conrad is with Penelope, and Doyle...well, he's agreed to be an usher, so that's improvement, but..." She lifted a shoulder. "I don't know. I guess you two were the only ones unmatched."

Jack made a noise, deep inside his chest, but swallowed, nodded. "It'll be fine, Brontë."

She glanced at Harper.

Harper's turn to act like all the air hadn't left the room. "Sure. Of course—no problem."

"Perfect. Great. Okay, Harp, I have you upstairs with Penelope. Jack, can you grab her bag?"

"Oh, no—no worries, Boo, I got this—" Harper turned toward the door.

Jack reached for the knob the same time she did, and her hand landed on his. He jerked away as if she might be a flame, about to burn him.

Nice.

She glanced at him. "Really, I can do this." Then she opened the door and headed outside.

She could lie with the best of them too.

Because she'd clearly been lying.

No, she couldn't do this.

THREE

"THIS IS GOING TO BE AMAZING!"

Penelope Pepper sat cross-legged on one of the twin beds in the guest room to which Boo had helped Harper—and Jack, of course—carry her bags. Because Mr. Save the World couldn't stop himself from following her outside, despite her protest, and grabbing her satchel and carrying it inside.

Which left her with her backpack and the wedding gift, wrapped and stowed in a large paper shopping bag. Oh, and her blue bridesmaid dress, still in the bag sent to her apartment in Nashville. Boo had grabbed that as she led them upstairs to one of the gorgeous bedrooms. Light-blue velvet curtains, plush twin beds with thick white comforters, bulky knitted blankets at the end, overstuffed pillows, and a vintage restored dresser with a spray of fresh flowers between the beds.

Yes, this was better than a closet.

Penelope hugged one of the linen pillows to herself, looking radiant, her dark-brown hair cascading down her back, a hint of a Caribbean glow on her skin. Clearly, she'd escaped with her family down to their vacation home in in St. Kitts, in the Caribbean.

Hard times, although Penelope had given it her best go to break free of the Pepper mantle and forge her own path.

Hence, the *Penny for Your Thoughts* murder podcast.

Harper cast her a wry smile as Boo set the paper bag on the bed next to her satchel. Jack had nearly left a breeze when he escaped the room, and Penelope had raised an eyebrow.

Clearly he was brimming with joy about hanging out with her.

Boo hung the dress in the wardrobe attached to the wall. "I'm so glad you guys made it." She glanced at Penelope. "Oaken loved the podcast, by the way. He listened to it during his tour last fall. And we're both listening to 'The Case of Sarah Livingston.' I love how you've narrowed down the suspects to her ex-boyfriend, her obsessive neighbor, and her so-called platonic friend Kyle. So, who do you think it is?"

"Can't say." Penelope grinned. "You'll have to keep listening."

Boo rolled her eyes. "Be prepared for Oaken to corner you."

"I still can't believe you're marrying Oaken Fox," Penelope said. "My sister is a huge fan. Especially after the social media about his attending the birthday party of the girl paralyzed by his sister's accident."

"Maggie Bloom. We're hoping that Maggie and her mom can attend the wedding." Boo sat on one of the leather benches under the window. She looked at Harper, frowned. "Harp, you okay? You look a little pale."

Harper *felt* a little pale. She'd closed the door behind Jack's escape and sunk onto the bed, her stomach churning, her heart pounding against her chest.

"Yeah. You look like you've seen a ghost," Penelope added.

"More like a haunting," Harper said.

Boo stared at her. "Wait—is this about *Jack*? I mean, I thought you put that all behind you. That was . . . years. Ages. Eons ago."

Harper didn't mean to gape, but, "Really? Boo. I have never been more mortified in my life than when Jack laughed—*laughed*—at me when Doyle suggested we go to prom together. It's a watershed moment in my life that still makes me pull the covers up over my head."

"You asked Jack Kingston to your *prom*?" Penelope said. "What is he—four years older—"

"Six. Six gigantic, millennial years older than me."

"Which would have made him twenty-four when you were a senior."

"Actually, at that time, he was twenty-three, but I had only just turned eighteen, so..." She lifted a shoulder. "I was young and..."

"She had a major crush on Jack most of our childhood," Boo said.

"Really." Penelope raised an eyebrow. "Well, what's not to like? He's... off the charts. Those blue eyes, that dark run-your-fingers-through-it hair, and he clearly works out. What does he do for a living?"

"He finds lost people," Boo said.

"For money," Harper added. "He's a rewardist."

"What is that?" Penelope shoved the pillow behind her and picked up her phone, as if to search.

"It's a person who makes a living off the reward money people put up asking for information leading to... you know, the recovery of someone who has gone missing."

"That's a profession?"

"You've heard of Crime Stoppers, right?" Boo said.

"Of course I have. But I thought they just aggregated tips."

"They also organize all the postings and manage the rewards. Jack has a husband-and-wife team, both lawyers, who find him jobs. Lives in a schoolie that he renovated himself when he finished law school."

"So he's like a PI," Penelope said, putting her phone down.

"Sort of, but he's not credentialed. So he has to be careful. He can't make arrests, can't interfere with a police investigation, and has to share with the police everything he digs up. He was top of his class at the U, so he knows the law, even though he didn't pass the bar."

Penelope held up a hand. "Okay, so—I'm going to need more about this prom thing."

"It's nothing." Harper had opened up her satchel, started to unpack.

"It's obviously something. Why would you ask a guy out of college to your senior prom—"

"I didn't ask him. But . . ." She glanced at Boo, sighed. "I did think he liked me."

"Why?"

She shook her head. Even now the reason seemed so . . . immature. "Because I live in fantasyland—or did at the time—and I'd talked myself into a happily ever after with Big Jack—"

"Big Jack?"

"It's a family name," Boo said. "He's the oldest and in-chargest. Or was."

"Was?"

"That is a different, also long, story," Boo said. "But—the reason that Harp here is freaking out is that she and Big Jack kissed."

Harper looked at her, horror on her face. "Thank you for that."

Penelope's eyes widened. "You did not."

"Did," Harper said, sighing. "Again, all on me, but when he found out I was still in high school and that I'd only just turned eighteen—"

"How *only just*?"

"Two days before the trip."

"Maybe that was my fault," Boo said. "I had turned eighteen early in the year, and I think he just assumed that Harper was the same age."

"Actually, after I thought about it, I don't think he even realized who I was. I was twelve when he went away to college, and he didn't come home much. I don't remember really seeing him at all during those years. And I might have changed a little between twelve and eighteen. Got braces, grew out my hair, added some curves." She shrugged. "And I was part of a humanitarian team that Doyle put together, all from his college buddies, so . . ."

"Wait. When was this?" Penelope asked.

"Senior year, spring break," Boo said. "A hurricane had ravaged Grenada, and Doyle led a team from his college group to help rebuild a children's home. I'm not sure how he talked Jack into going, but Harper went too."

"And he thought you were one of the college kids."

"I might have tried to hide my age. And when he knew me at the age of twelve, everyone else called me—"

"Bee." Boo grinned.

"As in busy bee—something my dad called me. I didn't hate it until later. But Jack never called me Bee. He called me Pigtails."

"Cute."

"Yeah. For a *child*. When I saw Jack again, I didn't want him to think that, so I introduced myself as Harper. He didn't remember my real name." She hung up a sweater in the closet. "Like I said—my fault."

"But he kissed you?" Penelope had pushed the pillow behind her, leaning forward.

"Please don't put this in a podcast."

She laughed, flipped her dark hair back. "Not unless you murder him."

"He might be the one to murder me. I've never seen a guy so embarrassed." She hung up a black jumpsuit, then dropped the bag onto the floor. "I don't know what I was thinking."

"You were thinking my brother was . . . well, Jack's always been a little larger than life."

"Yeah. And here he was, donating his spring break to rebuilding an orphanage. We'd had a fun week, laughing, working together.

He never once asked me about home, and maybe I thought . . . *Good. He's trying to start over."*

"Get to the kissing part." Penelope drew up her knees, clasped her arms around them.

"Okay." Harper sighed, but why not? "It was a couple days before we flew home, and we were working on rebuilding the roof, and he'd come down wearing a cutoff T-shirt, all sweaty and hot and perfect, and I just said, 'Hey, will you walk out on the beach with me tonight?' And he said yes."

A beat.

"And—"

"And during that beach walk, we kissed. And I thought . . . oh so many things. And then the next day, we were standing in the shade, and he was smiling and laughing and maybe flirting with me a little, and I think he might have even put his arm around me . . ."

She sank down on the bed and grabbed her own pillow for protection. "And then Doyle came up and clamped him on the back, laughing, and said, 'Hey, Bee, so, looks like you found your prom date.' And then he laughed and said to Jack, 'You and Brontë can double-date.'"

"I didn't know that part," Boo said. She made a face. "That Doyle."

"Yeah. Well, that's when it sort of all clicked. Jack just . . . stared at me. Like I'd slugged him. I could actually see the horror playing on his face as the recognition set in. And then he said, *'Pigtails?'* and his voice shook a little, and I knew, right then, it was bad. Very bad. And then it got worse."

"Oh no," Penelope said.

"He was horrified." Harper said.

Boo turned to Harper, wearing a pained expression. "I'm sorry. I heard the entire thing from Doyle, and he just said you both shrugged it off, no big deal."

"Yeah, well, that's because Jack laughed," Harper said. "Like, really laughed, like it might be ridiculous that he'd even be seen with me. And maybe it was to cover up his embarrassment, but everybody heard it, everybody saw it, and then he shook his head, like, *stupid little girl* and then *never spoke to me again*."

Silence.

"Ouch," said Penelope.

"I think all he saw from that moment on was me with braces, twelve years old, my hair in pigtails." Harper looked at Boo. "And now I have to walk down the aisle with the guy."

"And . . . um, dance with him." Boo made a face. "Sorry. I didn't know about the laughing. Or the ghosting."

"I tried very hard to never talk about it again."

"Doyle just said that you two had sort of gotten close and that Jack had a crush on you."

She stared at Boo. "What?"

"Yeah. And then Doyle said that he laughed at the prom joke and I thought . . . oh, Bee, I am so sorry. I didn't realize it was so traumatic. I can see if we can switch things—"

"No. It'll only make it worse. People would ask why, and then the story would have to be told and . . . Let's just leave it. I'm a big girl. I'll make it work." She drew in a breath. "Like you said—it was a misunderstanding, years ago."

"Well, I can definitely say you've grown up since then," Penelope said, and she waggled her eyebrows.

Harper threw a pillow at her but laughed. And maybe now, with the story out, it wasn't so horrible. Maybe it *was* fully in the past. And this was only for five days, and really just a few hours of bridal-party duty.

And then she never had to see him again.

"You can do this," Penelope said, as if reading her mind. "Maybe even show the guy what he's been missing."

"Oh, please. Don't go there. Jack is so far out of my league."

"No one is out of your league," Boo said. "Especially Jack. He lives in a school bus. You write for an international magazine."

Which, by the way: "Boo, can I talk to you about something?"

"Sure. I mean—if you don't want to do the dance—"

"No. Of course I'll do the dance. It won't be pretty, however. But..." She glanced at Penelope, back at Boo. "So, *PopMuse* magazine fired me after the Bliss article."

Boo's eyebrows rose.

"Bliss is mad that I did research. Talked to her dad about the death of her mom and her relationship with Chase Sterling—"

"I loved him in *Eclipse Protocol*. I heard they're coming out with a sequel."

"Yeah, well, they were on and then they weren't, and her publicist shut down all my queries—anyway, I might have dug too deep, and now I need a gig. A good gig. Something that will make *PopMuse* or *Inside Nashvegas* bite." She took a breath. Here went nothing. "Can I have the exclusive on your wedding story?"

Boo stared at her, then frowned—

Oh no.

"What exclusive?"

"Oh..."

"Really?" Penelope said. "The one that the entire world is waiting for? Don't tell me that you haven't been approached by *People* magazine, or *Vanity Fair.*"

"I have no idea. I've been head down, working on the wedding. And it's way out of control, with all of Oaken's country-music buddies showing up. Did you know that Benjamin King will be here?"

"Oh, I have all of his albums," said Penelope. "I can't wait."

"Yeah, well, there are so many security requests that we had to hire our own crew out of Minneapolis. A recommendation from my cousin Ranger, so they gave us a discount, but—no. No exclusive."

Oh. Harper drew in a breath.

Boo's eyes widened. "I mean—not from *People* magazine. I'll talk to Oaken and see if he knows what you're talking about. Maybe Goldie's been handling all those requests. But yes, if it's up to me, of course you can write about the wedding, Harp." She stood up. "In fact, if there has to be an article, I want you to write it. I know this is crazy talk, but I'm trying to keep this wedding as tame as I can. We got the guest list to less than a hundred, and I'm hoping to keep it drama free."

"That'll be hard with all the paparazzi."

"No paparazzi. All of Oaken's friends and family are at Grover House. My family is here at Doyle's, and Dodge and Echo and the rest of the Alaska Kingstons are staying with Dad and Mom when they arrive. Security will be on-site the day of, checking off guests with their digital invitation . . ." She sighed. "Maybe we should have eloped."

Harper came off the bed, walked over to take her friend's hands. "Listen, as your friend, I promise to keep anything I write sweet and chaste and perfect. You're going to have an amazing, drama-free week. I promise."

"I don't think you can promise the drama-free part, but . . . thanks."

"Well, don't worry about me and Jack." She glanced at Penelope. "And I'll make sure Penelope doesn't run off with one of your brothers."

"What? Me?" But Penelope grinned. "It's hard to be beautiful." She tossed her hair.

It worked, because Boo laughed. "Okay. I'll meet you downstairs in a half hour. Dance rehearsal is in town, with dinner for the entire party at the Moonlight Supperclub." She glanced at Harper. "I'll make sure you don't have to ride in Jack's ancient green Geo Tracker."

"He still has that?"

"Saw him pull up in it today."

Harper laughed. "Be still my heart. I used to think that car was so cool."

"I think he still does." Boo winked and headed toward the door.

Which left Harper the next twenty-eight minutes to stare at the stupid party outfits she'd brought, wondering which of them might make her feel less naked in Jack's arms.

She finally decided on the one-piece black jumpsuit with wide legs, and a long-sleeve white turtleneck, short boots. Felt like enough armor.

Of course, Penelope rocked her outfit in a white V-neck shirt, matching white pants, and an oversized black suit jacket, the sleeves rolled up. She wore her dark hair down, spike boots, and looked like she'd just walked off the runway.

So not fair.

Penelope hooked arms with Harper and leaned in. "He's going to regret laughing."

Sweet, but hardly.

They came downstairs, where Boo had divided up rides. Doyle's SUV took Austen and Penelope, Boo's hockey-star brother Conrad, Harper, and former SEAL Steinbeck. He climbed into the back seat next to Harper, and she barely fit against his broad shoulders.

Why all Boo's brothers had to be built like action heroes, she didn't know, but Steinbeck had actually been one, for a while.

"I didn't know you were back."

"Couldn't miss Boo's wedding." He looked over at her with those blue Kingston eyes. He still had a tan and maintained his military build.

"So you call her Boo too."

"Why not?"

"After the fight between her and Jack—"

"Yeah, Jack was way out of line. Doyle and I—and Austen—call her Boo. It was a nickname her Marine team leader gave her, and she liked it, so . . ." He lifted a shoulder. "Mom and Dad and Jack still call her Brontë. Jack can't get past the Boo thing—"

"They seem to have gotten past the fight, though. They're pretty friendly now." In fact, Boo was riding with Jack in his crazy little Geo.

Steinbeck's mouth tightened. He shrugged.

Interesting.

They rode into town. So much had been remodeled after the tornado, including the old supper club, now with a new exterior of stone and reclaimed wood beams, probably from the previous building. It sat on the edge of town with a panoramic view of the lake and stars.

Austen parked, and as they got out, Harper spotted Jack in the moonlit parking lot. He wore a pair of jeans, black boots, and a leather jacket. Not a hint of a smile on his face.

Yeah, well, me too, pal.

They went inside, where Boo talked with one of the managers, who then ushered them to the adjoining ballroom.

Harper stopped off on the way to the coat-check room—*isn't that a blast from the past?*—and left her black puffer jacket there.

Country music drifted from the ballroom with its gleaming, polished wood floor, chandeliers dripping from the timber ceiling, and round tables pushed to the sides.

A man waited for them, wearing a pair of black dress pants, a white shirt, and a vest. He clapped his hands. "My name is Julian, and I'll be your instructor over the next few days. We'll be learning two dances. The two-step, so everyone can keep up with the groom and his bride." He glanced at Oaken Fox and Boo.

Oaken might be even more handsome in person with that dark-blond hair, the way he stood behind Boo, his hands on her shoulders, grinning.

"And then the *Dirty Dancing* crew dance."

She stilled. *Wait—what?*

"Okay, everyone grab your partner. We'll start with the two-step."

She still couldn't move. Especially after Jack turned to her, his face stiff, like he might be walking toward execution.

Nice.

He held out his hand.

She took it, horrified that hers seemed clammy and slick.

And then, because she couldn't keep her mouth shut, or maybe her brain had already fled the building, she heard herself say, "Looks like we're going to get that dance after all."

Oh no, no—

He flinched. And she froze. And then, before she could flee, he took her hand and said, "At least you're not in high school."

Maybe Penelope would have new fodder for her murder podcast after all.

———•———

At least you're not in high school.

Those words. They'd just sort of fallen out of Jack's mouth, probably because they'd been sitting in his head—or his heart—since the moment Harper walked in the front door.

Seeing her took him out. Really, he simply had nothing—no breath, no heartbeat, no thought. Because sure, his mother had let down the boom, but . . .

Harper was, well, not a high schooler by any stretch of the imagination. .

First, she'd changed her hair. A little blonde pixie cut that turned her cute, like Tinkerbell or something, and made her pale blue eyes zing right through him.

And she had curves. Not that he'd missed those a decade ago, but it seemed she'd grown into her adult body, strong and lithe but with hips and . . .

Oh boy.

And then there was that little spit of determination, almost anger, that he hadn't seen before but maybe deserved because, well, he'd been a jerk. His over-the-top laugh had burned inside him like acid for a decade.

Now his hand brushed her back, his arm outstretched so she could rest hers in the cup of his hand, and he tried not to step on her toes as Julian directed them to move in a circle around the room, two-stepping.

So far, so good. He didn't want to think about the next dance. Because suddenly all he was thinking was . . .

That kiss. And other things he'd shut away. And probably shouldn't think about ever again. Like what-ifs and tomorrows.

"You're a good lead," she said, looking at his shoulder.

"Thanks. Mom's instruction in the kitchen as a kid. All the boys know how to dance."

She nodded, casting her gaze around the room. He followed and spotted Conrad dancing with Penelope Pepper, who practically glided along the floor, and then Steinbeck and Austen, who had that twin thing going on that made them immediately in sync. And finally his eyes landed on Brontë and Oaken. Brontë was laughing, her eyes light, and the look of it twisted inside him.

Yeah, he'd been a jerk, and not just to Harper.

Harper stepped on his foot and they nearly tripped.

"Oh! Sorry!"

He grabbed her around the waist, moved her out of the circle while they caught their balance. "It's okay."

"Aw, this is stupid. I can't do this." She untangled herself and walked away.

Could be she was talking about the dancing, but maybe—

"Harper. Um, can we talk?"

She looked at him, her eyes wide. "No. No, we're good. It's fine. Let's try it again."

Oh.

She came back to his arms, and right as they entered the circle, Julian clapped his hands.

"Okay, that's enough for today. We'll pick it back up tomorrow with the *Dirty Dancing* routine."

Harper let go of Jack like he had a lethal disease and walked away.

And there went that chance at redemption.

"So. You apologize to Boo yet?"

Jack sighed and turned to Steinbeck. The man wore a pair of dress pants, a white oxford, and despite the fact that Steinbeck was younger, he could crush a man with a look. Now he leveled it at Jack.

Who gave him the same look back. "We're good."

"Maybe, but you threw a cluster bomb into the middle of this family. I think that's going to take more than just a *we're good*."

Jack shoved his hands into his pockets, glanced toward the door of the restaurant. "I was wrong, okay?"

Steinbeck blinked at him.

"I didn't want her getting hurt." And mostly he was talking about Brontë.

"She served with the Marines—" Steinbeck started.

"As a Navy corpsman. Vast difference between what you did and her job."

"She still deployed into combat zones. Still had to keep up. Keep a pig alive, if you remember."

Of course Steinbeck had to go there.

"I remember," Jack growled.

"Even the part when you said she could barely keep herself alive?"

He shot his brother a look. "Not here."

Steinbeck's eyes narrowed. "Four years is a long time to let something fester. Boo might have acted like it's all good, but you left an open wound when you basically dared her to go on that reality show."

"I didn't dare her—"

"'Brontë, you couldn't keep a pig alive—'" Steinbeck finger quoted the words.

Jack held up his hand. "I know what I said. At the time, I thought it would keep her from doing something stupid."

Steinbeck cocked his head. "You do know her, don't you? You might as well have driven her to the audition."

Maybe he didn't know her. Maybe he just thought he did, based on his own fears and assumptions. But it wasn't like he'd stuck around..

"That show completely derailed her, wrecked her life."

"I know."

"So, could be it might take more to get to a *we're good*."

"You guys need to be separated?" Conrad had walked—no, swaggered—up, the hockey hotshot he was. He wore a black button-down, black pants, his hands in his pockets, and now bumped shoulders with Jack. "Glad to see you made it."

Steinbeck held up a hand. "Apparently it's all good."

Conrad raised an eyebrow. He'd grown his ruddy beard out, his hair behind his ears, deep in the middle of hockey season. "Boo's changed." He looked at Jack. "You might consider that she's grown all the way up, big bro. She's not the little girl who got lost in the woods when she was eight." He clamped him on the shoulder, squeezed. "Doesn't need you to find her anymore."

Jack nodded. "I know."

"Hey. Was that Aggie I saw sitting in the market parking lot?" Doyle came up, wearing a blue dress shirt, a suitcoat, dress pants. Looked like he might be on his way to a fundraiser.

Probably wished he was.

"Yeah. I stopped in Ankeny last night to see West and Nat and forgot that I use water in my radiator hoses."

Even Steinbeck made a face.

"You blow the head gasket?" Doyle asked.

"I don't know. Maybe. I might need a tow to the inn."

"If you can find a parking space," Doyle said.

They headed toward the dining-room entrance.

Conrad's attention seemed to fall on Penelope, who stood by the entrance, talking with Harper, of course.

The Pepper woman was a heart-stopper for the right guy.

Which, of course, was why Conrad stopped to talk.

Jack headed inside the restaurant. The party had rented out the entire space, and now long tables held candles with greenery nestled around gold chargers. Chandeliers hung from the ceiling, and country music played in the background. A fire flickered in the massive hearth on the other end of the room.

Servers walked the room with silver trays of appetizers. Fish on a cracker, white cheese, arancini with ham.

Brontë—the name Boo just stuck to his mouth after their epic fight—stood with her hand in Oaken's. He wore black dress jeans and a crisp gray shirt, a fancy bluish suit jacket. Her fiancé seemed fit, with light-brown hair and an affable smile. The tame side of country music, apparently. He was missing his Stetson, though.

They talked with a man with brown hair, early thirties, holding hands with a woman wearing pants and tied-back auburn hair.

Jack walked over, waited until Oaken stopped talking, and then stuck out his hand. "Jack." He nodded at Brontë. "Oldest brother."

"I know," Oaken said, but smiled. "Good to meet you. We missed you at Christmas."

Him too? Wonderful.

"This is my friend Axel Mulligan, from Alaska," Oaken said. "And his girlfriend, Flynn."

Jack shook hands. Then Axel turned to Oaken. "Later." He walked away.

Oaken turned to Jack. "So glad you could make it for the wedding." Oaken glanced at Brontë. "Boo was worried you'd be tied up with a case."

Jack gave him a smile, his throat too tight. Brontë grinned up at him. Okay, maybe he didn't have to constantly listen to the guilt. "Just finished one. But it's not a case, really. I'm not a PI."

Oaken gave him a blank look. "Oh."

"I hunt for missing people. I follow leads and unearth information and hand it over to the right authorities." He gave them a wry smile. "Usually without trouble."

"Oh, right," Brontë said, laughing. "What*ever*. You're like a basset hound. Trouble is like a steak."

Oaken grinned.

"I think *basset hound* might be a little strong, sis." But okay, the laughter made him breathe. And kept his gaze from drifting over to Harper again.

Maybe he was like a dog with a bone.

"Jack wrote a book about his first find. It was made into a movie. Now he's famous."

"Not famous."

"A super sleuth."

"No. I just . . . listen. And people tell me things. And most of the time, it's because they have a problem."

"That you *solve*," Brontë said.

"Only if there's a reward involved."

She gave a huff.

"I'm not the savior you think I am. Never was." He made a face, feeling the heat in it.

She rolled her eyes. "Tell that to any of my friends. They all fell under a spell when you walked into the room."

Now *he* rolled his eyes. She turned to Oaken. "It didn't help that he was the one who found me when I was lost."

"I remember the story," Oaken said, considering him.

"Yeah. It was his face I saw when I climbed out of the sleeping bag. And then he went on to save some Boy Scout two years later. That time, he made the news, local and statewide. Probably what launched his itch to find missing people."

Her words found a place, warmed him. "First, the kid was a Cub Scout, and that was pure luck. And second, to survive, you have to be smart. Like Brontë was, to dig a hole, climb into a sleeping bag, and stay put. Clearly she knew how to take care of herself."

Brontë stared at him, a tiny frown playing over her face.

He smiled at her, shrugged. "You did real good, Brontë."

"You did too."

He nodded, glanced at Steinbeck, who'd wandered over to the serving bar with Doyle. He'd picked up a fancy drink from a server who'd walked by.

Brontë stepped up and put her arms around Jack's neck. "It's okay to call me Boo."

Right. "Sorry, sis," he said, his arm around her.

"I forgive you," she whispered back.

Now, that felt right. And maybe he could breathe deeper.

She let him go. "By the way, Harper told us what went down between you two."

Oh, right for the jugular when he wasn't looking. "That was a long time ago."

"Yeah. Probably you could let that go?"

He nodded. *Probably.*

"For my sake, please just get along and stay out of trouble. She's my best friend. You're my big brother. I don't want bloodshed."

"If you make us dance together, that might not be possible. She stepped on my foot twice."

Right then, Harper came into view, walking with Penelope to the buffet.

She was like an accident—he couldn't look away. "What is she doing now?"

"Freelance writer. She wants to cover our wedding." Brontë gave Oaken a side-eye. "By the way."

Oaken raised his eyebrows. "We're going to need to talk."

"And that woman with her—Penelope Pepper," Jack continued. "I didn't realize you two were friends."

"She came to us about six months ago, asked to tell our side of the Mike Grizz attempted murder."

"She did a great job," Oaken said.

"I know. I heard it. And I'm listening to the new one."

"About the girl in Minneapolis who got killed in her apartment? I tried to get the name of the killer out of Penelope, but she wouldn't tell." She glanced at a man walking up to her. "Moose, you made it."

She turned to the big man, dark hair, holding hands with a pretty woman and a little girl, maybe eight years old. He *looked* like a moose, all burly muscle and dark gray-green eyes.

Jack stepped away as Boo hugged Moose and Oaken shook his hand, and Jack's gaze fell again on Harper.

That black jumpsuit hugged her body, brightened her blond hair. And her entire face lit up when she laughed, maybe at something Penelope said.

He was about to turn away when another man walked up to Harper, tall, with a sort of regal Henry Cavill jaw and demeanor.

Let it go.

Let her *go.*

He hadn't realized until now that he hadn't.

His father whistled from the front, and the room quieted as he greeted the guests and led them in a prayer for dinner.

Jack stood in line for the buffet and loaded up his plate. He found a seat beside the guy he'd met earlier, the man named Axel, and learned that his girlfriend with the auburn hair was a cop who talked about some drug dealer she was hunting in Anchorage. On the other side of her, Doyle was engaged in a conversation with some blonde woman with a hint of a British accent about the need for funding for more international search and rescue teams. Probably doing his spiel about the tragedy of international trafficking, which of course Jack could agree with.

But he couldn't tear his gaze off Harper, really.

Sheesh, she'd thrown him off his game so many years ago. Crept inside his brain and sat there, stirring up the what-ifs and should-haves.

Just survive the next five days without doing something stupid.

Toasts, and more toasts, and then the rundown by Bron—Boo—of the week's activities. Then they were dismissed to the dance floor, the music by some local country band.

Harper had vacated her seat.

Jack got up. *Shoot*—with the list of activities and a broken schoolie to fix, he didn't know when he'd get a chance to . . . what? Apologize? Maybe yes, because apparently, he was on a roll.

He got up, bid Axel goodbye, slapped a hand on Doyle's shoulder, and then headed for the dance floor.

Harper wasn't in the group of dancers, and he hadn't really expected her to be, so he rounded back to the lobby. Not there, either, although he did spot Penelope, standing with her jacket on. He came over to her. "You leaving?"

She nodded, her mouth a little pursed, as if stressed, and weirdly, it nudged all his trouble buttons.

Stay out of trouble.

Not his business.

"Have you seen Harper?"

Penelope raised an eyebrow, her mouth loosening into a smile.

"Yeah. She's getting her jacket." She motioned toward the coat check down the hallway.

So they were *both* leaving.

He headed down the hallway, back toward the dance hall, and found her at the coat-check booth just as an attendant handed over her jacket.

"Sort of like a car valet," she said as she reached for it.

The handoff missed, and the jacket fell to the floor inside the booth. The attendant retrieved it again with her apologies.

Jack reached over, took the jacket, and held it open for Harper. She cocked her head. He found a smile.

She shrugged and slid into the jacket. *Okay,* this didn't need to be terrible. "Let's hope they don't take the coats for a test drive."

He stood there, blocking her path.

"Excuse me—"

"Listen. I'm sorry I laughed."

Oh. Whoops. No preamble. Just like that. But that was the important part, right?

Still, his words must have hit her like a slap because she recoiled, then looked away, as if hurt.

Aw. "I mean . . . I was . . . surprised. And caught off guard. And . . . fine. I didn't know you were . . . *Bee.* I thought—"

"I know. It was my fault." She looked at him then.

His eyes widened. "What? No. That—what happened was *not* your fault." He lowered his voice. "I was there. And I do remember, um . . . well, I was the one who . . ."

"Started the kiss?"

He drew in a breath. "Yes. But to be clear, if I'd known—"

"Nice. Because of course, you couldn't fall for your little sister's best friend—"

"You were a baby!" He kept his voice low, but just barely.

"I was *eighteen.* By a whole week—"

"And still off-limits. C'mon, Harper. You were in high school . . .

and you still . . ." *Aw.* This wasn't going at all how he'd wanted. "It doesn't matter—"

"I still what? Led you on? Came on to you?"

He looked at her then. "You had a crush on me for years. So . . ." Her eyes widened.

"I didn't mean—"

She pushed past him, but he reached out, grabbed her arm, whirled her around. "I didn't mean you were to blame. I was the older one. I should have thought before—"

"You kissed me." She yanked her arm out of his grasp. "Seriously. Listen." She held up her hand, her voice shaking. "I did have a crush on you. Yep. Guilty. And maybe, yes, when I showed up in Grenada and you were on the team and you looked at me like you'd never seen me before, I thought . . . great. See. Maybe he won't see Bee. He'll see someone who . . . isn't a twelve-year-old girl."

"You most certainly did not look twelve," he growled. "I did think you were . . ." He let out a shaky breath. "Older."

"We aren't that far apart in age, six years—"

"It might have been a *decade.* Don't you know the math? Half your age, plus seven. You were still at least a year too young for me—and what am I even saying? You were still in high school! You're *Brontë's best friend.* Off-limits. Full stop."

She just stared at him. "That's the stupidest thing I've ever heard. But don't worry. I'm so over you, Jack Kingston. Like you said, a *decade* over you. So thanks, apology accepted, but there's no need." She held up her hands as if to stop the crazy. "Let's just get through this week, and then we can walk away and never talk to each other again."

"Fine."

"Perfect." She swallowed, her jaw hardening, then whirled around and headed to the door.

He watched her go.

Wait.

Um.

"Harper, come back." He took off after her. Because no way, no how was this what Boo wanted. *No bloodshed* meant a truce. And the expression on Harper's face looked like anything but armistice.

Harper had already stepped outside, so he pushed through, out into the cold.

He found her standing in the overhanging front entry, frowning.

"Harper?"

She looked at him, then back to the dark parking lot. "She left me."

"What?"

"Penelope. She left me. Took the Uber and didn't wait for me." He let the door close. Shivered. "Really?"

"Weird. I mean . . ." She shook her head, clearly flummoxed.

He could solve this. "Wait here. I'll get my keys."

She glanced at him. "You don't have—"

"No. I'm done with this party. Let me drive you back to the inn."

Her shoulders rose and fell, and finally she nodded. "But no more apologizing for the past, okay?"

"I can live with that." He held out his hand. "Truce?"

She considered it a moment, then took it. "For Boo's sake, yes."

At least that was a start.

She'd nearly blown her one chance to save the world.

Maybe she'd assigned too much pressure to herself going in. Because she'd told herself two hours earlier that Emberly—a.k.a. Ashley, for this night at least—had one shot to get this right.

It had started off so easy.

"Ashley, grab a tray and get back out there."

Orders from the catering boss, Nolan, who engineered the delivery of the walleye cakes, the wild-rice arancini, and the baked cranberry Brie to the guests in the dining room.

She'd picked up a loaded silver tray, held it in one hand, and pushed her way through the swinging door into the room.

Country music played on the overhead speakers, and in the massive dining room, guests of Fox's private wedding-kickoff bash stood with fluted champagne glasses, signature mules, and hot buttered rum in apple cider.

The place smelled festive, with the scent of a fire in the giant hearth, the cinnamon, nutmeg, and cloves from the rum mix simmering in a hot pot near the bar, and sprays of calla lilies and bright pink peonies, probably flown in from places south of the Mason-Dixon.

No expense spared for the wedding of a rising country-music star who looked like he belonged on the cover of a magazine. No doubt *People* had photographers lined up, and the paparazzi would be out in droves.

Which added an element of difficulty to this gig. But if Emberly did this right, she'd be in and out, information acquired, and back on the road by tomorrow. She'd make her delivery, disappear, and never again have to look over her shoulder.

At least, in her wildest dreams.

Of course, even as she walked around the room, guests picking up her offerings, her gaze landed on *him*. Her target.

Declan Stone.

She'd looked at his picture—*pictures*—for so long she could find him with her eyes closed, simply feel his presence in the room. Dark hair with hints of red, clean-shaven tonight but usually with a thin scrape of dark whiskers to match. Square jaw, a little cleft in the chin, and bone-jarring deep-gray eyes that could look right through a man—or woman—and dissect his soul.

Thanks to his elaborate home gym and the hours he spent there, probably thinking through his cyberweapons-of-war designs, he had barely an ounce of fat on his sinewed washboard frame. Wide shoulders and standing a good six foot two, his mere presence in a room took the air from it.

Or maybe it was simply the way he held himself. Arrogantly confident, slender fingers on the stem of his red-wine glass, his feet braced, listening with a slight cock of his head to a woman in a garish gold dress as she gestured with her hands. As if he might not be actually plotting his next double-crossing move against his country.

The traitor.

Three months of surveillance, and finally, *finally*, Stone had stepped out of the cover of his Batcave, into the light.

And it wouldn't last long. Four days, maybe five, max, during which Stone turned from cybertech inventor to dashing philanthropist, glad-handing country-music stars who might endorse his favorite charity, Maggie's Miracles.

The same charity that groom Oaken Fox helped fund, giving over fifty thousand last year to help children who suffered spinal-cord injuries. She blamed Oaken's fiancée for the connection—Stone owned an estate on his own private lake some twenty miles east, between Duck Lake and Minneapolis.

Yada yada yada, hooray hooray. She hated do-gooders who tossed out money and then stepped into the limelight.

The real heroes were the people who stayed in the shadows. Who did the grunt work that kept the world from self-destructing.

Emberly had already seen the Kingston parents talking with Stone, laughing, enjoying the wedding festivities.

Everybody happy. Nobody paying attention to the thief—actually, she preferred Artful Dodger, thank you—in the corner.

She spotted the groom now, standing with his pretty bride—short dark hair, wearing a dress, a thousand miles from the tough survival-reality-TV star who'd gotten a bad rap. At least in Emberly's opinion. Not that she paid attention, but again, *research.*

There was a reason her country had picked *her*.

"These are so nummy!" A woman plucked the last two walleye crackers from her tray. Reddish hair, almost like Emberly's—although tonight Emberly was a dark-haired brunette. "I'd forgotten how good walleye is. Here, Axe, you need to taste one of these." She handed a cracker to a man standing next to her, dark blondish hair, the build of a man who worked outdoors for a living.

Emberly-Ashley offered a tight, polite smile and kept moving. She just needed to offload the last of the Brie bites, then she'd figure out a way to get close to Stone. Grab that wineglass from his grip.

Step one: fingerprints.

She offered a Brie bite to a woman with long blonde hair, who shrugged and took it. One more to go—

She turned and nearly crashed into a man standing right behind her. He caught her tray, then her arm as she overcorrected, nearly falling backward.

"Hey—you okay?"

She might call him good-looking, with his light-brown hair, short and tousled. He wore a hint of the same brown on his chin, his five-o'clock shadow kicking in. He wore black dress pants, cinched around a trim waist, and a white oxford, open at the neck, his sleeves rolled up his forearms, like he'd been working. Mr. Reflexes let her go, gave her a smile, and it was then that she noticed his eyes.

Blue—like the color of the ocean at dawn, deep and layered and possessing an ability to capture her.

Look away.

She'd seen him before. She knew it in her bones, like an ache deep inside that she couldn't place.

"Sorry," she said. "My fault."

"No, that was mine. I was looking at my watch." He held it up.

Nice watch. No, a *really* nice watch. A Rolex Submariner with a green face, silver cybersteel design, luminescent hands, waterproof at three hundred meters.

A dive watch.

So, a former spec ops guy. Or a wannabe? Even so, the watch landed at a solid ten G's, so clearly Reflexes was part of the rich-and-famous club.

She might've considered lifting it if she weren't already on a job. Flashing a quick smile, she stepped back. "Brie bite?"

"They're really good, Steinbeck," said the woman behind her.

"Okay," he said and took the bite. "Thanks."

"Here to serve." She winked then—*oh, good grief*—and walked away. Way to make herself memorable.

But she'd dumped her tray, which meant focus on the job. It was just a matter of timing. She glanced at Stone—he had maybe three, four sips left of his wine, depending on the degree of interest he had in the blonde's riveting monologue.

She kept one eye on him as she slid by a couple just finishing their mules. They added their empty copper mugs to the tray.

One sip—no, two.

Time to angle toward the hearth—

"Did you nearly knock over a guest?"

She glanced up, jolted. Nolan had come up behind her.

"Sorry. I turned too fast."

"Slow down. Be invisible."

She nodded. "Yes, sir." Usually, *invisible* was her middle name.

"Fill your tray, then help fill the buffet trays in the kitchen."

Her mouth tightened, but she nodded and yes-sir'd again. Glanced at Stone.

One more sip. Another server had started picking up glasses, heading down his row.

Probably wouldn't be a good look to hurdle tables. But she needed that glass.

She smiled as she held up the tray to a big man, dark hair, a bit of beard growth, a lumberjack's build. He gave her his empty can of Diet Coke. Hilarious.

But she'd managed to edge near the hearth.

The other server had stopped to allow a woman to finish her champagne. *Bam,* and fast-break to the goal.

Emberly stepped out, quick-walking toward Stone and his group—

Stone left the group, heading for the bride.

And that's when Mr. Reflexes nearly took her out. How he'd moved from over at the bar to right in front of hearth, she had no idea, but he jerked back, hands up. "Sorry!" He again caught her tray. "I guess I'm destined to take you out."

She had steadied herself before the empty glasses toppled onto him, and now fabricated a smile. "No problem."

Except Stone had dumped his glass, and there went her future.

Reflexes had gone to the front, whistled, and introduced his father, who stepped up to pray.

She headed back to the kitchen to regroup.

In the end, it was easier than she thought. She simply walked around after dinner with coffee, sidled up to Stone and offered him decaf or leaded.

"Full strength," he said, glancing up at her.

She didn't look at him. *Invisible.* But as she caught the extra drips with her other napkin, she removed his butter knife.

That should work.

She just needed a thumbprint.

For tonight.

She had four days to get the rest.

It would help if she didn't feel eyes on her as she finished serving the coffee. If, as she exited the room, she didn't glance back and see *him.*

Reflexes—what had they called him? Steinbeck?—his blue eyes

on her, connecting with hers—*oops!*—for a long second before she disappeared into the kitchen.

That was close.

She wrapped the knife into her napkin, then, while the rest of the servers trafficked through the kitchen, she stepped out into the entryway, grabbed her jacket, and exited the supper club.

As she disappeared into the night, toward her rental, she took off the wig and shook out her short red hair. Then she took off the apron and dropped it all into the dumpster.

Now that was what she called invisible.

FOUR

THE DRIVE BACK TO THE INN, TRAPPED IN the car with Jack, didn't hurt quite as much as Harper thought it would.

In the dim light from the dash, she had only his low tenor and the outline of his face to remind her of the terrible dream-come-true moment of finally sitting in his cute little—and yes, ancient—Geo Tracker.

It wasn't quite as romantic as she'd dreamed, the heater barely keeping up, the seats narrow and cracked. But he still had those amazing hands that could catch a football and . . .

And that's when she pulled herself out of her high-school fantasy and back to the present, to the casual catch-up conversation that Jack was attempting.

"I hear you're freelancing. I thought you were working for some magazine in Nashville."

Interesting. He knew that? "I'm in between gigs. Are you still doing the missing person's thing? What do you call it—being a rewardist?"

"I don't call it anything. I just . . . show up and help if I can."

"So, what is that—professional nice guy?"

He glanced over at her then, something of darkness in his eyes, and of course it only ignited the investigative journalist inside her. *Something . . .*

"Depends. Sometimes yes, sometimes I get sued."

Hello, darkness, my old friend. "Sued?"

He shook his head. "Hazard of the trade. Which is why I don't do contracts. I can't let people down if they don't depend on me."

"Interesting way to live."

"Truth." He had turned down the road to the inn. "I don't make promises. And I don't have any power, really. I carry a gun—I have a concealed carry for Florida, which is good in thirty-seven states but not Minnesota, so it stays in the lockbox in the trunk. And I'm not bonded or licensed and—"

"But you're a lawyer."

"Nope."

Right. He'd failed the bar, according to Boo. Harper had that information tucked away somewhere in the Never Open file on All Things Jack.

"So, just a vagabond. A finder of lost things. A sometimes nice guy, sometimes troublemaker," she said. "Got it."

And there it was, a rare smile.

"Why are you getting sued?"

His smile vanished. "Someone got hurt."

He went silent then, and she opened up another file in her brain called Things I Shouldn't Care About.

"In Florida?"

He gave her a glance. "How do you know I live in Florida?"

"Plates on the Geo. And you mentioned you had a concealed carry permit from Florida."

The sides of his mouth lifted again. "Right. And yes."

"You mostly work in Florida?"

"I work where there's a missing person. I spend a lot of time in

Arizona, New Mexico, Oklahoma, Missouri, and Louisiana. But I like Florida."

"Too much snow?" She gestured to the dark, frozen banks lining the road.

He drew in a breath. "Too cold, yes."

Interesting, and it only brought up, well, The Fight.

The one that'd caused Boo to join the reality-television survival show. And then, after the disastrous social media, to flee to Alaska. Maybe it had also caused Jack to flee.

"I saw you and Boo tonight, embracing. So . . ." She glanced at him. "You two okay?"

"I hope so," he said softly, and it found all her unguarded places. The guy actually sounded . . . humble. Sorry.

He glanced at her. Maybe he knew that of course Boo had turned to her best friend with the sordid details. "I was out of line. It was right about the time Steinbeck got wounded, and then Brontë came home from the military after being with the Marines, and I just saw her getting hurt too. So I opened my big mouth and said something that I thought would shut her down."

"Yeah, not so much."

"Mm-hmm." He sighed. "I was just trying to . . . Never mind. Anyway, yes, I think we're okay."

She glanced at him. He appeared actually in pain.

Trying to . . . what? She wanted to follow up, but she still had the memory of the look in his eyes back at the supper club when he'd apologized. The one where he'd looked nearly wrecked, the guilt from the past rising in his eyes.

So maybe the guy had had enough of walking through the shards of yesterday for one night.

She nodded, looked away, let the quiet fall between them.

Slowing, he pulled past the inn and then down the road to Doyle's place. "What do you write?"

"Culture pieces. Personality articles. I recently did one on Bliss."

"The actress? She was in *Main Street Blues,* right?"

"The Broadway show, then the movie. She's from Minnesota, did you know that?"

He shook his head.

More silence settled between them.

"It's weird, right? That Penelope left without me?"

"Dunno. Does she do that?"

"Disappear?" *Oh.* "Actually, yes. She's done it a couple times, but those were different."

"Really." He pulled into Doyle's drive.

"Yeah. Once in college, for a weekend with her boyfriend. Her father sent a security team to find her."

He braked in front of Doyle's house. "A security team."

"She's . . . wealthy . . . But she's sort of trying to make it on her own. Although, she still has security that checks in on her."

"And the second time?"

"Publicity stunt to promote *Penny for Your Thoughts.* She left clues and asked her audience to find her. Whoever won got to join her for a posh weekend in Paris. It worked."

"I'll bet." He turned the car off, held onto the steering wheel. "I saw her talking with Conrad earlier. Maybe he charmed her away from the party."

"Yeah." She reached for the door handle. "Thanks for the ride, Jack."

He didn't look at her but nodded, then backed the Geo out of the driveway and headed down the road.

Doyle's stairs creaked as she went up to her bedroom and turned on the light.

No Penelope.

Maybe Jack was right. She'd been standing with Penelope when Conrad came up and complimented her on her dancing. The man, center for the Minnesota Blue Ox hockey team, had charisma—charisma that occasionally appeared on social media.

Oh brother. Why couldn't it be easy—just let a guy in, enjoy his company without analyzing his every motive?

And then there was Jack's laughter, playing like a siren to warn off her attempts at relationships.

No, this was her future—pajamas and her article.

She changed, then got into her magnificent plush velvet-covered bed and pulled up her laptop.

A Moonlit Prelude to the Main Event

It is a crisp, starry evening in the quaint town of Duck Lake, Minnesota—just three days before Oaken Fox and Brontë Kingston are set to exchange vows, then celebrate at the grand King's Inn on the shores of Duck Lake. As the sun dips below the horizon, a palpable sense of anticipation and excitement fills the air.

Earlier in the day, the soon-to-be newlyweds gathered their bridal party for a private dance lesson...

She closed her eyes, searching for words, feeling Jack's hand on her back instead. *Oops.* And then suddenly she was in the Geo, listening to his soft voice.

"Someone got hurt."

Aw. She minimized her document and opened up her search bar.

It wasn't hard to find the article in the *Gainesville Sun* about a hunt gone wrong for a missing person. According to the article, an eighteen-year-old girl, the daughter of a state senator, had gone missing, and Jack had answered a posting offering a reward.

The sheriff hadn't been kind about Jack's profession or his assumption that the girl hadn't been kidnapped—something the local sheriff didn't buy into. Jack found the girl and her so-called kidnapper at a local farmhouse. According to Jack, he found them in an embrace—something the parents denied. By the time SWAT got there, it was out of his hands. Mostly because Romeo also happened to be a convicted felon out on parole and the sheriff had no time for Jack's theories.

The alleged kidnapper died on site, Tansy shot and in a coma, and Jack ended up behind bars for obstruction of justice and reckless endangerment. Never mind that he'd been the one who'd called the cops, according to his statement.

And now the parents were suing him. Just ignore the fact that he could have been killed . . . and had been the one to find her.

It all put a burr inside her and fired her instincts to defend him. Which he clearly didn't want or need, if she tracked back to his matter-of-fact but chilly responses in the car.

Interesting. And, fine. Back into the Not Her Problem file. She went back to her article, tried to focus.

Oaken, ever the natural performer, effortlessly leads Brontë in a series of two-step twirls and dips, and magic twines through the building.

By the time the evening draws to a close and the last guests have bade their farewells, an air of giddy anticipation has taken hold. For Oaken and Brontë, their fairy tale is about to reach its pinnacle. And for everyone who has the privilege of bearing witness, the weekend's festivities are shaping up to be unforgettable.

Slightly sappy, but *PopMuse* would love it.

She sent the teaser off to Clarice with a request for a release to give to Boo and Oaken, and closed her computer. Then she turned off the light and walked to the window.

The moonlight stretched a luminescent finger along the pristine white of the lake, the trees reaching their dark arms into the velvety night. And in the distance, the undulating pink and green ribbons of an aurora borealis rippled through the sky.

It felt strangely magical.

She climbed under her warm comforter and watched the sky until sleep found her.

And then, of course, the files in her brain opened and she was a teenager on spring break, kissing a boy that could never be hers.

Her subconscious was such a traitor.

Dawn, and the aroma of eggs simmering in butter, maybe bacon on the stove, slipped into her room, and she woke, having slept hard.

Dreamed hard.

So hard she hadn't heard Penelope come in. She rolled over, the light wan but enough to see—*wait.*

She sat up.

Penny's bed remained untouched, although her suitcase still lay open, the insides tumbled, the debris of last night's clothing changes spilling out onto the floor.

Harper got up and went to the bathroom. The door hung ajar, but she knocked anyway. "Pen?"

No answer, and she pushed it open. No fresh haze from a recent shower. Just Penelope's makeup scattered on the counter—brushes and liner and mascara.

Harper headed back to her bedside table and picked up her phone. Dialed Penelope's number.

Hellooo—it's me. Do that thing you do and I'll call you back. Toods!

Harper hung up and dropped her phone on the bed.

She heard Jack in her brain. *"I saw her talking with Conrad earlier. Maybe he charmed her away from the party."*

She brushed her teeth, fluffed her short hair, then dressed in a pair of jeans and a sweatshirt and headed down to the kitchen.

Time stopped, right then, as Harper entered the doorway.

Five of the Kingston siblings sat around an old oak table—laughing, passing syrup, Doyle serving up eggs, Austen adding pancakes to a plate. Steinbeck sat beside Boo, reaching over her for the butter.

Jack had taken the end chair, wearing a flannel shirt, his dark hair wet as if he'd showered, still wearing the dark beard.

Sure, they were older and grown up, but seeing them together—almost healed from the terrible rift that had torn their family apart—stirred old longings inside her.

From back when she'd had a place at the table, her feet swinging from a chair, hoping eighteen-year-old Big Jack might walk into the room, his hair mussed.

For some reason, his mumbled words from last night about the fight raked up. *"I was just trying to—"*

What?

She didn't have time to pull the words apart because right then, Conrad walked into the room, showered and wearing a Blue Ox pullover. "Wow, you guys are loud."

"What are you doing here?" The words just spurted out, and maybe she wore a hint of horror in her expression, because even Steinbeck put down his fork.

Quiet.

"What do you mean? I'm here for a wedding?" His brow rose.

"No, I mean—you're not with Penelope."

He stilled. "Should I be?" He looked at his siblings, back at her.

"Penelope didn't come home last night."

Conrad frowned, his blue eyes wary. "Why are you giving me that look?"

"Because . . . well . . ." She glanced at Jack, then back to Conrad. "We thought that maybe you two had . . ."

"We?" Conrad glanced at Jack. "What?"

"Hey," Jack said, lifting a *whoa* hand. "Her friend disappeared from the restaurant. I just said that maybe you . . . might have . . . um . . ."

Conrad shook his head. "Don't believe everything you read online." He turned back to Harper. "I haven't seen her since last night at the restaurant."

Boo got up. "She didn't come back?"

"Her bed isn't slept in. We ordered an Uber last night, and she left without me." Harper glanced at Conrad again.

"I promise you, I don't know where she is." He folded his arms across his athletic chest. "And I know better than to do some late-night field trip right before a game."

"You have a game?" This from Austen.

"A doubleheader. Tonight and tomorrow night." He held up a hand. "Don't worry—I'm stopping by the tux rental today on my way back to St. Paul. And"—he pointed his gaze to Boo—"I'll be back for the rehearsal dinner."

Boo shook her head. "Fine. Whatever. What about Penelope?"

Steinbeck had risen with Boo, his question directed to Harper. "Did you try calling her?"

"Voicemail."

Boo walked over to her, her eyes wide. "Okay . . . so . . . don't worry, we'll find her."

And then she turned and looked at Jack.

His mouth opened, and Harper could nearly see the under-standing washing over him. "Wait . . ."

"Jack. She's missing."

He looked at Harper. "She's done this before."

"What? This is not that."

Boo pleaded now. "C'mon, Jack. Please. You have to find her."

He drew in a breath. And in her head, Harper heard, *I can't let people down if they don't depend on me.*

And just like that, in a moment that should have been accompanied by bright lights and singing, she got it. The fight. The rift. And now, after four years, healed or on the way.

"*I was trying to . . .*"

Protect my sister. Yep, that was the probable end to that sentence. And now he didn't want to promise something that might end up . . .

No. Penelope was fine. Probably on a shopping trip to Minneapolis. But even Harper's brain said that didn't make sense.

Still, the realization of all of it made her open her mouth, made the words come out almost on their own. "I'll offer a reward."

Even Boo gave her an incredulous look.

Jack shook his head. "No, that's not—"

"A hundred bucks if you can find Penelope."

He shook his head.

Boo rounded. "He'll take it."

"What?" Jack had risen. "No, I won't—"

Boo spun to face him. "Please. Jack. Find my friend."

Harper's heart nearly went out to him when he sighed and then nodded. "Of course I will."

But only *nearly*, because he got up, pushed his chair back, wiped his mouth, and looked at Harper when he said, "But I have three rules."

"Oh goody," Harper said.

He narrowed his eyes. "One, no promises."

She could have guessed that.

"Two, I don't make arrests. And I don't rescue anyone. I find them and let the authorities do the rest."

"Fine. And three?"

He met her gaze. "Rule three. I work alone."

She stilled, then, "In what world?"

"In my world." Then Big, Arrogant Jack pushed his bossy self past her and out of the room.

———————●———————

Perfect. Just when he'd found his footing in the family again. Sort of. Maybe.

At least he hadn't promised. *Aw.* But now he looked like a guy who had to be bribed to help. Not that he intended to take Harper's money. And he *was* going to say yes—

"Where do you think you're going?"

And here came trouble. He turned as Harper came in hot on his tail. "What do you mean you don't want help?"

He stopped, right there in the living area of Doyle's renovated, restored home with the gleaming oak woodwork and the marble-tiled fireplace, the plush velvet sofas that bespoke a time of elegance.

His mother's touches, for sure—Doyle was only caretaking the place for now while he tried to get his feet back under him. Maybe a better choice than jumping in an old school bus . . .

Whatever.

Jack rounded on Harper. "I mean—I work alone. *Help* means I have to watch your back, and some of these things can get out of hand—"

"I'm worried, okay? I called her, and she's not answering."

"Did you call her house? Her family?"

Her mouth opened. "No. She doesn't live at home . . ."

"We should call the cops."

She stared at him.

"What?"

"What if I'm wrong? What if she's . . . I don't know, in Minneapolis, shopping? And suddenly there's cops everywhere, right during Boo's wedding."

"Why would she be in Minneapolis *shopping*?"

"I don't know—it's Penny. She does what she wants." She looked at her phone. "I'd call her mom, but Penny would murder me if I worried her without proof."

"Why?"

Harper sighed. "Reasons. I will try and get ahold of Franco."

"Who's that? Boyfriend?"

"Assigned personal security. Although, she's sort of recently shrugged him off, so . . ."

"She shrugged off her personal security?"

"Long story, but I did mention she's a Pepper, right?"

"Yes. From the Pepper family billions. . I did make that connection." Could be, however, that he wasn't the only one. Right. "Fine. Okay. I got this. The last thing I need is—"

Her eyes narrowed.

"—a reporter detailing everything, maybe giving anyone a reason to suggest that I might do something out of bounds."

"You're talking about the lawsuit over the girl who got shot. Your belief that she wasn't kidnapped."

He stilled. "You googled me."

Her mouth pinched.

So yes.

"You made my point. I'll call Bront—ah, *Boo*—if I hear anything." He turned to go upstairs, where he shared a room with Conrad, who, yes, had been tucked in bed sleeping when Jack arrived back at the house last night after checking on Aggie.

He'd wanted to spend today getting her towed to the inn. Or at least somewhere that wasn't the market parking lot. But by the looks of the parking lot at the inn last night, as well as at the Grover, the Norbert, and even the smaller Rudolph House, he'd need to find a place at the market, out of the way.

Of course, Harper wouldn't leave his dismissal there. She scampered up behind him. "She's my roommate. My friend. And I'm not going to write an article about searching for her—"

"Or about me?" He glanced at her. "Even if it could get you clicks?"

"Why would I write an article about you?" She met his gaze.

Her eyes stirred something inside him. He drew in a breath. Maybe she didn't know. Hadn't read his book.

Wouldn't make the recent hiccup in his career into a reason for the media to drag up his mistakes. What he'd been thinking back then still eluded him.

So. "No reason. Just . . ." He shook his head. "I move faster on my own."

"Not this time. You're on my dime." She pushed past him. "I'll meet you out front in five." She beelined to her room.

"You didn't hire me—aw."

He had four minutes to lose her.

He stalked to his room, grabbed his wallet and phone, brushed his teeth, and then headed downstairs for his boots and jacket.

Whoa, she was fast. Dressed in leggings, a white parka, boots, and a hat, her short hair curling out from the back.

He glanced at her, said nothing, and she waited while he put on his work boots and grabbed his jacket.

Then she followed him out to the Geo, and when he unlocked the car, got into the passenger side.

"Fine. Don't get in the way. People get jumpy when they see a reporter."

"I'm her best friend. Not a reporter."

He sighed and nodded and pulled out into the blue-skied, white-scaped day. "We'll start at the Moonlight Supperclub. Talk to the manager, maybe any valets that might have been on duty."

"What about contacting Uber and seeing who might have picked her up?"

"We'd need a warrant. Although, if this turns out to be an actual kidnapping, we'll *have* to contact the police."

"If?" She looked at him, but he didn't meet her gaze.

"If." He turned out of the inn's drive, down the street, past her parents' little yellow house. Yes, he knew where she'd lived—had cringed every time he'd driven past it for a couple years after that spring. "You said she'd done this before. A stunt. I was listening to the podcast on the drive up. I know she's about to announce who she thinks is the killer in the Sarah Livingston case."

"So?"

"So, what if this is just publicity, to get more attention on the podcast before the big reveal?"

"C'mon. She has a half million listeners. I doubt—"

"Or a stall technique? What if she doesn't know . . . and is buying time?"

"She wouldn't do that."

He raised an eyebrow. "Even for publicity?"

She rounded on him. "She didn't alert the press, did she?"

"Um . . . you're the press."

Great, now she clenched her jaw and turned away.

"Listen. I've learned that we don't know people as well as we think we do. And when people get desperate, they do things they never thought they would."

"She's not desperate," she snapped. "She's . . . smart."

He made a noise of disbelief, mostly because she might be right. And he didn't have a gut feeling about anything right now.

Except, maybe, that he didn't want to let Boo down. Not when she looked at him with so much hope. "The last thing Boo and Oaken need is scandal around their wedding. Brontë's had enough scandal with the whole Boo Hoo Kingston thing."

"She likes the name Boo. Or did until social media made a meme out of her name."

"They made a meme out of the reality show and the fact that her boyfriend from the show dumped her on air and she made a stink about it. I hate social media. And the last thing I'm going to do is let Penelope turn *Boo's* event into a circus."

Harper said nothing. But she sighed, her breath fogging up the windshield. "I hope, for Penelope's sake, that you're right and this is just a publicity stunt."

They drove through town, then out to the supper club, and pulled into the empty parking lot. Just a couple cars near the employee entrance, and the main door was locked.

He went to the employee entrance, Harper following him, and knocked on the door, then poked his head in.

He saw an entryway into a hallway that led back to offices, and the kitchen in the opposite direction. He held the door for Harper, then headed toward the offices.

Doors hung open around a small reception area with a desk and chair, a window that streamed daylight into the dark, wood-paneled space. Clearly, they hadn't updated the administration area during their big post-tornado overhaul.

The receptionist looked up from where she worked on a laptop. Midthirties, brown hair, too much time staring at a computer, maybe. "Can I help you?"

He glanced at the nearest open door and spotted Julian from last night, dressed in a vest and a clean shirt, his blond hair groomed. "I need a moment with Channing Tatum over here." Then he walked into Julian's office.

The man had risen and now came around his desk. On the walls hung pictures of what looked like Broadway dancers in costume. *Chicago, A Chorus Line, Cabaret, 42nd Street, The Wiz,* and of course, the newest hit, *Main Street Blues.*

"You're with the Kingston-Fox bridal party, right?" He held out his hand.

"Jack Kingston. This is Harper." Jack glanced at her, and she extended a hand for Julian to shake. "We have a member of our bridal party who is . . . let's say AWOL, and we are trying to track down her last knowns. Did you have any valets working last night around nine p.m.? She was waiting for an Uber at the door."

Julian folded his arms over his vest and leaned on the front of his desk. "Yes. We have a couple valets, but with such a small party, we only had one on duty. He should have been at the valet box—so maybe he saw her. I'll get his name and number for you."

Huh. Well, that was easy. "Mind if we take a look around the entrance, just to see if . . . I don't know—"

"She left a note behind?" Julian grinned. "Listen. We're a small town. People trust each other here. But it is a getaway, and people meet people, especially on vacation. Or at a wedding, where romance is blooming. Magic happens." He winked at Harper.

She stared at him, a look of incredulity. "My friend is missing, and you're joking—"

Jack grabbed her arm. "We'll be back."

He ushered her out into the hallway. "Listen. You make him mad and we get nothing. I don't have any jurisdiction here, no power of warrant. I can't 'drag him down to the station for questioning.'" He finger quoted the last words. "It's just me and my charm. So if you're going to be my sidekick, you need to work with me."

"I'm not your sidekick." She wrenched her arm from him.

He held up his hand. "Fine. But if you want to find her, you need to do it my way."

Her mouth tightened, but she nodded.

He thought.

Hopefully.

He checked back in with Julian, who was on the phone—hopefully to the valet—then headed down the hallway to the entrance where he'd seen Penelope last night.

"What are we looking for?" Harper asked.

"Anything. Once I found a broken bike light that led to a woman trapped in a culvert, nearly dead from exposure. Another time I found a vintage gold chain and traced it to an online estate sale, which led me to a Realtor who had decided to take out her competition."

"Dark."

"You have no idea." He was looking through the fronds of a plant while she picked up the cushions of a bench. "People are capable of terrible things when they are pushed." He stood up. "Nothing here. I'm going outside."

He stepped out into the cold, the wind burning his nose despite the sunshine. A thin layer of ice and snow covered the lot, tire tracks indented in the blackened grime. He walked over to the valet stand, but it was empty.

Harper pushed outside too. "Nothing."

"No, there's something." He pointed to the camera aimed at the parking lot. "Security footage. C'mon."

He headed back inside as Julian came down the hallway holding a Post-It note.

"I called Ethan, and he said he didn't see her leave. But you can talk to him yourself."

Perfect. A call from the boss about a missing person. Now, even if Ethan had seen something, he'd be loath to admit it. Jack managed a smile and took the paper. "Thanks." He pocketed it, then glanced outside. "I noticed you have security cameras. I don't suppose you'd let us take a look at the footage?"

Julian raised an eyebrow. "I think maybe that request will have to come from Sheriff Davidson."

Right. Or, "Sure. Although the request could leak, and then you'll have the news sniffing out that Penelope Pepper, the famous murder podcaster, has gone missing from the Moonlight Supperclub and . . ." He lifted a shoulder.

Julian sighed. "Let me make a call. All our footage is stored on our server in the security office. I suppose if Marcus is there, watching . . ."

"Marcus?"

"Alvarez. He'll be in after lunch. We have another event tonight."

"We'll swing back around then. Thanks." Jack pulled out his cell phone and stepped outside.

"That's it?" Harper followed him. "What if he changes out the tapes between now and then?"

The call rang.

"This isn't the eighties. Everything is digital and probably uploaded to the cloud, and why would Julian do that? He has nothing to hi—Hello, is this Ethan?"

The voice seemed groggy, as if he'd woken the kid, so maybe there hadn't been a previous phone call. "Yeah, sure. What do you need?"

"I'd like to talk to you about a woman you might have seen last night—"

"I already told my boss, I didn't see her."

"Perfect. I'd like to swing by just for a short chat." He looked at the name. "Lockwood. Your dad is Tom. You're over on Willow?"

A beat. "Who is this?"

"Jack Kingston. Just a friend of the missing woman."

Another beat. "Okay. Fine." He hung up.

Jack pocketed the phone.

"I remember Tom Lockwood," said Harper. "Science teacher."

"That's the one. He was a track coach too." He headed toward the Geo. "Taught me how to run."

"Now we know who to blame."

He glanced at Harper, frowned.

She grinned at him, then got into the Geo.

Oh, this would be a long day.

FIVE

S HE REFUSED TO ADMIT THAT MAYBE, JUST A little, she might be having fun as they drove through the city of Duck Lake, partners on the hunt.

Jack emanated a devastating hotness when he turned all focused and driven, and of course she knew that, but seeing it again, up close . . .

"What are you thinking?" His question drew her out of her thoughts. She made a tiny noise of surprise and then scrambled for an answer because, well, she couldn't tell him what she'd *really* been thinking. Or remembering.

Totally inappropriate to be stuck in the sweet memory of watching him water-ski on Duck Lake, the wind in her hair, tangled around her face as the man did jumps and flips and turns and all manner of daredevil tricks behind his father's Yamaha ski boat.

Tanned, muscled from working landscape for the inn all summer, that dark hair short, wet, and tousled, laughing and thumbs-upping Stein and Conrad, who sat on the back deck of the boat.

"Nothing," she finally said, her voice a little tweaked.

Focus! Because hello, Penny was *missing* and . . . and . . .

He glanced at her. "Still think she's been kidnapped?"

She raised a shoulder. "Do you?"

"We'll see. Ethan might have answers."

"He said he didn't know anything."

"He lied."

She frowned.

"Everybody lies. It's just a question of how much."

"I don't remember you being this cynical."

He turned off Main, headed toward Willow Street. "Realistic. Honest. And blame years of missing-person cases where the missing person turns out to have simply absconded with the contents of a bank account. Or worse, committed a crime and struck out on the lam, trying to fake their own death."

"You get those?"

"A lot of people want to be dead and start over as a new person."

"Sometimes it could be nice."

He sighed. "Yep."

Silence, and she glanced at him. "Is that what you did after you ran from law school? Start over?"

He sighed. "I didn't . . . Listen, I graduated. Finished law school. But I couldn't seem to . . ." He tried again. "Sticking around was too hard after Sabrina's death."

The name landed like a thud between them. "Sabrina?"

He turned onto Willow. "My study partner. If you say you didn't read the book, I won't believe you."

"I saw the movie."

"Bad version of the book. They changed her name."

"Stella, I think? And you were Jason."

"Like the Friday the 13th murderer, so that was a nice reference. I think that's the house. We had a pizza party after practice here once."

"It was her case that made you decide to be a . . . professional nice guy?"

"Finder, if we have to call it something. But no—that started when Boo went missing back when she was eight."

Right. Also when she'd first decided that she could give Jack her heart. "She told me about it."

"Went to my head. Listen, let me do the talking." He'd pulled into the plowed driveway, bordered on either side by snowy banks. A shoveled trail led up to a white ranch home with a wreath still hanging on the door, the pine tips turning to rust.

"Hardly—"

He looked at her. "Listen. If she has disappeared, then I don't want him spooked. It won't matter what we say—he'll think we're cops and that's the end. This isn't the movies. I can't *make* him talk."

"I wasn't—"

He turned and headed up the porch, knocked on the door. A few pine needles spilled into the snow.

Footsteps inside, and the door unlocked, eased open.

Ethan, she supposed. A lanky teenager who'd clearly had a hard sleep, his hair spiked, wearing a pair of faded jeans and a T-shirt. Clearly out of his persona as Supperclub valet. "Kingston?"

"Yeah," Jack said. "We just need a couple minutes."

It might take longer than that to get him to talk, but she held that in. She wasn't leaving without answers, so it didn't matter what the boss ordered. She didn't have to follow his crazy rules.

A purple haze lingered in the house, and the moment she stepped inside, the sweet, rancid odor of now legal cannabis filled the hallway. Jack glanced at her with a raised eyebrow, and she shrugged as they followed Ethan into the great room.

Heavy on the 1970s decor, a thick shag carpet covered an original wood floor, light-tan leather furniture, and large picture windows overlooked a river, frozen out back.

In the center of a wooden coffee table, an ashtray held a couple crumpled, burnt butts.

"Your dad around?" Jack asked, his voice easy, hands in his pockets.

"Cancun," Ethan said and dropped onto the sofa, picked up one of the burnt butts and a lighter and started to fire up breakfast.

"Dude—can you wait on your high for a minute?" Jack said, his voice easy.

Ethan doused the flame. Set the joint down and leaned back against the sofa. Shrugged. "Whatever."

Jack's jaw tightened, but he still managed the smile.

So many layers to this man.

"So, you were working valet last night."

"What of it?"

That thrummed a tight string in her. And she might be getting stoned just standing here.

Jack seemed unfazed. "Listen. This is a private conversation, just you and me—"

"And the babe."

The what?

"Yeah," Jack said. "So what you say here doesn't get back to your boss, ever."

Ethan gave him a look of disbelief.

"And I don't tell your dad. The coach. My coach."

His eyes narrowed. And then he let out a dark word. "Fine. I didn't have anything to do with your missing friend."

"This is her," Harper said, having pulled up Penny's picture on her phone. "Penelope Pepper."

Ethan seemed to focus on it for a moment. "Yeah, I remember her." He glanced at Jack. "Hard to forget. She's got rizz."

What?

Jack just nodded.

"She was waiting for a car."

"No Uber?" Harper asked.

"Yeah, Uber. Whatever. I think Ty drives Uber and Lyft—I've got his number. He does a lot of pickups at the Moonlight."

"Ty?"

"Bowman. He was supposed to pick her up."

"You're friends?"

"No. He's like . . . old."

"I know, Ty," Harper said. "He was in my grade."

Ethan focused on her. "Are you from here?"

"Duck Lake Storm, bay-bee."

He held out a fist. She met it. Whatever helped her get information.

"So Ty picked her up?" Jack said, ignoring her.

"Dunno. I had to grab a car—nice ride. Mercedes. Rental, though. I saw the tag when I drove it up. Guy who picked it up was big, reminded me of that actor who plays Jack Powers."

"Winchester Marshall?" Harper said.

Ethan snapped his fingers. "Yeah, that's the guy. Anyway, I got back and she was gone, so . . ." He lifted a shoulder. "That's all I know."

Jack said nothing.

"Really, man. That's all."

More silence.

"Fine. She was on the phone talking to someone when I left. Kinda sounded mad."

Now Jack nodded. "Upset."

Ethan pointed at him. "Right. Anyway, when I came back, like I said, she was gone."

"Ty picked her up?"

"I guess."

"Can you give me his contact?"

Ethan pulled a phone from his pocket, scrolled. "Give me your number, I'll text you."

Jack had pulled out his phone. Rattled off the numbers, and Ethan thumbed in the message.

Jack's phone dinged.

"We done?" Ethan reached for his joint.

Harper felt woozy, so hopefully, yes.

Jack gestured to her and headed for the door as Ethan lit up.

"No business card, no *call me if you think of anything*?" Harper said.

"I'm not a PI." He held the door open. "Besides, what would said card say? Professional nice guy?" He smiled then.

She rolled her eyes. "So, we talk to Ty?"

"After we stop at the market. I need to talk to Gordo Martin about Aggie camping out in his lot."

Aggie?

He wove his way from the snowclad neighborhood to Main Street, then over to the market. A renovated school bus, painted white, sat in the lot.

He parked next to it.

She got out. "So, this is Aggie."

"Sweet Aggie," he said, putting his hand on her hood. "I had this crazy idea to fix up a schoolie the summer after law school. Not sure why." He went around and unlocked the door. "Want a tour?"

Really? She followed him up the steps, past the driver's seat, and paused, a little undone.

Look who has a decorator's touch. It was the perfect man cave, with a leather sofa and an oversized flatscreen that hung from the wall over a long butcher-board countertop. A farmhouse sink, low white cabinets opposite the black leather sofa. A dishwasher, a clear corner cupboard that held jars of spices as well as dishes, a stainless steel fridge, and an electric stove.

"My office is in the back, along with the bathroom, the shower, and my bedroom."

"This is incredible, Jack. And here I felt sorry for you, living in a bus. I imagined an old mattress on the floor, a small tin-can fire."

"Definitely less maintenance."

"Missed opportunity, I think."

He laughed. "She looks humble on the outside, but inside, she's all state of the art. I keep tinkering, but yes, she's home." He ran a hand over the butcher-block counter. "I did her wrong by stopping in Iowa."

"What's in Iowa?"

"Oh, my lawyer, and manager. Husband-and-wife team. They find work for me, handle any legal issues, and do some online hunting when I need it. Sort of my backup."

So, not the loner she'd thought, either.

"I need to run inside the market and talk to Gordo."

She headed out, and he shut the door behind her. "Want something?"

"What, a Hot Pocket?"

He raised an eyebrow. "Maybe a salad?"

"Aren't I supposed to be paying your expenses?"

"For the love—you did not hire me. This"—he gestured between them—"is not a binding contract. I made no promises—"

"Right. The rule."

"The number one rule." He drew in a breath as if it mattered, a lot.

She held up a hand. "Okay. You don't work for me. But—I could still buy you a Hot Pocket."

"I don't want—never mind. Do you want anything?"

"I'll wait for one of your mother's cinnamon rolls."

He considered her. "Maybe a better idea. I'll be back."

She got in the car and pulled out her phone, checked her mail. Opened a message from Clarice.

Good start. Fun. Find the release forms attached. I reached
out to PopMuse. They'd like to put your articles on their blog
this weekend. Forward the releases to Goldie if they agree.
Don't hold your breath, but I like your tenacity. K.

She downloaded the releases, then called Penelope's phone again. *C'mon, Pen, where are you?* The same voicemail message played. She tried a text—again.

Harper
_____
Please check in. I'm worried.

Jack was talking with a man she didn't recognize, so she opened her Instagram and scrolled through the postings. Mostly celebrities, but a few posts on travel locations, some food bloggers, and a couple song drops from indie songwriters. Bliss had posted a clip from her upcoming performance in *Leap of Faith,* a rebooted Broadway musical.

She was about to close her phone when she spotted a post from *@PennyforYourThoughts.*

**Ready for the big finale to "The Case of Sarah Livingston"?
Listen to PFYT on Monday night!**

Then a shot of Penelope, bundled up, holding a coffee in a place called Echoes Vinyl Café.

She looked up to see that Jack had come out and carried two cups of coffee. She leaned over and opened the door.

He handed her a cup as he got in.

Oh. Sweet.

"You still a candy-coffee girl? Because I doctored it."

Time stopped, hiccupped. And maybe he realized it too, because he swallowed, then set his cup into the holder and put on his seatbelt.

"Thank you."

"Mm-hmm." He took a sip of his. "Gordo said if I can't tow her, I can move her to the back lot. Hopefully she can limp that far."

Harper nodded and flashed the picture at him. "Have you ever heard of Echoes Vinyl Café?"

"I saw Echoes on my way into town yesterday. Why?"

She looked at the picture. "Penelope just posted something from there."

He glanced at her. "Just now?"

"It's in my feed. She could have prescheduled it."

He put the car into reverse. "Or," he said, pulling toward the exit, "she could be hanging out at the coffee shop while we're running all over town looking for her." He pulled out. "Hate to say I was right, but . . ."

Then he looked at her and smiled.

Smiled.

Not a laugh, a smile, like . . . well, with the coffee, maybe he was attempting *friendship*?

"We'll do a drive-by."

He headed toward the shop, which stood where the old Duck Lake Diner had stood. *Shame.* The lot was scattered with a few cars—an orange Subaru, a beater sedan hand-painted and graffitied, and a grimy blue Taurus that had seen better years.

Pulling into a space, he put the car into Park. "Run in and check."

She nodded and got out.

Inside, the place smelled like old records, probably the array of LPs that hung against a backdrop of orange walls. A long counter that held thousands of records lined the far wall. A real trendy feel. An LP played on an old-style console phonograph. The Beatles' "Yellow Submarine."

In the middle of the room, a number of round wooden tables and molded vinyl chairs, also orange, filled the space. A few patrons, mostly millennials, sat at tables, typing into their laptops, nursing mugs of coffee.

A real Penelope vibe, but no Penny.

A coffee counter on the other side of the room listed the specials, scrawled on a black chalkboard wall. At the counter, a woman with short purple pigtails and an orange apron greeted her, the name Quinn on her tag.

Harper flashed Penny's picture. "Hi. Have you seen this woman?"

"Why?"

"She's missing."

"Like as in—"

"Like she might have been kidnapped." She lowered her voice, and Quinn's eyes widened.

Quinn, too, lowered her voice. "Sorry, no. I've been here all morning, but I'm filling in for Tallulah. She usually works the morning shift. She should be in this afternoon."

"Would she have been here last night, or yesterday morning?"

Penelope had gotten to town before Harper, so the post could have been scheduled yesterday.

"Yes," Quinn said.

"Okay. I'll be back. Thanks."

Jack was reading his own phone when she climbed back inside. He looked up at her, startled, then tucked the phone away.

"Everything okay?"

"Mm-hmm. What did you find out?"

"No luck. But Tallulah is coming in this afternoon."

He raised an eyebrow.

"Problem is, it seems like she took this shot during the day." She showed him her phone again. "See the light? It's daylight."

"So . . . yesterday, before the event?"

She nodded. Okay, here went nothing. "Let's go talk to Ty. This time, you let me do the talking. Ty and I have history."

———•———

History? What kind of history?

Harper's words sat inside Jack's brain, burning as if they might be, yes, a Hot Pocket.

Next to him, Harper had pulled up GPS, was now directing him to Ty's home, or at least the home of Ty's parents.

"Take a right up here," Harper said, pointing ahead.

They were driving around the smaller, older communities of Duck Lake, located near the central park that had been destroyed by the path of the tornado so many years ago. Bungalows and cottages and a few ranch-style homes. He hadn't come home after the tornado hit, but he'd called his parents for updates and read about it online.

That hadn't been the first time he'd regretted his lifestyle. But Doyle had moved back around then and had saved Jack from having to step back into his oldest-brother shoes.

"What kind of history?" He couldn't stop himself, apparently.

She gave a small snort that did not sound like laughter. "The kind of history that says the guy owes me."

"So not . . . um . . ."

"Romantic?"

He couldn't say the word, but, "Yes."

"Hardly. He drove me crazy. He was a hunter, a real outdoorsy guy. Wore camo to school. Loved his classic rock—was the kind of guy who blared the radio in his ancient Ford pickup in the school parking lot. Unfortunately, we were paired up for a mock debate in our senior year English class. It was a big school event every year, and everyone had to deliver a persuasive argument. It was a disaster from the beginning. He hated public speaking, and he did none of the research."

"I've been in a few group projects. One person does everything."

"Me. I did everything. But we both had to give a speech. Which I knew would be an epic fail. I'd seen him give speeches before. He'd get up and sort of ramble and sweat and . . . it wasn't pretty."

"Wow."

"Yeah. I'm not being mean—in fact, I tried to be a good partner. Stayed after school to help him write his speech, practiced with him, everything. And then, the day of the presentation, the guy took me out at my knees."

"Ouch. How?"

"What I didn't know was that he stole *my* speech during our study sessions, and when the event came, he got up and delivered it. Rote memory, perfectly, as if he was acting."

He slowed as they turned onto Birch. "I've heard about that phenomenon. That people who are introverts, who fall apart in public, can put on a different persona and become someone confident and amazing onstage."

"Oh yeah. He acted his way through the speech. And it was brilliant. I'd written it, and it was supposed to be my finale speech. We performed in the school auditorium, and I'd planned to videotape it for college entrance applications. My mom was even in the audience. But there it was, already given, and I had nothing." She paused. "It's up ahead."

She pointed to a story-and-a-half bungalow, gray exterior, white door, the mailbox at an angle, jutting from the snow, the victim of a snowplow. The house sat in a row of identical bungalows, probably built in the fifties when so many of these homes had gone up after the war.

"What did you do?"

"Oh, I got up and totally made up my speech on the spot. Embellished, lied, and basically told a story."

"So—"

"The other team killed me. Took out all my arguments, made me look like an idiot."

Oh.

"Is it some comfort that he's an Uber driver now?" He pulled into the driveway.

"Not even a little. They can make a lot of money. I'm an out-of-work journalist. Let's go." She opened the door, slammed it behind her.

Ho-kay. Maybe he should stop her before Ty took off running. He got out. "Harper—slow down."

But she was already at the front door, knocking.

He ran up behind her, but the door opened to an older woman, early sixties, maybe, in a pair of leggings and an oversized pink sweater.

"Mrs. Bowman. I'm looking for Ty," Harper said.

The woman squinted at her. "You seem familiar."

"Harper Malone. I went to school with Ty."

"Oh, yes. Ty and you were friends. I remember."

Jack lifted an eyebrow.

Harper sighed.

"I'm sorry—he's not here."

"Can I get his address?"

"Oh, he lives here, but he went to Minneapolis for the Blue Ox game tonight with a friend."

Oh.

"When did he leave?"

Mrs. Bowman glanced past Harper, her gaze landing on Jack. Her mouth opened. "Jack Kingston?"

Um . . . "Ma'am?"

"Oh, you look just like your book jacket cover."

Shoot.

"Wait here—will you sign it?"

"Oh, uh . . ."

Harper turned to him. "Yes, Jack, sign Mrs. Bowman's book."

"Come in," Mrs. Bowman said, and Harper walked right in.

Great. His mouth pinched. Mrs. Bowman had left them standing in the entry.

"Apparently I need to read the book," Harper said.

"It is better than the movie. Has the facts instead of fiction."

"Like what fiction?"

"Like she wasn't my girlfriend—"

Mrs. Bowman returned with the, *yikes, hardcover* version of *Sabrina's Last Case: The Search for Answers,* by Jack Kingston.

She flipped it open to the front, and a receipt fluttered out. She handed him a pen. "To Marjorie. And write something pithy."

Oh brother. But he signed it, with a *Happy reading*, because that's all he had. "When did Ty leave?" He handed the book back.

"Oh, yesterday. After work, I think. Thank you."

"Can you have him call me when he gets back?" Harper took the pen from Jack, then picked up the receipt and wrote on it. "I'm only in town for the weekend, so I'd like to catch up." Her smile matched her coffee—sweet.

"Of course. Ty will be so happy to see you. He still has your debate-team picture on his desk."

Harper practically pushed Jack out of the house.

"I forgot that Conrad has a game tonight," Harper said.

"You keep track of his game schedule?"

She followed him off the step. "Oh yeah, I'm a total hockey groupie. Glued to the television—"

He stared at her.

She laughed then. Really laughed. "Oh, your face. No, Jack. I have a normal Minnesotan's love of hockey—that's it. Conrad mentioned it to Penelope last night. She said she'd watch it if she could. I forgot that when he mentioned it this morning."

"If she could?"

"Yeah. I thought she meant all the wedding stuff, but maybe . . . I don't know . . . she had plans?" She sighed. "Maybe you were right.

Maybe she's not missing at all. She is a little ... quirky. Maybe she got Ty to drive her to Minneapolis to go to the game."

"Would she do that?"

"She bought tickets on the spur of the moment to a Wrexham match two years ago when they toured the US, just in hopes of seeing Ryan Reynolds, so yes."

He considered her for a moment. Funny, but he'd gotten exactly the opposite feeling in his gut. She had not taken a joyride into the city. "Let's check out the security footage."

He climbed back into the car.

Maybe he just didn't want to go back to the house. Maybe he'd liked the fact that Mrs. Bowman had his book and he'd signed it in front of Harper.

Maybe he liked the fact that Harper had told him about Ty, like ...

Shoot. Maybe he just liked her, the old feelings from the past stirring to life like an dormant ember.

She *so* wasn't an eighteen-year-old spring breaker anymore.

He pulled out and drove back through town to the Moonlight.

"So, what facts are different?"

He glanced at her.

"The book versus the movie."

Oh. "Well, first, I wasn't the last person to see Sabrina. She'd gone out with some girlfriends after our study session, and a bouncer at the campus pub saw her leave."

"But you were the first one to notice she was missing."

"She'd asked me to go with her somewhere the next morning, so yes. Except I was about an hour late. I went for a run, showered, changed, and went to her apartment. She'd left without me. I called her—no answer. So I waited there about an hour before her roommate came home."

"In downtown Minneapolis, in the height of winter."

"They got that wrong too. It was March. The snow was melting." He turned onto Main again. "And I didn't search for her by myself. Not at first. Like I said, I called her and called her and then contacted campus police. But I had nothing but a gut feeling that something wasn't right. And then, forty-eight hours later, I checked, and the campus police hadn't found her—and hadn't contact the Minneapolis police, so I did. They found a cam shot of her car leaving the neighborhood early the day she disappeared—a bank cam caught it. So they decided she'd gone home."

"To Iowa."

"Yes. And that's when I picked up the case and stopped studying for the bar exam."

He said it quickly, easily, as if it weren't a knife to his soul.

"And after that—the trip to Iowa to visit her family, and then you finding her car by the side of the road at a Minnesota rest area. The interview with a couple OTR truckers who saw her car there that morning, smoking. Did the movie get it right?"

"Yeah. I finally got the footage from the rest-area cameras, identified the trucker who picked her up."

"The movie had you tracking down the trucker."

"Nice guy. He brought her to a nearby town, where she got a tow-truck operator to pick up her car. Then she went to a local café to eat, and from there—"

"Vanished again."

"Yeah. Took me two weeks to figure out that she'd gone to meet with a witness. She was working for a law firm as a clerk, and I'm not sure why she went to talk to Hinkle, but she met him at the diner, then went back to his farm, where he showed her the radiation poisoning to his cows."

"Which eventually killed Hinkle."

"Yeah. I talked with him before he died. He filled in the blanks of how she went to the nuclear plant, got inside with the help of a local security guard, got samples, and was all set to deliver them to officials when she was caught."

"The movie ends with her running for her life through the woods in the dark."

"Actually, it ends with me—or my character—finding her body at the bottom of the cliff, but with the evidence intact. She saved lives."

"So did you, by finding her."

Her words found raw places inside, scraped up by the story. "Yeah. I can't help but think that if I hadn't gone for that run . . ."

"Jack. You have to forgive yourself."

He had turned into the Moonlight parking lot. Eight years since Sabrina's death, and he didn't have a clue what *forgive yourself* meant.

Now he just looked at Harper and must have worn his thoughts on his face, because she reached out and touched his arm. Sweetly. Like they were friends.

"Just saying that maybe the professional nice guy deserves some grace."

He glanced at her touch, heating his entire body, then blew out a breath. She let him go, and he unstrapped his seatbelt. "Let's find your friend." He got out and headed for the supper club.

Julian rose from his desk when he spotted them. "I talked with Marcus. He pulled up the footage and found your friend." He came around and led them back through the building, past the ballroom, the coat-check closet, and the dining room, all the way to a locked room, where he knocked.

A man answered, military vibe, built, and stuck out his hand to Jack. "Marcus Alvarez."

Jack introduced himself and Harper. "What did you find?"

"I pulled it up for you." The office held flatscreens with multiple cameras, a few rolling chairs, and in the next room, an office with a conference table, a whiteboard.

Now, Marcus offered Harper a chair and she took it. Jack stood behind her, arms akimbo.

The center flatscreen held a still picture of a woman getting into a white Toyota Camry. Definitely Penelope, dressed in that all-white outfit, the oversized man's jacket.

"Is that someone in the car already?" Harper leaned forward, and Marcus enlarged the screen. Hard to tell.

"Any shot of the license plate?"

"I already got that." Marcus handed him a piece of paper. "I ran the plate. That's definitely Ty Bowman's car."

"Play the footage," Jack said.

Marcus pushed play, and Jack watched as Penelope got into the vehicle and closed the door. It drove off-screen, darkness, the red lights flashing, then disappeared into the night.

Something didn't feel right. He couldn't put a name to it, but . . .

Harper shook her head. "Okay, I'm calling Franco." She got up. "See you tonight for your next dance lesson?"

Oh no.

"Perfect," Harper said and opened the door, holding her phone.

Jack thanked Julian and walked out behind her. She paced the hallway, nodding, talking to someone on the phone. She finally hung up and headed back to him.

"Okay, I called her house and talked with her security guy. He said that he'd heard from her—that she'd gone back to Minneapolis to chase a lead for her podcast." She pocketed her phone. "Maybe she found out something that she had to edit before the show dropped."

"Feels like she'd say something," Jack said.

"I know, but . . . she's a little over dedicated to her show—" She pulled out her phone. "It's a text from Boo. I need to go back to the inn for a dress fitting, and you're due at the tux rental place in town."

Right. Fine.

He headed down the hallway, the image of Penelope standing by the door, texting, reaching back to him. "She was upset."

"That's what Ethan said. But given his state . . . who knows?" She reached the door, but Jack put his hand on it.

"Call her again."

"Fine." She pulled out her phone as she headed outside, and dialed. "See. Voicemail." She started across the parking lot, hanging up.

A sound trilled from nearby, and he stilled. "Is that a phone?"

"Sounds like 'Bohemian Rhapsody.'" She, too, stilled.

Is this the real life? Is this just fantasy?

He put his hands on his hips, scanned the empty lot. Rounded back to Harper.

"Queen," she said.

"I know." He shook his head.

The song kept playing. *"No escape from reality . . ."*

Pine trees in planters lined the front walk of the supper club, and he walked near. The song died and then revived again. He searched the planters. Nothing.

The phone kept playing, and he walked down the row of pine trees.

"Because I'm easy come, easy go . . ."

He stopped at the end of the row, where the driveway turned toward the street.

The song had died.

Silence, just the shifting of the trees.

He listened a bit longer, searched the snowbank, but found nothing.

"We need to go," Harper said.

He nodded and turned back to the car.

But he couldn't ignore the fact that his gut said that Penelope might actually be in big trouble.

SIX

J ACK WAS HERE FOR A *WEDDING.*

Just in case his brain had forgotten. But standing in front of the three-way mirror at Dapper Duds Rentals in his penguin suit should jolt him back to reality.

Not here for a hunt. And definitely not here for romance.

Although, his instincts argued with him on at least one point, and his heart had thoughts about the other.

A midtwenties female clerk named Shelly stood behind him, smoothing down his shoulders, his arms, pulling on the back of the jacket. "Good fit."

"If you like sweating, strangulation, and fear." He mumbled it, but Doyle looked at him from where he stood, next in line for the fitting for his usher role.

"Fear?"

"Have you seen the price tag on this rental?" Jack lifted his arm and took another look at the rental price.

"Since when does Mr. Reward care about money?" Doyle looked every inch the kind of guy who hobnobbed with billionaires, comfortable and dashing in his tux. He wore an easy, relaxed smile and had cut his dark hair to a perfect trim. Mom always said that Doyle and Jack could be twins, with the same hair color, the stormy blue eyes, although Doyle had a hint of hazel in his. But that was where the resemblance stopped—Doyle had the easy charm and refinement of a humanitarian philanthropist. Jack preferred to get to the point, although he did know how to ease into it, when needed.

The rest of the groomsmen—Steinbeck and a guy named Shep—were still changing.

Apparently, Conrad had kept his word and stopped by earlier on his way to Minncapolis.

"Since Aggie decided her days were numbered."

"Whatever. Like you don't have a tidy ETF gaining millions," Stein said, coming out of the dressing room, something of a warm smile in his countenance.

And the terrible fist inside loosened even more. Maybe Jack would survive coming home. After all, he'd survived the last six hours with Harper.

More than survived.

Enjoyed.

Oh boy.

But she was smart and easy to talk to. They made a good team, and that thought jolted him. There was a reason he worked alone, and her name was Sabrina.

"You need to stop pretending you're a hobo," Doyle said. "I've seen your house in Florida. On the ocean."

"Not on the ocean. I'm two blocks off."

"Whatever."

"Fine, yes—I invested the money from the book sales, but showing up in a bus puts people at ease. I'm not a slick operator—I'm just a guy trying to help. Besides, I like having my own place to stay when I'm on the road."

Professional nice guy. Okay, maybe.

And now Harper's words found him. *"Just saying that maybe the professional nice guy deserves some grace."*

It wasn't that he didn't want grace—he just didn't believe it could ease the grip of his mistakes.

"Or you're desperate," Steinbeck said.

"Which makes them think I'll put everything into getting the reward."

"You're all set," said Shelly, and stood up. "Let's get this jacket off you." She pulled it off his shoulders.

"How goes it with finding Penelope?" Doyle asked.

"Not sure. We think she might have gotten an Uber ride to Minneapolis."

Shelly put the jacket on a hanger and handed it to Jack. "Next?"

Doyle stepped up to the podium. "Minneapolis?"

Jack unbuttoned his cuffs. "Maybe shopping. Maybe to watch the Blue Ox game. Harper says she's pretty impulsive . . ."

Stein stood at parade rest, watching them. "But you don't believe that."

Jack glanced at his younger brother. In a way, Stein seemed the oldest—his demeanor, his confidence. He always managed to show up when Jack didn't, at least after . . . well, Sabrina's death had really derailed Jack. And then the Big Fight had sealed the deal.

"I don't know. Apparently she does this—disappears on a whim. But there's something about the whole thing that feels . . . not right. I think we need to keep looking."

"You just want to spend more time with Harper." Doyle met his gaze in the mirror.

Jack stilled.

"Please. Remember, I was there, at the beginning. I saw you two during the mission trip."

"I'll give you a thousand dollars to never talk about that again."

Doyle held up a hand. "Just saying that I haven't seen that version of you in a long time."

"What version is that?" Jack's voice had turned a little dark.

"The happy, laughing, not-so-tightly-wound, less bossy version of Big Jack Kingston."

His mouth opened.

"Ditto," said Steinbeck, lips in a grim line. "I miss that guy."

"That guy went missing a long time ago." Jack turned toward the dressing room.

Ten minutes later, he sat watching Steinbeck get fitted. Stein still held his SEAL build, even after his injury and two years in the civilian world. And a tan, evidence of the last year working as a dive instructor on some remote Caribbean island.

Talk about running.

And now, of course, Harper stepped into his brain again and lingered. Maybe he *had* run a little—or a lot—after the debacle in Grenada. Definitely after Sabrina's death.

Stein looked over at him as Shelly pulled off his jacket. "We need a bigger size," she said and draped it over her arm, disappearing onto the showroom floor.

Stein grinned at Jack, gave him a thumbs-up.

"Get over yourself."

He laughed, and Jack let the sound of it sink into him, bathe a few wounds. Stein stepped off the platform and came over to him.

"So, what on earth is Doyle talking about? You and Bee?" He raised an eyebrow. "Seriously?"

"And now I have to murder Doyle, leave his body where no one can find it. I can do that."

Stein rolled his eyes.

"Fine. So, in my second year of law school, I came home for spring break, and Do-Gooder Doyle had arranged this mission trip to Grenada to clean up after an earthquake. I'm not sure how, but he got me to sign on, and I spent the week with a bunch of his friends. Or I thought. Harper was there—I totally didn't remember her as Bee." His brain, for a second, returned to the snapshot he kept tucked away. The one with her long, beautiful blonde hair in a braid down her back, her skin tan, those pale blue eyes bright, alive. The way she'd razzed him, made him forget the weight of his studies, at least for a week.

"And?" Stein looked at him, an eyebrow raised.

"And she was fun. Smart. She laughed at my jokes."

"I thought she was smarter than that." Stein grinned.

"Oh, you're hilarious. But yes, I . . . there were sparks. Something. And . . ." Here went nothing. Still, better for him to say it than Doyle. "I kissed her."

Steinbeck's grin vanished. "You didn't."

"It was an impulse. But to be fair, I thought she was older—at least Doyle's age."

"Not Boo's best friend. Which made her too young—"

"She wasn't too young, technically, but she was still in high school. *And* Brontë's best friend—I suddenly saw her as twelve."

"What was it that you used to call her?"

"Pigtails."

"Oh, that—that's bad."

Jack nodded. "I couldn't end it fast enough. I ignored her the rest of the trip, and ever since."

"Until yesterday."

He met Stein's eyes. "The problem is—"

"You've never forgotten her."

He lifted a shoulder. "Tried. Failed. And hated myself for that. And now . . ."

"And now she's back, and hot and smart and definitely not in high school." Stein shook his head. "This is what we called a major snafu—"

Shelly returned. "Try this size."

Stein took the jacket. "So, what are you going to do about it?"

"There's nothing to do. Four days until the wedding, and then I hit the road, so . . ."

"Mm-hmm." Stein stood still as Shelly smoothed his shoulders. "This is a good fit."

She nodded, appreciation in her gaze. *Oh brother.* She worked the jacket off him. "I'll get your order ready."

Stein stepped off the podium. "Unless you *don't* hit the road."

"Um—"

Jack's brother held up a hand. "There's a season for everything. Maybe Aggie's demise is a sign. You go back, take the bar—"

"And spend my life being strangled by the legal system?"

"Hey, you're the one who went to law school."

"Not sure why." He got up.

"I know why." Stein headed for the dressing room, stepped behind the cloth curtain, his voice rising from within. "It's because you're a Boy Scout, trying to change the world. Always have been. I blame Grandpa and all that time you spent with him fishing."

"He did like to tell stories while we waited for the walleye to bite."

"Yeah, legal-eagle, crime-fighting, evil-versus-the-good-guy stories." Steinbeck pushed back the curtain, now in his street clothes. "It's what made Dad run for mayor all those years ago, and after Dad retired, Grandpa turned his sights on you."

"Oh please," Jack said. "Don't tell me Grandpa's war stories are *not* why you went into the military."

"No doubt. But you, big bro, had big dreams. And be honest—none of them included you sitting behind a desk. You loved arguing cases."

"I loved a good story. And winning. And hanging out with Grandpa." He grabbed his tux and followed Stein to the front, where Doyle was finishing up his rental order. Outside, the sun had started to wane, sending firelight into the snowbanks.

"See you at dance lessons." Harper's words to him as he'd dropped her off at the bridal salon lit a terrible warmth inside him.

Down, boy. Four days. Then back on the road.

"I miss Gramps," Stein said as he handed over his credit card. "And hanging out with him in his shop, working on his boat."

"I can still smell the barn sometimes," Doyle said. "The diesel fuel in the air, or wood shavings from his projects."

"He had that old transistor radio with the cloth cover." Stein signed the receipt. "Used to listen to the local station—for fishing reports."

"And classic rock." Doyle hoisted his garment bag over his shoulder as Stein joined him. "Journey. Queen. Boston. I knew all the words. It's crazy how many old bands are reused in video games today. I'm constantly hearing the classics when I'm down at the Hub."

Jack stepped up to the desk, his credit card in his hand. "You're still volunteering at the Duck Lake Youth Center?"

"He's practically running the place," Stein said.

Doyle shrugged, and Jack spotted Doyle's own version of running in his gesture.

Jack paid for the tux, picked up the garment bag. "Thanks." And just like that, with Doyle's words, Harper's story about Ty rounded back to him. *Loved his classic rock.*

Queen, playing in the snow.

A phone? He looked at Stein. "I need to swing by the Moonlight before it gets dark."

Stein followed him outside. Jack hung his garment bag on the hook in the back seat and slid in, Stein on the passenger side.

"What are you looking for?"

"A phone. I think."

"Penelope's?"

"No. I think it belongs to an Uber driver—Ty Bowman. Maybe. Just a gut feeling." He glanced at his brother. "How are things going in—where are you at?"

"I've been working as a dive master in St. Lucia." He looked out the window. "But I think I might look into a tactical job.

Did you know our cousin Ranger lives in Minneapolis? He's on a private tactical team. They do SAR and security work and need contractors."

"So, personal security?"

"Maybe. Could be defense work overseas."

"How are the knees?"

Steinbeck ran a hand over both replacements. "Today, okay."

"Good enough for security work?"

"We'll see."

The amber rays of the sinking sun bled through the skeletal maples and oaks as he pulled into the lot of the supper club. Jack parked near the edge of the pine trees, where he'd last heard the ringing. Getting out, he turned on his phone's flashlight. Stood on the drive.

"So?"

"He's the Uber driver, so it doesn't make sense that he'd ditch his phone. So, let's say that someone took it and threw it. When we looked at the footage of Penelope getting into the car, Harper thought she saw a person already inside."

"Shared ride?"

"Maybe. Small town, so could be. But why throw out the phone?"

"You heard it ring? Where?"

He pointed to the edges of the pine-tree-lined drive. "Could be anywhere."

"Probably not in snow," Stein said, also shining his flashlight onto the bank. "To hear it, it would have to be on—"

"Pavement." The road was clear, just ice, some salt, a dark path that ran out from the supper club to the road. But over the years, ruts and cracks had formed. He walked to the edge, shone his light along the cleared area. "Sometimes, when I don't have a speaker, I stick my phone into a glass to amplify the sound. Hard surfaces can do that."

He focused his light on the broken edges, where the pavement had cracked, some of the spaces wider than others.

The light glinted against something and he leaned down.

The phone, black, lay on its side, wedged into a crevice. "Got it." He pulled it out with his gloved hand. "Screen's cracked. But it still has juice."

Steinbeck walked over, flashed his light on the webbed screen. "You need someone who can hack it internally."

"Nat could do it, but she'd need the phone."

"Our cousin Ranger. He works for that security outfit I mentioned. He has a connection with a white-hat hacker, a woman named Coco Marshall. She could take a run at it. I'll reach out to him." He turned off the light and pulled out his phone to text.

Jack looked at the damaged screen. The picture still bled through along with a text, almost unreadable. He shone his light on it.

Mom
Where are you? Because I'm
done lying for you.

Aw. Sometimes he hated it when his gut was right.

The whole thing had started to irk her.

Harper turned to allow a fellow bridesmaid, a woman named London, to unzip her gown in the dressing room at Blossom Bridal Boutique.

Penelope's dark-blue V-necked velvet gown hung on a hanger, and sure, she'd probably slide into a perfect fit, but the woman should have been here.

"Kudos to Boo for finding dresses we can wear again," London said. She wore her blonde hair back in a messy bun and was another one who could slide into a sample dress without adjustments. But

Harper liked her. No nonsense, the kind of person you could count on. Boo said that London worked as a pilot on their SAR team in Alaska, so clearly brave and smart too.

"Although, I'm not sure where I'm going to find a place to wear a tea-length long-sleeve velvet formal in the Keys." This from Boo's older sister, Austen, who'd looked stunning in her dress, her auburn hair down, her skin tan. She had already climbed out of her dress, and reappeared from the dressing room wearing jeans and a sweater.

Harper headed to a dressing room.

"What do you do again?" asked London, to Austen.

"I work for a dolphin and sea lion show. I'm a trainer."

"And she hunts for sunken treasure," Harper said, fixing the dress on its hanger. "Don't let her fool you. She's a master diver." She pulled on her jeans, her black sweater, and wished she'd worn something nicer, because next stop was the dance lesson.

With Jack.

"Find anything cool?" London asked.

Another voice answered. "She found a couple gold coins from the *Atocha*."

Harper emerged from the fitting room, where Boo had come in.

"The what?" London asked.

"It's a Spanish galleon that went down in 1622 about thirty-five miles off Key West, This"—he gestured between them—"is not sure they were from the *Atocha*, although it was in the area where the stern went down. But there are other shipwrecks up and down the coast. And it's a hobby, not a side hustle."

Boo held up her hands, but grinned. "Someday you'll find a lost treasure and strike it rich."

Austen laughed. "I'm happy with my dolphins." She pointed to Penelope's dress. "Should we bring this with us?"

Harper had already updated them on Penelope's whereabouts, based on her security detail's words.

She'd left out, of course, any details about Jack.

Details about how he'd listened when she'd told him about Ty, and even filled her in on Sabrina and the truth behind his hunt. It felt, just a little, like they'd found a friendship. Or maybe just partnership. Still, when he'd dropped her off, he'd met her eyes, holding on a little when she'd said *"See you at dance lessons."*

Dance lessons. The first time in his arms had roused the old crush. After today, tonight might do her in.

"I'll take it," Harper said. "I still can't believe she did this." She picked up the dress.

Boo nodded. "She probably wasn't the best choice for a bridesmaid. I only recently got to know her. But we needed someone to walk down with Conrad, and Oaken really liked how she handled the Mike Grizz case on her podcast. She's funny and sweet, and I don't know—it was a bit of an impulsive ask, but . . ."

"She'll be here," Harper said, putting her arm around Boo's shoulders, pulling her close. "It'll be fine."

"I hope she's back for tomorrow's spa and manicure day." She glanced at Harper. "Thanks for looking. I hope spending the day with Jack wasn't a total nightmare."

"I managed. Although I've decided that getting him to smile might be a personal goal."

Boo laughed and headed out of the dressing area. "He's always been serious—comes with being the oldest, I guess. But yeah, he was a lot more fun before law school and Sabrina's death." She reached for her wool coat, hanging by the door.

Harper grabbed hers as well. "He told me the real story in the car."

"Did he mention that after he finished school, he didn't attend graduation and completely abandoned his future?" Austen said.

"Not really, but I got that gist. Feels like he blames himself."

"They were study partners, so maybe. He's been a bit of a loner since then. He's a thinker and super loyal and probably spends way too much time in his head. Which is why he likes traveling, helping people that he can walk away from."

His words bumped into her head. *"I can't let people down if they don't depend on me."*

Boo stepped outside, holding open the door.

The setting sun had unleashed the wind, now burning against Harper's neck. "You couldn't have picked a destination wedding?"

"This is a destination," Boo said, winking. "The King's Inn is a famous wedding venue."

"In *June*." Harper shook her head. Austen cracked a smile.

"It's warmer than Alaska," London said and climbed into the back of the rented Escalade.

Boo stopped Harper with a hand on her arm. "Did Jack mention that he also hasn't had a girlfriend since Sabrina?"

"He said he wasn't dating Sabrina."

"Yeah, well, maybe not, but the fact is, he's a closed book. Don't get hurt, Bee."

Harper raised an eyebrow. "Don't worry. I'm over your big brother. Really."

Boo narrowed her gaze. "Right."

Harper rolled her eyes and got in. The car rumbled, started by remote, already warm.

She sort of missed the adventure of the Geo. *What?* No, she did not.

"By the way," Boo said, her voice lowered, "Oaken and I talked, and he talked with Goldie, and you're in."

In?

Boo smiled.

Oh, in. "You'll let me have the exclusive?"

"The article, yes. Pictures are already promised to *People*, but I'll give you a couple exclusive shots." She winked.

"Oh, Boo, thank you. I promise, I'll write you something beautiful."

"I know you will. I trust you." Boo gave her hand a squeeze, then shut the door.

The words wound down into her soul. *"I trust you."*

As they pulled into the parking lot of the Moonlight Supperclub, she spotted a couple cars as well as the Geo.

She tried to ignore it, along with the stupid rush of anticipation. It was just a dance lesson, not a date.

Not anything.

She got out, followed the troupe inside, and spotted Ethan by the door, dressed in his uniform. He smiled at her, nodded, seemed to have sobered up. Or maybe he just faked well.

Inside, she checked her coat and headed to the dance floor.

The men stood in a circle, talking and laughing—well, almost all of them. Jack stood, arms folded, legs spread out, as if he might be assessing their conversation.

Or a million miles away, thinking.

Boo walked up to Oaken, who kissed her, and then the one named Shep, with his dark hair and denim shirt, pulled London close. Romance hung in the air.

Austen looped her arm through Stein's, which left Harper to walk up to Jack.

"Hey."

He blinked at her for a moment, then pulled a long breath, didn't smile. She frowned.

"We need to talk," he said, just as Julian came into the hall.

"Okay, dancers, today we'll run through the two-step, then start working on the choreography of the *Dirty Dancing* crew." He clapped his hands and arranged everyone in a circle.

"What's going on?" she said to Jack softly as she put one hand on his shoulder, settled the other into his grip. He smelled good—she hadn't noticed that before. And being this close to him, the sense that he'd matured in the last ten years—filled out, become solid, muscled, capable—stirred inside her.

Nope, not a twenty-four-year-old spring-break fling anymore. *"He's been a bit of a loner since then."*

Shoot. Now she cared, thinking of him in that old bus, rumbling around the country. She absolutely would not take that as another personal challenge.

Would *not*.

The music started, one of Oaken's hits, and Julian had them moving around the floor. She counted in her head, quick-quick-slow, quick-quick-slow.

"I found the source of the song," Jack said, low, under his breath.

She'd been counting and now looked up at him, his words jolting her. She lost count, stumbled, and nearly went down.

He caught her, pulling her against his chest.

His amazing, solid, muscular chest, with the hard planes of his torso. "Gotcha."

Her heart did a crazy, unforgiving leap.

And then she looked up at him. His blue eyes held hers, and for a second, a long delicious second it looked like . . . maybe . . .

His gaze dropped to her lips and she swallowed, wanted to nod—

"Keep moving, over there."

Julian.

She pushed away, righting herself.

"You okay?" Jack said, and it seemed he sighed just a little.

"Perfect."

He'd stopped, now waited, then moved her back into rhythm. They nearly slammed into London and Shep, but Shep piloted away just in time, navigating around Jack and Harper.

"What song?" she finally said, feeling the beat again.

He blinked as if catching up, then, "'Bohemian Rhapsody.' The one we heard earlier today."

Oh, right.

"Now, men, it's time to learn how to twirl her out and back in."

Julian stopped the music, then demonstrated the spin with Boo, who seemed to already know the move.

Jack tried it, spinning Harper out, close again, catching her. "You need to hold on," he said, indicating her loose grip. "Otherwise you'll go spinning out into space."

Probably already was, given his piercing gaze on her, the way he'd secured her back in his grip.

He tried it again, and this time she held on. The music started, and they moved into two-step. After a few moments, he spun her out, then in, caught her, a perfect move.

Julian even called them out. "I think we have a natural couple here."

Aw . . .

Jack's smile dimmed.

"So, what's the source of the song?"

"A phone."

The music stopped and Julian called them in. "Okay, let's work on the ensemble moves for the signature dance."

He had brought in a flatscreen television, and now, as she stood with Jack, they watched the sequence with Patrick Swayze and Jennifer Grey. He paused it when the men lined up behind Swayze.

"Okay, the entire wedding party will line up behind Oaken, and this is the dance we'll learn today." Julian pushed play, and she wondered if Jack could feel the way she held her breath, her body coiling as they watched the dance troupe from the movie follow Swayze.

She could do this.

Julian then made them line up and taught them the steps.

Step, touch, step step, wiggle, step, touch—it turned to a jumble in her head.

She'd never thought of herself as a klutz, but this felt—

"You've got this."

She looked over, and Jack glanced at her, a surety in his expression.

"I'm going to fall on my face."

"Step kick, look back, step, hip thrust . . ." Julian at the front.

Hip what?

She glanced over at Jack, who looked just as traumatized. Still, she attempted the moves.

Anything for Boo. Who was letting her write about her wedding.

"Repeat, and this time end with a spin," Julian said, moving ahead, but now Shep, and maybe London, had started to laugh, and that sent Boo doubling over as she watched from the side, and then Steinbeck and Austen, and finally even Jack grinned.

Julian stopped the music.

"I think we can just improvise," Jack said.

Julian gave him a withering look. "Let's at least try the angel lift. Jack and Steinbeck will run over, grab Brontë's arms, and pull her toward Oaken." He turned to the groom. "Remember to brace your legs, one in front of the other, solid stance. Find her hip bones, press up through your core, keep it strong. And Brontë, keep your arms wide, your back arched. You're flying. Ready?"

"Let's do this." Oaken walked over to his position, and Boo grinned at him, her eyes shining.

Maybe that's what love did. Made you sparkle, gave you courage to . . . what? Run into a man's arms, trusting he'd hold you up?

Apparently, because as Julian hit play, and as Jack and Steinbeck drew their sister onto the floor, she broke out into a run, her arms out, leaping into Oaken's arms.

And he lifted her perfectly above his head.

"Holy smokes," Steinbeck said. "Way to go, Boo."

Oaken held her there, his gaze on her face, and maybe it would be nice to find someone who looked at Harper that way, as if she might be his whole world.

They twirled around, and then Oaken let her go and Boo laughed.

And only then did Harper realize she'd been holding her breath.

Julian let the music play, and maybe it contained a little magic, because Shep pulled London onto the dance floor, and Boo and Oaken started to sway.

The words sang in her head.

In the golden glow of the reception hall, under a canopy of twinkling fairy lights, Brontë and Oaken find themselves at the heart of their own love story, dancing as if the world has melted away. As the iconic opening notes of "(I've Had) The Time of My Life" fill the air, the newlyweds step onto the dance floor with an air of excitement and a hint of mischief in their eyes.

The chemistry between the couple electrifies the atmosphere, turning their performance into more than just a dance—it's a celebration of their journey, their challenges, and their victories. Oaken, with a confident smile, guides Brontë through each step, his support unwavering as she leaps into the iconic lift. Time seems to pause, their friends and family holding their breath as Brontë soars above the dance floor, radiant with joy.

"Harper?"

Jack stood in front of her, and for a second, she thought he might be asking to pull her onto the dance floor, to wrap her in his arms, hold her close, maybe mimic some of the moves—

"Let me show you what I found."

Oh. Right. She nodded and followed him away from the studio, into the hallway. He reached into his back pocket and pulled out a phone. "This is Ty's phone."

It took a second. A *long* second to pull herself back, to hear his words, to plug them into today's events.

Ty's. Phone. "Wait—what?"

"And it's dying, but I took a shot of the text on the screen. It says—"

She read it aloud. "'I'm done lying for you'? What does that mean?"

"I don't know. But look who sent it."

She took the phone, studied it. "Wait. Does that say *Mom*?"

"Yeah, it does. I think we need to go back for a chat with my biggest fan."

And Harper had absolutely no power to resist following him out into the night.

⎯⎯•⎯⎯⎯⎯⎯•⎯⎯

"Are you trying to get me killed? Or just incarcerated for a good ten to twenty?" Emberly leaned over her computer, her earwig in, seated cross-legged on the sheets of a queen-sized bed. The other bed was made, neat and tidy and free of any critters that might decide to emerge from the corners of the bad paneling of the Duck Lake Motor Lodge.

The place made her want to bathe, over and over, but it had ended up being the only gig in town that took cash and didn't look too closely at her ID. Not that it wasn't a perfect forgery, thank you.

The place reeked of burnt coffee—her fault—and maybe mildew from the grimy shower curtain. She'd pasted the floor with the thin towels and asked the desk for more. It wasn't like they had a plethora of guests—one guy, who'd gone out earlier today, his room still uncleaned given the Do Not Disturb sign on his door.

Orange carpet, brown covers on the beds, gold lamps—the place had embraced the resurgence of the midcentury modern vibe, although Emberly doubted they'd done anything but stay the course from the original motif.

Reminded her too much of the old shows she'd watched while waiting for her mother to come home from work.

So yes, the Motor Lodge lacked charm, and even warmth, the heater on the wall fighting to kick out enough breath to cut the frigid January wind.

But she couldn't go far, not with the job still ongoing, so she'd had to stick around this one-stoplight town and regroup.

"You always say I make it too easy. You're the one who didn't grab the phone." Nimue, in her ear, laughing, her voice sweet and betraying nothing of her true identity as a hunter on the dark web. Nimue could spot scammers, posers, and catfishers with a glance at her screen and knew how to creep out of their ISP into real life. Bring down the predators, terrorists, and trackers.

But once in a while, when Ember needed her, Nim poked apart security systems and helped her strategize her next move.

Because that's what sisters did.

"I got kicked out of dinner before I could find it."

"Good thing he's hosting the bachelor party."

"At least you don't want me to go in wearing a cake."

"Please, please do that."

She laughed. Wow, she missed Nim.

"Listen, wear the blonde wig, add some glasses and contacts, don a suit—you'll be part of the security. In and out of Stone's office, phone in hand. Order a pizza on your way home."

"Is that like saying 'Bob's your uncle'?"

"The guys on the team say that. It's a thing."

Ambient sounds through Nim's microphone suggested she might be sitting outside, maybe in the sunshine of some tropical café, enjoying an umbrella drink.

"Where are you?"

"A place on the river. I needed to get out of the bunker. It's seventy-five and sunny, and there are a few manatees floating around near the dock."

"I think I hate you."

"You could actually quit, join me down here in Florida."

"Pick up a waitressing job?"

"No. You're a terrible waitress. Didn't you nearly get mowed over twice last night?"

"Yes. Same guy. Like he had me on radar."

And for a moment, Mr. Reflexes entered her brain. Steinbeck, someone had called him. Brown hair, blond highlights, dark beard, and those eyes—oh, she'd seen those ocean-blue eyes before. Still couldn't wrap her grip around the memory, however.

"I hope not," Nim said. "Okay, I found the blueprints of Stone's estate. I'm sending them to you. It's gated, of course, and he has a handful of security personnel, so obvs, they'll know you're not with them. But the guests won't, so just avoid outside security and you'll be fine."

Emberly pulled up the blueprint of the estate from her email. "That's a lot of room for a single guy." She did the quick math. Six bedrooms, seven baths, twelve thousand square feet on thirty acres. "He bought it six years ago for four mil."

"Originally built in 1928, so it needed a lot of upgrades. But I found a few holes in his system."

She could almost hear Nim crack her knuckles.

"First, there's a caterer coming in tomorrow with a delivery, so that's easy."

"Right. Carry in some canapés, hide, don my security suit, sneak out during the party—"

"Find his office, find his cell phone."

"He might have it on him."

"He might. But the house has spotty cell service, so he installed a booster in his office, along with broadband. According to the usage from his provider, he syncs his computer—and I'll bet his phone—every night. Probably on a base charger."

"Brilliant. So I get in, duplicate the phone."

"Download the vault information. All you need is the passcode from his app. That and the print you lifted should get you into the hard-copy cyber vault in Montelena."

"And order me a pizza."

Laughter. "Please come to Florida. Think beaches and surfing and good-looking tanned men—"

And right then, bam, she *knew*.

Oh no. She practically groaned, looked up at herself in the mirror, wincing.

She knew where she'd seen Mr. Reflexes before.

Please, please let him not remember.

Nim was still listing off beach perks. "And I mentioned the seafood, right? And ice cream—there's a homemade-gelato place beachside that will make your eyes roll back into your head."

"I mentioned that I'm freezing my tuchus off here, right? Reminds me of that double-wide we lived in for a while. In—where was that?"

"Rapid City, South Dakota. Buffalo Acres. An orange buffalo statue stared at me every night at the edge of the trailer park. I still have nightmares." A slight chuckle, and then it died.

Oops. Maybe Emberly shouldn't have brought that up.

"Anyway, so, don't get caught, okay?"

"Nope. I got this."

Her sister hung up.

As long as one former Navy SEAL didn't suddenly remember the woman who'd left him for dead.

SEVEN

I F THEY COULD FIND TY BOWMAN, JACK COULD stop overreacting.

He sat nursing his coffee at the table in Doyle's kitchen in dawn's early light, trying to get his brain to stop whirring on the what-ifs. Most of them about Penelope.

No, *most* of them about Harper. Like, what if he'd kissed her, last night on the dance floor? That one took up most of the room in his brain, forbidden, delicious, terrifying—

And too easily, he could find himself dragging up the past, the kiss on the beach so long ago, her long hair woven through his fingers, the smell of the ocean on her skin.

He'd spent years tucking away that memory, and yet it roused, unblemished and vivid in his brain, as if it had been waiting to ambush him.

Better to focus on her quiet disappointment at seeing the dark Bowman house last night. Mrs. Bowman had vanished. Maybe she'd gone to the store, although they'd sat outside for a good hour waiting for her before giving up and returning to Doyle's to grab pizza with the rest of the wedding party.

Harper had said nearly nothing, and he hadn't known what to say except a lame "We'll find her" as she escaped upstairs.

The others stayed up late to play a game of Mexican Train.

He'd retired, too, to the bedroom he shared with Steinbeck, and had lain on the bed, staring at the ceiling, listening to the *Penny for Your Thoughts* podcast.

He'd fallen asleep too early, halfway through the third installment.

Now, he put his earbuds back in and pushed play on his phone, trying to catch up, hating the way his gut tightened with each episode. Mostly listening to the callers who added their "pennies" at the end of each episode. He thought maybe she taped the callers and played out the armchair detectives' theories later instead of taking live callers.

Everybody had a thought, each one wilder than the next, and that brought him around to the fact that maybe he was overthinking all of this. What was Occam's razor? The simplest answer is usually right?

What was the simple answer?

Dawn scattered gold and rose hues over the oak kitchen table, the wooden floor, the white quartz island. Doyle—or rather his dad—had done a decent job of remodeling the old Victorian's kitchen.

Made a guy nearly want to sell the old bus and settle down in his own planted-in-one-place house.

"You're up early."

The words were spoken by Boo—he was finally getting it—coming into the kitchen. She wore flannel pajama bottoms and a sweatshirt, her dark hair crazy around her head.

"Yeah," he said, lifting his coffee and pressing stop on the podcast on his phone. "Just . . . looking for ideas."

She opened the fridge and pulled out orange juice. "On Penelope's podcast?"

He glanced at his phone. Oh, she must have seen his screen. "It's a place to start."

She closed the fridge door. "Harper said that she'd gone shopping in Minneapolis. Or maybe to Conrad's game." Taking out a glass, she filled it, then braced a hip against the counter. "She told me when she agreed to be a bridesmaid that she would be in and out and not to expect her at all the events. She's a big-deal podcaster, so . . ." She turned to him. "Should I be worried?"

He had finished his coffee, so he picked up his phone, pocketed it, then walked over and put his coffee mug in the dishwasher. "I'm not sure. Harper says that she contacted her security and that she's in Minneapolis. And if she told you that she'd be in and out . . . so maybe not." But he wanted to circle back to Bowman's this morning, with or without Harper.

Boo stopped him from walking past her with a hand to his arm. "For the record, I never thought you didn't care."

Her words made his throat thicken. He nodded. "The last thing I want is for you to get hurt, Boo."

"I've known that my entire life," she said quietly, the past in her gaze.

His hand covered hers. "Don't worry. Just focus on your wedding. It's going to be perfect, I promise."

She arched an eyebrow. "You don't have to promise, Jack. But I do appreciate you enacting your super tracking skills on my behalf."

"Always." He winked, and she nodded, the word settling, eliciting a smile.

She let go of his arm. "Don't forget the bachelor party tonight."

"Right. Where is it?"

"I don't know—that's Shep's deal. But my bridesmaids and I are going to the Lumberjack's Table for karaoke."

"I'd rather have toothpicks shoved under my fingernails."

"That's a nice word picture." She added her glass to the dishwasher, grinning. "I'll need Harper back for spa day this afternoon."

He had started out of the kitchen, now turned. "What? Harper back?"

She laughed. "Whatever. She's up, taking a shower. Also listening to *Penny for Your Thoughts,* by the way." She gestured to his phone app.

Really. And just like that, a spark lit inside him, that moment last night on the dance floor when she'd tripped. *Gotcha.*

Sheesh.

It was like one part of his brain simply deleted all the warning sirens blaring in the back of his head to set the other side free to party.

Boo's smile at him, the shake of her head, lingered as he headed upstairs to shower. Twenty minutes later, he found Harper in the kitchen, finishing off her coffee and a bagel. Of course she smelled fresh and clean, floral, her short hair curly. Her blue eyes sparked with something he couldn't place as she saw him. She wore a pair of leggings and a white flannel shirt, and he had the craziest urge to call off this morning's house call and just . . .

What? Hang out by a cozy fire, playing a game of gin rummy?

Yeah, that would be good idea, and would not at all send him back where everything had gone south.

She might not be way too young for him anymore, but she was still Boo's best friend. And like a sister to the rest of the family.

Besides, three more days and she'd be heading back to Nashville. And he and Aggie had a date with a wrench and his grandfather's barn and then, maybe, the road.

"Ready to head back to the Bowman place?" She'd gotten up, tossed her remaining coffee into the sink, then loaded her mug into the dishwasher.

"Have you tried calling Penelope again?" He followed Harper as she headed out to the entryway for her jacket.

"Yes. Voicemail."

Shoot. Still. "Conrad isn't back yet. Maybe she met him after the game and they went out."

"Did you call him?" she said, pulling on her UGGs, then winding a scarf around her neck.

"Left a voicemail." He shrugged on his jacket. "But Steinbeck got in touch with our cousin. He works on a tactical team and they put me in touch with a white-hat hacker named Coco. Ranger texted that Coco said we could drop the phone off with her today—she'd see if she could get into it."

Harper pulled on her white puffer jacket, then grabbed a hat. "Maybe we should go to the police."

He had his hand on the door, now glanced at her.

"If Mrs. Bowman isn't there."

He sighed. Nodded.

The Geo fought awakening but finally turned over, and he slid the heater on full. The sun had started to thaw the frost gathered on his window. "I should check on Aggie. I was able to limp her into the market's side lot last night, but I should probably swing by and make sure there are no vandals."

"Why a schoolie?"

He glanced at her and read her real question in her eyes. "Because I needed something to consume my brain after Sabrina's death. Fixing up Aggie worked. As did writing the book. And then I answered my first reward posting, and I guess that's when I dove in. It felt right."

"Looking for missing people?"

He'd pulled out of the driveway. "Not just missing people. I once answered an ad to find a missing pet goat."

"A goat."

"She was the school mascot. Turned out an opposing team had kidnapped her. I was the town hero."

"The goat rescuer."

He laughed. *Oh boy.*

"But I follow up on rewards for information on burglaries and murders, and even hit-and-runs. Things the police are too busy for or have lost leads on."

"Professional problem solver too."

"I need to hire you as my PR person."

"Maybe. But if you do, you'll have to smile every once in a while. Lose the grump."

"I'm not a grump. I'm just . . . driven."

"By what?"

He hadn't meant to go here. He let her question sit as he turned down Bowman's road, back through the sleepy cottages under the towering oak trees.

"Jack?"

"Helplessness." *Oh.* He hadn't meant to bark it. But she didn't recoil.

She nodded, as if she understood.

He glanced at her.

"I'm onto you, Jack. Just so you know."

What—

"I know that your interest in being a tracker didn't start after Sabrina."

"Oh?"

"My dad was on the callout volunteer team when Boo got lost. He said you refused to quit, even when the other searchers had worn themselves out."

"She's my sister."

"Mm-hmm."

He had pulled up to the Bowman home, with the dark windows. Not a good sign.

"Fine." He gave her a hard look. "Dad told me to stick with her on the portage. But I didn't, and she took a wrong turn, and . . . anyway, yes. I couldn't let go."

"Just like you couldn't let Sabrina go."

He glanced at the dark house. No movement. "It sits inside me, an ember, getting hotter and hotter until I *do* something."

"And now?" She, too, looked at the house.

"Now the ember in my gut says we need to go to the cops. But let's check one more time." He got out and headed to the door. She followed him.

They stood on the cold step for a good five minutes, leaning on the doorbell.

The police station smelled of burnt coffee and small-town business, with BOLO posters on the bulletin board. BOLO for Daisy, the lost goldendoodle. BOLO for a 1998 Ford Bronco, gone missing from Mattson's Motors, right off the lot. BOLO for a set of keys with a boat float on them, missing from Echoes Vinyl Café.

Which reminded him. They needed a chat with the barista.

He recognized the deputy who retrieved them from the waiting area. "Jenna Hayes. Since when did you become a cop?" She wore her dark curly hair short, her brown eyes warm as she shook his hand.

He noticed, however, the way the warmth died, a chill entering, as she looked at Harper. Nodded.

"Jenna," Harper said, her mouth pinched.

Interesting.

They followed Jenna into an open room, to her desk. She pulled up a folding chair and set it beside a straight chair next to her desk. Harper took it as he sat in the other one.

"We're here because we're looking for Ty Bowman. He might be missing," he said.

She raised an eyebrow, folded her arms, leaned back. "Ty Bowman has a history of getting himself in over his head. Some petty theft a few years ago, and then he ran drag races out in the country, *Grease* style. It became a ring—until a teenager got hurt. And Fish and Game found him night hunting a few years ago. Recently, he was caught fishing out of season. And of course, there's the drugs."

"Drugs?"

"We've suspected for a while that he uses his Uber operation to transport drugs. We just can't catch him. He's probably lying low after grifting someone. What makes you think he's in trouble?"

"We found—" Harper started.

"Him on camera picking up a friend of ours," Jack said, glancing at her. *Ixnay on the onephay.* "But we also can't get ahold of our friend."

Jenna glanced at Harper, back to Jack. "Who is this friend?"

"Penelope Pepper."

"From the Pepper family? Why is she in town?"

"She runs a podcast—she's here for Brontë's wedding."

This seemed to perk Jenna up. "Is Oaken Fox at your place? I love—"

"Yes," Harper said. "But he's not missing."

Jenna's mouth made a tight line. Apparently to match Harper's. *Huh.*

"How long has she been gone?"

"Since Tuesday."

"You should have come to us sooner." Jenna wiggled her mouse to wake up her computer.

"We weren't sure she was in trouble. Still aren't." He had lowered his voice, but it came out sharper than he wanted.

Jenna considered him. He offered a smile. She sighed. "Let me take some notes." She pulled up a blank page on her computer. "Okay, so you said Bowman picked her up? When?"

"Tuesday night. Around nine p.m. at the Moonlight Supperclub," Harper said.

Jack ran down the details of her disappearance, with Harper interjecting as Jenna typed.

"We went to Bowman's house last night and this morning, but no one is there."

"Of course not." A voice sounded behind him, and he looked over to see Sheriff Davidson. He carried a cup of coffee.

Jack stood, extended a hand. Harper smiled at him.

Portly and bald, he was stern and fair. And had been one of the few adults who'd believed a sixteen-year-old kid when he'd given his theory about where a lost Cub Scout might be.

Harper stood and the sheriff nodded to her. "Good to see you, Harper."

"Sir."

"How's your father?"

She seemed to pale at that. "Um. Last I checked, fine."

Jack frowned, but he turned to the sheriff. "Why 'of course not'?"

"Ty Bowman is in critical care at the Waconia hospital. Was found in his car, shot in the head, last night. I personally brought his mother to the hospital."

"Holy cats," Harper said quietly.

What she said. He turned back to Jenna. "Now can we put a BOLO out on Penelope?"

"Is there any reason to think that she might be in danger?"

He stared at her. "Gunshot to the head?"

"Twenty-four hours after she was picked up. I don't see the connection, Jack."

He stared at her, back at Harper.

The sheriff lifted a hand. "Yes. We can put a BOLO out for her. Do you have a picture and a description?"

"I've got one," Harper said and pulled up her phone, handing it to Jenna.

Ten minutes later, they walked out of the station into the blue-skied, frigid day.

Jack couldn't stop himself. "What's with the chill between you and Jenna?"

Harper looked at him. "Really?" She reached for the door handle of his Geo. "Jenna is the reason my parents are divorced. She completely wrecked my life."

Please don't ask. Please don't ask.

But what was the man going to do when she made a statement like that, let it fall between them like an unpulled grenade?

Why couldn't she keep her mouth shut?

She looked out the window as Jack drove them to Waconia, some thirty miles down the road. He made no comment.

"I didn't realize you were friends," she said. *Whoops.*

"We're not, really. She and Doyle went out for a little while, in college. I saw them on campus at the U a few times. She was pursuing a law degree."

Oh. She shook her head against her stupid overactive imagination. And really, she had no claim on the man, despite what her heart said.

"How old were you when your parents got divorced?"

"Twelve, but they had years of separations before that. First one was when I was eight."

"That's young."

"Third grade. I still remember watching out my attic window as he drove away." She sighed. "That time, it was my fault."

He glanced at her. "It's never the fault of an eight-year-old child, Harper."

She said nothing, the words roping inside her.

"What happened? And what does it have to do with Jenna?"

She made a wry face. "Okay, that might have been an oversimplification of the truth. But it felt real at the time."

"Still does, it seems."

"Caught that, huh?"

"Hard to miss the cold front. I'm still shivering." He winked. "For whatever it's worth, I remember Jenna being a little demanding, according to Doyle."

"We were never friends. But one day on the school playground—"

"Oh no. This is a school-playground story?"

"It is, so hold tight and picture in your mind's eye two eight-year-old girls having a brawl. Over a swing, mind you. I took her swing; she wanted it back."

"High crimes and misdemeanors."

"No statute of limitations on that. I might have been a little stubborn. She had small gang with her, and they surrounded me and demanded the swing back. I said no way, and she said she'd punch me in the stomach. And I stared right at her and said, 'Do it.'"

"I can see that." He looked over, winked again.

What—? Oh, if he wanted her heart to stop holding on to him, he needed to stop the winking, pronto. And maybe he could tame those curls a little, shave, and stop smelling like some sun-dappled forest.

Made a girl want to get lost just so he'd find her.

Enough.

"Don't think I was too tough. I *was* crying at the time. But I refused to move. And I was so scared she'd actually punch me that I got angrier and angrier. I'm not sure who made the first move, me or Jenna, but we were suddenly pulling hair and kicking and pushing and slapping—it was an ugly girl fight."

"Drama at Duck Lake Elementary."

"It got worse. They dragged us into the principal's office and called our parents. Her mom was freshly divorced and my dad came in as my representative, and instead of standing up for me, he said that we both probably needed anger-management counseling."

"Oh no."

"Ten weeks of after-school, once-a-week meetings with Jenna as we talked through our feelings and learned how to manage our anger."

"It didn't take, I see."

She laughed. "We didn't get into any more fights. At least on campus."

"So, Rocky Balboa, how does your dad leaving fit into this story?"

The way he said it, with the nickname, softened the blow of the question.

Along the highway, the fields glistened under the bright sunlight, the sky a wispy blue. A perfect January day.

Penny, where are you?

"While we met in one room, my dad and Jenna's mom met in another to learn techniques on how to help us. It turned into coffee, and then one-on-one chats to discuss their wild children. Although I'm not sure they talked at all about us."

He'd gone quiet, all teasing gone. "I'm so sorry."

"My mom found out and kicked him out."

"That's not on you." He looked at her. "Or Jenna, really."

"I know." She leaned back. "But I was scared. I thought maybe he wanted a different daughter. Jenna was prettier and had better grades—Dad liked good grades—and I thought maybe if I did something amazing, he'd choose me."

He'd turned off the highway, toward the town of Waconia.

"I don't love where this is going."

"All the way to seventh grade when I entered a book-writing contest. First ever in our community, and oh, I wanted to win. Badly." She drew in a breath. "So I plagiarized a book I'd gotten from the library."

"That, I didn't see coming."

"It got worse when I won. That's when my mother read the book. She realized quickly that I couldn't have written the story, got the librarian involved, and they sleuthed it out."

"Your *mother*? Ouch."

"She wasn't wrong, but my father was not on board when she went to the principal. They took away the award, gave it to the second-place winner—"

"Please tell me it wasn't Jenna."

"No. Thankfully. But oh, that was the fight that finally ended it. My dad said that Mom should have had more loyalty and grace, and she said he was impossible to trust, and both of them blamed each other for my lack of ethics, and . . . anyway, six months later, they were divorced. My father moved to Minneapolis, then to Arizona with Jenna's mom, and I really haven't seen him since."

Silence beside her. Finally, "So he just . . . ghosted you?"

"Walked away without a word."

He swallowed, then looked over at her. Another beat, and he turned his gaze back to the road. "I shouldn't have done that."

She blinked at him.

"After . . ."

"I know when."

"Yeah. Well." He stopped at a light, sighed. "I might have over-reacted. At the time . . . I was mortified."

"I know." She gave him a sad smile. "I should have told you I was Bee."

"No. You *weren't* Bee. Bee was a twelve-year-old girl who used to camp out in the backyard with Boo and made cookies with my mom and was sort of like a kid sister. You showed up at spring break with your long blonde hair, tan and smart, and any hope of me seeing Bee vanished." He offered a small, wry smile. "I liked what I saw."

Everything inside her stilled—her breath, her heart, her regrets.

He met her eyes then, something in them that she hadn't seen . . . well, since that spring break, maybe. A glimpse into the man behind the persona.

The look he'd given her right before he'd kissed her. Desire, curiosity—

Wait. "Liked." Past tense.

"Which made finding out you were actually *Bee,* my kid sister's best friend, that much worse, of course."

Of course.

He blinked, and the look vanished. "I never meant to hurt you. I just didn't know what to do. So I panicked. But I'm . . . I'm sorry I hurt you."

He just might be breaking her heart all over again. But she wasn't eighteen with a head full of fairy tales anymore. Somehow she managed to nod.

The light turned green and he turned, the hospital in sight.

Good thing, because she might need resuscitation. Mostly because her brain was caught on . . . *liked.*

He'd liked her. And sure, his kiss could have told her that, but . . .

But maybe it hadn't been just a spring fling. Maybe . . .

Oh, no, no. Pay attention to the grammar!

"So, you still went into journalism, despite the debacle?"

Right. They were still catching up. Her heart thumped, finally. "Yeah. Turns out I can write a pretty good story. Without copying it. I entered the contest the next year, under a pen name, and won."

"Attagirl."

Aw, and now he'd lit a full-out fire inside her.

"I got a part-time job at the *Duck Lake Currents,* and that seeded in me a love for story."

He pulled into the lot and parked. "Here goes nothing."

Bowman. Girl, get your head in the game.

She followed him into the hospital, and at the desk, they asked about Ty. The receptionist gave them passes to the second-floor ICU waiting room.

Mrs. Bowman sat on a vinyl chair, her eyes closed, clutching her purse, wearing jeans and her boots, a jacket over her like a blanket. Fatigue lined her face.

She roused at their footsteps, blinked and sat up. Her red eyes suggested she'd been crying.

Harper sank into the chair beside her. "Mrs. Bowman. We heard about Ty."

The woman glanced up at Jack, then at Harper, and her eyes filled. "Oh, he'll be so glad you're here."

Harper looked at Jack, not sure—

Jack crouched in front of her, his voice soft. "Ma'am. We . . . we found this." He pulled out the cell phone. Held it up to her.

"That's Ty's phone."

"Yes. And there's a text frozen on the screen. From you." He raised an eyebrow.

Her eyes widened. "I didn't . . . he is . . . I . . ."

"It's okay," Harper said. "You're not in trouble, but we are looking—"

"Working with the investigation into the shooting," Jack said. "And we need to ask a few questions in order to find the shooter."

"I already gave a statement to Sheriff Davidson."

"I know," Jack said, nodding. "Would you mind terribly if I asked some follow-up questions? Just to help our search."

Oh, he was good at this. Not lying, but not letting her think they were rogue, either. She should take notes.

"I guess not."

Harper got up and went to a vending machine, put in a couple dollars, and returned with coffee.

Jack had taken her chair after swiping the tissue box from a nearby table. He handed Mrs. Bowman a tissue. She blew her nose into it, then took the coffee from Harper.

"We just need to know what you were referring to when you said you weren't going to lie for him anymore."

She wiped her eyes with the wadded tissue. "He sometimes does airport runs."

A beat, and Jack frowned. "What?"

Harper had also expected something more epic.

"Yeah. Airport runs. All the way into Minneapolis." She shook her head like *What a disappointment.*

"I don't understand," Harper said.

"He's on probation," Mrs. Bowman whispered.

"Oh," Jack said. "I see."

Harper didn't see. "What does that have to do with—"

"He's not allowed to leave the area without permission." Mrs. Bowman's voice contained an edge. Then she held up her hand. "Sorry. He turns off the location on his cell, and that's usually when he's out of the area."

"How do you know he turns off his location?" Jack asked.

"I have a family finder app on my phone. He's connected. Unless he turns off his location. I saw that he did it on Tuesday night, and I just knew . . . airport run."

Harper glanced at Jack, whose mouth made a grim line. She could almost read his *Dollars to donuts, it wasn't an airport run he was making to the cities*, but she also said nothing.

"This was Tuesday night? What time?"

"About six p.m. I called him a couple times after that, but no answer, so I started to text." She covered her mouth, shaking. "I had no idea that he was . . . he was . . ."

Jack put his arm around her. *Professional nice guy.*

"I'm sorry I lied to you." Mrs. Bowman blew her nose again.

Now Harper crouched in front of her. "When did they find him?"

"Yesterday, maybe around noon? It took them a while to identify him. He didn't have his wallet. But they ran his plates, and

Sheriff Davidson came to get me about five, I think. He was just out of surgery. They have him in a medical coma because he keeps having seizures." Her eyes filled again.

"Where did they find him?" Jack asked softly.

"Oh. At the Duck Lake boat ramp."

"What would he have been doing there?" Harper asked.

"He likes to ice-fish and sometimes spends the night out at our fish house, but . . . it's not on Duck Lake."

"Your fish house isn't on Duck Lake?"

"Oh no. We have land on Loon Lake. Used to spend our summers there, at a cabin, when his dad was alive. But the cabin was destroyed in the tornado a few years back and I never rebuilt. He stores the fish house at a boatyard there." She wiped her eyes. "He so loves to fish."

Jack nodded. "Thank you, Mrs. Bowman."

"Marjorie."

He repeated the name, and it elicited a smile. "Can I get your number, in case I have any more questions?"

She rattled it off to him, and he typed it into his phone.

Then he rose. "Can we get you anything?"

Her face hardened. "Just find the person who shot my son."

Jack nodded, then reached out and pressed a hand to Harper's shoulder as they walked away. He wore a hint of urgency in his expression.

"What?"

"What she doesn't know is that you can track a phone's location even if location services are turned off. Cell phone providers are required by law to track for emergency services. Which means the phone still communicates with nearby towers."

"Which also means that we'll be able to figure out where Ty was before he picked up Penelope and the other person in the car."

"And if he might have picked up someone from the airport." He got off the lift. "We need to get this to Stein's hacker friend,

Coco. And then we need to start asking—who would want to hurt Penelope?"

The question chilled her through.

He pushed out of the hospital and his phone rang. He pulled it out, answered. "Conrad." Stopped walking. "What?"

Another pause, and he looked at Harper, held up his hand. "Where are you?"

He started walking—no, jogging—for his Geo. "Okay, stay there. I'm on my way."

She caught up to him as he unlocked the door. "Where are we going?"

"Sammy's Bar and Grill, downtown St. Paul."

"Um, why?" She slid into the car.

He turned the car over, flicked up the heat. "Because Conrad got a voicemail from Penelope. And he needs us to hear it."

"Can't he forward it to us?"

"He can. But my cousin Ranger texted me, and he's set up a meet with this hacker, Coco, in St. Paul." He turned to her. "Which we need to do ASAP."

"Why?"

He pulled out. "Conrad thinks she's in trouble."

EIGHT

JACK DIDN'T KNOW WHAT TO BELIEVE.

"Play it again, Conrad."

His brother sat across from him in a massive booth tucked into a corner of Sammy's Bar and Grill, an iconic sports bar dedicated to the fandom of the Minnesota Blue Ox hockey team. Once a shipping warehouse with high steel beams and brick walls, now promo posters, signed photographs of the greats, and framed jerseys plastered the walls. Flatscreens handing from the ceiling and tucked into every corner, played the various games in the league as well as a rerun of last night's matchup against the Colorado Sting.

The owner, Sam Newton, still working behind the long oak bar, had once played defenseman for the Blue Ox.

Most of the players hung out here after the games, getting another taste of the cheering. Now, Conrad sat, his dark-blond hair still wet, curly on top and around his ears, his beard full and tinged with rust, wearing a black button-down shirt, a pair of black jeans, fresh from a short practice before tonight's game. He wore his superstar aura easily, as if it fit him like his jersey, like he belonged under the limelight.

No wonder Penelope had reached out to him.

"That's not the crazy one," Conrad said. "There's another."

Conrad's phone sat beside a basket of wings, an appetizer Jack had found Conrad eating when he walked in with Harper.

"Just play the first one again. I want to listen for any duress."

Conrad pushed play again, and Penelope's voice came through.

"Hey, Conrad, it's me, Penelope. I'm heading to Minneapolis tomorrow, so if the offer is still good, I'd love to see your game tomorrow night. Maybe catch a bite afterwards. So, call me when you get this. Toods!"

Conrad paused before the next one started.

"That sounds like Pen," Harper said. "Just . . . you know. Happy."

"Except clearly she was planning on driving in yesterday, not vanishing on Tuesday night."

Jack met her eyes. She swallowed, her face a little pale.

He nearly reached out, took her hand under the booth. *"I liked what I saw."* No clue why he'd let that tidbit sneak out. And he should probably forget the way she'd looked at him in the car, her beautiful eyes widening, maybe the smallest spark inside them.

No, no, he couldn't go back to the past. Three more days, and he would hit the road. Except, the words that he'd shot across the bow to West and Nat had roused inside him during his drive to St. Paul. *"I've been thinking that it's time I hang this gig up. Maybe retake the bar."*

And then what? Hang out a shingle in some low-rent building in Minneapolis? Take on insurance claims and speeding-ticket defense?

Or become a prosecutor, maybe, going after domestic abusers and shoplifters?

No. He liked what he did. Even if he did occasionally scrub up against the law.

Still. He hadn't exactly hated hanging around Harper again.

"She never showed up for the ticket I left at Will Call," Conrad said. "Admittedly, I never listen to voicemails, so I only got her text." He opened his texting app and showed them the text of virtually the same message as the voicemail.

He took the phone back. "So when I checked my voicemails today . . . well, you listen to it."

He put the phone back on the table, jacking up the volume against the noise in the bar—the games, people chatting, laughter.

Muffled sounds, as if the phone might have been in Penelope's pocket, and then, "No, don't stop, why are you stopping?" More sounds—a male voice, another yelling—"No!"

A gunshot.

Penny's scream. And then more muffled sounds, more shrieks—

The message ended.

Harper appeared stripped, and Jack's chest turned hollow.

Conrad leaned back, pressed his hand over his mouth. Then, "That's why I wanted you to hear it, in person. I think she pocket dialed me. My guess is that I was the last person she'd called or texted, so—"

"So the phone redialed," Jack said.

"Maybe she did it on purpose," Harper said, her voice shaking. "Let's not forget she's a murder podcaster. She's probably learned a little about how to leave clues."

Jack looked at her. "You said she's disappeared before—"

"Before, there wasn't a guy in a coma!"

He held up a hand. "Hey. I was just agreeing with you."

She winced, looked away, her eyes glistening. "Sorry."

And now he couldn't help it—he did take her hand. Squeezed. Maybe he was a professional nice guy.

He turned to Conrad. "What's the time stamp on that?"

"Tuesday, around eleven p.m. I was back at the house, my phone off when it came in. It goes onto Do Not Disturb at ten p.m."

"Good to know. I'll make sure, if I ever need you, to call before ten."

Conrad gave him a withering look. "You're in my favorites, so I'll get your call regardless. Not that you ever call." He raised an eyebrow.

Ouch.

"Do we go to the police?"

"We already did," Harper said. "In Duck Lake. They put out a BOLO."

"This needs more than a BOLO," Jack said. "She's missing, a guy's been shot, and her last known location was in the car with a shooter? So, yeah . . . now I'm officially worried."

He still held Harper's hand under the table, and she gripped it tighter. "What do we do?"

"We need to get Ty Bowman's phone to Ranger's hacker friend."

"What hacker friend?" Conrad asked, leaning back as the waitress came by the table with fresh sodas and another basket of wings, this one for Jack. Harper had ordered fries and now pulled the basket to herself and grabbed the salt and ketchup.

Jack watched as she made a small pool in the middle of her fries and filled it with ketchup.

"Going to have some fries with your ketchup?"

"Don't judge. My friend is in mortal danger. I need this."

He glanced at Conrad, who smiled. "I remember you downing chocolate chip cookies like an All-Pro defenseman."

She gave him a smile despite the pain on her face. "Who can say no to your mother's cookies? Besides, my mother doesn't bake. Or cook. She just . . . fixes people's problems."

"Why do you think my mother bakes so well? Cookies after every hockey game, a double batch when we lost. Problem solver."

She laughed, and Jack scurried around in his brain for that memory Conrad had stirred up. But Conrad was three years younger than him, so he'd been a senior when Harper had entered her freshman year.

Jack hadn't been around to see this side of her.

And by the way, she was not too young for Conrad, then or now, and that truth grabbed hold and twisted. Especially when Harper looked at Conrad, warmth in her eyes.

Aw. Stop. Jack had no claim on her. Besides, his brother might be wise to be with someone like Harper.

He returned to Conrad's previous question. "Ranger set us up with a white-hat hacker named Coco Marshall. He said she lives in the area and could take a crack at getting information off Ty Bowman's phone."

"Ty Bowman? I remember him. Skinny kid. Boo's grade."

"*My* grade," Harper said.

"He was the driver who was shot." Jack had picked up his phone, started to dial Stein.

Conrad leaned back. Looked at Jack, who listened to Stein's phone ring. "My goalie is married to a girl named Coco."

"Your goalie?"

"Wyatt Marshall—wait—did you say her last name is Marshall?" Conrad leaned up. "She's sitting right over there." He pointed to a booth across the room.

Jack glanced over and spotted a woman with dark hair, purple at the roots, seated with a boy, maybe ten. Across from her sat a bigger man, hockey build, and yes, he looked the size of a man who could stop pucks.

"Is she a cyberhacker?"

"How would I know?"

He pulled out Ty's phone. "I'll be right back." Sliding out of the booth, he wove his way across the restaurant.

When he spotted Jack heading his direction, the big hockey goalie leaned back in the booth, his jaw tight, probably ready to fend off a request for an autograph, or maybe a picture, given that Jack held the damaged phone.

He even slid out of the booth, as if to stop him.

Jack turned then and waved to Conrad, who thankfully had eyes on him. Conrad frowned, lifted a couple fingers in a courtesy wave.

It worked. Marshall relaxed, his hands in his pockets by the time Jack walked up to him. Jack stuck out his hand. "Jack Kingston. Conrad's brother."

Marshall met his handshake and offered a smile. "Wyatt Marshall. Nice to meet you."

"I'm actually here to talk to your wife, Coco."

Wyatt frowned, and Coco looked up at Jack at the mention of her name.

"My cousin Ranger sent me your direction. Said you could help me with a small problem."

She glanced at Wyatt, then back at Jack. "He texted me. Something about a phone?"

He handed her the smartphone, now dead. "There's a missing woman, and this phone is from her Uber driver, who is fighting for his life after being shot in the head."

Coco glanced at her son, back at Jack, one eyebrow up. The boy played a handheld video game, his earbuds in, but still.

"Sorry."

"It's all right. We usually don't let him play videogames at dinner, but it's been a long couple days, with back-to-back games." She took the phone, then pried off the rubber case and opened the back. "SIM card is still here. I should be able to get the information from it."

"What we really need is the GPS. His car was found out at the Duck Lake boat launch, but we need to know the route it took on Tuesday before he was . . . um . . ." He glanced at the kid. "Relieved of his driving position."

Coco arched another brow but nodded. "Okay. It'll take some time."

"We don't have a lot of time."

"I see." She glanced at Wyatt.

"I'll catch a ride home after the game," he said.

She set the phone down and turned to Jack. "What's your number? I'll contact you when I get the information."

He gave it to her, and she put it into her phone, then sent him a text. His phone buzzed and he confirmed her text, adding her into his contacts. He dropped the phone back into his front pocket. "Thanks."

"No guarantees, but I'll do what I can."

Jack headed back to his booth, and when the waitress swung by, he handed her his credit card to pay for the Marshalls' lunch.

Meanwhile, Harper had been texting. She looked up. "I'm late for the spa day. Boo texted me. What do I tell her?"

He glanced at Conrad, back at Harper. "Nothing."

"I'm not lying to my friend."

"Listen. You're not lying. You're dodging." He leaned forward, including Conrad in his huddle. "The last thing Boo needs to worry about is where Penelope is. You know her—she's an SAR professional. She'll activate her search and rescue gene, and suddenly her wedding won't be on the radar. I don't want anything to destroy this week for her."

"She has a right to know—"

He held up his hand. "Of course. But there is nothing she can do. We're fresh out of leads. Until Coco comes back with a route, we need to keep this under our hats."

"What about the police?" Conrad said.

"We already talked with Jenna. Can you forward me the second voicemail? I'll swing into the sheriff's office and give her the update." He looked at Harper. "Without you."

Her mouth opened. "Why—"

"Because you have a spa date."

She pursed her lips.

"And maybe Jenna will cooperate a little more if her nemesis isn't doing the asking."

"I'm not her nemesis."

A beat.

"Fine. Whatever."

He directed his words to Conrad. "You're coming back tonight, after the game?"

"Maybe." Conrad raised a finger to the waitress, who came back around with Jack's credit card and the check. "It'll be late, though."

Jack signed the receipt, then shoved the customer copy into his pocket. Slid out of the booth.

Harper followed him out to the car. "Maybe you're right. I'll dodge. But not for long. Keep me posted if you get any information."

"Will do." West nudged into his head. *Maybe what you need is a partner, though. A Watson to your Sherlock.*

Stop.

But as they walked out to the car, under the fading light of the late-afternoon sun, he knew one thing . . .

He'd been lying to himself, and his heart, for years.

He'd never gotten over Harper Malone.

———•———————•———

A domestic terrorist didn't deserve a twelve-thousand-square-foot mansion on the shores of his own private lake, filled with stone fireplaces, leather furniture, and the delicious smell of tomahawk steaks grilling on the massive outdoor grill.

Then again, she wasn't in charge of fate, and it certainly didn't listen to her.

Emberly crept out of a closet in a second-floor bedroom, where she'd managed to slip in after Nim's clever plan had played out.

Emberly had had to do a smidgen more homework—starting with locating the catering company, their location, and the rental vans they'd use for the event, and then posing as a driver.

That got her through the gate. Carrying a tray of thick seasoned steaks got her into the kitchen, and the memorized layout of the house landed her upstairs in one of the spare bedrooms.

Nim had connected her to the security feed, and she spent most of the next three hours watching on her phone as the guests arrived—the Kingston boys, all four of them, swaggering in like they owned the place. Stein came in wearing a pair of black jeans, a form-fitting shirt. No limp, so that was interesting.

But her research suggested he'd actually requalified for operational duty, so maybe she'd overreacted to the whole left-for-dead thing.

Oaken's SAR crew arrived not long after. She'd done her research on them too. A search and rescue team out of Alaska, and sure, they had *the last frontier* written all over them. Led by a big guy named Moose—the name felt accurate—who came in with his brother Axel, grinning and slapping Shep Watson on the shoulder as they entered.

So that was Shep. She'd heard stories. *Huh.*

And with them arrived Oaken Fox and his band. Oaken wore a little less swagger, but he had a quiet confidence about him that suggested he wasn't intimidated by the military and SAR types around him.

The party also included a couple of Brontë's cousins—one from Alaska, a dark-haired guy, cool in his aviators, and a local named Ranger. Nim had clued her in on Ranger, and he looked like the former SEAL he'd been, although maybe leaner.

Music played through the house, and the caterers had started the smoker hours earlier, popping in the ribs. She could almost smell the hickory from here. That and the steaks and a tray of homemade brats suggested a man's party.

Not a piece of chocolate to be seen.

She'd spotted Stone, of course. No feeds to his office, but one in the hallway, and he'd come out of the upstairs roost a couple hours ago. The office sat in a separate wing, in a massive third-floor room with picture windows that offered a 360-degree view of the lake and surrounding forest. According to the blueprints, the roost was accessed by a private set of stairs that connected to the rest of the house via a long balcony landing that overlooked the main floor, the arching two-story picture windows, and the lake.

She'd have to cross the open balcony, then access the room with the thumbprint lock, which might have been tricky had she not lifted the thumbprint and reapplied it to the thumb of a latex glove.

She'd wait until dark—which wasn't hard, given the early sunset. And according to the screen on her phone, the lake already waxed deep orange across the snowy face.

Meanwhile, the guests congregated on the lower floor, where they played pool. A few had gathered in the hot tub, a few more hanging out in the sauna while the chefs doctored the ribs and prepared the steaks.

Now felt right.

She slid out of the closet, wearing the suit of the local security team. She'd even found a patch and had it made to look like the private firm Stone employed.

No gun—but she did carry a Taser, just in case.

She stopped for just a second to check her attire. Blond wig, although not the one that Nim had suggested. This one was short and utilitarian, and yes, she wore glasses, and green contacts over her gray-green eyes.

Black long-sleeve shirt, black cargo pants, boots.

Slipping out of the bedroom, she stepped into the dark hallway.

It led down to the balcony, then opened to the stairwell to the upstairs office.

"Don't get caught, okay?"

She took a deep breath, then walked down the hall. No need to creep, she was security. Doing rounds.

She paused at the opening to the balcony.

A few men had ventured to the main floor, their conversation lifting. The scent of hickory smoking nearly caused her stomach to give her away.

Don't look. Keep walking.

She headed across the balcony, eyes on the office door.

It sat recessed in the stair's landing alcove. She'd already slid on the latex thumb and now pressed it against the lock.

The door unlocked, and she rolled the thumb off and headed upstairs.

Her surveillance yesterday had netted a few pictures of the office from a distance, but now it felt bigger, more open, the night pressing into the windows.

Now this was an office. A seating area looked out to the lake. A massive custom walnut desk wrapped around the other end of the office, with monitors—now dark—that rose from the desk. Sleek, contained, Stone's weekend retreat.

Probably he didn't plot *all* of his terrorist activities here. Just the really important ones, like developing an army of cybersoldiers.

Who could be programmed by the highest nefarious bidder.

She didn't turn on the light, of course. Instead, she pulled out a night-vision monocular and held it to her eye. Scanned the desk.

Found the charging pad.

No phone.

Breathe.

She should have known something like this would happen. Why hadn't she just lifted it at the party? She was better than this.

Giving the room one last scan, she found nothing. Turned to go.

Footsteps on the stairs.

She stilled, then pocketed the monocular, and searched . . . *There*. Behind the stair railing, a small bookshelf, maybe waist high.

Hustling over, she knelt behind it. Tucked herself in.

Please let it not be Stone—

The light didn't flick on, didn't suddenly expose her, which meant—maybe she wasn't the only one sneaking around.

This could work for her.

In the moonlight, she caught a glimpse of the intruder—the, *ahem, other* intruder. Big guy, built, he wore a dress shirt, pants. One of the guests.

Which meant—"Stop where you are." She'd stood up and grabbed her Taser, held it out.

The man stiffened, turned, his hands up.

And her heart nearly punched through her chest.

Of course. Steinbeck Kingston. She must have left the door open.

He held his hand out in front of him. "Hey. Sorry—I saw someone come in here, and I thought maybe . . . Never mind. I can see I was wrong."

She nodded. "Are you a guest here?"

"Yeah. But . . . sometimes catering crews can be a front for a different kind of crew—anyway." He gestured to her weapon, obscured by the dark. "Clearly that was a leap."

"Clearly."

It wasn't lost on her that the longer she stood here, the greater the chance that *real* security might roll up, and with them, Stone.

Who probably didn't know who she might be, and if she hoped to get that phone, she needed to keep it that way.

"Okay." She sheathed the Taser. "Thank you, Mr.—"

"Kingston. Steinbeck Kingston." He lowered his hand and held it out to her.

Oh no, she wasn't that stupid. "You can just go back to where you came from. I'll finish up here."

He lowered his hand, then nodded, backed away. "I trust Stone is in good hands."

With friends like Stein, yes.

Except, cold thought slithered through her as he took the stairs down.

Stein wasn't . . . *working* for Declan Stone, was he?

Please don't let him be a terrorist too. She just might give up on humankind. Because she remembered the man he'd been. Or she'd *thought* he'd been.

She followed him down, closing the door.

Only when she turned did she see that he'd paused at the end of the landing, near the other stairway, watching her.

Then he lifted his chin and headed down.

And as she strode down the hall, descended the far stairs all the way to the main floor, as she got into the rental truck and drove through the gates, it occurred to her.

Steinbeck Kingston was going to be a problem.

●————————————————————●

As she sat in a padded chair while a pedicurist filed her toenails, Harper couldn't shake away the memory of Penelope's scream through the phone.

Crazy.

Worse, she sat in a puffy white bathrobe, with mud drying on her face and her hair wrapped up, so it wasn't like she could suddenly jump up and run from the room.

Besides, she had no transportation, Jack having dropped her off at Serenity Spa.

The place smelled of lavender, a waterfall rushing down a half wall that cordoned off the massage rooms. Her skin smelled of lemongrass and eucalyptus, and if it weren't for the knot in her gut, she might have actually enjoyed the one-hour working of her tense muscles.

Except . . . *Penny*.

Brontë had asked whether she'd heard from her and . . .

She'd lied. Okay, not exactly *lied*, but, "Conrad got a text from her. Said she was in Minneapolis."

So, a half lie.

It burned like a coal inside her, but watching Boo's face as she leaned back and let the pedicurist massage her feet and legs—*yes,* her friend needed this day, without fear. Besides, like Jack had said, what could they do? He was probably sitting with Jenna right now, tracking down leads.

As the deputy flirted with him.

Harper closed her eyes, trying to relax into the leg massage.

"Okay, Mom, give us your five best tips for a long and happy marriage." This from Austen, who sat in the next chair, wearing the same attire, same mud pack. Beside her sat London, who also sat with her eyes closed.

Emily Kingston leaned forward in her chair from where she sat at the end, on the other side of Boo. "Seriously?"

"You've been married for nearly forty years, Mom," Boo said. "Certainly you have some tips."

"I don't know. Forgive, maybe? Yes, that's the right color." She nodded as her attendant held up a deep red.

"Racy, Mom," Boo said.

"It's the only shade I wear. It's called I'm Not Really a Waitress." She winked. "Even if sometimes your dad thinks I am."

"And you think he's your personal handyman."

"What? He is." She grinned. "Okay then, my tips." She looked at Boo, so much love in her eyes.

Oh, Harper had wanted Emily Kingston for her mother. It wasn't just the cookie comfort food—although Conrad's words had struck home. Mama Em listened. Cared. And after Harper had won the sixth-grade spelling bee, she'd found her picture and the article cut out and displayed on the fridge along with the rest of the family's accolades.

She'd belonged.

So maybe Harper did have something to contribute to Boo's beautiful wedding week . . . her silence.

"First," Mama Em said, "remember that men are built to protect. So don't be whiny and needy, but also let him step in for you when he wants to. Sure, you can pump your own gas, change your own tire, and open your own door, but it doesn't make you weak to have your man do it for you. In fact, it makes you honored."

So different from the advice Dr. Phillipa Malone would have offered. *"Stand on your own two feet. You don't need a man."*

"Then, remember that you're partners, not adversaries. He's on your side, and you're on his. Listen to him, seek to hear his point of view, and work with him to solve problems. The more you work together, like a team, the stronger your bond will be."

And just like that, she could feel Jack's hand on hers, under the table, squeezing.

"Be team Fox. Just like we were—and still are—team Kingston." Nothing of the Big Family Fight reflected on Mama Em's face, and maybe that was the point. Teammates fought, but they didn't betray each other. And in the end, they showed up.

Like Jack, back for Boo's wedding, despite the wounds he'd caused.

Harper had clearly misjudged him.

The pedicurist held up a color for Harper. Harper had picked blue but now pointed to the wild red on Emily's toes. "I'd like to not be a waitress too."

"Me too," Boo said.

"Not me," said Austen. "I'm getting Barefoot in Barcelona."

She held up the pale pink color. "I've always wanted to go to Barcelona."

"It's beautiful," London said beside her, her eyes still closed. "Especially for a romantic getaway."

Harper noticed a purple color on her toes. "What's yours, London?"

London opened her eyes, wiggled her toes, wearing a grin. "Shaking My Sugarplums."

Laughter.

Harper wished she knew the story of Shep and London. He seemed so solemn and unshakable against London's mystery.

"Okay, Mom, that's two," Austen said. "I want three more."

"I did mention forgive, right?"

Forgive. The word ribboned around Harper's heart. *"I'm sorry I hurt you."*

Oh, why hadn't she said she'd forgiven him?

"And . . . embrace adversity together. Which means trust each other. Am I repeating myself?"

"Is this like—couples who wallpaper together stay together?" Austen said.

Mama Em smiled. "Yes. And couples who tackle tough things, holding hands through them—they stay together too. You learn to lean on each other but also to hold each other up. And how will you become the dynamic duo without facing challenges?"

And just like that, Harper was back in Grenada, helping Jack rebuild a roof, handing up tiles and nails and . . . laughing with him. Sharing a can of grape Fanta. Hauling water to the worksite together, one hand each on the handle.

"Just keep loving, keep trusting, even if you get burned," Mama Em said. "Keep believing the best; keep taking risks. And if you get in a fight, be the first to apologize, even if you were mostly in the right. A soft answer turns away wrath, and someone has to go first."

Not ignore the problem and walk away? Right.

"Most of all, remember this. He's already said 'I do.' Or he will—and then it's done. You're his and he's yours, and now you start to dive deeper into the joy and wonder of your love. You stop trying to earn it and start the tending of it." She reached out and took Boo's hand. "And then you live happily ever after."

They laughed. Even Harper, but for some reason the words lodged inside her.

They finished the pedicures, moved to the salon for their facials, and two hours later, as stars burned in the sky, they headed out to the Lumberjack's Table.

Harper seemed to have lost her appetite, or maybe the fries from Sammy's had filled her up. She watched as the other ladies took the mic.

London sang a version of "I Will Always Love You" by Whitney Houston that brought the house down, and then Austen and Boo offered up a hilarious version of "Wannabe"—"I'll tell you what I want, what I really, really want—"

The lyrics managed to add to the quagmire inside. "If you want my future, forget my past . . ."

Even Mama Em got up to sing and brought it home with Celine's finest. "Near, far wherever you are . . . I believe that the heart does go on . . ."

"C'mon, Harp—you gotta sing." Boo handed her the song-choice book.

Perfect. But Jack was in her head with words about not wrecking Boo's wedding week. She gave Boo the list. "Pick one."

"Anything?"

"I'm living on the wild side."

"Since when?" But Brontë opened the book, found a song, and went to the front. "Tee up, Bee."

Harper rolled her eyes but went to the front.

The first bars played, and Boo folded her arms, almost a dare. And then the song sank in. *Seriously?*

Boo arched a brow.

Dare accepted. Harper stepped up to the mic. "I heard that you're settled down . . ."

Adele's lyrics seemed to land right in her soul, about a woman singing to her first love, the one she never got over.

"I hate to turn up . . . but I couldn't stay away . . ."

Harper's throat tightened, but she swallowed it down, belted out the song, her voice rising and falling, even slowing . . .

"Never mind, I'll find someone like you . . ."

She looked out into the crowd, the room a little hazy in the dim light. Her gaze cast to the door, where a group stood, and for a second, just a flash, she thought—

No. Jack was with Oaken, at the bachelor party.

She closed her eyes and finished out the song. "Sometimes it lasts in love, but sometimes it hurts instead . . ."

The song finished, and she hung her head as the crowd erupted. Then she looked up, grinned, and held up her arm.

Met Boo's eyes and tried not to cry.

She got off the stage then, and Boo walked up to her. "That was amazing."

"And that was mean."

Brontë's eyes widened. *Oh,* Harper hadn't meant—"Sorry. It's just, I . . ."

"Don't let him go. For you, it isn't over. And I saw how Jack looked at you last night, when you were dancing. Maybe for him it isn't over either. I made you sing that song so you wouldn't have the same regrets. You have two days left. Don't let him walk away unless you want him to."

Then Boo pulled her into a hug.

Aw. Harper hugged her back.

Boo's words clung to Harper all the way home, and even after she'd changed into her flannel pajamas and a sweatshirt, wool socks. She took off her makeup and couldn't bear the empty bed beside her, so she went downstairs to the fire, taking her laptop with her.

She sat on the plush leather sofa and opened it up, trying to capture today's events.

In the lush tranquility of the Serenity Spa, reality TV star Brontë Kingston and her closest friends celebrate the dawn of her new chapter with a day drenched in relaxation and laughter. The serene day unfolds with massages that untangle the knotted anticipation of Brontë's upcoming union with country-music sensation Oaken Fox. As the spa's natural light filters through gauzy curtains, Brontë's mother, with eyes twinkling, gathers the group, imparting pearls of wisdom about marriage. "Just keep loving, keep trusting, even if you get burned."

She stared at the blinking cursor. Then she saved the document and headed over to a different file.

The forbidden file.

A Thousand Summers

Aw, why not? She clicked it open.

Twelve chapters of her unfinished book about the spring break—now fictionalized into one tumultuous summer—that'd changed her life. Not a memoir, but fiction about unrequited love, a forbidden romance, and giving away your heart.

Although, she should probably change the names to protect the innocent. Or guilty.

She opened her last chapter.

The kiss.

The sun sets, casting a golden glow across the

beach, turning the gentle waves into molten light. I stand close to Jack, my heart racing as I lose myself in the deep blue depths of his eyes, so like the ocean sprawling endlessly before us. His dark hair catches the breeze, a striking contrast against the sky's softening hues. I've dreamed of this moment for so long, and now, enveloped in the twilight's embrace, my fantasy edges toward reality.

Jack turns toward me, his expression hesitant yet filled with a longing that echoes my own. He leans in slowly, his lips meeting mine with a tender hesitance that sends shivers down my spine. The touch is a whisper, cautious and exploring. Yet as I respond, something shifts. The kiss deepens, fueled by my eager reply. His arms wrap around me, pulling me closer, the rhythm of the waves syncing with our burgeoning passion. My mind whirls—this is the man I've adored from afar, now kissing me with a fervor as vast as the sea itself. I'm overwhelmed by disbelief and joy, hardly able to grasp that this moment, so beautifully perfect, is truly mine.

She read it again, caught in the memory, the scent of the salty air, sand between her toes, cool to her bare feet. He had smelled slightly of sawdust, a little of coconut sunblock, and tasted of the sweet lemonade from dinner. He'd said yes to her invitation to meet her on the beach through a trail in the lush grasses, and as the sun set, they'd sat, talking. His fingers had combed the sand as he'd told her about law school, and she'd told him about her college classes at Gustavus—just two days a week—where she pursued her associate's degree.

Yes, she could see now how he might have been confused about her age.

But maybe he'd just seen what he'd wanted to see— *"I liked what I saw."* And she'd liked the desire in his eyes, and that, along with the scent of the night, the adventure of their spring-break trip, and even the magic of her crush, had all made her lean in.

She'd invited it, even if he'd reached for her, pulled her to himself.

Magic.

No, not magic. A mistake. A terrible mistake that could have hurt him. Because technically, she had still been in high school and, yes, been too young for him.

No wonder he'd run from her. Boo's words wound through her. *"For you, it isn't over. Maybe for him it isn't over either."*

She stared at the crackling fire. *"Don't let him walk away unless you want him to."*

But maybe it wasn't up to her. Like the saying went—if he was into her, she'd know.

She opened a new document, watched the cursor blink, but she had no words.

Instead, she opened her email, attached the little blurb about today's bachelorette party, sent it off to Clarice.

Closed her computer.

The door behind her opened and she turned.

The guys, coming back from the bachelor party. Doyle, laughing, and then Steinbeck, pulling off his shoes and heading upstairs. Shep, and behind him, Jack.

Shep also headed upstairs, behind Doyle.

Jack, however, glanced her direction. The firelight caught his expression, a small flicker of something in his blue eyes, pulled out a few russet tones in his dark whiskers. He'd tugged off his coat and hung it on a hook by the door, then removed his shoes, and now he came walking over to her in his stocking feet, wearing jeans and a thermal shirt that outlined his amazing shoulders.

Sheesh, she didn't know who she liked better—the Jack of her beach memories, or this one, so much older, his edges a little softened, but still fierce and determined and possessing the ability to sweep her heart from her chest.

"You're still up."

She nodded, not sure what to say.

"Good." He sat down on the chair. "Because I think I found a lead. Wanna do some tracking?" Then he smiled, and all she could think was . . .

"And then you live happily ever after."

NINE

P ENELOPE HAD A DEATH THREAT." JACK SET
down his coffee, recently brewed and steaming, and sat on the
chair next to Harper, who had pulled up the *Penny for Your
Thoughts* podcast.

Harper wore her pajama bottoms and an oversized white-and-
maroon University of Minnesota sweatshirt, her short hair tousled, no makeup. Sweet. Simple.

Honest.

Twenty-eight. Not *eighteen.* His brain had finally sort of settled
on that fact, so no, he wasn't going to run. In fact, when he'd arrived
home from the bachelor party and spotted her sitting in front of
the crackling hearth, he'd thought—

Two days.

She'd walk out of his life in two days. And he didn't know what
to do with the punch that landed in his gut, then swept his breath
out.

It hadn't helped that he couldn't take his mind off her all evening, even as he'd hung out in the steaming hot tub and watched
the Blue Ox game on a massive theater screen at Declan Stone's

impressive lake home. He'd finally suggested going over to the Lumberjack's Table to throw axes.

Stein had agreed, apparently itching to leave, and they'd walked in right as Harper was singing the Adele song, and didn't that take a piece out of him? *"Sometimes it lasts in love, but sometimes it hurts instead."* She'd had a soulful longing in her voice, and if it hadn't been for Steinbeck tugging him to the pool tables in the back, he'd have found a chair, kept listening.

Maybe come up to her and said . . .

What? Because he couldn't have dated a high-schooler. Even if she had been eighteen years old.

Now, however . . . well, the math felt different today, sitting with her at the kitchen table, the night pressing against the windows, the bracing scent of fresh-brewed coffee in the air. She kept playing with a bracelet she wore, running the charm over the chain, clearly a thinking habit as she read through the comments from the most recent episode.

"Most of these are just people speculating on who killed Sarah Livingston," she said.

"It's not in the comments. It's on the show." He reached over to move the cursor toward the end of the podcast, where Penelope played the various voice comments. They listened for a moment, and then the voice he'd heard before came on.

A medium tenor, the voice sounded in his late twenties, maybe early thirties. "You got it all wrong. And if you don't figure it out right, Sarah won't be the only one to die."

He paused it.

"That's not a death threat," she said. "He could be talking about anything."

"I thought so too, at first. Just a listener's concern that if she gets it wrong, a killer could run free. But the more I hear it, the more I feel like it's a threat. Listen to the way he says it—" He replayed the recording. "That's not a concern. That's a threat."

She leaned back in her chair, let go of her leg, folded her arms over her chest and gave him a look. "Now who has the overactive imagination?"

Oh. Right. He'd said that to her. "Listen, at the time, I thought she might be pulling a publicity stunt."

"And now?"

"Now we have a guy in a coma and a scream on voicemail." He, too, leaned back in his chair. "Maybe we need to take a closer look at the case she was working on."

"The murder of Sarah Livingston? Sure. I haven't listened to all the podcasts, though, so—"

"I have. Or most of them." He got up, grabbed her empty mug. "More coffee?"

She nodded.

"Okay, so here's what I know," he said as he poured. "Sarah Livingston was a just-starting-out real-estate agent who was found dead in her apartment from an apparent break-in. Except, all her valuables were untouched, and there was no sign of a forced entry. Investigators initially pointed to her former boyfriend, a real-estate developer named Holden Walsh. His car was seen in the parking lot that night. The only other suspects were a friend Sarah called that night and her neighbor, who had a key to her apartment. Nothing led to either of them or further implicated Walsh, and the case died."

He had fixed her coffee and returned to the table, set it in front of her.

"Penelope picked up the case and started to look into Walsh. Apparently, he had some shady financial records and a history of violence. Penelope's initial thought was that Sarah had something on him that he didn't want to get out, that he entered her apartment with a spare key and silenced her."

"So, it's Walsh."

"Or not, because Penelope confirmed his alibi. And she found evidence that pointed away from him." He pulled out a chair, sitting in it backward, bracing his arms on the back. "First, there was a masked man seen on footage near Sarah's apartment around the time of the murder."

"Like Zorro?" Harper took a sip of her coffee, looking at him over the rim.

He smiled. "I don't know. I was thinking more like a hosiery guy, but let's go with Zorro."

"So, Zorro. Who else?"

"Her neighbor Tommy. Turns out he's an ex-con with a rap sheet that includes burglary. They were seen fighting a couple weeks earlier."

"Over what?"

"Her cat. It got out and she blamed him. Penelope got the information from Kyle, Sarah's longtime friend from college. Sarah's phone records suggest they might have been becoming more than friends after she broke up with Walsh."

"Do we think Kyle's a suspect?"

"According to Penelope, he had a domestic-violence complaint against him back in college, but it was dismissed. She did some sleuthing and found it was from a former girlfriend who accused him of losing his temper in a jealous rage."

"You think he could have done that to Sarah?"

"Records show that Walsh visited her apartment only two days before the break-in and murder, so . . . maybe?"

"Four suspects. And according to Penelope's podcast, she was going to implicate one of them in her next show." Harper opened up the schedule. "Which drops tomorrow night."

She clicked on the icon and then stilled.

"What?"

She turned her computer around. "She posted about the podcast on Instagram earlier tonight." Clicking on the feed from the podcast page, Harper opened her IG page.

Don't miss tonight's podcast with a surprise guest! This changes everything!

"She could have scheduled this before she went missing," Harper said.

He took a sip of his coffee. "Maybe."

"You still don't think she's really missing." Something sparked in her eyes.

He held up a hand. "I didn't say that. I think it's pretty clear that something isn't right. I just want to keep an open mind."

"You're the one who said she had a death threat."

He blinked at her, then stood up. "Since when am I the bad guy here? I've been traipsing all over the county for the past two days. I'm in, okay?"

His own words pinged through him.

"I'm in."

Aw. Next thing he'd be making promises.

She studied him for a moment, then sighed. "Sorry. You're right. I'm just . . . worried."

He turned his chair around, sank back into it. "And your brain is playing what-ifs."

She nodded grimly.

"Sort those what-ifs into scenarios. Possibilities. Then you'll start thinking like me."

"Lots of what-iffing going on up there?" She pointed to his head.

"It's chaos. And loud. Especially when I'm on a hunt."

"But you like it."

He gave it a moment. "Yes. I do. Just because I get a reward for finding someone doesn't mean I don't care."

"You just don't want anyone to depend on you." She arched an eyebrow.

He had said that, hadn't he? "I don't like letting people down."

His words emerged soft, and he looked away, toward the dark window.

The one that reflected the sadness in her expression.

He turned back to her. "It was my fault that Boo nearly died out there."

She frowned. "What?"

"I was supposed to stay with her. Keep up with her. But I was mad that she kept running ahead, so . . ." He blew out a breath. "If we hadn't found her, I don't think my dad would have ever forgiven me."

"That doesn't sound like your dad."

"Oh, you didn't hear him after we found her. He took me apart."

"I've never heard your dad shout."

"Oh no. He gets lethally quiet. And it's scary. But more, I was fourteen, the oldest, and he said that as the oldest, I needed to take my responsibility seriously. That my siblings were depending on me."

He swallowed, shook his head. "And maybe it went to my head. I thought—okay. I'm not going to screw this up. I'm going to protect them all."

"And now it makes sense."

"What does?"

"Two days in the woods, hunting for your missing Cub Scout."

"Yeah, well, that was different. I was in charge; he was a kid—"

"And you found him. And became a town hero. I know. I was there."

A great warmth had filled her tone. It reached in, and he didn't have the power to stop it.

"Which is why Sabrina's death did a real number on you."

Oh.

"I spent a lot of time with your family. Waterskiing, fires by the lake. And growing up, you were larger than life. The leader of the pack. Then suddenly . . . you were gone. Out of their lives."

He started to shake his head, but she held up a hand. "Why do you think the entire family fractured when you walked away four years ago?"

"It didn't fracture—"

"You haven't had a full family Christmas since then. Everyone scattered."

"You're blaming me—"

"No. I'm saying that they depend on you more than you think. You are, and will always be, the oldest brother. You can't abdicate that, Jack."

He had nothing.

She shut her computer and got up. "You've been all over the nation, searching for lost souls. But the one you should be hunting for is right here." She put her hand on his chest.

The warmth soaked through him, burning as he stood up.

She met his eyes.

He met hers.

And she was right there, just inches from him. Full-grown woman, looking at him as if she . . . well, *knew* him. Not in the hero-worship way of so many years ago, but with depth and understanding and . . .

The old spark had already flamed inside him, the one she'd lit so many years ago, and now it simply flashed over. He lifted his hand, touched her face.

She didn't move, just drew in a breath, and her gaze fell to his mouth, back to his eyes, telling him yes.

So, of course, he kissed her. Because all other thought had abdicated and, *aw*, he was tired of trying to hold back the fire. He leaned forward and pressed his mouth to hers, gently, searching—

She stepped up, put both hands on his chest, and kissed him back. Not searching but responding, gas to his fire. Especially when she wound her arms around his neck and pressed her body against his.

The action ignited everything inside him, all his senses, and he simply tried not to combust as he wrapped his arms around her, angling his head down, breathing in the smell of her, tasting coffee, nearly engulfed by the sense of how well she fit against him.

Like she had always belonged in his arms.

He emitted a groan deep inside his chest, aware, so very aware, that no one, ever, had had this terrible, wonderful, terrifying effect on him.

No, he'd never forgotten her.

"Pigtails?"

Oh—

And just like that, the fire doused, a cold wash. He jerked, lifted his head, and stared down at her, wide-eyed.

She stared back, frowned, then took a breath. "Oh no . . . you have that—"

"I shouldn't have—"

"For the love!" She pushed him away. "I am not in high school anymore."

He took a step back, breathing hard. "Yep. Yep." Then he shook his head. "Super aware of that right now."

She raised an eyebrow.

"Except, for a second there, you were, and—"

"Get over it." She stepped up to him, trapping him against the table. Put her arms around his waist.

The fire relit, the embers stirring. Oh, she smelled good, something playful in her beautiful eyes. "You're not lost anymore, Jack Kingston. You're right back where you're supposed to be. So stop running."

Then she kissed him.

He closed his eyes, let her explore his lips, let her nudge his mouth open, let her take control. She wound her arms around his neck again, and he sighed and pulled her into his arms.

And for a long time, he simply stopped thinking and let himself be found.

She finally pushed away, and a slow smile slid up her face. "Tomorrow, we hunt down that death threat."

What?

She walked to the sink, poured out the rest of her coffee, then with a wink, she headed upstairs.

Wait. What just happened? His heart thumped, the taste of her still on his lips.

He should clearly stop thinking of her as *Pigtails.*

Turning off the lights, he headed out to the family room. The fire had died to a simmer in the hearth, and he sank onto the leather sofa, stretched out, staring at the embers' pop and glow.

"The one you should be hunting for is right here."

Maybe he couldn't abdicate his position. But maybe he didn't have a right to it, either.

He didn't realize he'd nodded off on the sofa until the soft thud of firewood falling into the hearth basket made him open his eyes.

Sunlight streamed into the room, the fire cold, and he blinked at the form until he recognized his father arranging the wood into the copper log basket. He wore a canvas jacket, a wool hat, boots, and gloves.

Jack sat up, ran his hands over his face, and his father turned.

"I didn't see you there. Sorry to wake you." He took off his gloves and smacked them together over the basket, chipping off the wood shavings. "You okay?"

Jack nodded. "Up late working on a project. Didn't want to wake Stein."

His father nodded. "I got another couple loads to bring in." He gestured with his head toward the door, and Jack got up, followed him out, donning a coat and boots on the way.

The inn's pickup backed up to the house, the tailgate open, firewood stacked in the back. Jack held out his arms as his dad piled wood in. "Still at it every morning."

"It's the charm of these old houses. A fire in the hearth, your mom's fresh-baked cinnamon rolls." He gestured to the cab. "She sent some for the crew."

His stomach nearly clenched, hungry.

Going inside, he let his father unload the logs from his arms. Then he followed him back out to the truck. His father opened the door. A casserole dish with a towel over it sat on the bench seat. Jack held up his hand. "I'll help you with the other wood deliveries. Earn my breakfast."

His dad nodded, warmth in his eyes.

Jack got into the passenger side. His father always reminded him a little of Russell Crowe, salt-and-pepper hair now, and gray whiskers, but he had a perpetual grin that took up all the space on his face, a low laugh, and Harper was right—the man never raised his voice.

Maybe that's why his disappointment sat in Jack's soul.

They drove to Grover House, the childhood home of his father. Similar to Doyle's place—the Norbert—Grover House possessed a wide front porch, a turret, a parlor, dining room, five bedrooms, and a third-floor ballroom. They sometimes brought in a caterer for bigger groups. Now, a few shiny Escalades sat in the driveway, belonging to Oaken and his friends.

His father backed the truck in and got out.

He loaded Jack up with more wood, then grabbed his own armful, and they headed inside.

Bacon frying in the kitchen, conversation, laughter. Weirdly, the fact that Jack's sister was marrying into a sort of found family settled a peace inside him.

They arranged the logs, then his father stirred the fire to life.

"Thank you, Mr. Kingston."

Jack looked over to see Oaken entering the room, holding a cup of coffee.

His father got up. "We've been over this. It's Grover." He winked at Oaken.

Oaken lifted his coffee, glanced at Jack. "Have you tracked down Penelope yet?"

That's right. Oaken and Penelope were friends. Jack had worked the fire into a blaze and now set the poker back with the fireplace utensils. "Working on it."

Oaken's mouth made a tight line. "If you need help, let us know."

And by 'us' he meant Boo's search and rescue team. "Maybe. We have a couple leads we're checking out today."

Jack followed his father back out to the truck. His dad looked over as he put the tailgate up. "I didn't know she was missing."

"Yeah. We thought she went to Minneapolis, but"—he shook his head—"I'm not sure."

"If anyone can find her, it's you, son." Then he winked and headed to the cab.

And Jack just stood there, wanting for the first time to make promises.

His father fired up the truck, and he slid into the front seat. They motored over to the Rudolph, the third home, this one more of a cottage, built for great-great-grandfather Bing's youngest son, who'd remained a bachelor all his life. A porch, of course, a small turret for the parlor, two bedrooms, and a great room with a marble fireplace in deep mahogany.

"The band is staying here." His father got out and they repeated their resupply of the firewood.

They got back in the truck, and Jack wanted to round back to his father's earlier statement, but the older man turned on the radio to the morning news from KDUC. Something about vandalism at the market this morning, police on the scene.

His father turned off the radio. "Kids today need something

to do. Outside. Something to fill up their time more than video games."

"Like building firepits?"

His dad glanced over at him, grinning. "It kept you boys out of trouble."

Jack shook his head, also grinning. *Maybe.* "That's Doyle's job now."

"He's a big help. But he's getting restless, I can feel it." He pulled back into the drive for Grover House. "Sort of like you."

"Me? I'm not restless."

"Son. You've been restless your entire life." He turned to Jack as he put the truck in Park. "But it's good to have you home."

Maybe Jack was tired, but the words nudged in beside the others, filling his chest.

"Conrad's here," his father said, looking up at the porch.

Indeed, his brother, dressed in a black parka and jeans, came down the stairs to the truck. He came over to the driver's side, and his dad rolled down the window. "Hey. You just get here?"

"Came in early this morning instead of driving in last night." Conrad wore a grim expression and glanced over at Jack. "What are you doing here?"

"I, uh . . . well, I'm here for a wedding. How about you?"

Conrad rolled his eyes. "Dude. Did the sheriff not call you? I drove through town, and your school bus . . . Sorry, man, but it's incinerated."

───────────●───────────

Today, she would find Penelope.

Harper transferred the photographs she'd dug up of Holden Walsh, Kyle Brunley, and Tommy Fadden to her phone and closed her computer.

She hoped Jack was up—she wanted to track down Kyle Brunley

and talk to him. According to her search, he lived in Bloomington and worked for a law firm in downtown Minneapolis. Handsome guy, brown hair, grew up with Sarah Livingston.

She'd found clips of him speaking at their high school graduation. He matched the caller's voice on the podcast; she knew it in her gut.

Jack would flip. *See,* she could find people too.

Her words from last night kept thrumming through her. *"You're not lost anymore, Jack Kingston. You're right back where you're supposed to be. So stop running."*

Wow, she didn't known where that had come from, but hello. She'd kissed Jack Kingston. Again. Only this time, he hadn't run.

Yet.

No. She'd seen the look on his face when she'd left him. Shaken, maybe, but also intrigued, those blue eyes following her.

Intrigued was good for a man who liked solving mysteries.

She'd showered, dried her hair, and now headed downstairs in her black pants and a bulky blue sweater. Conrad and Stein stood in the kitchen, leaning against the counter, nursing coffee as she came in.

Clearly, she'd interrupted their conversation, because they both cleared their throats and summoned up smiles. "Morning, Bee," Stein said.

"Harper," Conrad corrected. Winked. It didn't have the same effect as a wink from Jack, but a familial warmth swept through her. He must have gotten in last night, after she'd gone to bed.

She'd spent way too much time thinking about Jack, of course, and the way he'd looked at her when she'd suggested he might be searching for himself.

Sort of made her wonder if they all were hunting for pieces of themselves, really. Like Penny and her podcast. And Boo, when she'd signed up for a reality show after a dare from Jack. And maybe even her mother, remodeling her home, finally.

Harper didn't have a clue what she might be looking for. Coffee, maybe. She headed for the machine. "Is Jack up yet?" She picked up the pot, grabbed a mug.

Silence and she turned. "What?"

Conrad stared at his mug. Steinbeck drew a grim line with his mouth.

"Sheesh. You act like he left town or . . ." She set the coffeepot down. "Did he leave town?"

"Nope," Conrad said.

"Gonna be hard to do," Stein added.

She frowned. "I don't—"

"His schoolie was torched last night," Stein said.

The words dropped through her, hollowed her. "*What?*"

"Not sure what happened, but when I drove by the market this morning, the bus was still in flames, fire trucks and everything. Jack left about twenty minutes ago."

She didn't have time for coffee. Instead, she walked to the door, grabbed her jacket.

Conrad came behind her. "Where are you going?"

She shrugged on the coat. "To the market. Everything he owns is inside that schoolie. And . . ." She didn't know why her voice shook. "I just . . ."

"Care. Okay, I get it." Conrad walked over and grabbed his jacket. "I'm going with you."

"You don't—"

"I think I do. You're not the only one who is worried about Jack."

"I'm going too," Stein said.

"It's a party," she said and grabbed her keys. "But I'm driving."

She headed outside, the guys on her tail, her heart thundering. "Who would want to burn Jack's schoolie?"

"No idea," Conrad said.

"Maybe it has to do with your missing friend," Stein said, wedging his body into the back seat.

"Penelope? Why would—" She exhaled. "I hope not."

"Still missing, huh?" Conrad said. "That's disturbing."

She glanced at him. Nodded.

"How do you two know each other?" Conrad asked. If she thought Stein was big, Conrad barely fit in her Chevy Sonic, his thighs the size of timbers, his presence taking up most of the front seat. She'd seen him get into more than a few fights on the ice, so he could probably handle himself just as well as Stein, or nearly.

The thug squad, these two, and she suddenly realized they'd tagged along for protection. For her? Probably for Jack.

Still, sweet.

"We were roommates in college at the U of M and for a year after we graduated. She moved home when her sister's fiancé was murdered, and that's when I headed to Nashville, but we stayed close. She reached out to me to do the murder podcast on the Mike Grizz case, and I connected her to Oaken and Boo."

A line of smoke trailed up into the sky, still dissipating as they drew near town.

She slowed. Traffic backed up around the market, gawkers.

Sheriff's cars and a fire truck still sat on the lot.

Only blackened shells remained of the schoolie and the car parked next to it, clear casualties of the flames. She parked next to Jack's Geo and got out, the air soggy, sooty, and redolent of burnt rubber.

Jack stood, his hands in his back pockets, talking with a deputy.

Jenna. *Of course.* Harper took a breath and walked up to them, followed by Stein and Conrad. She stopped next to Jack. Might have reached out and taken his hand if it hadn't been tucked away.

He appeared grim, his jaw tight, the loss reflected in the hard stare he gave his former home. What had he called it—Aggie?

"You okay?"

He nodded, drew in a breath. "They're still trying to track down the owner of the other car." He shook his head, looked at Jenna. "Let me know when you locate that car."

"What car?"

He turned and hooked Harper by the arm, walked her away from Jenna. "They caught a car on tape driving by the front of the market this morning. Of course, they don't have any cameras in the back lot, but they think it might be the arsonists." He had slipped his hand down to hers, gripped it. Maybe for moral support, but she gripped it back.

Conrad glanced at Stein, who lifted a shoulder. "Were you able to salvage anything?"

Jack shook his head. "It's all gone. But you know, it's just stuff." Still, his mouth pinched at the edges.

Right.

He'd kept walking and now opened the market door and headed right up to the clerk. "Hey, Anna. Is Gordo here?"

Anna nodded, her attention casting over to Stein and Conrad, then to Harper, back to Jack. "In back."

Jack headed behind the checkout counter, knocked on the doorframe, and a man, early forties, a little extra padding, a full head of gray hair, got up from his desk.

"Jack. So sorry. Do the police have any leads?"

Jack had reached out to shake the man's hand and now stepped back. "No. But I was wondering if I could take a look at that footage."

"I was just looking at it." Gordo returned to his desk and moved the computer around. A camera had stopped on a white sedan with an orange door, graffiti on the body. "Seems I've seen that car before, but—"

"I have too," Harper said. "At Echoes Vinyl Café."

Jack nodded, looked at her. "Yes. That's where. I knew I'd seen it, but I couldn't . . . You're brilliant, Harper."

She just stared at him. He'd called her *brilliant*?

Jack turned back to Gordo. "Can you text me that picture?"

"I don't want to get in trouble with the police."

"I'm just helping out. I'll call them if I can track down the car."

Gordo nodded, and Jack pulled out his phone, rattling off his number. A moment later, it pinged with the text.

Jack held out his hand again. "Sorry for the mess. I'm just glad it didn't affect the shop. I'll get a wrecker in here to tow Aggie away after forensics have their turn."

Outside, the sky had begun to clear, the day crisp. He turned to Stein and Conrad. "Thanks for coming, guys, but really, I'm okay."

"Yeah, we know," Conrad said. "So, to Echoes then?"

Jack spiked an eyebrow, and Harper hid a smile. Then she reached into her pocket and pulled out her keys. Tossed them to Conrad. "Try to be nice to her. I'm riding with Jack."

Conrad nodded.

"I'm a better driver," Stein said. "Have you seen him?"

She got into the Geo; Jack got in the other side. Put both hands on the wheel.

She touched his shoulder. "You okay, really?"

He drew in a long breath. Swallowed. Then cast her a glance. "Good thing I wasn't sleeping in her."

"That's not remotely funny."

"But true." He turned over the engine. "It's not the first time someone has tried to hunt me down. She once took a bullet near the door."

"What?"

"I camped in the wrong place for the night. Private land."

"You need a safer life."

He pulled out, gave a small chuckle, and it stirred something inside her. So maybe he'd survive this.

"You have insurance?"

"Of a sort."

"What does that even mean?"

"It means that book royalties are still good." He pulled into the Echoes parking lot, and Conrad pulled in beside them.

"They're like a couple bulldogs."

"They're your brothers. You might consider that when a guy's home blows up, people get worried."

"Fine." He got out, and she followed him inside the store. Same vinyl smell along with coffee, but a different woman stood at the counter. She wore her hair in long black braids, pulled back, a purple shirt with the Echoes logo on the front, an orange apron. Her nametag identified her as the missing Tallulah.

Jack introduced himself and Harper and mentioned they'd been in on Wednesday.

"Yeah, Quinn told me," Tallulah said. "You were looking for someone."

"My friend Penelope." Harper had pulled up her picture from the podcast site and now showed Tallulah.

"Who's asking?"

"I'm her roommate, and she's gone missing."

"Sure, she was here. Sat at that table in the corner." She pointed to a booth. "With a guy. Good looking. They talked for about an hour, I guess."

"A guy," Jack said. "Can you describe him?"

"I don't know. Brown hair?"

"How about this?" Harper opened up a picture of Holden Walsh.

Tallulah frowned. "No."

"How about this one?" Kyle Brunley.

"Yeah, that looks like him."

Jack frowned. "Who is that?"

"Kyle Brunley. The man behind the voice."

His smile came slow but sweet and poured through her. "Good work there, Watson."

Watson?

He pulled out his phone and flashed the picture of the graffitied sedan to Tallulah. "When we were here, we saw this car outside Echoes. It's pretty distinctive. Any idea who it belongs to?"

"Why?"

"We love the paint job," Harper said.

"They did it themselves," Tallulah said. "That would be my cousin Elton and his buddy Job."

"We'd love to talk to them," Jack said, tagging onto Harper's vibe. "See if they might do some work for us."

"They're in most mornings. Hanging out with Dylan and Van Morrison." She pointed to a corner of the shop, a vinyl getaway, with a couple plush bouclé sofas and big, bulky headphones.

In most mornings. "Were they here the same day my friend Penelope was here?"

"Sure. I guess so. Yeah. The place wasn't very full. Just them and your friends and another guy, if I remember. Suit and tie. He did some computer work, then left."

"Before or after Penelope?"

"I don't know."

"Did she grab an Uber?" Jack picked up a card from the counter. He handed it to Harper.

Ty's Rides. And a phone number.

"I can't remember. Listen. I hope you find your friend, but I'm not here to rat out my customers."

Jack held up a hand. "You're not ratting out anyone. Penelope is in a wedding, and we're just trying to catch up with her."

His phone rang and he swiped it open, stepped away.

"The Oaken Fox wedding?" Tallulah had brightened up. "I thought I saw Ben King in town earlier. He's here, right?"

Harper shrugged. "I don't follow country music."

"Word in town is that it's going to be at Heritage Church. I hope there's security, because there will be paparazzi—"

"We have security, but it's all very tame. And the reception is at the house, so invite only, very private, very low key."

"That's no fun," Tallulah said.

Harper laughed. "I don't think we can take any more fun. Thanks for your help." She stepped away, after Jack.

Stein, however, had followed them in and now ordered a tall coffee to go.

Conrad followed with a breve.

Jack had gone over to stand by the door, his voice low into the phone. Harper shoved her hands into her pockets, feeling like an eavesdropper.

And she got nearly nothing from him.

"Wow. Really? Oh boy. Yes," and, "Thanks."

Stein had joined her, blowing on his black brew. He seemed to be looking at someone on the far side of the room.

She followed his gaze and spotted a woman in a booth. Short red hair that poked out from under a white stocking cap, a black jacket, jeans, boots. She nursed a cup of coffee, reading her phone.

When Harper turned back, Stein seemed like he'd dismissed her.

Jack came over.

"I'm not a fan of that look," Stein said.

"Reminds me of those days when he'd get us out of bed to shovel," Conrad said. "I don't want to shovel. I pay people for that."

"I'm sure you do, bro," Jack said. "But no, I need you to take Harper home."

She stiffened. "What?"

He ran a hand behind his neck, winced. "This just got serious." He looked at Stein. "That was Jenna."

Of course.

"There's been another fire."

"Where?"

"That's the thing. It's out at Duck Lake Motor Lodge. And there's a victim."

Harper stilled. "That's right near the landing where Ty's car was found."

"It is," he said. "And my gut says that it's connected."

Oh, for—"That's it? Your *gut*? You're abandoning me because your gut says it's connected? Seriously." She looked at Conrad, then Stein, who shrugged. Back at Jack. "This is my hunt too. So get used to me tagging along there, Sherlock."

He raised an eyebrow. *Well, two could play at the nicknames.*

"Fine. But first sign of trouble—"

"You'll what? Have the brute squad drag me home?"

His eyes darkened and his voice quieted. "Maybe. Because the last thing I want is for you to get hurt, Bee." Then he walked away, toward the door.

Oh great. Here they went again.

———•———

She hated fire. So when Emberly had woken up to the smell of ash and burning plastic, she'd shoved everything into her backpack, pulled on anything she could find, and hightailed it to her rental.

Her tires screamed as she pulled out of the parking lot. She dialed 911 in case no one had noticed that there were flames breaking glass and crawling out of unit 3.

She hated the Duck Lake Motor Lodge. *Next stop, a tidy Airbnb.*

No, next stop had been the Echoes Vinyl Café, where she'd ordered a jumbo piping-hot vanilla mocha and tried to tell herself not to panic.

Except that's when He Who Seemed to Have Radar on Her sauntered through the door, easy as pie, like it was no problem that he kept showing up in the same places she was like he might be stalking her.

Only, maybe not stalking, because Mr. Reflexes was with two of his brothers—

Jack Kingston, who'd been some kind of small-town royalty here so many years back. Football captain. Hockey captain. Track captain. He'd probably played both defense and offense in football, which meant he could slap down a ball as easily as he could catch it.

And then there'd been the big front-page article nearly eighteen years ago, about how he'd saved some Cub Scout. *Cub* as in kid, age seven, who'd gotten lost at Boy Scout camp. Two days later, Jack had found him.

With Jack now was Conrad, center for the Minnesota Blue Ox hockey team. He had too many online mentions to count, with his shots record soaring over twenty percent. *Impressive.*

And finally, Stein, who'd vanished from the radar when he graduated from Duck Lake High. Emberly knew some of the pieces, although the big jump from the moment she'd seen him bloody and dying to the one with him running a blocking route between her and mission success was a big ugly gap. She wanted to refuse to believe that he might be mixed up with Stone. Then again . . . well, he'd seen some stuff.

And now he'd seen *her*. Because of course as she sat in the booth, sipped her coffee, and tried to pretend she might be doing something riveting with her phone, all she could feel was Steinbeck's gaze on her.

Burning.

Unpacking.

Oh, she was so made here.

Made and without the foggiest idea how to get close to Stone to get his phone. And without the password, the entire op was shut down.

And Declan Stone would get away with murder. *Murders.* Plural.

Except, Steinbeck had seen a brunette and a blonde, and unless he was an owl, he might not have gotten a good enough look at her at Stone's party to remember her.

Fate seemed to be on her side for once, because the conversation with the barista had carried and Emberly had picked up some tidbits. *"No. It's a low-key wedding. Heritage Church, reception at the house. We have security, but it's all very tame."*

Tame. As in, could a girl simply walk in carrying a gift?

She could if she had an invitation, maybe.

When Stein turned away, she thumbed open her text app.

Nim answered almost immediately.

Nim
_____

Sure, I can make you an
invitation.

And then her phone rang.

She swiped it open, kept her voice low even as King Jack strode out of the coffee shop, the woman and his brothers hot on his tail. *Interesting.*

Nim, in her ear. "The key is to figure out what they sent out. Who is on the guest list? It would be super special and terrific if it was someone without encrypted email."

"I have a list of guests from Stone's party. I'm sure someone on there might have a copy of the email."

"Text it to me." A pause. "You okay? You sound . . . weird."

"I . . . it's nothing."

"Tell me!"

"The motel I was in caught fire this morning."

"What?"

"Yeah."

"How?"

"I don't know. It was in the room a couple doors down. But we were the only guests at the hotel, I think, so . . . yeah, creepy."

"Did anyone get hurt?"

"I don't know. I called 911—but I left."

A sigh. "Could Stone have . . . I don't know . . . found you, and maybe tried to . . . you know . . ."

"I don't know. I thought he was just this tech guy, way behind the scenes, but . . . I'm not sure."

She watched as Stein got into a Chevy Sonic and pulled out behind a green Geo Tracker.

"You remember that guy I told you about? On the botched job in Poland?"

"The SEAL. The one who got his legs nearly blown off."

She refused to let the image, the memory, the smells, the screaming take over. "He's alive."

"No."

"Yes."

"That's a good thing, right? No more nightmares—"

"I think he's working with Stone."

A beat. "That can't be right. He was a SEAL."

"People change. But . . . I think he knows who I am."

"You need to leave, Ember. What if—"

"No." She cut her voice low. "I need to get into that wedding. Get the phone. Stop Stone. It's more important than . . ."

"Than your life."

"If it comes to that."

"Because you can't see me, let me say that I'm raising my hand to disagree."

"Just get me into the wedding. And then get me to Florida. I need a beach."

She hung up. Finished her coffee.

And then she picked up her phone and went shopping.

TEN

WHY DO YOU HAVE TO BE SO STUBBORN?"
Jack glanced at Harper now as they drove to the Duck Lake
Motor Lodge.

Aw, it shouldn't have come out like that, but—

"Why do you have to be so bossy?" She arched a pious eyebrow.

"It's just like . . ."

"What?"

"Nothing. It just . . . you don't . . . you don't give up. And then—"

She turned to him. "Wait one second. Are you talking about
what happened *ten years ago*?"

"No." *Yes. Maybe.*

She had followed him out to his car again, with Conrad and
Steinbeck in hers, and he'd had the terrible urge to lock the door
and leave her standing in the Echoes parking lot. *Or not.* Because
the other urge was to keep her Velcroed to himself, make sure that
whatever game Penelope's kidnapper might be playing, it didn't
end up with Harper shot or in a coma or—

"Breathe." She touched his arm, shaking him out of himself,

and he swallowed. "Everything is going to be fine. I'm not in any danger."

His mouth pursed. He didn't know what to trust, his gut or his head. But Occam's razor said that the simplest theory was probably right. And the simplest theory in this case said that someone was trying to eliminate Penelope and anyone associated with her, and that included Harper.

Thankfully, before he said anything stupid, his phone rang. He went to pick it up, but Harper held up her hand. "You're driving." She answered it, turned it on speaker, and held it up between them.

He glanced at her. Then, "Jack here."

"It's Coco. I got into his phone. And I mapped his route."

Jack wished his chest would loosen at that news. "And?"

"No airport trips. But he did get a call from your friend Penelope and pick her up on Tuesday in Duck Lake."

"At a place called Echoes?"

"Huh. You might not need my help."

"I do. Keep going."

"So yeah. He had a few other rides, mostly from town. One from an apartment complex to a church, another from the market out to the Duck Lake Motor Lodge. That was Tuesday night before he picked up Penelope."

Aw. Now acid filled his chest.

"His final ride ended at the supper club."

"In every sense of the term."

She made a sound of agreement.

He'd reached the highway that circled the south end of the lake, driving past the Moonlight Supperclub on the way to the boat ramp. "Any other calls or texts?"

"That's it. How's he doing?"

"I don't know. Thanks, Coco."

"Anytime. Any cousin of Ranger's is a friend of mine."

"Thanks." Then he hung up.

"The motor lodge is right down the road from the supper club," Harper said.

"Yep." His mouth pinched at the edges.

"What if the killer called him to pick him up and drive him to the supper club, and then he pulled up, saw Penelope, and . . . what?"

"You saw the tape. She leaned down and opened the door, no coercion."

"As if she knew the guy in the car?"

"Maybe. Or maybe she just trusted Ty."

They'd reached the entrance to the motor lodge, a painted wooden sign out front next to a giant carved duck. The long timber building was filled with one-unit rooms with outside doors, recently updated by the look of the new windows, the lighting along the edge of the roof, the Adirondack chairs on the shoveled porch.

Above the blackened unit, smoke still scattered in the sky. A fire engine was parked out front, hoses trailing into the charred open door. Two cruisers from the local sheriff's office and a coroner's van were parked outside, a body on a yellow board, covered in a tarp.

Jack spotted Jenna outside the room, talking with another deputy.

"I can't seem to escape that woman," Harper said under her breath.

Jenna clearly felt the same, because she shook her head as Jack and Harper crossed the parking lot toward her. Behind them, Conrad and Stein rolled in—their backup, apparently. They lumbered up as Jack stood at the edge of the crime-scene tape.

"What are you doing here, Jack?" Jenna said, casting him a look. *What, no flirty smile?*

"Who's the vic?"

Jenna shook her head.

"C'mon. We're still on the hunt for Harper's friend, and . . ." He turned, his hands in his pockets, spotted the landing just across the street. More crime-scene tape flapping in the wind. He turned back. "Was this arson?"

"Too early to tell. Fire chief thinks it was slow-burning—might have started from a space heater that shorted."

"That's not what my gut says."

"Then your gut needs to spill." She stepped up. "What aren't you telling me?"

And just like that, he was face-to-face in his memory with Sheriff Wade as they wheeled Tansy into an ambulance. *This is on you.*

He held up a hand. "I'm not withholding anything. It's just a little . . . fishy." He glanced at the lake and back. "Where's the victim's car?"

She, too, looked around the lot.

"You talk to the motel clerk?"

"Yes. The deceased checked in Tuesday night, spent the night, and no sighting of him after that. The clerk said that Wednesday morning she saw that his car was gone, so she charged him for the night and thought he'd left. The cleaning service came in this morning. In the winter, they come every Friday, in case there are weekend motorists."

"So, his car was gone by Wednesday. What kind of car?"

She gave him a look.

"I'm just trying to help. Listen, there's a woman missing, a shooting, and a murder in this very small town on the very week that Boo Kingston is marrying a country-music superstar. You don't think that's a little worrisome?"

Her mouth tightened. "Yes. Fine. Sheriff Davidson is aware of this. He's already met with the security team for the event. He's probably with them now—"

"Who's the victim, Jenna?" Harper, her voice sharp. "Please."

Jenna looked at Harper. "You back for good?"

"No."

Jenna nodded. Glanced inside, then back at Jack. "Okay. The news will pick it up later today anyway. According to the front desk, his name is Kyle Brunley, from Minneapolis."

Jack tried not to stiffen, not to let the name find his solar plexus. Maybe he'd been expecting it, just a little. Still, he let a beat pass, then another.

Jenna frowned. "You know him?"

"No."

"Yes," Harper said on a wisp of breath. "He was last seen meeting with Penelope at Echoes Vinyl Café."

Jenna looked at Jack, almost accusingly.

"I don't know that that was the last known sighting of him," Jack said. "But yes, I think he came to town to meet her."

"Why?"

"He was a suspect in her murder-podcast case." And now his breath returned to him, along with a dark swirl deep in his chest. He reached out and found Harper's hand. "Any idea of when he might have been murdered?"

"Hard to say."

"Could it have been Tuesday night?"

"No way to tell. He's . . . there's not much left."

"Okay, that's it." He turned and practically pulled Harper away from the crime scene, into the parking lot. Stein and Conrad, who stood sentry behind him, parted, then followed like Dobermans.

Good. He'd need them to wrestle her into the car. "You're going back to the inn."

She yanked out of his grip. "Have you lost your mind? Maybe you haven't caught on yet, but you're not the boss of me. In fact, you *work* for me."

"No, I don't, and yes, I am the boss of you. Starting right now."

"No—"

"Yes," Conrad said.

She tried to level him with a look. Good thing Conrad knew how to take a hit.

"He's probably right," Stein said, a little more calmly.

Thank you, bros.

"But mostly because it's rehearsal night, and Boo is going to start wondering where you are."

She stared at Stein. "I don't have to be at the rehearsal for eight hours."

"Don't forget dance lessons," Conrad said.

"What is wrong with you people? My friend was with a guy who was shot and a man who was murdered, and you want me to learn how to dirty dance? Wow." She held out her hand. "Keys, please."

Conrad dug them out, and as he did, Jack wanted to grab them from his hand because—

"Thank you." She swiped them from him. "I'll do my own investigation."

"Harper!" Jack started after her. Grabbed her arm. She whirled around, a terrible glint in her eyes. The keys fell from her hand. Stein picked them up.

She reached for them, but he held them back.

"Seriously?" Her voice shook and she rounded on Jack. "I'm not a high-schooler anymore!"

"I know!" He ran his hand across his mouth, nearly shaking. "Don't you think I know that? Sheesh—" He shook his head. *Not now.* "I very much, clearly know that you're not a high-schooler." He held up his hands and took a breath. "You don't have to be a teenager to get in over your head."

"And you're here to make sure that doesn't happen—"

"Yes! Okay?" He dropped his voice low. "I'm just trying to—"

"Protect me?"

He gave her a look that once upon a time might have shut her down. "Yes."

"So you're just going to send me home, like a child, like *Pigtails*, while you and your brute squad—"

"Hey—" Conrad said, but Stein put a hand out.

"—hunt down . . . who? *Who,* Jack? Because I'm the one who did the research, found the suspects, and downloaded the pictures."

"Gimme your phone."

"Not on your life."

"Text them to me."

She shook her head, her blue eyes hot, a little spitfire staring up at him.

He stood there, the wind around him, and tried to wrap his brain around the terrible, wretched urge to pull her to himself, to kiss her—and to show her exactly why she had to go home. Stay where he could find her.

I can't lose you again.

The words entered his brain then, solidified, and he knew—just *knew*, like a blinding light that zinged through him—that he'd been running hard, just like she'd said.

Running from the crazy sense that they belonged together.

Denying it. But even as he looked at her, he saw them—a version of them that could be. Playing games in front of the hearth, maybe caretaking Rudolph House. Making dinner together . . .

He wanted something out there that he couldn't put his hand around. And it started with Harper.

"I'll take her home," Conrad said. "Give me your keys."

"I can drive myself," Harper said.

"Not a chance." Jack looked at her, and Conrad nodded. "I'll take your car. Conrad, get her home."

Jack gave his keys to Conrad, and just as he did, Stein tossed Jack Harper's keys.

"I hate you all," Harper said.

"I can live with that," Jack said evenly.

"You're fired," she snapped.

He rolled his eyes. "Finally."

She shook her head, walked to the Geo, got in. Slammed the door.

Conrad glanced at Jack. "You sure you want this to go down this way, bro?"

"Keep an eye on her." Jack turned to Stein. "Ready to hunt down a couple of local firebombing terrorists?"

"Just when I thought Duck Lake was boring. High drama and suspense." He glanced at the Geo. "She'll get over it if we find her friend."

As Jack got into Harper's little Sonic, he watched Conrad drive away in his Geo. Harper looked like he'd broken a piece of her soul.

Just like she had a decade ago.

"No, bro. She won't." Then he pulled out and headed back to Duck Lake.

———————•———————

And now she was twelve, being hauled home by one of the Kingston brothers, as if she needed babysitting.

Conrad brought her to the Big House, as it were. Tonight's big rehearsal-dinner event was being hosted by Oaken and his team at the Paddle House after the dance class. The Kingston team would decorate the third-floor ballroom for the private wedding reception. She didn't wait for Conrad as she headed inside through the kitchen.

Mama Em stood, aproned, at the massive stainless-steel kitchen island, frosting a layer of wedding cake. Already, over sixty cupcakes sat frosted, with Austen decorating the tops of the blue swirls with white edible glitter.

Boo, too, wore an apron and was frosting tiny pink, yellow, and green macaroons. The kitchen smelled of celebration and cut into the jumble of her hot emotions enough for her to take a breath.

Mama Em looked up at her arrival. "Bee! Good, you're here. I need floral arrangements put together. Just for the guest rooms—Dodge and Echo are coming from Alaska, and Ranger and his wife, Noemi, will be spending the night, since they're coming from Minneapolis."

Being pulled back into the Kingston vortex of activity might be exactly what Harper needed.

Conrad came in behind her, hung Jack's keys on a hook, then shrugged off his coat. "Smells great, Ma. What can I do?"

"Go upstairs and help Doyle set up all the tables and chairs for the reception."

Conrad walked away, and Harper eyed the keys just for a moment, then spotted the bouquets of flowers seated in buckets near the floral workstation. Two crystal vases sat on the counter.

She grabbed the flowers, unwrapped them, then sorted them out into sections. Blue anemones, white roses, blue carnations, mini calla lilies, cedar branches, and purple hyacinths, along with a bouquet of baby's breath. She measured the vases, then trimmed the stems under running water and removed any leaves below the rims.

"So you're just going to send me home, like a child, like Pigtails..."

He'd blinked at her then, as if she'd slapped him, but she'd been too busy retorting to Conrad to respond.

Now her words burned inside her. And it reminded her of Jack's statement two days back about his fight with Boo four years ago.

"I was just trying to protect her."

Yeah, well, Harper didn't need protection. She wasn't a child.

She used the cedar as a base, then started with calla lilies, then the roses, then carnations. She added the anemones last and put the bouquet into the vases.

"Don't you think I know that? Sheesh!"

She'd missed, also, the drop in his voice, the tremor.

Still, *hello,* they were partners.

"Rule three. I work alone."

So apparently, she'd ignored that.

"Those are beautiful, Bee."

She nearly jumped out of her skin at Mama Em's voice. "Thanks."

"I could always count on you to get these right." Mama Em leaned in. "You have just the touch."

"They need the baby's breath, and maybe a raffia ribbon around the vase."

"Perfect." Mama Em put her arm around her. "I've missed your touch around here. You've always been a part of the team." She let her go and headed back to her cake.

And now Harper's stupid eyes decided to water. She blinked back the burn, added the final touches, then picked up a vase. "I'll deliver these to the rooms?"

"Perfect." Mama Em had started added the frosting to the second layer of cake.

"I'll go with you," Boo said, and walked over to get the second vase. She picked it up and followed Harper from the room.

The door closed behind them. "Okay, so what's up?"

Harper glanced at Boo. "What?"

"You and Jack. Inseparable for the last two days, and then . . . what? You're here? Alone?" She led the way up the wide mahogany stairs. "And by the way, where is Penelope?"

Harper followed her down the hallway on the second floor. Boo went into a room, the Gatsby suite, decorated in the black and gold of the era—long black curtains with gold tassels, and on the four-poster bed, a red brocade coverlet, again with gold fringe, and a green chaise lounge. Boo set the flowers on a black lacquered dresser.

Then she looked at Harper and raised an eyebrow.

"I don't know," Harper said. "Jack is . . . looking for her."

"Jack, whose schoolie was torched today?" Boo put her hands on her hips. "What am I missing here?"

Harper sighed and headed to the next room, the Fitzgerald. A carved four-poster bed in rich mahogany with a navy coverlet, pale-pink art-deco wallpaper, gold velvet drapes, and a love seat facing the candle-filled hearth. Harper set the vase on a writing desk, next to a vintage gramophone.

She turned to go, but Boo grabbed her hand. "Harp."

Shoot, now her eyes burned again. She met Boo's gaze. Swallowed. "I'm not supposed to tell you, but Penelope is . . . maybe in trouble. We tracked her down to a coffee shop, where she met with a guy named Kyle Brunley—"

"The friend of Sarah Livingston."

"Yes—I didn't know you listened to the podcast."

"Of course I do." Boo pulled Harper over to the love seat. "He's a suspect in the murder."

"Except he's dead."

Boo's mouth opened.

"And Ty Bowman was shot."

"Ty—wait, from high school?"

"He's an Uber driver in Duck Lake. He's in a coma at the hospital in Waconia. Shot in the head and left at the Duck Lake Landing boat launch. Kyle was found at the Motor Lodge."

"They are right across the street from each other."

"Penelope was in the car when Ty was shot."

Brontë just stared at her.

"I'm sorry. Jack didn't want you to worry—"

"Are you kidding me? Why hasn't he called the police?"

"He did. He's working with Jenna."

An eyebrow arched. "Really."

"It's fine. But . . ." She sighed. "He sent me home with Conrad. Like I'm twelve."

Brontë took her hand. "He's just worried—"

"He's not my big brother." Harper looked past her out the window. "Or at least, I was hoping not . . ."

Her gaze flicked back to Boo, who now did a poor job of hiding a smile.

"It's like I can't seem to quit him. Like . . . I don't know. He was more than my first crush. I built a happily-ever-after world around him." She didn't know why she was saying this to Boo, but, well, her best friend probably already knew. "I even wrote a romance novel about . . . well, a guy named Jack. Only, it ends up happily ever after too." Her eyes burned again, and she swiped her cheek. "And it's not just that . . ." She sighed. "I feel so helpless. So . . . angry. I know I could help find her if he would let me."

"How?" Boo wore a little fire in her eyes.

"Tommy Fadden, the neighbor, said he saw a masked man leaving her apartment the night of her murder. Penelope said that the police had discounted his testimony because he was sort of obsessed with Sarah, but what if . . . what if he has more to say? Something that could help us find this Zorro guy..."

"Zorro?"

"Sounds better than 'masked man.'" She finger quoted the last words.

"You're such a storyteller. No wonder your blog post about the wedding dance rehearsal got so many likes."

"It posted?"

"Yeah. *PopMuse* picked it up and it's trending, along with an engagement photo. And a few memes of our faces over Patrick Swayze's and Jennifer Grey's."

"Nobody puts Baby in a corner."

Boo laughed. "Yeah. So"—she looked at her watch—"you have exactly six hours to find Tommy Fadden, interrogate him, and get back for the wedding rehearsal. Hopefully with Penelope in tow."

"At least with information I can give to the police." She took Boo's hand. "I'm sorry we didn't tell you."

"Jack's on it. I don't know what I could do to help anyway." She met Harper's gaze. "Find Tommy. I'll cover for you. Maybe Jack deserves a little taste of his own medicine." She winked.

Harper took the Geo, because what else did she have to drive, thank you? Listened to the radio—classic rock already preprogrammed into his radio.

"Don't Stop Believin'."

Whatever. She probably needed to give up on her fairy tale.

An hour later, she pulled up in front of 56th Manor, a small three-story apartment complex with a mansard roof and outside parking cordoned off by tall, grimy snowbanks. An entry allowed for mailboxes, with a list of names on a buzzer panel. She found the one for Tommy Fadden and pressed the buzzer. What were the odds that he might be home on a Friday—

"Yo."

She leaned in. "Tommy. My name is Harper Malone. I'm . . . a friend . . . of . . . well, Penelope Pepper. Can we talk?"

Silence.

More silence.

Then a buzz and she pushed inside. The place smelled tired. Orange-and-brown patterned carpet, no elevator, open stairs in the middle of the landing, and past that, a hallway toward the units. Sarah had lived on the ground floor, Tommy beside her, and now Harper found his apartment, gold number three on the door.

It opened before she knocked.

Tommy Fadden had seen better years, a look in his eyes that suggested bad choices and even worse consequences. Early thirties, maybe, wearing a pair of faded jeans, a black long-sleeve shirt, barefoot, a faded tat on his neck, bald, unshaven. His gaze darted down the hall, back to her.

"Harper?"

"Can I come in?"

He drew in a breath, then opened the door further.

What are you doing? But she'd told Boo where she was going, and really, Penelope had already interviewed him.

And it was daytime.

Aw, her gut fisted as he shut the door.

A bachelor's apartment. Flatscreen on the wall with cords hanging down, leading to some sort of gaming controller. Tweed sofa, a scuffed coffee table hosting a can of Red Bull. A single bar stool sat next to a counter that overlooked a tiny kitchen. A Styrofoam container with the words *The Anchor* sat on the counter, half open, with the remains of tangy chicken wings. The smell still hung in the air.

He offered her the sofa.

"I won't bother you for long." She remained standing.

He folded his arms and sank onto the stool. The man clearly worked out. "I already told Penelope everything I know. She didn't use half of it, though."

"Really."

"It wasn't the first time Sarah's place was broken into. Her back French door was jimmied a couple weeks earlier and her laptop taken."

Maybe she should sit down.

"I work late shift down at the Anchor bar."

"I've heard of it." Rough, down in the warehouse district. Maybe he was the bouncer—

"I'm a bartender, so I have to close. She had a cat, and Sarah was gone—one of her overnight real-estate events with her ex. Never liked him."

"Walsh."

"Yeah. A big real-estate developer. Hotshot."

"The podcast said he was her boss."

"She was a freelancer, so not technically, but . . ."

Maybe she'd misjudged him, the way his jaw tightened. *Not a thug. A protector.*

"That night of the . . . murder. What did you see?"

Tommy looked back at her, his eyes a little reddened. "Same thing I did before. I'd gotten home, was going over to feed her cat when I saw her French door hanging open. I thought maybe she'd forgotten to lock it, so I went in." He rubbed the back of his head. "Got beaned. Not sure with what—could have been the laptop. But it knocked me over long enough for the guy to get away. Big guy, built. Bigger than me."

"Really? That's a big help."

"Fine. Six three, six four. Burly. All black clothes, and he wore a mask."

"Like a Halloween mask?" She refrained from the Zorro description.

"No. Like a . . . special ops kind of mask. With a thermal eyepiece, mouth guard, hoodie. Like he might be military."

"Thermal eyepiece."

"Night vision, maybe, because he had good aim. I still have a bump."

"No idea who he might have been?"

"I wish it were Holden Walsh, but he alibied out both times, according to Penelope."

That jibed with what Penelope had said on the podcast.

"Any other ideas? Kyle Brunley?"

He almost laughed. "That guy? No. Let's just say he's built for running, not fighting." He got up and walked around the counter. "Naw." He opened a drawer and pulled out something. Dropped it on the counter. "And there's this."

He held up a matchbox with a logo on it, a blue-and-black swirl. "*Turbo*. What's that?"

"It's a nightclub. Downtown."

"Where'd you find this?"

"On the floor of Sarah's apartment, after the guy got away. I'd gotten ahold of his pants pocket as he was running away, and it ripped."

"And you didn't give this to the police?"

He cocked his head at her. "And have them look at me? C'mon—I already have a rap sheet. Burglary, back when I was eighteen. Did two years in Saint Cloud. I've been clean since then—head down, got my bartender's license. I don't want any trouble." He held out his hand for the matchbox. "I did take a trip down to Turbo, though, had a look around. The building is under Swindle and Walsh—S & W Management."

She handed the matches back to him. "Really."

"Yeah." He met her eyes.

Something had shifted in his, and she frowned. Swallowed. "Okay, well, thank you." She held out her hand.

His hand closed around hers. His eyes narrowed just around the edges. He didn't let go.

"Um. I need to go—"

"Sorry, honey. You're not going anywhere."

ELEVEN

"HELP ME UNDERSTAND WHY WE'RE TRACKING down your old hockey coach?"

They had driven out of Duck Lake, twenty miles east to the town of Chester, taking the county road south and then back west toward the Marshall Fields Winery.

"Because there was a sticker for North Star Arena on the bumper of the car in the video."

"The ice arena?"

"Where all the county hockey teams practice, and Garrett Marshall still runs the arena, I think. Or he might know who does now." Jack turned onto the long, snowy road that led to the river valley winery. The red barn rose from the snowy white fields, the immense farmhouse seated beside it, having been added on to over the years. A pavilion, probably for weddings and tastings, sat snow-covered, huddled in the yard. The fields lay barren and snow-cast, row upon row of frigid, gnarled vine.

He pulled in, then got out and went to the door under the covered porch. Knocked.

It opened, and a man stood in the doorway, salt-and-pepper

hair, muscular upper body, wearing a black pullover with a Vikings emblem.

Instinct had Jack standing up straight. "Coach."

A blink and then, "Jack Kingston?"

"Sir." He held out his hand. Garrett met it, grip firm.

"It's been, what, maybe fifteen years? What brings you to my doorstep?"

"I'm back for my sister's wedding, and . . . well, I'm trying to track down someone who might have done a little damage to my wheels."

"I'm sorry to hear that."

Steinbeck had walked up behind Jack. Garrett looked at him. "Steinbeck, right?"

"Sir. Good to see you. I served with your son, Fraser." He held out his hand.

"I heard that, I think. He's separated from the Navy."

"Me too." Steinbeck didn't add on anything, so maybe he wanted that part of his life locked down.

Garrett Marshall glanced at Jack. "Jack, I'm going to need your promise that when you find these guys, you'll call the cops, not try and take anything into your own hands."

Right. "I've grown up a little bit since my hockey days."

Garrett said nothing.

Jack held up a hand. "I just want to see if he might have any insurance information for me. He drove away before we could exchange information."

Steinbeck gave him a look, but he didn't meet it.

"Come in, boys." Garrett opened the door, and Jack stepped in, followed by Stein. The smell of something baking filled the house, grabbed Jack's stomach.

"How can I help?" Garrett said.

"He had a North Star Arena sticker on his car, and I wasn't sure if you were still coaching—"

"Not anymore." Garrett sighed. "These bones are too old. But . . . I do run the Zamboni, and I'm familiar with the teams and the rosters."

"His name is Elton. But he also had a buddy with him named Job. We're not sure whose car it might be."

"Elton Bridges and Job Ramsey."

Just like that.

"Elton played until he was a senior. Defenseman. Job was a winger. If I remember right, Job got hurt, dropped out his sophomore year. Elton was hoping for a scholarship to the U, but I don't think he made it."

"Thanks, Coach." Jack was turning to go when Garrett put his hand on his shoulder. "It's good to see you back here. Let me know if you ever want to slap around a puck."

He laughed. "Yeah, Doyle was talking about clearing the ice back home, maybe having a game of broomball."

"How is he?" Garrett's voice softened.

"He's . . . I think he's better." But he wouldn't really know, would he? A hand reached in, clenched his gut.

He really didn't know any of his siblings. Not anymore.

I work alone. He pushed the rule from his head and met Garrett's outstretched hand.

"Not everyone is raised a Boy Scout, Jack. Go easy." He winked at Jack, then shook Stein's hand.

"What did he mean by that?" Jack said as they walked out, got into Harper's car. *Sheesh,* he was a jerk for stealing it. He'd have to go home, trade it out for the Geo.

"I think he means exactly that—you were raised to be the kind of person people can count on."

Jack looked at Stein. "Right. Hardly." He pulled out.

"Are you kidding me? Until you walked out of our lives after Sabrina's death, I thought you might be up there with . . . I don't know. A superhero?"

He gave a laugh.

Stein didn't. "Dude. You were my big brother. You were larger than life. Even before you saved that Cubby. I mean—you found Boo. That sort of cemented it for me. You were—"

"I lost Boo. You know the truth."

Stein frowned.

Jack glanced at him. "I was the reason Boo went missing. Because I was angry that I was assigned to babysit her. And I was carrying a canoe, so, hello, I might have been in pain and impatient. I told her to go ahead without me. Just in case you have any lingering ideas of me and my awesomeness."

A beat. Then, "But you fixed it."

He glanced at Stein.

"And you learned from it." Stein sat with his hands in his lap.

"Oh, please, now you're going to do some SEAL speak, like fall seven times, get up eight."

"I think that's some Japanese proverb or something, but yes, I've heard it. Here's the one you should hear—God has a plan for your life, and even you can't screw it up."

Oh.

"I don't know, Stein. Feels like I've been living in the alternate plan, the one I did screw up."

"The one where you don't become a lawyer?"

Jack shrugged.

"What if that *is* the plan? What if you're really good at this gig, and this is what you're supposed to do. What if this *isn't* the mistake?"

They'd left the county roads, back on the highway toward Duck Lake.

"I hate you all."

No, he couldn't live with that.

He handed Stein his phone. "Speed dial number one."

Steinbeck pressed it, and then put the phone on speaker.

"Please tell me you're at a wedding and not tracking down a missing person." Nat, and in the background, crying lifted.

"Sorry to bother you."

"No problem. West! Come and get your child!"

Muffles, and then Nat came back on the line. "'Sup?"

"I need an address for an Elton Bridges and a Job Ramsey."

"Who are they?"

"The people who torched Aggie."

Silence. Then, "Are you kidding me?"

"Nope. They threw a rock into her back window, followed by a firecracker. *Boom*. She died a valiant death."

"Oh, Jack, I'm so sorry."

"I'll figure it out." He refused to go there. The feelings could wait.

"Okay, I have addresses, but be careful."

"Don't worry, Stein is with me."

"Oh, great. Nothing like a couple tough guys to keep the tensions low."

"Hey. We come in peace."

"You'd better. I've texted you the addresses. Stay frosty."

"Frosty?"

"Just don't end up in jail." She hung up.

"Jail?" Steinbeck raised an eyebrow.

"Long story. Get me directions to Elton's place."

Ten minutes later, they'd pulled up to a gray two-story bungalow with a small white front porch and a maroon Caravan in the driveway. They got out, crunched through a half-shoveled walkway trampled by an army of boots, and Jack rang the doorbell. Shoved his hands into his coat pockets.

The door opened—a woman in her early forties, holding a toddler. The kid sucked on two fingers, and a little girl in a yellow princess dress hid behind the woman's legs. "Listen," the woman said, "I already love Jesus, so you don't have to sell me."

Stein smirked.

Jack shook his head. "I'm looking for Elton, if he's here."

She rolled her eyes. "What's he done this time?"

"He . . . um . . . I just need to talk to him about a little fire incident down at the market."

"Fire. Ho-*ly* cow. That kid. Ever since he lost his hockey hopes, he's been fooling around town—" She put up her hand as if to stop herself. "Nope. I have lunch burning. He's probably with his friend Job. Now, he's a real catch." She shut the door.

Ho-kay.

"Job lives on the other side of town," Stein said, already pulling up his phone, where he'd forwarded the directions. "In the Eagle Lake gated community."

"You're kidding."

"I'm thinking graffiti car belongs to Elton here." He got into Harper's car.

"Job probably drives a Porsche, got his keys taken away." Jack said as he pulled out.

Stein smirked.

"You laugh, but I dated a girl from the Eagle Ridge gated community. She was . . . high maintenance."

"I remember. What was her name?"

"Gemini. Ashton."

"Oh yeah. Redhead. Hot."

"Yeah, and I was broke after our first date. We went to the state fair."

Stein laughed. "That's what happens when you're captain of everything. You had the ladies snowed."

"Hey—is it my fault that Dad paid us minimum wage?"

"What are you talking about? You got use of the boat and his truck, and I know you got out of at least two speeding tickets."

"One. The other ticket was for making out with Clarissa Fairmont."

Stein grinned. "She was a year older than you."

"I know." Jack laughed. "That relationship lasted one date too. I was so mortified about being found out that I drove her home and never called her again."

"You let your mistakes have too much power over you." He shook his head.

But the words found Jack, burrowed in.

He glanced at Stein as they left Duck Lake and headed south for the gated community. "I thought you said that maybe my mistakes can be God's plan."

Stein lifted a shoulder. "Sure. But only if they don't turn into a bullet that sits inside you, infecting your insides."

A gate cordoned off the entrance to Eagle Lake as if it were a high-security compound. Never mind that the fencing ended at the forest, some fifty yards on either side of the stone pillars and wrought-iron gate.

A coded box sat at the entrance, which meant . . .

"We need an inside man," Stein said. "Keep driving and drop me off."

"Are you going to do some super sneaky SEAL stuff?"

"Something like that." He winked. "Circle back around and wait down the street until you get my text."

"Please don't break any laws."

Stein grinned, slid out, and disappeared into the woods.

Jack kept moving, parking down the road on a semi-cleared forested road. From here, the stately houses that lined Eagle River rose, many of them made of brick, all of them with three-car garages, basketball courts, and theater rooms, and there was a pavilion in the center of the neighborhood for picnics.

A bedroom community for the wealthy who worked in Minneapolis. Or now, remotely.

Ten minutes. C'mon, Stein, don't do something stupid—

Jack's phone buzzed and he picked it up.

Stein_____

Now. Hurry.

Jack pulled out and spotted the gate opening as he drew near. He rolled through, kept going, and then spied Steinbeck emerging from the booth. He slowed, and Stein slid into the passenger seat.

"Go, go."

He hit the gas—not hard, but enough to keep them winding into the community. Maybe thirty homes, but he lost himself in one of the streets, per Stein's direction.

"How did you do that?"

"These places have no security, although they promise it. I walked up from the inside and told the attendant that I was a resident and I saw a couple kids setting a fire down at the pavilion."

He pointed to a line of smoke, now dying.

"Did you start a fire?"

"In one of the grills."

"With what?"

"You didn't see the pile of old Christmas trees? That's the house." He pointed to a house at the end of the cul-de-sac. Beautiful white-brick house, with columns flanking the front door, a basketball hoop in the drive. It overlooked the lake in the back and what looked like a swimming pool to the side. Two stories, with a long room over the garage, it had the space of the third-floor ballroom of the King's Inn.

Jack parked in the drive and got out.

"Here goes nothing." He knocked at the door. Glanced at Stein. Knocked again.

Footsteps, and then the door opened.

Job Ramsey stood in the opening. Or at least a man Jack thought might be Job. Tall, wiry, with the build of a former athlete, maybe, but a guy fighting to sprout into a man, with a scant array of whiskers, long blond hair, wearing a pair of sweatpants and a black hoodie that said *Hang on, let me overthink this.*

"What's goin' on?" he said.

Jack put a foot in the door. "Is your buddy Elton here too?"

Job took a step back, and Jack walked all the way into the house. Put up his hands. "I'm not looking for trouble. I just want to talk."

"Get out of my house!"

Stein had entered also and now put a finger to his mouth. "Calm down. We just want to talk."

Job had backed up and leaned against the counter.

"Nice house," Jack said. He put his hands in his pockets. He hadn't wanted to do this outside. Now that he was in, he kept his distance, his voice easy. "Mom and Dad home?"

Job's mouth tightened.

A two-story ledge-rock fireplace soared to the roof in the great room, surrounded by black leather furniture, white carpet. Job leaned against a massive onyx island surrounded by white cabinetry. A giant chandelier the size of a buffalo dripped from the ceiling.

Money.

"I just need to know why you threw a firebomb into my school bus."

Job's eyes widened. "What?"

"Yeah, we got you on camera," Stein said. "Torching the bus."

"That was an accident. We were supposed to get the Taurus, but Elton missed—"

A word sounded from behind Jack, an opinion about Job's accusation, and Jack spun just in time to turn his shoulder into a blow that might have broken his spine.

So Elton still knew how to handle a hockey stick.

Jack staggered to one side but rounded and caught the next blow mid strike.

He'd had a few turns at goalie over the years.

He jerked the stick forward, wrenched it from Elton's hand, and Elton shouted, falling.

Jack didn't hit him. He was a kid—a gnarly, angry kid, but still—so Jack pushed him down to the wood floor, landed next to him, grabbed his hand, and twisted it into a submission hold.

Elton howled.

"Calm down. You're not hurt—yet."

Scuffling. Jack looked over to find Job fleeing through the side door.

Steinbeck took off behind him.

That would be a race he'd like to watch. Instead, Jack looked down at Elton. "Let's do this again. You torched my schoolie today. Why?"

"It was an accident!"

Elton was struggling, so Jack pressed his knee against his lower back. "Calm down and I'll let you go."

Elton had an opinion on that that Jack suspected his mother might not like.

"Fine—it was an accident. What do you mean?"

"We were hired to fire the other car. We missed."

"You missed—"

"Yeah, okay. We threw a rock—it bounced off the car and hit your window. It broke. We blew up the other car—but then Job said that we needed to cover up our fingerprints, so he threw in the firecracker. It was a junker, dude. Seriously—we thought it was abandoned."

No comment. "Who hired you?"

"This guy—I don't know his name. We met him at Echoes."

"When?"

"Thursday morning. He gave us each five hundred bucks to torch the car. That's all I know."

"Thursday." Jack sighed, rolled off him, let him go.

Elton scrambled away rubbing his arm. "What's your problem?"

"My problem is that I'm homeless, thanks to you."

And right then, the front door banged open. "Down, get down!"

Jack turned, his hands up, and Jenna came in, followed by a cadre of local deputies. She held a gun. "Jack. What are you doing here?"

"I'm having a chat with—"

"He assaulted me!" Elton pointed at him. "He hurt my arm!"

Jenna lowered her gun. Sighed. Then looked at Elton. "Yeah, well, you're both under arrest."

"What?" Jack practically shouted.

"Elton Bridges, you're under arrest for arson. And you"—she turned to Jack—"are under arrest for obstruction of justice."

"I haven't obstructed anything." He turned as Jenna pushed him to the island. "We were just chatting."

"How about trespassing?" she said.

"I didn't—"

"We received a panic-button alert," said someone behind him. He glanced over—Eagle River security.

"Obstruction, trespassing, and given the complaint of the suspect, assault."

"He hit me with a hockey stick!"

She grabbed one wrist, then the other, cuffed him. "Tell it to your lawyer."

Aw.

"You don't have to be a child to get in over your head."

For a long second there, Harper had thought—*yep, in over my head*. "You're lucky I didn't use my ninja moves on you."

Next to her, in the passenger seat, Tommy laughed. A low rumble that even now sounded a little menacing, but she kept trying to see past the burliness and tattoos to the teddy bear inside.

The guy who'd started to tear up with worry in his expression when he'd told her that she couldn't leave—not when she might be the only connection to Penelope and, most of all, to answers to Sarah's murder.

"Sorry to scare you. You're just the only one who knows how to find Penelope. Her listeners—which include me—know something is wrong."

And that had had her sticking around because—how did he know that Penelope was missing?

He'd unhanded her nearly immediately, hands up, as if realizing his own actions. And then he'd made her coffee and spent the last hour scrolling through the fan comments on the *Penny for Your Thoughts* forum.

"She usually posts every day, and especially on Fridays, before her podcast drops, but we haven't heard a thing on her forum since Tuesday. And there is *a lot* of speculation. Some think it's a publicity stunt. Others are sure she got grabbed."

"She has a lot of fans." Harper had been on the forum before with Jack and now searched for any posts that might look threatening.

Which of course allowed Jack to walk into her head. *"I don't like letting people down."*

She'd shaken him away and asked Tommy again about Turbo. He'd pulled up the nightclub's website on his laptop and checked the hours.

"I need to be back at the rehearsal long before this opens," she'd said to his suggestion that they go there and ask about the security team.

"Turbo is owned by Holden Walsh's management company. What if we talk to him, ask him if anyone on his staff matches the description of the intruder?"

She'd given him a look that made him raise his hands in defense.

"I'm not suggesting we accuse him of anything. Maybe we're

searching for a guy that Sarah saw at Turbo. Walsh was her ex—certainly he wants her murder solved."

"Unless he did it," she said. "We could be setting ourselves up for trouble."

"Then," Tommy said, "he gets nervous and sloppy and next thing we know, he leads us to our masked man."

"Zorro."

He'd smiled at that. At least *someone* thought she was being cute. *You're brilliant.*

Nope. Not brilliant. A dreamer.

And maybe foolish as she drove with Tommy, an hour later, through the tangle of traffic leading to the S & W Development office in St. Paul. She still had over an hour before her dance lesson with Jack.

But finding Penelope took priority. Jack probably wouldn't want to dance with her anyway.

"You know, I would never hurt Sarah." She glanced at Tommy now as he looked out the window, away from her. "She didn't see the guy I'd been. Just the guy I wanted to be. We were friends, and yes, I hated that she was with Walsh, but . . . she'd never go for a guy like me anyway."

Traffic had slowed to a standstill on 94, but they'd nearly reached the Wall Street exit.

"What do you mean?"

"She was educated. Beautiful. And I'm an ex-con who works in a bar." He lifted a shoulder.

"I think that there are no rules in love." She turned onto the exit.

"What are you talking about? There are all sorts of rules—especially the ones a guy makes in his head. And they don't come down without a fight. Take a right on Kellogg."

"Maybe nothing we believe about ourselves comes down without a fight, even if it's a lie." She turned right, and he pointed to a three-story building. A sign to the parking ramp led under the building.

No ticket at entry meant a public lot, so she descended and found a space in the darkness of the lower level. She unhooked her belt, turned to him. "But some wars are worth the fight."

Her own words tunneled back through her as they took the elevator to the lobby. Again, Jack's words. *"I very much, clearly know that you're not . . . a high-schooler."*

He was built to protect, so maybe she could take a breath, give him some grace.

Maybe.

They walked out into the sleek vintage lobby of what looked like a former bank or post office. Polished oak flooring, open ceilings with painted black industrial piping, and the logo for S & W Development on a wall leading back to some offices. A few potted plants, pictures of local developments along the walls of the waiting area, some blueprints, some aerial shots. She perused them as Tommy walked to a long mahogany counter topped with white marble. A receptionist sat behind it, and he asked if Holden Walsh was in.

But Harper's gaze had caught on a development called Loon Lake Estates. A blueprint of lots with a gated entrance connected to a yacht club and a fenced-in boatyard seated on the south shore of Loon Lake.

Just a few miles up the road from Duck Lake.

A couple of model homes surrounded the blueprint, expensive, lavish.

Other property projects also hung on the wall—Turbo night club among them, along with a few multifamily properties and apartment complexes, another office building, as well as retail spaces.

"I got his card," Tommy said, coming up to her. "He's not in. Neither is his partner, Derek Swindle." He handed her the card.

"Of course not." She sighed, looked at her watch. "I have to get back to Duck Lake. I need to be at a dance and wedding rehearsal in less than an hour."

"Sorry. I thought this would be something." He pushed the elevator call button.

"He does tenant services as well as property development," she said, looking at the card.

"Sarah was one of his real estate agents."

The door opened, and they got in, rode down.

"Why the laptop, I wonder?" Their feet echoed in the dim parking garage. A couple of lights were out, something she hadn't noticed before, and for the first time, maybe, she didn't hate that Tommy looked like a guy you wouldn't want to meet in a dark alley. Or parking garage.

"She reported it missing, but she said that she had everything backed up to the cloud, so . . . "

Harper unlocked the car. She slid into the driver's seat as Tommy belted himself in.

Movement behind her caused her to jerk, scream as a man sat up. He wore dark glasses and a stocking hat, and he shoved a gun against the side of Tommy's head.

"Everybody stay calm."

Tommy put his hands up. Glanced at Harper, his mouth pinched.

"Take the car," she said and reached for the handle—

"Who are *you*?"

She jerked and glanced at the man. "Who did you expect?"

"Stay put. We're going for a drive."

Tommy rounded in his seat, lunging for the gun.

"No!" Harper shouted.

A shot. It exploded through the car, and Harper put her hands over her ears, screaming.

"Shut up!" the man said, but Tommy was shouting too—more of a keening as he doubled over.

"Tommy?" She turned to him, and Tommy leaned back, his hands to his stomach, breathing hard.

"You shot him?" She turned to the man. "You shot him!"

He'd shot Tommy through the seat and now sat back and leveled the gun at her. A big man dressed in a black turtleneck, suit pants, a wool coat, gloves. "Drive."

"To the *hospital*."

"Nope. Just drive." His voice emerged low, unshaken.

Her hands shook so much that she barely gripped the wheel as she pulled out, grinding the gears as she fumbled with the stick shift.

"Calm down. You follow my instructions and no one dies."

"Tommy's going to die!" She glanced at the man in the rearview mirror as she stopped at the exit.

He lifted his shoulder. "But you might live."

Her eyes burned as she pulled out into traffic, her heart choking her. Next to her, Tommy groaned, his hands bloody. They stopped at the light, and she unbuckled and pulled off her puffer jacket. Shoved it at him. "Use this."

He had closed his eyes, and now took the jacket, slumping back.

It wouldn't absorb anything, but it might add pressure to the wound. *Please, God—if you're watching—*

"Drive!" The light had turned green, and she took a left on Mounds Boulevard.

"Get on 94 going west."

So, back toward Duck Lake.

The man sat in the middle, the gun on her as she pulled out onto the highway and merged into traffic.

Think. Her phone was in her parka, so that hadn't been a bright move. If she could pull up beside a cop—

"Just drive, Harper," Tommy said quietly, barely breathing.

Her vision glazed as she nodded, tried to keep them between the yellow lines.

Talk about over her head. And Clarice, of course, wormed her way in. *"One of these days you're going to go too far, dig too far, and I'm not going to be able to rescue you."*

Tommy had gone quiet beside her, his eyes closed. She put her hand on his chest. Still breathing, but barely. "Please let me drop him off at a hospital."

"Take the Highway 7 exit."

She got off, her gut tight. The sun had settled low in the west, a simmer of fire along the horizon, red bleeding out through the birch and evergreen trees, then over the whitened landscape. She passed Excelsior, then Victoria, and finally headed toward Carver.

"Where are we going?" Her voice had lost its gusto.

"You should have left it alone."

"Left what alone?"

He drew in a breath. "The podcast case."

She couldn't stop herself. "Did you kidnap Penelope?"

He made a noise she couldn't decipher, so—

"Did you kill Penelope?"

He met her eyes in the rearview mirror, dark and fierce in the fading light. "No."

She wanted to believe him.

Farmland, vast fields of white, peeled out around them, the light fading fast. A few miles out of Duck Lake, he directed her north on a county road toward Loon Lake, and her brain went to the blueprint she'd seen in S & W Development.

She glanced again in the mirror. Could he be Holden Walsh himself?

They cut south, around Loon Lake Drive, and she passed a boat-yard full of motorboats, and yachts on stands, many covered in canvas.. Small fishing boats were stacked three high, all dark outlines against the gray sky, the rising moonlight. A fence cordoned out would-be vandals.

Farther, a snowy construction street veered off the main road, and of course—she just knew it—they drove past a sign for Loon Lake Estates.

A few skeletal homes, draped in winter, stood half-completed along the shoreline. A lonely excavator rose, cold and abandoned, against the night.

He directed them toward one of the houses, the basement dug but not poured, and suddenly old mafia stories thudded into her mind.

"Stop here."

In the drive, by the open grave.

"Get out."

He slid toward her side, got out, holding the gun on her. The light of the open door illuminated Tommy, gray and maybe not breathing.

Oh. She fought her rising scream.

"Get him out of the car." He motioned with his gun.

"So, we're upgrading from when you shot Ty, huh? No more just leaving a dead guy in the car—he might live."

She glanced over. Not a flicker of a response, but then again, darkness hid his face. Opening the door, she crouched next to Tommy. He still clutched the parka to himself, but as she drew it away—*find the phone!*—his hand fell.

"Pull him out!"

She stood up, gripping his jacket. "He's too heavy."

The man cursed, then walked over, and before she could brace herself—*totally didn't see that coming*—he pushed her. Hard. She flew away from the car, landed with a splash of pain on the frozen, rumpled ground.

He reached in and grabbed Tommy. Yanked him out.

Tommy fell like a sack of sand onto the snow.

Harper rolled, found her feet, and took off.

Run! A shot destroyed snow just ahead of her, so she aimed for the excavator, took cover behind it.

She wished she'd scooped up her parka. But she wore a blue sweater and black pants, and maybe they would hide her.

Another shot. It pinged against the metal, so she scrambled to the far side. Tripped. Her hand caught the grimy, frozen wheel before she went down.

"You can't get away. There is nothing out here. You'll freeze to death—"

Her wrist caught on the tread of the wheel, and she wrenched it free, then crouched and took off toward the shell of a nearby house.

Another shot—wide—and she dove over a snowbank, then into the garage of a house, feeling along the edge before she came out the back and took off again.

Her feet crunched, her breaths puffing out in the cold, but she kept low and kept running.

Along the block foundation of a third house, and then up the shoreline, she spotted the clutter of the boatyard.

She kept to the debris of the worksite, hiding behind dumpsters and half-built stacked-block walls, and then finally broke out into a run toward the fence.

Scale the fence. Hide in the boatyard—

A shot, this time just ahead of her, and she yelped and dove onto the ground.

Her black attire against white snow—in the moonlight, he'd see her.

So, not over the fence.

She spotted a long building, probably the administrative offices. Shadows on the far side might hide her—

Scampering into the shadows, she leaped up the fence. A drainpipe helped her climb. She spidered up, threw a leg over—her sweater caught, ripped, but she clambered over the other side, slid along the building all the way to the front.

Maybe if she got inside she could call—

"You can't hide from me!"

She pressed herself against the building, his voice way too close—maybe on the other side of the fence—

Why hadn't she listened to Jack and stayed put?

Pushing herself away from the building, she sprinted toward the racks of boats, then dove between them, ducking, then sliding under their elevated keels, working her way deeper into the yard. She emerged between a couple of boats, one of them a motor yacht rising high on a lift above her. A swim platform jutted from the back.

Hide.

Here went nothing. She loosened the bottom strap, then pulled herself up onto the swim platform. Ducking under the canvas, she crawled into the back of the yacht, along the deck, and then— *there.* The cabin.

She opened the door and climbed down the stairs. Then she slid onto a bench, her back to the wall, pulled her knees up against herself, held her breath, and hoped very, very hard that Jack would miraculously come and find her.

TWELVE

A BOUT TIME."

Jack rose from where he sat in the lobby of the Duck Lake sheriff's department, having been released thanks to Elton's admission of swinging at him.

Or maybe thanks to that moment in the back seat of the cruiser, before Jenna and her partner got in, when Jack had suggested that he might be willing to drop his charges if Elton dropped his accusation of assault.

Done. Now he'd have to deal with the B & E, but with no evidence of forced entry, and the fact that Job *had* opened the door for him—

In the last hours of the day, Nat had gotten the local judge to release him on the basis of Boo's wedding tomorrow, Jack's longtime ties to the community, and the fact that the minor offense of trespassing would probably be dismissed.

It helped that Jack had played hockey with Judge Darlene Strickland's son.

But the release had left him waiting in the lobby for rescue.

Last thing he wanted was to call Boo or Austen or even his father. Which left one of his brothers.

And as he waited for Conrad to show up, he practically memorized the bulletin board. Same notices as yesterday—a 1998 Ford Bronco, Daisy the lost goldendoodle, whose poster had been updated with a one-hundred-dollar reward, and the set of keys with the boat float. He'd gotten a close look at it—loon-shaped foam with a number imprinted on the back. And, more interesting, in the description of the theft from Echoes on Tuesday night was a note to call Tallulah.

Now, Conrad walked over to him, his rescuer. "I had to sneak away, otherwise I would have raised questions. This is a little different for you." He gestured to the manila envelope with Jack's possessions.

"Not as different as you might think." Jack walked through the open door that Conrad held for him.

"Really?"

"In this case, the arrest might have been providential." He noted Conrad's sleek Dodge Charger in the lot. Along with his brother's dress clothes. "Aw, I'm late."

"Very. Everyone's at dance practice. Except, of course, Penelope and Harper."

He stopped. "Harper? Where is she?"

"Dunno." Conrad's car beeped as it unlocked. "I dropped her off at the inn and went to help decorate for the reception, and when I came downstairs, she'd left."

Jack stared at him, nonplussed. "I thought the point of dragging her home was to keep an eye on her."

"I'm not her keeper, bro. She's a grown woman. Something you might want to get through your head."

Yeah, thanks, Jack had already noticed that. But he shut his mouth as he climbed into the passenger seat.

"Boo said that Harper promised to be at the rehearsal, so keep your hat on, bro," Conrad said.

"Fine." But something else gnawed inside him. "Let's stop by Echoes on the way."

They pulled out, night already settling over town. "Is Stein at the dance place?"

"Of course."

Interesting.

"What happened?"

"I found the guys who torched Aggie. Had a little chat."

Conrad glanced over at him, eyebrow up, a half grin.

"What's with that face?"

"Just nice to see you."

Whatever that meant.

Conrad pulled into Echoes.

"I'll be right back." Jack got out, went inside. No Tallulah at the counter. Purple pigtails—Quinn—stood at the counter.

"You're back."

"Tallulah gone?"

"Yeah. Morning shift."

The place seemed deserted, and he noted the late hour. "You're nearly closed."

"Can I get you something?"

"Tallulah posted a BOLO for keys that went missing."

"Yeah. Right off the counter at the end of her shift. She had to get a ride home."

"Does she own a boat?"

Quinn frowned.

"I saw the boat float on the chain."

"Oh, right. Yeah. Not a boat—a fish house. It's her dad's. He keeps it up at Lilly Lake, in the boatyard. At least in the summer. It's probably on the ice now." She lifted a shoulder. "Why? Did you find them?"

"No." He rapped his knuckles on the counter. "Thanks, Quinn." A smile.

She smiled back.

"So?" Conrad said when he got back in the car.

"Dunno. Just a gut feeling." He stared out the window as Conrad pulled out, toward the Moonlight Supperclub.

"Like when you know a fast break is coming and you can't stop it?"

Jack laughed. "Something like that."

"Does it have anything to do with Penelope?"

"I don't know. Maybe." He looked at Conrad. "Okay, here goes. Penelope is getting ready to name her suspect in the Sarah Livingston cold case. I think she got a call from Kyle Brunley—"

"The dead guy at the Duck Lake Motor Lodge."

"Yep. Sarah's platonic friend who might not have been platonic." Jack's brain landed on Harper for a moment, then he shook it away. "I think Kyle knew something about the crime. Maybe even something about Tommy or Zorro—"

"Zorro?"

"The masked man who was seen leaving Sarah's apartment the night of the murder."

"Zorro. Got it."

Jack missed Harper. Really, he should be talking this out with *her*.

"So, Penelope meets Kyle at Echoes on Tuesday,, then heads out to the Inn and gets settled in before everyone else arrives," Jack said. He pulled his phone from the manila envelope. No missed calls from Harper. "Meanwhile, Kyle drives out to the Motor Lodge."

"Where he's murdered."

"Right. Maybe before Penelope is picked up. My thought is whoever murdered him called Ty for a ride. But why? Why not drive his own car?"

Conrad's eyes widened, and yes, an answer clicked in. "Maybe the torched Taurus—"

"Belonged to the killer." Jack pointed at him. "All rentals have GPS built into them. Which could put our murderer at the scene of the crime. Instead, he parks at the market, takes an Uber to the Motor Lodge, kills Kyle, gets back in, and rides to the supper club."

"And waits?" Conrad said.

"He gets lucky. Penelope calls Ty again. Or maybe not lucky—smart—because Penelope was in Echoes the same time Job and Elton were, the same time the man with the suit was."

"The man with the *suit*?"

"Just stay with me," Jack said. "He watched Penelope and Kyle, watched her get picked up by Ty. He might have grabbed the man's card. And who knows what they talked about in the Uber ride out to the Motor Lodge? Maybe Ty had already gotten the call to pick up Penelope . . ."

"And he saw opportunity. But what is the motive?"

Jack sighed. "The podcast." *Wait.* "What if this wasn't about Zorro but Tommy? What if Kyle had something on *him*?"

"Tommy?"

"The ex-con neighbor. With an assault record."

"An *assault* record?" Conrad turned into to the supper club. Jack spotted Harper's Chevy Sonic in the drive.

Please.

Except . . . wait . . . Something nudged at him, but he couldn't . . .

"Yeah," he said, turning back to Conrad. "Maybe Tommy took Kyle out and then Penelope because he was trying to silence them."

Conrad pulled up to the Sonic. "Yeah. Except what about Ty?"

Ty.

"Why shoot Ty?"

Jack shook his head. Got out. Looked at the Sonic, and it hit him. "She's got my car."

SUSAN MAY WARREN

Conrad had hiked up the collar of his wool coat. "Yeah. She swiped your keys from the house."

No Geo Tracker in the lot. His mouth pinched as he followed Conrad inside. "(I've Had) The Time of My Life" floated out from the dance hall, and he walked in and spotted the wedding party nailing the steps behind Oaken.

Across from her groom, Boo was grinning, wearing a dress. *Wow,* he hadn't seen that coming, but then again, maybe he didn't know her as well as he thought.

Maybe he didn't know any of them, really.

His fault, and he meant to change that.

He walked up and Boo spotted him, then ran over to him. Julian called after her.

"Jack! I'm so glad you're here. Did you find her?"

"Penelope?"

She frowned. "No. Harper. She was supposed to be here a half hour ago. And you're late too. I'm worried."

He put his hands on her shoulders, leaned down. "Okay. I'll find her. Any idea where she might be?"

"There was a guy she wanted to interview. She thought he might be able to help her find Penelope." Behind her, the music had stopped, and Oaken and Stein walked over.

Jack glanced at Stein, who just gave him a nod. Whatever that meant.

"Who did she go talk to?" And his stomach was already clenching when she said, "A guy named Tommy."

He closed his eyes. Then he stood up, turned away, and put a hand to his mouth.

Stein followed him. "You okay?"

Probably not. "I don't know."

Julian was clapping his hands, trying to round them in, and Jack really wanted to put a hand around the man's throat. Instead, he turned back to Boo, found his voice, the one that he should have had days ago. "I will find her. And Penelope. I promise. You just nail that dance for tomorrow's reception." Then he winked.

Boo stared at him as if she really needed his words, so he smiled. An easy *I got this* smile.

She took a breath. "Okay."

He gestured with his head to Stein and Conrad, who walked away with him. He pulled out his phone and tapped open an app.

"What's that?"

"I've got a GPS tracker on my Geo." A map opened, and he widened it, zoomed in. Stilled.

"Yeah?"

"The car's parked at Loon Lake. Near the boatyard."

"That's ten minutes away from here."

"Fifteen," Steinbeck said.

"Not if I drive." Conrad pulled out his keys. "Let's go."

"Wait—wait. Where do you guys think you're going?" Austen had walked up with Doyle.

Oh. Conrad looked at Steinbeck, who looked at Jack.

"What about the dance?" Doyle said, clearly reading them.

Jack faced Austen. "We need to take care of something."

"But the rehearsal is next. At the church."

"I think we can figure out how to walk down an aisle. Just point and push."

Her mouth made a tiny bud of annoyance. He'd lit something inside her. He met her gaze, no blinking. "Sis, I need you and Big D to stay here and keep Boo calm." He glanced at Doyle.

Austen's voice thinned. "Why?"

"Just . . . trust us." He glanced at his brothers, back at her. "Trust me."

She considered him for a moment, then smiled. "I never stopped." Then she turned and hooked Doyle's arm. "Let's keep this show moving."

Jack didn't know why her words settled inside him, a boulder to ground him.

"Don't drive like a grandma," he said to Conrad.

"Do you even know me?" Conrad got into the driver's seat.

Stein squeezed himself in back, and Jack kept his phone out as he strapped into the passenger front. "The Geo's not moving. Let's roll." He looked over at the speedometer twice as Conrad pushed the Charger up the highway toward Loon Lake.

"How'd you get out of the clink so fast?" Steinbeck said.

Jack turned to Stein. "Where were you?"

"Just had a little chat with Job." He wore a slight red mark on his chin. "They were paid to torch the car next to yours."

"I got the same story."

"He's got a theory. It's long," Conrad said.

"My guess is that it involves Tommy Fadden?"

"He's a suspect in the Sarah Livingston case. And Harper went to talk to him." Jack said.

Stein looked over at the speedometer, nodded, then leaned back. "Why is she there?"

"I don't know." Jack turned. "A set of keys with a key from the Loon Lake boatyard was stolen from Echoes on Tuesday."

"The day Penelope went missing," Conrad said. "So, what does that have to do with your theory?"

"Maybe Tommy—the guy in the suit, who killed Kyle and kidnapped Penny—brought Penny to the boatyard to kill her. Except, why didn't he just kill her when he shot Ty?"

"Maybe he didn't want her found?"

"Why the stolen key?"

Silence. They wove into the countryside with the moonlight glinting on rumpled pewter fields of snow. Here and there, lights shone from farmhouses, all the way until the land turned forested.

"Turn here," Jack said.

"I know the road to Loon Lake," Conrad said. "Some developer is building houses out here. He had a reception for the team about a year ago to try to sell lots. A few of the guys bought."

"Not you?"

Conrad lifted a shoulder, no comment. *Interesting.*

"They're up here if I remember the presentation correctly."

Jack sat up as they drove past the Loon Lake Boat Works. But according to his app, the Geo sat farther up the road.

Just beyond the boatyard sat an unfinished housing development—half-framed houses, piles of dirt, a mutilated shoreline for future million-dollar lake homes.

Conrad's lights scraped across the little green Geo.

Jack pointed.

"I see it," Conrad said and pulled up.

Their headlights illuminated a body lying in the snow, and even though Jack's brain screamed *too big, not her*, he scrambled out, running toward the body.

Blood saturated the ground. He knelt next to the man—a big man, clutching a bloody white puffer jacket.

He rolled the man over, leaned in. "He's still breathing. Call 911!" He grabbed the jacket and recognized it immediately.

Harper.

He stood. "Harper!"

"He's been shot," Steinbeck said, coming up on the other side. He'd moved the man's jacket aside. "Kidney shot. He's lost a lot of blood." He put a finger to the man's carotid. "Still pumping, but barely. The nearest life flight is Waconia—they're at least thirty minutes out."

Conrad had stepped in front of the headlights, a phone to his ear.

"Call Boo. See if her SAR team can get here."

Stein had also stood up. "Boo's a field medic. Get *her* here." He turned to examine the car. "The gunman shot through the seat."

He turned to Jack. "Which means whoever shot them rode here with them."

Jack froze.

"You don't happen to carry a gun?"

"Trunk. Lockbox."

Stein had retrieved the keys, but Jack had already started to study the ground. He opened his glove box, grabbed a Maglite and twisted it on.

Bloody shoeprints in the snow, about Harper's size. Running, given the lengths of the stride. Right toward—*there.* An excavator. He tromped over the frozen ground, found a trampled area, and his light pinged off something.

Gold, in the snow. He picked it up, and while he knew in his head that she was out there, seeing her bracelet put a fist through his heart.

Harper. But he didn't yell, because what if she yelled back and got shot for her efforts?

More shoeprints leading away, and this time trampled by bigger shoeprints. He tracked hers to the boatyard fence, the end of the building. Shone his light on it.

A piece of black yarn flapped, caught by the wind. Until now he hadn't even noticed the breath off the lake, brutal against his skin. But with the temperature falling . . .

What was one more B & E for the day? Again, he wanted to shout her name but held it in as he landed on the other side of the fence.

Bigger steps here too, and his gut clenched.

He stared out at the yard, the rows and rows of stored boats, most with canvas covers tied down tight. A marine rack held smaller speedboats, three stories high. He shone his light across it, then down the rows.

Her shoeprints led away, toward the racks, but vanished in the harder pack of the yard. *Harper, where are you?*

The boats loomed over him, the wind—or his heartbeat—in his ears and . . .

Please, God. Don't let me screw this up. He shouldn't have shoved her away, shouldn't have made her feel small, incapable—

Shouldn't have let his fears push her away.

Now. Or maybe even back then . . .

"God has a plan for your life, and even you can't screw it up."

He shot a glance at the moon, his throat tight. *I might be in over my head here.*

The wind answered, gusting off the lake, lifting snow and ice and scattering across the yard, into his open coat.

And then he saw it. Down at the end, the cover flapped on a large motor yacht. Someone had untied it.

Maybe sneaked inside.

He took off, jogging on the ice.

Oh, she was smart. He ducked under the edge of the canvas, found a swim platform, and then climbed up the back edge of the boat.

The yacht shuddered when he landed on the deck. No Harper. His light scraped across the boat's cabin door. He knelt and tugged at it.

It opened. He stepped back, about to peer inside.

A canister slammed through the gap, nearly connecting with his forehead. He jerked back and slapped it away. It rolled out across the deck.

His light clattered to the ground, and he turned back just in time to see Harper barreling out of the cabin, wielding what looked like a can of peas.

She pounced on him, her weapon held back, ready to strike. He caught her wrist on its downward swing.

"It's me! Jack!"

She stilled, breathing hard, her eyes wide, and lowered the can.

She sat back, looked at him for a long second . . . then her face crumbled.

Aw.

He sat up, scrambled over to her, and pulled her against him. "It's okay. You're safe. You're safe."

She let him hold her, her body trembling. Hiccupping. "You're here." Her voice broke. "You're here."

"I'm here."

He leaned back, caught her face in his hands. Met her eyes.

And then he kissed her. A full-throttle, wow-you-had-me-scared kind of kiss that also included a hint of why-did-you—and then he stopped thinking and just *kissed* her.

He drank her in with all the desperation of a man who didn't want to let her go. Not again. Not ever.

She kissed him back, just trying to keep up, it seemed, but he couldn't get enough, pulling her closer. She tasted of her tears, and that slowed him down a little, and when she leaned away, he was breathing hard.

"I'm okay," she said. "I'm okay."

So now it was apparently her turn to rescue him.

He swallowed. Let her go. A fire extinguisher lay in the glow of his discarded torch. "That could have really hurt."

"That was the point."

He wanted to smile, but . . . "What happened?"

Her eyes widened. "Tommy!"

Tommy? "He's been shot."

"I know—" She scrambled up.

He caught her arm. "Let me go first."

He put her behind him as he crawled out of the boat cover. Steinbeck ran down between the boats, holding a light. "What are you doing?"

"Just a little boat tour." This from Harper.

Stein was breathing hard and put his hands on his knees. "I see how it is. Leave me to find the bad guys while you guys neck in the back of a boat."

"We weren't—" Jack started.

"'Bout time," Stein said. "You okay, Harp?"

"Yes," she said as Jack helped her down.

Stein stood up. "No sign of the shooter."

"Maybe. But it's dark. Let's get out of here."

Sirens sounded in the distance. Jack took Harper's hand. "Let's go."

They reached the gate as a cruiser turned into the housing development, the lights sweeping across the entrance. Another cruiser pulled up just outside the gate.

Jack's grip tightened as Sheriff Davidson got out of the car. He looked at Jack, then Stein and Harper. "Aren't you guys supposed to be at a party?"

But Jack looked at Harper. "I think I know where Penelope is."

———•—————————•———

If she were dreaming up what-if scenarios, she might conjure exactly this one.

Harper stood, a blanket over her shoulders—her jacket thick with Tommy's blood—as a chopper from the nearby Waconia hospital lifted off from the road. It stirred up all the debris, snow, and dirt from the worksite, and she turned away, leaning into Jack.

Who stood behind her. Who'd found her, rescued her.

Who'd kissed her like he never wanted to let her go.

She didn't know what to do with that. Instead, she focused on his words about Penelope, and his story, the one he'd unwound for her as she'd watched Boo and Doyle and Boo's SAR friend Shep try to stabilize Tommy, whose chest had filled with blood, his breathing down to wisps. They'd arrived still in their wedding-rehearsal attire, armed with a first-responder kit that Doyle kept in his car, of course. It wasn't much, but it had a long bore needle and a catheter, and Harper couldn't tear her gaze off Boo doing the initial work of saving Tommy's life.

The EMS team on the life-flight chopper had done the rest, inserting IVs, packing his wound, strapping him onto a stretcher for transport.

She'd listened to Jack's story, and now, as the chopper arched away, she turned to him. "You think Zorro stole the keys from Echoes and was intending to break into the boatyard and leave Penelope there?"

She noticed he hadn't said *body*, or *corpse*, but she got it. No way Penny could survive out here in the January cold for three days, three nights, without shelter. She tried not to let her throat close.

He didn't seem to be in a hurry. "My guess is that he shot Ty, and then, so the crime would seem random, he walked across the street, with or without Penelope, picked up Kyle's car, put her in it, and transported her here. Used the keys to enter the boatyard, and . . ." He looked over into the darkened yard.

Sheriff Davidson and Jenna stood in the circle of Jack's listeners, along with Oaken and Boo, Austen and Doyle, Stein and Conrad, even Boo's SAR team, who'd arrive during the search.

There went the dance rehearsal.

"So you think she's in the yard somewhere?" Sheriff Davidson asked, his mouth pinched. He'd read between Jack's words too.

"Dunno. Maybe. But . . ." Jack looked at Harper. "Are you sure you want to be here?" He looked at Boo too. "And you?"

"I want to find my friend," Harper said, and Boo nodded.

"Okay, let's spread out," Sheriff Davidson said. "Jenna, let's grab a couple Maglites from the cruisers."

She crunched away through the snow.

Jack turned to Harper, pulled her blanket close. "You sure you don't want to wait in the car?"

She nodded, her throat tight.

Jenna came back with flashlights and handed them around.

It seemed like some kind of horror movie, all the lights flicking on, illuminating tragedy in the darkness.

Sheriff Davidson had called the owner of the boatyard before, when he'd been debating arresting them. Jack had done some fast talking to wriggle his way out, and the sheriff now reopened the gate.

The searchers fanned out into the yard.

Jack took Harper's hand, and she walked, the blanket still over her shoulders. He led her down a row of storage units, slowing at each one to examine it.

"Do you have an insider trading tip?"

He glanced at her. One side of his mouth tweaked up. "There was a number on the boat key. I thought maybe . . ."

"He stashed her body in a storage locker?"

His smile vanished. He gave a nod.

"That's dark."

"Mm-hmm." He kept walking, kept looking. "I keep thinking— how did he know about this place? I mean . . ."

"I know. The boatyard is next to a Holden Walsh development."

He stopped. "It had to be someone who knew about the development."

"Yeah. That's how Tommy and I got taken. We were at Walsh's office in downtown St. Paul."

"Why?" He'd turned to her.

"It's a long story. Just . . . we have reason to think that Zorro was connected to Holden Walsh. Maybe even *was* Walsh."

Jack just stared at her, breathing. "He could have killed Sarah. And then you."

She had no words when he closed his eyes, then pressed his forehead to hers.

Oh.

Then he lifted his head and kissed her on the lips. Something short, as if almost reassuring himself that she was okay.

Huh.

He leaned away. "The boat float is in the shape of a Loon. And it has a number on the back. In this case . . ." He pointed to a number painted on the front of a yellow storage unit.

Except, no lock hung on the door.

"Are you allowed to open that?"

"I'm not a cop. If I find Penelope, I'm just a guy getting into my storage unit."

"No wonder you get sued."

He stepped up to the door, lifted the handle, and swung it open.

She held her breath.

"Empty." He flashed his light inside, just to be sure. The light skimmed across a couple cans, a shovel.

She let out the breath she'd been holding. "There is a master push code for the sliding gate, so the key can't be for that. My guess is that the key is for the lock on the door. But this one is open, which means someone left it open and took whatever had been in here."

He nodded. "An ATV."

"Yeah? I was thinking snowmobile."

He glanced at her. "Not bad, but this"—he walked into the unit and picked up a can—"is a corrosion inhibitor. It's added to gas to prevent corrosion of a metal surface. Used in high-humidity places for vehicles that are not meant to hang out in the snow."

"Like an ATV."

He pointed at her.

"So why would he steal an ATV . . ." Even as she said it, her heart fell. "To hide the body."

He walked out, shut the door.

She had turned, looking at the space across from the storage unit, and her eye caught on something shiny and yellow on the ground. "What if the key isn't just for the storage unit?" She pointed to the spot, and he shone his light on it.

A number, painted yellow on the ground, broken by snow and ice that partially concealed it.

"What are you thinking?" he said.

"A parking space for icehouses."

He took her hand, and they walked down the row, out to the lake. The moonlight shone on a village of houses, maybe two hundred yards out.

"We need the sheriff," he said. "And you need a better coat."

Thirty minutes later, she sat in the Geo, the heat blasting as Jack drove them through the darkness, behind Sheriff Davidson's car, searching for house number 132.

It felt like searching through a pile of laundry for a lone sock.

No, she was simply cold.

Worse, Boo refused to go to the church, joining with Oaken and the others on her team, searching the boatyard.

The sheriff stopped in front of a large orange icehouse that reminded her of a tow-behind camper trailer, parked in a neat row of other icehouses.

"Stay—" Jack turned to her. "Forget it."

She gave him a bleak smile and slid out. He'd found a canvas jacket for himself in his car, making her wear his parka, which hung on her, the arms dangling. She joined him in the bath of headlights as Sheriff Davidson knocked on the door.

No answer, and one of his deputies handed him a phone. He nodded, then handed it back and proceeded to attack the door with a door jack.

"S'pose that was a judge, issuing a warrant?" Harper asked.

"Or Tallulah, giving her permission," Jack said. "I find that people are pretty willing to help when they think someone is in trouble."

The door swung open, and Harper drew in her breath as the sheriff went inside.

He emerged, shaking his head. Came over to them. "Empty. And now the county owes Tallulah a new door."

Jack gave him a grim look.

"She's not here, Jack. And it's cold out." Davidson walked to his car.

Jack didn't move.

"Jack?"

He looked at Harper. "I just . . ." He shook his head. "I'm sorry, Harper. I thought I could find her."

She stepped close and put her floppy-coat arms around him. The night whisked up wind and snow around them.

Sheriff Davidson had already started back to the frozen shoreline, and as she and Jack got into the Geo and Jack turned around, she spotted the searchers headed for their cars.

Not like this.

"This isn't . . ." She looked at Jack. "Stop."

He obeyed, put the car into Park.

"Why would Walsh try to kill Tommy if Penelope was dead?"

"Maybe he thought Tommy could identify him?"

"No. Tommy already gave his statement to the police. However, he did leave out a break-in and stolen laptop a couple weeks earlier. Penelope knew about it. So maybe he thought she'd found something on the laptop. Maybe from her conversation with Kyle. Maybe something else, but Walsh was looking for it, or looking for *her*. That's why he tracked down Tommy. Because he knew Tommy was sweet on Sarah, would protect her." Her breath caught. "He asked me who I was."

"What?"

"In the car—I think he thought I was Penelope. At first—and then, yes. He didn't expect me to be there. He expected Penny."

"Which means she's still alive."

A beat as his words settled. "Maybe she got away that night, took off. And he thought she went to Tommy?"

Jack nodded. "Okay, let's what-if," he said. "I'll start. How did she survive?"

"What if she got away?" Harper said. "We know she was in the car with Ty, saw him get shot. What if she got out, ran away?"

"But that was at the Duck Lake dock."

"Maybe she'd gotten all the way to the Motor Lodge."

"Sure. Kyle was already going to kill her, leave her body there."

"So he what—hits her? Because he can't kill her in the Motor Lodge parking lot. Too many lights."

"He gets his car, runs her down."

"Yeah, but then, still, she doesn't get away. He can't think she's with Tommy."

Jack looked toward the dark boatyard. "What if she wounded him?"

Harper sat up. "Which could be why Kyle burned the car—his blood in the seats."

"Good. Then what?"

"She runs."

He gestured to the darkness, the forest. "Where?"

Right. Not a light to be seen. Except . . . "Wait. Ty. *He's* the link here."

"How?"

"She was in the car with Ty once before he picked her up. And I know Penelope—she's a talker. And his mother said he loved his fish house. Spent all his time there. What if that came up? Penny asked about it. It's possible she even knew about the Loon Lake housing project. Could be that Ty even complained about it."

"Now you're reaching."

"Maybe—but I also know Ty. Remember our high school project so many years ago? It was about the Eagle Lake development and how the pollutants from the houses killed all the fish. He was pretty angry."

"Okay, so she knows about the Loon Lake development and the boatyard."

"And what if"—she leaned in—"Ty had a Loon Lake boat key?"

He considered her, light in his eyes. "And what? She took it?"

"Maybe Kyle did catch her, maybe she did wound him, but he still grabbed her and took her to the housing project, to finish his plan."

"And she got Ty's keys, somehow . . . Didn't Mrs. Bowman say he stored his icehouse at the boatyard?"

"Marjorie."

"Right."

She rolled her eyes. But a heat of hope had stirred in her as Jack took out his phone.

The woman answered on the second ring, sounding tired. "Hello?"

"Mrs. Bowman—Marjorie—this is Jack Kingston." He put the call on speaker.

"Jack. Did you find him?"

Oh, the hope in her voice could make Harper wince.

"Working on it, ma'am. How's Ty?"

A sigh. "They found brain activity today." Her voice shook. "But he's still in a coma."

"I'm so sorry. We . . . we were wondering. Does Ty store his icehouse at the Loon Lake boatyard?"

"I think so."

"Do you . . . happen to know the number of his parking space?"

A pause. "I don't."

"It would have been on the back of his Loon Lake boat-float key chain."

Another pause. "I'm so sorry. I don't know. But I do know that he recently painted his house blue. Like Blue Ox blue. He's a fan."

Blue Ox blue.

"Thank you, Marjorie." Jack hung up.

Harper had already grabbed the flashlight, was getting out.

The lake was covered with icehouses, set at angles, with ice roads between them. Skid houses and wheeled houses.

"Wheeled or skid?"

"Probably the bigger ones. She said he spends a lot of time there. A few of these are like small cabins, with beds and televisions."

She walked down the row—a bright green house on wheels, a white-paneled skid shack, a couple of silver houses. All snow-covered and crusted with ice.

"There must be fifty houses here, and the team looked in nearly all of them."

"Yes, but only one is Blue Ox blue."

"Like that one?" He pointed to a small house seated behind a garish purple ice castle with a bay window and a porch.

The house behind it seemed forlorn and forgotten, a box on ice.

Except for the door, a set of black stairs that had been pulled in.

A boot print was pressed into the snow below it, but that could belong to anyone.

She headed toward it, but Jack caught her.

"Please let me go in first."

She read his face, nodded, and he stepped up to the door. Knocked.

No answer. Leaning up behind him, she shouted, "Penelope. It's Harper!"

More silence.

"I'm getting the tire iron," he said and headed for the car.

Harper took his place in front of the door and hoped, *please,* that someone was inside to listen. "Pen. I know you're scared. I don't know what happened, but I do know that you're safe. You're found. You can stop hiding. Come out—"

The door shook.

She stepped back.

Jack ran up, breathing hard, holding the tire iron.

The door opened just as he reached it.

Penelope took one look at him, held out a fire extinguisher, and sprayed.

He pulled Harper away, turning her, his back to the foam.

"Penelope! Stop! It's Jack!" Harper untangled herself from his arms. Turned.

Penelope stood on the steps, still dressed in her white shirt and white dress pants from Tuesday night, although now in men's boots, a hat, and a wool jacket. She wielded a half-empty can of fire retardant and stared wide-eyed at Harper.

She dropped the can, stepped down, and flung herself into Harper's arms. "Oh, you're okay. I was so worried—"

"*You* were worried!" Harper pushed her away. "You vanished. For *three* days."

Penelope's mascara had bled off long ago, black streaking down her face. "I know. I'm so sorry—that wasn't the plan. And I was so worried he'd find you looking for me and . . ."

"Who'd find her?" Jack said, foam on his jacket, around his ears. He was wiping it off, shaking his arm.

She met his gaze, her pale brown eyes wide, her dark hair down, and of course the woman could look beautiful even disheveled, wearing oversized SORELs and a grimy flannel jacket that smelled like fish. "I don't know."

"Well, that's a big help," he said. He took off his jacket and shook it out, the foam flying into the night. "What is it with you two and fire extinguishers?"

"Self-defense training, sophomore year, Mrs. Runyon's class," Penelope said and held up a fist.

Harper bumped it, unable to sort through the emotions in her chest. "Are you *okay*?"

"Starved. I've had nothing but canned sardines, saltines, and dried pork rinds for three days. I think I've lost ten pounds. At least I'll probably fit into my dress." She winked at Harper, gave a shaky smile.

What? "Penelope—what's going on?"

Penelope looked up at Jack. Back at Harper. "We should go." She closed the icehouse door.

"Do you need to stop at the trauma center, maybe get checked out?" Harper said.

"I'm fine. Just smelly." She wrinkled her nose.

Jack had picked up his tire iron and now walked to his Geo. "Get in the car. I'm freezing."

"Bossy," said Penelope to Harper and slid into the back seat. "But I like it."

His angry expression met Harper's gaze over the top of the car. She shrugged. "I have no idea what's going on."

"I do not understand women," he said. "This suddenly feels like a publicity stunt."

"That got a man killed? And two more seriously injured?"

His mouth tightened and he shook his head.

But then she got in, and got it. Penelope had pulled the blanket to herself. She met Harper's gaze in the mirror, a haunted look in her eyes. Harper had seen this version of Penelope. The one who laughed off trauma, not sure how to handle it.

Okay. Harper knew how to get people to talk. *Slow down. Listen.* She cranked up the heat as Jack pulled out, then turned to Penelope.

"You've been missing for three days, Pen. And yet you seem to not be completely freaking out—what's going on?"

Penelope tucked the blanket under her chin, her voice now soft, almost contrite. "I know. I'm sorry. It was a desperate move, coming out here. I didn't know what else to do when..." She swallowed, her voice falling. "I should never have gotten into that car."

"Ty's car."

She nodded.

"Why *did* you?"

"Because the man—I still don't know his name—said that Kyle had sent him. He called himself Felix. Last name Johnson."

"That's the version of Smith here in Minnesota," Jack said.

"And then, of course, he pulled a gun."

Jack's mouth made a grim line. He arrived at the shore and took the boat ramp out, driving along the fence of the boatyard out to the road.

Penelope's gaze found Harper's. "Kyle is dead, isn't he?"

Harper nodded.

Penelope closed her eyes. "I told him he wasn't safe. That he needed to go to the police. But he said that he wanted to wait until the podcast dropped so that they wouldn't suspect him of trying to deflect suspicion from himself. He has evidence from the laptop that will point to Walsh."

"Until the podcast dropped—why?"

Her friend sat back, folded her arms. "Because in the podcast, I name the suspect."

"Holden Walsh."

"Not Holden."

Jack interjected—"Wait. So you've been *in hiding*?"

Penelope sighed. "Yes. Of course. Harper, didn't you get my note?"

"What note?"

"I left it in your jacket, back at the supper club. I figured you'd find it when you came back and found me gone." Her mouth opened. "Oh no. You didn't get it."

"No, I didn't get it. I was frantic. We both were."

Jack looked at her, raised an eyebrow. *Whatever.*

"Why would you do that?" Harper asked.

Penelope did look sorry. "I got a death threat."

"We heard it," said Jack. "On your podcast."

"Oh, not that one. It was an email that said if I released the name of the killer, he'd find me. Ty was going to drive me to Minneapolis. The plan was to stay in Minneapolis, show up for the rehearsal dinner . . ."

"Without telling anyone?"

"No! Of course not. The plan was to leave on Tuesday and then call Boo on Wednesday morning. I was going to tell her I was in Minneapolis for business, but when I met Conrad on Tuesday. . . well, I thought maybe we could hit it off, you know . . . an impulsive getaway. But it didn't quite go down that way."

"Seriously?"

"My life was in danger!"

"Then go to the police, for Pete's sake. Penelope, people were counting on you."

"To what? Dance? Get my nails done? I planned to be back for the rehearsal, right after the podcast dropped." She checked her watch. "In about an hour."

"I called and texted so many times—"

"My phone got lost somewhere between Ty getting shot and my escape."

"So, what happened?" Jack said. They'd turned onto the road, heading south for Duck Lake.

"I should never have opened the door to the Uber, but it was Ty, so . . ." She shook her head, the haunted look back. "The man with him had a gun on Ty. I panicked and obeyed. I couldn't believe it when he shot Ty." She shook her head, her eyes glossy.

"He's fighting for his life in ICU."

She drew in a breath.

"And then what?" Jack said.

"I got out of the car and hid. And saw the guy get out, search for me. And I thought, *Get back in the car; drive away.* But I couldn't move Ty from the driver's seat, and that's when the guy rounded back and grabbed me. I got ahold of Ty's keys and held on to them even when I was thrown into the trunk. When we got to Loon Lake, I remembered what Ty had said about his blue icehouse. I got away, hid, then made my way out here and hunkered down."

"Why on earth did you stay out here?"

"Because I knew the guy was looking for me, on an ATV, more than once. I figured, at the very least, there'd be people here over the weekend." Her face turned wan. "At least, I hoped so."

Harper couldn't help but reach back, take Penelope's hand. "You're safe now."

"Maybe. Because as soon as my podcast drops and I give all the reasons why it's not Holden, then there is only one person left."

"Who? Who killed Sarah Livingston?"

She met Harper's gaze. "The same man who killed my sister's fiancé."

A beat.

"Derek Swindle."

"What? Who—wait. Walsh's *partner*? Why? How?"

"The only thing the police had linking Walsh to Sarah that night was his car, caught on camera in her apartment parking lot after the gala. The time stamp has him there the same time that the man was seen fleeing her house. My guess is that it was planted there by Swindle."

"So Walsh is being framed."

"Yes."

"Why?"

"I think it has to do with information on Sarah's stolen laptop."

"Why did you never mention that in your podcast?"

"I was waiting until I found out what's on it. Which would lead me to why. And hopefully, to the intruder in her house that night, the actual killer." She looked away, out into the night, a look of determination on her face. "I don't know why Swindle wanted Sarah dead, but I'm going to figure it out."

Right. There was a story to tell, and Penelope wanted to be the one telling it.

They'd entered the town of Duck Lake. "Where to?" Jack asked.

"The sheriff," said Harper.

"The wedding rehearsal," said Penelope.

"Great," Jack said. "Fine. Wedding rehearsal, just so we can put Boo's mind at ease, then to the sheriff's office." His jaw flexed then, and he looked over at Harper.

And she didn't know if he was kidding or not when he said, "You owe me a hundred bucks."

THIRTEEN

H E WASN'T A CHUMP. HADN'T BEEN PLAYED.
The woman had truly been in danger.

At least, that's what Jack kept trying to get through his brain as he stared into the mirror in Doyle's master bathroom, tying and retying his stupid bow tie.

The sun cast its rays through the windows—a glorious day for a wedding.

"Can't we just have clip-ons?" He ripped the stupid tie from his shirt, wanting to crush it in his hand.

"Take a breath there, Goldilocks," Stein said, walking up to him. "Give me the tie. Simple knot tying 101."

Jack handed Stein the tie, lifted his jaw.

Through the open door of the bathroom, Jack spotted Doyle in his usher's attire, fixing his cuff links, his dark hair gelled, wearing a scrub of trimmed dark whiskers. He'd said little when Jack arrived at the rehearsal last night with Penelope—had simply given a tight nod and shaken Jack's hand.

Walked away.

Memories, maybe.

Sometimes—more often than not—Jack wished he could wind up the past, recast it.

Conrad sat on the bed, already dressed in his gray tux, the shoulders tight. *Someone* should have taken more time to get it fitted. He was texting.

Possibly Penelope, given the way he'd looked at her last night, the worry in his gaze. The woman might not have been wrong about an impulsive romance.

Except, everything about her explanation sat inside him like a burr. It didn't help that Harper had all but abandoned him at the rehearsal, and maybe that was petty, but—

"Chin up, bro," Stein said and finished tying. "Now, don't touch it." He turned Jack by the shoulders, back to the mirror. "Spiffy."

Whatever.

"What's that look?"

"Nothing." Jack headed out of the room. The sooner he could get this day over—

And then what?

Stein had followed him out of the room into Doyle's massive master bedroom, where the brothers were getting ready. Oaken was at Grover House with his team.

The ladies had left early this morning for the Duck Lake Heritage Church, the first church in town, now a historical site used for exactly these occasions.

Well, not exactly this occasion, because the town had started to buzz with the arrival of paparazzi and Oaken's celebrity guests. Even last night as Penelope was giving her statement at the sheriff's office, most of the conversation from the gathering of deputies had centered on the various celebrity spottings.

"I saw Glo and Tate Marshall and their little girl."

"And Kelsey Jones—she and her husband were here. She just dropped a solo album."

"Ben King was at the Lumberjack's Table tonight with some people. Saw it on Insta."

"Mike Grizz showed up . . ."

Jack had tried to block it out, his arms folded as he leaned against the doorjamb and listened to Penelope attempt to describe her kidnapper.

Tried to get past the fact that he knew it—just knew it.

She'd constructed the entire thing. Even if it had gone south on her.

"What has you all dark and broody?"

Stein had come up behind him where Jack now stood at the window overlooking the snow on the lake, the sun shining through the trees. A glorious, blue-skied day, and everything would be fine. Probably.

"I don't know."

"I do," Conrad said, pocketing his phone, getting up from where he sat on the end of the king bed. "It's the wedding day."

Jack frowned.

"Which means that tomorrow is . . ." He raised his eyebrows as if waiting for an answer.

"Leftover cake?" Jack offered.

Conrad laughed. "No, man. It's fish-or-cut-bait day."

"I don't even know what that means."

Conrad walked over to the dresser mirror, checked his appearance. "It means, what's up with you and Harper?"

Stein grinned. "Yep. That's it." He nodded. "That's what's got him all surly."

"I'm not surly."

Silence.

"Fine. If you haven't noticed, I'm homeless."

"You're hardly homeless," Doyle said, looking up. "You practically have a beachside home. And a pretty nice-looking vintage Alfa Romeo in the garage. And a sick-looking Victory Hammer S bike." He folded his arms. "You want to talk about homeless—try living in your parents' guesthouse like you might need an emotional Band-Aid."

Jack looked away.

"I know I need to figure this out. And I will because I'm not the guy I was five years ago," Doyle said.

"We know that. And Dad needs help with this place," Conrad said, his voice soft.

Doyle lifted a shoulder, directed his gaze to Jack. "I'm sorry about your broken-down old bus going up in flames, but maybe it's a sign."

"Of what?"

"That your running is over."

The words came from their father, who stood in the doorway. He wore his tuxedo, gray with a blue vest, a bow tie perfectly tied, his salt-and-pepper hair slicked back, clean-shaven, and walked into the room and shut the door.

Silence.

Conrad drew in a breath.

Stein folded his arms, looked away.

"Running?" Jack said.

"Let's cut to the truth, Jack. We all know that you blame yourself—not sure why—for Sabrina's death."

Jack shoved his hands into his pockets.

"It derailed you. And then it got worse when you failed the bar."

Jack glanced at Stein, who raised his hands. "I didn't tell him."

"Please. We're not stupid. Jack, you're an achiever. You don't fail. And when you do, you freak out."

"Not true."

His dad held up his hand. "Let me amend that. You hate to fail."

"Doesn't everyone?"

"Everyone isn't the oldest brother in the family. Everyone isn't the guy who was known as Big Jack." His dad's voice softened.

"Everyone isn't the son who showed up, shovel in hand, for every firepit I asked you to dig."

A smile from his brothers.

"Everyone isn't the guy who still shows up, even when all hope is gone."

"Let's not turn this into a hero thing. I get paid to find people. Some might call me a mercenary." Jack offered a smile.

His father shook his head. "I don't know who told you that you had to be the best—I hope it wasn't me—but you need to know that the only one looking at your failure, judging you by your failure, is you."

Jack looked away, took a breath.

"I know you hate being called out. You don't do vulnerable well—"

"I'm not a jerk."

"That's not what I mean. You hold everyone away because you think that your failures will make you less in people's eyes." His dad stepped closer. "You care very deeply about your people."

His chest clenched. He glanced past his dad, looking for escape.

"That's why you ridiculed your sister when she wanted to re-up with the Navy."

"She was going to join a Marine expeditionary unit! *Again.*" *Oops.* That might have come out a little too passionately.

"I know," his dad said quietly. "For the record, I'm not unhappy that she opted out of that. But I know you carried the rift between you and Brontë and in our family on yourself, and . . . well, you made it bigger than it should have been."

"I hurt her. I got that."

"You hurt *yourself.* You let your shame tell you that you weren't loved. Weren't eligible for grace."

"We fixed it."

"You might have fixed it with her, but you haven't fixed it between you and God, have you?"

He looked at his father, made to open his mouth, but his father held up his hand. Great, they were doing this in front of his brothers?

"God loves you very much, Jack. He made you for a purpose. And he's waiting for you to come to him, to stop running and discover peace. To take your rightful place in this family, as Big Jack."

Shoot. "I don't even know what that looks like."

"Maybe you won't until you get there." His dad had walked close enough to put his hand on Jack's shoulder. "You were created for the outrageous, overwhelming, wonderful love of heaven. Stop telling yourself what you're supposed to do and simply let God work in you *to do*. Then, and only then, will you truly stop searching and satisfy this restless itch. The greatest find is waking up every day to the excitement of seeing what God will do."

And just like that, Harper's words rushed into his head. *"You're not lost anymore, Jack Kingston. You're right back where you're supposed to be. So stop running."*

Except the voice sounded deeper, maybe a heartbeat or a thrum inside him.

He nodded as his dad squeezed his shoulder.

"So, ready to get your littlest sister married?"

"I can't believe she's getting married first," said Stein, probably without thinking.

Jack wanted to wince for Doyle, but his brother took a breath, found a smile. "Let's do this."

His father put his arm over Doyle's shoulder as they walked out. Stein and Jack followed, Conrad swiping up his phone behind them. They tromped out into the frigid, beautiful day.

Jack got into the front seat of his father's truck as his brothers squished into the back, shoulder to shoulder.

"It's like I'm five, pinned between my brothers," Doyle said, sitting on the hump in the middle.

Conrad grabbed one of his knees, and Stein grabbed the other.

"Get your grubs off me." He elbowed them but laughed.

Jack was right where he was supposed to be. *Maybe. At least for a while.*

And then what? Florida? He'd purchased the place for investment purposes after the success of the true-crime book.

But maybe his heart was here . . . or . . .

Harper certainly wasn't staying, so there was that.

Except, what if . . .

Maybe they should play the game again, this time at the reception, maybe where he could pull her into someplace private . . .

"After the wedding, Oaken and Boo will take pictures at the church, then more at the house before the reception starts. That was the memo that Boo's wedding planner gave me."

"Who?"

"A woman named Megan. She's from out of town but came highly recommended."

"What's for dinner?" Stein asked.

"I don't know. Mom brought in a caterer, a recommendation from Megan."

Yeah, he'd get Harper away from the reception and tell her . . . *what?* He looked out the window, trying out words in his mind. He didn't want this to end? He was in love with her?

Yeah, that was raw and terrifying. Maybe his dad was right about the running.

The historical church sat on the edge of a park in the middle of town, miraculously spared from the tornado six years ago. A simple limestone building with a tall steeple and a bell at the apex. The stone stairs that led up to double wooden doors were now flanked with tall cedar trees decorated with white ribbon and tulle.

A blue carpet, laid for traction, led up the stairs to the front door.

His father pulled into the lot, parked. "We're supposed to use the side entrance, sneak in." He grinned at them, a joy in his eyes that Jack felt down to his bones.

They got out, and Conrad put a hand on Jack's shoulder, pulling him away. "Hey. I need to show you something."

The wind shivered through him as Conrad handed him his phone. "This came through on my feed. It's a *PopMuse* blog about the wedding. They've been posting little blurbs every day, some insider point of view."

He might know who that insider was. "Yeah, that's Harper. She got permission from Boo to cover it."

"That explains it." Conrad nodded. "Didn't know you had it in you, bro."

Had what? Jack looked at the blog. His breath caught. "What?"

"Not sure what she was going for there, but I'd give you five out of five stars."

Jack's entire body turned cold as he read, the words like a punch to his sternum.

And he just wanted to run.

———•———

"Just stop thinking. Breathe. Enjoy." Harper stood in the bridal suite, a room in the back of the Duck Lake Heritage Church, holding Boo's hands, meeting her eyes, saying the words to herself just as much as to the bride.

They'd found Penelope. Safe and alive.

The lit candles in the hearth filled the room with the scent of lilies, competing with the array of blue-and-white rose bouquets delivered by the florist earlier. The flowers sat on a vintage coffee table surrounded by pale-pink Victorian parlor sofas.

Beyond the double doors, the hum of guests filling the sanctuary lifted and filtered into the former choir room. The room had been redone for exactly the purpose of these final moments.

Ornate full-length mirrors, one of them a three-way surrounding a dais. Plush white velvet straight chairs sat against makeup vanities with soft lighting and table mirrors, and along the wall, there were hanging stands for long dresses. More flickering candles in the windows and soft piano hymns playing turned the morning into a fairy tale.

Or maybe that might just be Harper's wild imagination having a go. *See, everything is going to be fine. Perfect.*

Magical.

So what that Jack had been acting weird—*very* weird—last night. Maybe he was as relieved as she was.

He'd driven them back to the inn in silence and hadn't even attempted to stop her as she followed Penelope to their room.

She'd sort of hoped for a late-night regroup in front of the hearth. Something that included his arms around her, telling her—*what?* That he loved her? That he wanted a future with her?

There went her imagination again.

Just stop thinking. Breathe. Enjoy.

"Nearly ready for the dress." This from Megan, their very busy wedding planner.

"Thanks for finding Penelope," Boo said. "If I'd known she was really in danger, I would have stopped everything and sent out a search party."

"Honestly, we thought she was fine. I called her security, and he said she'd checked in. And then Conrad got the scary voicemail."

"I told Franco that I was going back to Minneapolis," Penelope said, coming over. "But I didn't realize I'd sent the voicemail." Of course, her dark-blue V-necked velvet bridesmaid dress fit like a glove over her tall, slender body. The hairdresser had coifed her hair into a waterfall of dark curls and drips.

The poor woman had tried to do something—anything—with Harper's short hair, and in the end had added a few curls, flips, and a gold barrette.

Harper felt *cute*. Maybe *sweetly pretty*. The girl next door, standing on the edge of what she really wanted. So maybe this was the best Harper could hope for.

"With the extra security team that Oaken's crew hired, we're all safe now," Boo continued. "Everything is going to be fine."

Right. What she said.

"Okay, Bride, you're up." Megan had positioned Boo's shoes in the puddle of the dress and now took Boo's hand and helped her over to the dais. Then, while Megan held the dress open, Austen and her mother steadied Boo as she stepped into the gown.

Harper's throat filled watching Boo transform into a bride as Megan pulled the dress up around her. The beaded-lace sheath wedding dress framed her toned body, the long-sleeve arms ending in scallops. The deep V back, with covered buttons, formed a bodice with a lacy décolletage and cat-eye neckline.

"Wow, Boo," said London, also elegant in her gown and long blonde hair, swooped up. "That works."

Boo grinned. "It was my mom's."

"Oh," said Mama Em. "We updated it, a lot. Added sleeves and took in some around the waist. The chapel-length train is all hers. I wasn't that fancy when I married Grover." But Boo's mother wore a look in her eyes that made Harper wish . . .

Aw, she wished for too much, probably. Her wishes got her in too much trouble.

Just stop thinking. Enjoy.

"Something old," Boo's mother said and handed Boo a strand of pearls. "Your grandmother's." She attached them around Boo's neck as Megan buttoned up the back of the dress.

"And something new," said Austen. "Oaken asked me to give these to you." She opened a box, and inside sat diamond earrings.

"Wow," said Penelope. "Good man."

Boo lifted them out, affixed them in her ears.

"I got you the quote you wanted," said London, and lifted a small index card.

"What's that?" Harper asked.

"A line from *Wuthering Heights*." She read the card: "Whatever our souls are made of, his and mine are the same."

"I don't think you'll forget that," her mother said.

"Just in case," London said, "I'll stick this into the something blue." She folded the card and tucked it between the blue and white roses of the bridal bouquet in a stand on a table in the room.

And in Harper's mind, she was already writing her article.

In the softly lit bridal suite, a sanctuary of calm and beauty buzzes gently with the quiet excitement of a wedding morning. Here, Brontë steps into more than just a dress; she is slipping into a story woven from generations of love.

The air is scented with the subtle fragrance of roses, lilies, and anticipation. Brontë, standing gracefully in front of an ornate mirror, lifts the fabric of her gown— the same gown her mother wore decades ago, now altered to marry tradition with contemporary grace. The dress, a cascade of delicate lace and silk, whispers stories of the past as it rustles against the plush carpet of the dais.

She wears a pair of diamond earrings, a gift from her groom, Oaken. They sparkle under the soft glow of the chandelier, each facet catching light. Around her neck is clasped a pearl necklace, handed down from her grandmother. The pearls, each a testament to enduring beauty and strength, lie against her

collarbone—a touchstone to the women who have shaped her.

Her bouquet rests on a nearby table. White and blue roses cluster tightly, their hues a perfect echo of the clear January sky. Concealed among the blooms is a love note, a ribbon-bound excerpt from *Wuthering Heights*: **"Whatever our souls are made of, his and mine are the same." This quote now gains new meaning as she prepares to walk toward Oaken.**

Okay, even in her head that sounded over the top. But probably appropriate.

And now, as Boo took a long breath, the words in Harper's mind continued to pen the moment.

As the organ music slips in through the closed doors, building the anticipation of meeting her groom, Brontë steps fully dressed toward her reflection. She pauses, her heart a symphony of beats, her reflection a portrait of bridal beauty. The joy in her eyes mirrors the smiles of the women who surround her. Today, Brontë not only marries the man she loves but also steps into a new chapter of a love story that spans generations—her feet firmly planted in tradition, her heart soaring into the future.

Harper wanted to cry.

She wanted this. All of it. The tradition. The family. The groom. *Her own* groom.

Jack.

"Don't let him walk away unless you want him to."

"Bee, you okay?" Boo's gaze had fallen on her.

"Yeah. Great." She forced a smile.

Boo shook her head. "It'll all work out."

Harper raised an eyebrow.

"Jack will take one look at you, and he'll realize that he is crazy about you. Always has been. It's just taken this long for it to be right."

Yes. Maybe his walking away from her back then had been exactly the right thing. Had given her a chance to find herself—at least enough that she knew what she wanted. Who she wanted.

So no, she wasn't letting him walk away.

"Hey, how's the article going?" Boo asked.

"Good. They posted a couple excerpts on the *PopMuse* blog."

"I can't wait to read it. You always have a way of bringing out the magic."

A knock came at the door. The photographer, a woman from Minneapolis armed with a camera around her neck, stuck her head in. "Five-minute warning." She closed the door.

Boo inhaled, smiled, her gaze still on Harper. "I've learned that God has good things for those who trust His love for them."

Maybe she was talking about Harper, maybe herself, but Harper nodded.

Megan stepped up to the dais. "Time for the veil." She affixed the chapel-length veil with the embroidered edges and the tiny tiara on Boo's head.

"Gorgeous," Austen said.

"My sister is overjoyed that someone could wear it," Penelope said softly.

Boo looked over at her. "Thank you. I love it."

"She got it in Italy." She pressed her lips together, nodded, her eyes bright.

Aw, so there went any lingering anger toward Penelope.

Boo stepped off the dais, letting the veil cascade along the pale-pink carpet. "How do I look?"

"Oaken won't be able to speak," Austen said.

"I hope he can speak enough to say I do," Boo said, laughing.

"He'll be able to nod. Maybe grunt or something," London said.

The door opened and Megan, who'd stepped out, came back in. "We're ready for you. Bridesmaids, I need you in reverse order, like we practiced."

Penelope stood at the front, then London, and Harper lined up between London and Austen, who stood in front of Boo. Her mother kissed her cheek and exited.

And right then, Harper caught a glimpse of Jack, standing in the vestibule.

He could take her breath away. If possible, the tux only made his shoulders wider, his waist trimmer, sculpted his entire body. His hair hung just above his collar, dark and curly, and he'd trimmed his dark beard for the occasion. He stood, his hands clasped in front of him, and all she could think of was those hands pulling her to himself on the boat.

She may have crushed on him as a child, dreamed about him as a high-schooler, but the last few days, spending time with him, discovering him—no, *finding* him—had nourished in her feelings that had taken breath and life and . . . hope.

She loved this man. Loved him enough to . . . what? Stay in Duck Lake? Follow him around the country?

To find a life with him, wherever that might be.

"You should go," Austen said from behind, and only then did Harper realize that London had moved forward.

Shep held out his arm—he had cleaned up well too and wore a look of appreciation for London.

And then Harper searched for Jack's gaze.

No appreciation. Not even kindness. His mouth pinched, and he glanced away as she took his arm. His stiff, unmoving arm.

The arm of a man who wanted to ghost her.

He didn't spare her a look as they stepped up to the sanctuary door.

Inside, sprays of blue and white roses hung along the carved wooden pews. And at the front, an organist played "Jesu, Joy of Man's Desiring."

But in the back, a frost settled over her.

Megan nodded, and Jack stepped out, stiff, a soldier doing his duty.

Harper pinned her eyes to the front, glancing once at Oaken, dressed in a tuxedo, his face stalwart, as if trying not to weep.

Her too.

She looked away and spotted Penelope, all grins, having walked down with Conrad. And next to her, London, now taking her place on the stage, her smile aglow.

They reached the bottom on the stage and Jack simply dropped his arm. He held out his hand to help her up the steps, but she ignored it. Managed on her own, then took her place beside London. Somehow managed not to cry as Austen came down on the arm of Steinbeck, her brother. Then the congregation rose for Boo and, *aw*, now she had cover.

So many tears. At least she didn't blubber as Boo came down the aisle, glowing, and took Oaken's hand.

Beautiful. From the vows, with Boo's romantic quote, to Oaken's song, written just for her. A man, a guitar, and eyes only for his bride.

And then the pastor pronounced them married.

They walked back up the aisle to cheering, and the bridesmaids followed on the arms of the groomsmen, and if she'd thought Jack was chilly on the way down the aisle, she practically caught frostbite during the recessional. He couldn't get rid of her fast enough when they reached the vestibule.

He walked over to Boo, gave her a hug, along with Oaken, and stepped away, a strange expression on his face.

Whatever. She didn't care.

She hugged Boo. "Congratulations."

"I'm so glad it's over."

"Oh, it's just beginning," Oaken said beside her.

Harper forced a laugh, hugged him too, and then joined Austen, who'd already done the honors.

"Now what?"

"Now we have pictures at the house," Boo said. "And then the reception."

And then Harper could get into her Sonic and floor it back to her life in Nashville.

"There's a couple limos outside to take the wedding party to the house," Austen said. "Megan said that she'd bring our makeup and clothing bags."

Boo and Oaken stood at the doors, greeting guests as they came out. Sure, Harper should probably stick around and play brides-maid—and sure, she was overjoyed for Boo and Oaken—but at this point, she was over it. The sooner she could escape, the better.

Maybe she'd spend the night on her mother's sofa.

Harper followed Austen outside and found a limousine waiting for them, warming. Conrad helped Penelope inside, then held out his hand for Austen, who followed Penelope in.

He held out his hand to Harper. She took it.

"Great blog today," he said as she gathered up her dress.

"What?"

"On the *PopMuse* site. I have to admit, I didn't see that coming. Very . . . informative."

She just frowned at him. "What blog?"

He raised an eyebrow, then fished his phone from his pocket. Unlocked it and handed it to her.

She climbed in and settled next to Austen in the plush seats, then looked at the phone.

No. Oh no . . . What?

Conrad got in and shut the door.

"Where's Jack?" asked Austen. "And Stein?"

"They're driving Dad's truck back to the house. Mom and Dad are driving with Oaken's parents."

But Harper couldn't take her gaze from the blog—no, her *novel*.

Jack turns toward me, his expression hesitant yet filled with a longing that echoes my own. He leans in slowly, his lips meeting mine with a tenderness that sends shivers down my spine. The touch is a whisper, cautious and exploring. Yet as I respond, something shifts. The kiss deepens, fueled by my eager reply.

The *PopMuse* editor had written an introduction. Harper wanted to cover the phone as she read it.

Welcome to the juiciest slice of today's wedding insider—where the bride and groom aren't the only ones trying to stay warm in snowy Minnesota. Stay tuned as we dish out more from this wedding's exclusive "Private Moments with Brontë and Oaken" series.

Private moments? Oh no—

Don't say we didn't warn you—it's getting hot in Minnesota!

Not hot. Not. Hot.

Harper looked up at Conrad, who was watching her. He nodded to her silent question and she handed back the phone.

Just stop thinking. Breathe. Enjoy.
Hide.

FOURTEEN

I T WAS HIS FAULT, REALLY. HE'D BROKEN EVERY
single personal rule, starting with one of the most basic... *I work alone.*

Followed only by: *I don't make promises.*

He'd forgotten, however: *Don't give away your heart.*

"You're wanted for pictures in the parlor," Conrad said, coming
up behind Jack where he stood in the dining room, staring out at
the lake.

No, staring out at memories. Or maybe not memories but the
pictures he'd drawn of Harper and himself, building an imaginary
life inside his head.

"Right." He drew in a breath.

Conrad stepped in front of him. "You okay?"

"Yeah."

"You're a terrible liar."

"Whatever. I don't know what game she might be playing, but
fool me once, on her. Twice, that's on me."

"She didn't know about the blog."

Jack frowned at him.

"I showed her in the limo. She looked pretty freaked out."

"I don't care how it got posted—"

"You just care that . . . what? I'm not seeing the sin here."

"I'm the hero in a freakin' romance novel!" Jack hadn't meant to raise his voice. He lowered it. "Listen. Private stuff shouldn't be . . . public."

"You're embarrassed."

Jack caught a glimpse now of the bridal party gathering in the parlor. "Of course I'm embarrassed."

"Get over yourself. So what it's true? So what you lost your heart to Harper—"

"Except, all that time, she was writing a torrid romance about me."

"It's hardly torrid. It's sweet and maybe a little sappy, but hardly even PG-rated." Conrad leaned in. "The real issue is that you're scared."

Jack's eyes flinched.

"Dad was right. You're scared you're going to screw it up. That you're going to fail her—"

"I'm not—"

"Just like you did Sabrina."

Jack's mouth pinched.

"I was there. I don't care what you say—you had a little thing for her. And she had a thing for you. And you never acted on it. Why?"

He swallowed.

"I'll tell you why. Because you were secretly in love with *Harper*. And that horrified you."

"I barely knew she existed until that spring break."

"And then you really knew, until you told yourself she was off-limits."

"She was."

A beat.

"Okay, yes. I knew she had a little hero worship going when she was young. And I might have liked it—but she was a child, so . . ."

He lifted a shoulder. "And then she showed up, and yes, I didn't realize it was her . . . Bee. Pigtails. Whatever. I fell for her. Hard. She was fun and smart and easy to be around, and she listened to me, and I felt brilliant and like maybe I hung the moon in her eyes—*because I did.* And then I kissed her—and found out who she was—and all I could think was . . . I took advantage of her and that hero worship, and yes, I was ashamed of myself."

"But you never forgot her."

"I *should* have forgotten her."

"You did nothing wrong, bro."

Jack ran a hand behind his head. "But don't you see—I'm still that guy. The guy she crushed on—Mr. Hero Worship. And she's writing a novel—and now I'm Mr. Romance!"

"Novel, or memoir. Sounded pretty real."

Jack looked away. *It was. Oh.* He turned back to Conrad. "Yes, I'm embarrassed. But I'm also pretty sure that she's in love with a version of me that is not me."

"Despite your efforts to clue her in to the truth?"

"Yes."

Conrad laughed. Full-out laughed. "Seriously? Mr. I Promise I'll Find Your Friend? And Save Your Life Along the Way? Yeah, you're doing a bang-up job of making her see the truth."

Jack shook his head, made to push past Conrad, but his brother stopped him, his hand on his arm.

Jack stiffened.

"So what?" Conrad said.

Jack frowned.

"So what that the whole world knows you love her. And so what that she finds out that you're not really Big Jack. Or that you are but you are also Sometimes I Get It Wrong Jack. This woman loves you. And that is a rare and beautiful thing, bro." He let Jack go.

"I feel naked."

"You can choose how you feel. You might consider feeling honored, Fabio." Conrad winked and walked away.

Fabio?

Whatever. Jack followed him out to the parlor. The photographer had already finished taking shots of the ladies, and now she directed them to stand with their processional partners. He walked up to Harper.

She smelled good. Like flowers or something. And frankly, looked downright stunning in that V-necked dress, the fabric soft under his hand as he put it on her shoulder, as directed.

She stiffened.

Aw. "This woman loves you."

Maybe not so much.

Boo and Oaken took their spots, and Jack forced a smile, holding it for about twenty more minutes as the photographer repositioned them.

"We need to talk," he said to Harper at one point, bending down to whisper in her ear.

She ignored him.

The photographer had the men high-five, the women raise their bouquets in triumph as Boo and Oaken kissed, then she dismissed the women.

"Men, I need you with the bride and groom."

"I need a moment," Boo said and headed out of the room, her dress trailing after.

Jack took that moment to catch up with Harper as she walked toward the door. He grabbed her wrist.

"Can we talk?"

She drew in a breath, and only then did he notice her reddened eyes. It tempered his words, just a little. "I read the blog."

"Mm-hmm."

He still had hold of her wrist and now pulled her into the center of the home, by the stairs, near the bathroom.

He kept his voice low. "Why did you post it?"

She exhaled. Shook her head. Then she jerked out of his grasp. "Leave me alone—"

"No." He took her hand, and this time directed her toward the door on the opposite side, under the stairs.

The one that led to the family wine closet.

They stepped in and he let go, the chill of the room catching his breath. A wall of wine penned them in on all sides, a chandelier hanging from the ceiling.

"What were you thinking?"

She stared at him. "I didn't submit it on purpose! It was a mistake. I don't know how, but I uploaded the wrong file."

His expression didn't change.

"Fine. It was from . . . a novel I was working on."

"With me as the hero."

"Yes, okay. Yes."

"It felt pretty real."

She lifted a shoulder, and then her eyes filled. "I'm sorry."

He shook his head. "Why would you write all that down—"

"Are you kidding me right now? Because that was . . . that was the best week of my life—despite how everything turned out."

"It was just a kiss."

"It was . . . hope. It was . . ." She shook her head, then looked at the bouquet she held. Sighed. "You don't know what it's like to want something so much you dream it into existence." She looked up at him. "I wanted to be a Kingston more than anything in my entire life. And yes, I had a terrible crush on you. But more than that, I wanted what I thought you wanted. A family. A home. This. I wanted this."

He stared at her, nonplussed.

"My father walked away from me and never looked back. My mother . . . she would rather be with her clients than listen to her own daughter. And that was all fine because *your* mother listened. She loved me more than mine ever did—"

"So, what—you wanted to be my sister? Great. Now I feel gross—"

"Don't be a jerk. Of course not. But that night, when you kissed me, I thought ... I thought I belonged. I thought you wanted me."

He raised an eyebrow, hating the memory those words dredged up. Because yes ...

"In your life."

Right.

And then she took a breath. Sighed. Looked up at him, and he saw in her eyes the woman he'd discovered this week. Smart. Brave. Determined.

"I'm sorry you're embarrassed. But I'm not sorry that I kissed you. Then, or this week. I'm not sorry that I have an overactive imagination or that I wish for big things. Frankly, I thought I made you sound pretty good."

Then she turned and pushed through the door.

The cool breath of the wine cellar followed her out. He stood for a moment, then spotted Boo emerging from the bathroom across the hall.

Fine. He'd talk to Harper later.

He *had* sounded pretty good.

He returned to the parlor, followed the instruction of the photographer, Harper's words running over him.

"I wanted what I thought you wanted. A family. A home. This. I wanted this."

He did too. He just didn't know how to find it, to land it.

His dad found his thoughts, wandered around as Jack posed with the groomsmen. *"He's waiting for you to come to Him, to stop running and discover peace."*

By the time they'd finished, country music spilled out from the third-floor ballroom, down the winding stairs, into the foyer where guests started to arrive. Jack met a few of Oaken's posh friends, trying to keep an eye out for Harper, but he didn't see her.

He glad-handed his cousin Dodge, from Alaska, catching up for a moment on his family—Echo and baby Chase—and then met Noemi, the wife of Range.

Jack finally went upstairs. Round tables filled much of the room, with a band set up at the front along with a dance floor. Oaken and Boo's sweetheart table sat alone at the front of the stage.

The wedding party sat at one table, Oaken's family and Boo's SAR team at another. Jack took a seat next to Austen. "Where's Harper sitting?"

She picked up a name card next to her. "Here."

He frowned, again looked around for Harper. Most of the tables were filled, the band playing music in the far corner, the smell of dinner wafting up from the kitchen.

"Where's Penelope?"

Austen picked up her napkin, frowned at him. "Um, I think I saw Harper and her talking earlier, out on the porch."

"Outside?"

"Yeah. Wait—you don't think she *left* do you?"

He pushed his chair out, got up. "I don't know."

She put her napkin down. "You need us to find her?"

He looked at her. "No, but if I do, I'll let you know." He put a hand on her shoulder, then wove his way through the crowd.

He headed down to the second level, but the guests' doors were closed, so he descended to the first floor. Empty parlor, empty dining room. He pushed through to the kitchen, to the scent of roasted chicken—no, quail, given the golden-brown birds on the counter. Staff plated the food, then covered the plates and loaded them onto a dumbwaiter that lifted to the third floor.

He spotted his mother talking with another woman. *Oh, Oaken's mother.* Pretty woman. Blonde and tan.

"Mom, have you seen Harper?"

"Not recently. She and her friend Penelope were outside talking to some man earlier. Not a guest, but Penelope seemed relieved to see him. She gave him a hug."

A hug?

"I think Boo and Oaken are about to head in—you two better get upstairs." Jack brushed past them outside.

The sun had started to set, the wind stirring the breeze, creaking the trees. The parking lot was jammed full of cars.

He stood there, his hands in his pockets. *Oh, Harper, please don't leave—*

A moan lifted—deep and pained—and the sound landed in his chest, stirred—

He went to the edge of the porch and stilled.

Penelope lay in the snow, her face bloodied, her dress torn. "Penelope!" He scrambled down the steps, scooped her up. "Are you okay?" He started up the stairs, carrying her. "Where's Harper?"

He pushed into the house. "Mom, I need help!" He burst into the kitchen as his mother rounded the corner.

She took a breath at the sight of the wounded woman. "Not near the food. C'mon." She directed him to the nearby bathroom, just off the entry.

He set Penelope down, and his mother had already wetted a towel. She put it to Penelope's nose, still gushing blood.

Penelope pinched her nose, her voice stunted. "Harper and I were talking when suddenly he just showed up. Just walked up the steps and—I was so shocked I hugged him." Her breath caught. "I hugged him. Wow, I'm such an idiot. He completely played us and . . ." She looked up at Jack. "This is a lot bigger than I thought."

"Where. Is. *Harper*?"

"He said he needed to talk, and I started walking toward the car and then thought, *What am I doing? I'm at a wedding.* So I told him no, and that's when he tried to grab me. Harper got in the middle, and then he hit me—oh, I think my nose is broken—"

"Penelope!"

"I don't know! I heard Harper shouting. And then she came at us, swinging something—a shovel. Yeah, she hit him with a shovel."

Jack grabbed the frame of the door.

"I think maybe she hit him again—I don't know. I remember her running."

"Where?"

"I don't know—"

"Why didn't she go back to the house?"

"I don't know!" Her eyes filled. "She ran. And he ran after her."

Her words had the power to buckle his knees.

"Did he catch her?" His voice emerged on a whisper.

"I don't know—I didn't hear anyone drive away." She met his eyes then. "No. I don't remember them driving away."

"Who, Penelope? Who did this?"

Penelope lowered the towel. "Kyle Brunley."

He stilled. "What? He's dead."

She shook her head. "Not so dead."

"Then who was the dead body at the Motor Lodge?" He got up.

"I don't know."

"Maybe the guy who took you." He turned to the kitchen, spotted a waiter. "We need some ice."

He turned back to Penelope. "Do you think she could still be here? On the grounds?"

"Maybe."

"Jack? Everything okay?"

He turned and spotted Austen coming through the kitchen.

Aw. "No. Not even a little. Get the guys. I need their help." Then he turned to his mother. "Call the sheriff. Then tell Boo I'm sorry."

He left and stalked outside. Stood on the porch. *C'mon, Harper. Where'd you go?*

The sun still shone high, hitting the cars, the glistening snow.

She'd be barefoot, thanks to her bridal heels, so she wouldn't go far. And she'd go somewhere she could hide. Or defend herself.

His gaze shot to the trail. The one that connected their houses. Yeah, he knew about it—mostly because Boo had taken the trail sometimes, sneaking out after dark.

He'd been onto her then, had occasionally tailed her, making sure she got to Bee's house in one piece.

"Bro." Conrad, pushing out of the house, Stein behind him, then Doyle and Austen.

Jack turned to Austen. "Tell Boo what's going on. But tell her to sit tight. We'll find Harper."

Austen nodded, headed back inside.

"Jack?" Stein said.

"Grab a shovel and follow me." Jack headed off the porch onto the drive, headed toward the pathway to Harper's house.

Hang on, Harper. I'll find you.

—————•—————

She wasn't surprised that Jack had rejected her, frankly.

Because hopes and dreams did that.

She probably shouldn't have let it consume so much of her mind, however, because it took way, way too long for her brain to catch up when Penelope hugged Kyle Brunley.

Not dead Kyle Brunley.

The Kyle Brunley who then told Penny he needed to talk to her. Took her hand and pulled her from the porch.

Maybe it took a second for Penny to catch up too. Harper blamed it on their breeding—too much Minnesota nice. But by the time Harper realized he had ahold of Penny, that she had put on the brakes, they were down the stairs and in the parking lot.

Harper grabbed the shovel that had been used to clean the porch stairs, and maybe her brain had stopped thinking, but—

Well, it was just like that time with Jenna on the playground. No, she wasn't going to let someone get away with bullying. She launched herself at Kyle.

Good thing Penelope ducked.

The blow broke her friend free from Kyle, and Penelope spun, tried to run back to the house, but Kyle lunged for her, grabbed her, and somehow in there, managed to send a fist into her pretty face.

Blood. And Harper lost it. She hit him again, this time across the back, and his legs buckled.

But he turned and grabbed hold of the shovel, ripping it out of her hands.

Run!

Her only thought. And maybe she should have aimed for the house, but no, Kyle stood between her and the front porch. So Harper turned and fled, still wearing her pumps, which immediately morphed into skates.

She slipped, landed on all fours, then scampered up as she saw Kyle push Penelope so hard she hit the porch.

Then he rounded, his eyes on Harper.

She kicked off her pumps and scrambled to her bare feet.

And fled.

Through the snow as the fading afternoon light cast over the crusty surface, almost illuminating her path. She didn't need a map—she knew exactly where the forest floor dented, where it opened, and how far she'd have to run to reach 458 Whispering Pines Drive.

More than a few overgrown branches hit her face, her arms, and she'd lost feeling in her feet, but she kept moving.

Her pursuer thundered through the forest behind her, breaking branches, grunting.

She had never run so fast.

The cottage sat snow-covered and dark through the trees, no

smoke from the fireplace. Only then did she remember her mother's words about this weekend's conference.

Get inside. Barricade. Call the sheriff.

Her foot broke through a crusty edge, landed on a branch, twisted.

She tumbled through the snow, slammed into a tree. Lay dazed, breathing hard.

Get up. Get . . . up!

She rolled, tried to find her feet, but her ankle screamed. *Shoot. No!*

It would not end like this. She had a better—*much* better—future planned for herself. And yes, it might not include Jack, but she didn't have to stop dreaming. Stop hoping.

"God has good things for those who trust His love for them."

Maybe it wasn't about her dreaming but about her trusting. *Yes.*

But first she had to stay alive—

Branches breaking, feet thumping. She turned.

Kyle flung himself at her. She screamed and barely dodged his grip. He landed with a *whoof!* in the snow.

For a split second she debated turning, kicking him, fighting back, but—

But she was a reporter, not a superhero. She turned and fled, her feet breaking through, her hands slapping away branches. She held in a shout at the pain screaming up her leg.

She made it to her yard before Kyle caught up. He launched himself again and took her down.

The snow cushioned her fall, but it still jarred her breath.

He rolled her over, and she tried to backhand him. He caught her wrist, shoved it down. "I just want to talk!"

"This isn't talking!"

"No, I need it to be *over*," he growled, and brought back his fist—

She closed her eyes, bracing herself.

A shout, and just like that, the man lurched off her. She opened her eyes, spotted him on the ground, rolling with another man.

In a tux.

Dark hair, big, strong, and . . .

Angry.

Jack hit Kyle once, then again, and then Conrad was there, pulling him away as Stein grabbed the man and rolled him over, subduing him.

Jack stumbled back, breathing hard, his hair wild, his expression wrecked as he looked at her.

She pushed herself up, also breathing hard.

Then he walked over and dropped to his knees in front of her. "No one gets to hurt my girl."

She launched herself into his arms, burying her face in his shoulder. His arms went around her, crushing her to himself.

"Please be okay. Please. Be okay."

She leaned back, caught his face in her hands. "I'm okay."

His eyes glistened. "I'm so sorry. I'm not really mad about the story—I'm just . . . I don't want to screw this up. I don't want to hurt you—"

"Then don't," she said, and kissed him.

And he was every bit her superhero as he caught her up and kissed her back, his mouth desperate on hers, his arms crushing her to himself.

She held on as he scooped her up, then stood up, still kissing her, as if afraid to stop.

And she drank him in, tasting, letting her heart, her dreams, believe.

He finally leaned back, breathing hard, his eyes on hers, fierce, bold.

Big Jack was back.

She smiled.

"Totally Fabio," Conrad said from behind them.

Jack kept holding her gaze, but he smiled. "You liked that, huh?"

She wasn't sure who he was talking to. So she nodded.

"Yeah, well, pay attention." He looked at his brothers.

"What? You're going to lead by example?" Doyle said, giving him a look.

He waggled his eyebrows.

Wow, she'd missed him. This Jack. The Jack that knew how to charm his way, over and over, into her heart.

He addressed Stein. "Secured?"

"Yep."

Kyle was on his feet, his hands cinched behind him with Stein's belt. In the distance, sirens whined.

Jack didn't put her down. "We have a reception to attend. I hope you weren't going anywhere important."

"Nope. Just . . . you know. Next door."

He carried her then, back down the trail between the houses, back to the big inn on the lake, the home she'd always longed for, to the family she'd always belonged with.

Boo and Oaken stood in the parlor. Penelope sat on the sofa, cleaned up, her nose still reddened and swollen. They looked up as the group came in, Jack still carrying Harper. He put her down, his hand on her waist.

Boo came over. "You okay?"

"Yes."

"What happened?"

Harper looked at Penelope. "All I can think is that Kyle faked his death."

"But why did he come back for Penelope?"

"Because he's the masked man." This from Penelope, her voice tight.

And just like that, it clicked. "He was the one in Sarah Livingston's flat. He knew about Walsh—maybe Walsh *was* there, and that . . . that made Kyle crazy with jealousy."

"Crazy enough to kill Sarah?" Oaken asked.

"Maybe it was an accident. Blunt head trauma, right?" Jack said.

"And who was in the car with you? Because you would have recognized Kyle, right?" Boo said.

Penelope nodded. "Probably the man from Turbo. A bouncer. Working for Swindle."

"So Kyle worked for Swindle too?"

"He was a lawyer with the firm that S & W employed. According to his own testimony, he introduced Sarah to Walsh. I don't know why Swindle wanted Sarah dead, but I think Kyle went there that night, saw that Walsh had been there—at least recently—and who knows what went down? Maybe it was an act of passion. Maybe something else."

"Is that why he wanted to meet with you on Tuesday?" Harper asked Penelope.

"No. He met with me to give me the thumb-drive files that were on Sarah's laptop."

"He stole it?"

"No. I think he was trying to help her until it all went south, and then she was dead and he was a suspect."

"Then who was the dead guy at the Motor Lodge?" Jack had retrieved a blanket and now draped it over Harper's shoulders.

"The guy who shot Ty. Big guy—Felix Johnson. Probably followed Kyle out to Duck Lake," Penelope said. "My guess is that he worked for Swindle too."

"Kyle might have seen what went down in the parking lot, and when Felix returned to kill him, he reacted in self-defense."

"So then who took you and Tommy?" Conrad directed his question to Harper.

"Kyle," said Harper. "I didn't recognize him in the darkness, with his glasses and hat, but my guess is that he feared Tommy could identify him."

"And he didn't know where Penelope was. He might have thought she got away," Jack said.

"But it doesn't explain who killed Sarah," Harper said.

"Probably Kyle," Jack said. "It's possible he really loved Sarah. He went over to confront her and it just . . . got out of hand. He did things that he wishes he could change."

Penelope nodded. "Maybe that's why he wanted to talk to me—"

"No, Penelope," Harper said. "I think he wanted to make you disappear. He told me that he just wanted it to be over."

Penelope swallowed, looking a little stricken. Then, that familiar determined look came over her face. "Oh, it's far from over."

Uh-oh. Harper narrowed her eyes. "Sounds like another podcast."

Her friend winked.

Boo held up a hand. "Listen. My guests are hungry. We need a grand entrance. So, wedding party, let's get going."

"Bossy much?" Jack said.

"I get it from you, Big Jack," Boo said, and then looked at Harper, at Jack. "Finally."

"Right?" Austen said, standing on the stairs.

Stein grinned.

Penelope got up, made a noise, then flopped down on the sofa. "Head rush."

Conrad went over, bent down, and picked her up in his arms.

"Hello, muscles," Penelope said, grinning.

"You looked a little wobbly."

Doyle frowned. "I feel like I missed something."

Laughter.

Harper slipped her hand into Jack's as they headed upstairs.

"Your feet okay?" he said halfway up.

"Cold."

"I'll get you some socks."

"You don't have to."

But partway through dinner, before the toasts, he left their table. Came back ten minutes later with a pair of wool socks. Knelt at her feet and helped tug them on.

Boo, from the head table, caught her eye, shook her head, and grinned.

Toasts, from Oaken's best man, Shep, and from Austen. Then cake cutting, and then the guests were asked to go downstairs. They crowded the dining room, the parlor, and the entry as Ben King played an acoustic song on his guitar, something he'd written for the occasion.

Oaken stood with his parents, holding hands with Boo.

Harper, for one, had a firm grip on Jack. Who kept looking down at her, a mysterious smile playing on his face.

What?

The caterers had cleaned the ballroom, and now the crowd headed back upstairs for dancing.

Oh. Right. The dancing.

Oh no.

Boo had changed into a short pink dress and heels, and Oaken had taken off his jacket.

"Oh no, they're doing this." That from Conrad. He glanced at Stein, who appeared stricken.

"C'mon, guys. This is for Boo." Jack turned to Harper. "Can you dance in socks?"

"Watch me."

He took her hands, gestured with his head, and the guys followed him over to the side of the dance floor. Then he leaned down, put his voice to her ear. "Trust me."

Oaken had taken his position, to the cheers of the crowd, Boo on the other side of the room. The music started, and Harper watched as Boo swung her cute little pink dress.

Who was this woman? Boo had found a peace inside herself, or maybe outside herself, that radiated through her body, her smile.

And when she looked at Oaken, the entire room lit up.

The deep tenor stepped up to the mic. "Now I've had the time of my life . . ."

Oaken turned to Boo, beckoning her just like Swayze, and she smiled, swung her dress, shrugged.

Laughed as he walked over and took her into his arms.

The crowd hooted.

Then he moved her in front of him, put her arm up, trailed his down her side, then grabbed her hand, and suddenly, the room exploded in wild cheering, as they started to dance. Crisp and sharp, every step nailed—the twirls, the shimmies, the turns, even the side lift.

"Wow," Austen said, laughing, covering over her mouth.

Oaken kissed Boo's hand, turned, and started dancing toward the wedding party.

Oh, Harper didn't remember the moves. *What*—

"Just follow me."

She looked up at Jack.

He smiled, mischief in his eyes, then stepped in front of her. He glanced at Conrad, then Stein and Doyle.

They shrugged.

Oaken had danced over, turned, and then—

What? Jack stepped out behind him, with the music. Step, step, step, step, to the side, back. Repeat. Julian's instructions in her head, Jack and his brothers working it out.

She couldn't move, watching them nail the steps.

Austen, behind her, also stilled.

London stepped back, giving Shep room, and Penelope sat at the table, laughing, an ice pack on her nose.

Step, step, step, kick, ball change. Glance over the shoulder. Jack winked, turned back.

The music swelled, and even Boo had her hands over her mouth, her dress swishing to the music.

Apparently, the Kingston boys—and rest of the groomsmen—could dance.

When they'd had time to learn the moves, Harper couldn't guess, but Jack led them out, right, left, two little hip rolls, and then more steps, more hip rolls, a twirl, and Julian's words simply flew right out of her head.

Instead, she watched Jack become everything she'd imagined. Laughing, leading his brothers, joining in with the family that needed him.

He and Stein walked over to Boo, pulled her toward Oaken, and Boo launched herself into Oaken's outstretched arms.

Bam.

The crowd took the house down, cheering, the band still playing, and Jack danced over, pulled Harper onto the floor.

"I don't know how to do that hip thing," she said, but he laughed and put her arms around his neck.

"Just hold on, Harper. I got this."

"Oh no, that's how it's going to be?"

He laughed again, then bent down and kissed her. In front of the entire world. Or at least it felt like it.

And then he drew her in close, and they danced.

———•———

Research mattered. A girl did enough research and she could fabricate a digital invitation and use it, along with her ID, to get past the hired security at the gate.

Sure, they had a list. Emberly tried to help them find her name, getting out of her car, shivering by the side of the road in her dress pants and white cashmere coat—a find at the local thrift store—as other guests squeezed by the tall snowdrifts. She just kept apologizing and then, bingo—as she pointed to the name, she "accidentally" knocked the man's tablet into the snow, crashing the program, and he bent to retrieve it, trying to reboot it.

Then she waved at a "friend," who waved back—a reflex—and *bam*, the security guard waved her in.

And that was how it was done.

She'd left her coat in the car and walked in with her gift behind superstar Ben King and his wife. She put it down on the dining-room table, already piled high, next to a package from Glo and Tate Marshall. She remembered them from the big trial of Glo's mother, the former VP, a few years ago.

But terrorists just didn't give up. And tonight, Stone was going down.

Although, for a moment before she'd walked upstairs to where the music had started, she'd enjoyed the view from the back windows of the gorgeous inn. The setting sun turned the snow on the lake a deep, variegated amber with pink edges, the evergreens near the shoreline and in the yard frosted with white.

Not a terrible place to live.

She'd headed upstairs then, to the reception, on the hunt for Stone.

He sat near the front, at a table with the Fox family—handsome, suave, charming. A real chiseler.

It was then that the wedding party came in, but she ignored them, her gaze on Stone.

He used his cell at least twice, then dropped it into his suit pocket, his guard clearly down.

She waited until everyone sat, then found a table with an empty chair. Someone named Brett.

Quail, a fig and goat-cheese salad, wild-mushroom risotto, cranberry compote, baby carrots, beets roasted with thyme and honey, and a couple offerings of wine that she turned down.

Then toasts, and she kept her gaze on Stone.

The caterers asked them to exit while they cleared the tables, and fate couldn't have played a better hand. She just happened to scoot in behind Stone as they filed out and didn't even have to be the one to bump into him. Another woman did the honors and then, just like that, she swiped the phone and dropped it into her pants pocket.

The main-floor bathroom had a line, so that hideout wouldn't work. She spotted a small library slash office off the great room.

It practically beckoned her inside. She went in, closed the door, and set the phone on a writing desk by the window. Then she took out her own phone, hooked the two up—a cable was faster than Bluetooth—and started the download of the contents of Stone's phone.

From here, she spotted another house, just as stately, down the road, and yet two more farther on. A carriage house sat between them with its own stacked-stone chimney, clearly as well loved as the other homes.

Some people had no idea how the rest of the world lived.

Ten long minutes. Finally the phone dinged, and she walked out of the room.

And that's when the plan died. She'd stuck his phone back in her pocket, but . . . well, now she had to return it if she didn't want him asking big questions.

But as she stood in the foyer, she spotted Declan Stone shaking hands with his hosts, the Kingston elders, and then . . .

He walked out the door.

She couldn't rightly run after him shouting, "Your phone, your phone!"

Now what?

The guests had returned upstairs, and clapping sounded, along with music. *Wait.* Was that the song from *Dirty Dancing*? No, they were not doing the dance—

She headed back upstairs, not sure what else to do, and stood at the door, her mouth just a little ajar as she watched the wedding party—Stein included—dance out the song.

He didn't look injured to her. In fact, the man seemed perfectly, terribly capable.

And handsome. Way, way too handsome for her good.

Except . . . and it came to her.

Stone's phone sat in her pocket. But if Steinbeck worked for him . . .

Onstage, the band continued to play, and now the crowd streamed out, laughing, clapping, couples finding the rhythm of the song.

This didn't have to be that difficult.

Please don't remember me. He probably wouldn't since she wore the long blond wig, had done her makeup different, wore heels.

She stood at the edge of the floor, as if wanting to join in but not sure . . . her eyes on Stein as he danced.

Look at me. Look—

Weird how the power of suggestion seemed to almost conjure fate. Stein indeed turned, and his gaze landed on her.

She smiled, lifted a shoulder, and he frowned, but it seemed something of curiosity . . .

Here goes nothing.

She added some rhythm to her shoulders, and a laugh, and he held out his hand to her. "Wanna dance?"

She slipped one arm around his big shoulders, nodded, and then stepped right into his embrace.

He lifted an eyebrow. "Okay."

Then he started to move, and he was no Patrick Swayze, but he could groove, his hand around her back, holding her tight to himself, moving her around the dance floor as if they belonged together.

She spotted another couple and, as he turned her, deliberately bumped into them.

"Sorry!" Stein said.

She slid the phone into his trouser pocket, then bumped her hip against it, just in case he felt the weight of the phone.

He didn't. Instead, he gathered her back up, his arm around her waist, and moved his hips with hers. His other hand made a cradle for hers, his form driving them around the dance floor.

Good. He'd find the phone, return it to Stone, and it kept the phone from *really* being stolen. They'd both think he'd picked it up by accident.

No need to get suspicious.

She matched his moves, and then, weirdly, found herself relaxing. Enjoying the lead of his strong arms, his hand around hers. He smelled of the woods and snow, a little male musk, and when he pulled her closer as the song slowed, she rested her cheek on his chest, drew her arms around him.

Forgot, just for a second, her mission, her life, even her name.

And let herself forget his.

The singer came back, reprised the ending, slowly, sweetly, and Emberly backed away, taking his hands, met his eyes. Oh, he had beautiful blue eyes.

I'm glad you're alive. She wanted to say it but parked the words inside.

Then as the song died, he twirled her out.

She let go. And without looking back, walked off the dance floor, down the stairs, and out the door.

Mission accomplished.

FIFTEEN

J ACK COULDN'T STOP SINGING OR HUMMING the song, the lyrics stuck in his head. *"I've had the time of my life."* He didn't want the night—right now—to end. And maybe that was pitiful, but . . .

The wedding was over. Tomorrow Harper would leave and . . .

"Best part of the wedding is the leftover cake." Doyle leaned against a counter in the kitchen of the inn, his tie off, his shirt sleeves rolled up, holding a massive piece of cake.

"Right?" Conrad, similarly attired, unpeeled a cupcake.

Austen had changed clothes, wearing a pair of yoga pants and a sweatshirt, helping clean up the kitchen after the catering crew left. She was bagging garbage, tying it.

"Austen—sit down," said Harper, who sat wearing the big socks Jack had snagged from the emergency supply his mother kept for guests. "We can clean tomorrow."

We? He liked how that sounded. He set down his cake plate. "I want to know who Stein was dancing with."

He cast a glance at his brother, who had come back into the house after taking out one of Austen's garbage bags.

"What?"

"That beautiful blonde you danced with tonight. Who was she?"

Stein lifted a shoulder. "She looked like she wanted to dance, so . . ." He hoisted Austen's closed bag.

"That was some dancing. Who knew you had moves?"

"We have the same mother. Same dance classes."

"No way," Conrad said. "Mom never taught us *that*."

One side of Stein's mouth lifted up as he headed out the door.

"I want to know how you learned the crew dance, Jack," Harper said. She had finished off another cupcake too.

"YouTube video. Last night. Over and over."

"He practiced in the bathroom. The light was on after midnight," Conrad added. "Always has to be the best."

Jack gave them an *of course* lift of his shoulder.

Even Harper laughed.

And everything inside him longed to walk across the room, take her in his arms, and tell her he loved her.

Loved, yes. Enough lying to himself. He loved Harper Malone. And if that meant him moving to Nashville and setting up camp . . . well, there were plenty of lost people in the South, right?

Maybe he'd even take the bar. Again.

Doyle set down his plate. "So, Declan Stone offered me a job."

A beat, during which Stein walked back into the house, dragging the night and cold with him. He stamped off his boots. "The stars are out. It's a beautiful night for broomball."

Everyone looked at him, then back at Doyle.

"What kind of job?" Jack asked.

"His foundation runs an orphanage down on the island of Mariposa, in the Caribbean. He needs a director, and I need a change."

More silence.

"But I can't leave Mom and Dad with this place, alone." He stuck his hands in his pockets, then pointedly looked at Jack.

What? "Oh . . . bro."

"You should stay." This from Harper. She was nodding, something alight in her eyes. "You don't have a home, and maybe in the meantime you could buy a new bus, fix it up—"

"What are you talking about?" Austen said. "Jack's loaded. He's got a home in Florida, near the beach, a boat, vintage cars—"

Jack held up a hand. Too late—Harper's eyes widened.

"And here I was worried you were homeless."

"This is my home." The words just sort of slipped out.

More silence, and then Austen smiled at him. "Yeah, it is. Like that needlepoint Mom has, right? Near or far, wherever we are, all roads lead to home."

His gaze held Harper's as he nodded. *Stay here, with me, build a home.* The thought pulsed inside him. But how could he ask her to give up her life in Nashville?

But . . . maybe he didn't have to have the answers. Maybe, just like his dad had said, he should stop trying to figure out what he was supposed to do and simply let God work in him to do whatever came next. *"Then, and only then, will you truly stop searching."*

"Yeah," he said, his gaze still on Harper's. "I could stay for a while."

Harper smiled, warmth in her eyes. So, he'd said something right.

"Thanks, bro," Doyle said. "I have a few weeks before I'm going to fly out, so I'll teach you the ropes."

"I think I can figure out how to stack firewood and shovel the driveway," Jack said. "Since I'm the one who taught it to you."

Laughter, and Doyle rolled his eyes.

Conrad's phone buzzed and he pulled it out of his pocket, thumbed it open. Made a face of approval.

"Aw, now you have to tell us who is texting you that has put that grin on your face," Doyle said.

Conrad slipped the phone back into his pocket. "Penelope.

Wants to talk to me about something." His phone buzzed again, and again he pulled it out, swiped it open.

This time his face fell. "Oh no."

"What's *oh no*?" Stein asked.

Conrad flashed the group a picture. Him carrying Penelope into the wedding reception. Someone had snapped it, put it up on Instagram with the caption—

Has the center for the Blue Ox finally found a woman to focus on?

"So, maybe not a date," Austen said. "Sorry, Con."

He dropped the phone back into his pocket, his mouth pinched.

"Sorry, bro," Stein said. "This is why I don't have social media."

"You don't have social media because you're a stick-in-the-mud," said Austen. She'd finished cleaning and now came over and slid onto the counter, next to Harper.

"Speaking of Declan Stone, didn't I see you talking to him tonight, Austen?" Doyle asked.

"Not really. We wound up in the buffet line together, and he asked me what I did and seemed a little interested, although he might have been being polite. I mean, when I say I'm a marine biologist, I get a lot of rolled eyes. It's like when people say they're a rocket scientist. It sounds a little like I'm a nine-year-old girl wanting to play with dolphins."

"But you *do* play with dolphins," said Harper.

"Actually, *sharks*," Doyle said.

Austen grinned.

But Jack was watching Stein, who'd pulled his phone—no, two phones—from his pocket. He put one down and looked at the other, frowning as he pushed the power button. "I think this is Declan Stone's phone."

Jack walked over, looked at the screen. "Is that a dog?"

"Declan's dog—died last year. He has a picture of him on his wall downstairs by his pool table." Stein set the phone on the stainless-steel island. "What am I doing with Declan Stone's phone?"

Jack held up his hands. "This mystery is on you. I'm done." He stepped up to the door. Indeed, outside, the moon had sprinkled magic onto the snow on the lake, the stars a thousand diamonds, turning the night priceless. "Anyone want a game of broomball?"

Stein glanced at him, smiled. "Really?"

"We turn on the lights, clear a rink . . ."

"I'm game," said Conrad.

"Me too." Doyle answered.

Stein shrugged. "I'll deal with the phone tomorrow." He turned. "You're going down, Big Jack."

Jack laughed. "You think so."

"I'm in," Austen said, sliding off the counter. "But only if Harper plays."

"I wouldn't miss it." Harper held Jack's eyes as she joined Austen. "But I'll need to borrow some clothes."

"I have a stash at the carriage house," Austen said. "I got you. I'll meet you at Doyle's." She headed out the door, the boys behind her.

"Grab shovels on your way to the rink," Jack said as they left. He caught Harper's hand, however, and pulled her back into the kitchen.

She looked up at him, her blue eyes big, so much in them. And he couldn't stop himself.

"I love you, Harper. I just didn't want to admit it. And maybe I wasn't ready for it either, but I am now." He nodded, took a breath. "So if it means making promises, I'm in."

"Breaking all your rules."

"So many rules." He nodded. "I'm crazy about you, Harper."

She smiled, put her hands on his chest, then wound them around his neck. "I know."

Aw. He lowered his head to kiss her, but she lifted her chin away. "Ask me."

He stilled. Ask her—what?

"Stop panicking. Ask me to stay, silly man."

Oh. Raw. Terrifying. But maybe that's how he discovered the truth—by putting his heart out there. "Please . . . stay."

She wrinkled her nose.

"I don't want to lose what I found—what we found."

"Okay, Mr. Nice Guy, I'll stay." She shrugged. "Because I love you too."

"I know."

She laughed. "Whatever. Besides, I already told Penelope I'd help do research for her podcast."

He shook his head, grinning. Wow, she smelled good, all velvety and molded to him in his arms, like she'd been made for him, and he for her.

It'd just taken them this long to find each other.

"Where do we go from here?" she said softly.

"I think you should kiss me," he said.

"So bossy." But she lifted herself up and pressed her mouth to his. Sweetly, tasting of frosting and what-ifs and the tomorrows he could already see.

The back door opened, and Stein stuck his head in. "Are you coming already? Sheesh—you're not going to make us dig this rink all by ourselves, are you?"

Jack let her go. "Right behind you." He looked down at Harper. "By the way, you still owe me a hundred bucks. Don't think I'm letting you off the hook."

And as she laughed, he swooped her up and carried her out the door and into the gorgeous, starry, magical night.

Bonus Epilogue

Thank you for reading *Jack*. I hope you loved the story. Find out what happens next with a Bonus Epilogue, a special gift, available only to my newsletter subscribers.

This Bonus Epilogue will not be released on any retailer platform, so scan my QR code to get your free gift. You acknowledge you are becoming a subscriber to my newsletter. Unsubscribe at any time.

Meet Conrad, a hockey star meets celebrity romance in book two of the Minnesota Kingston series.

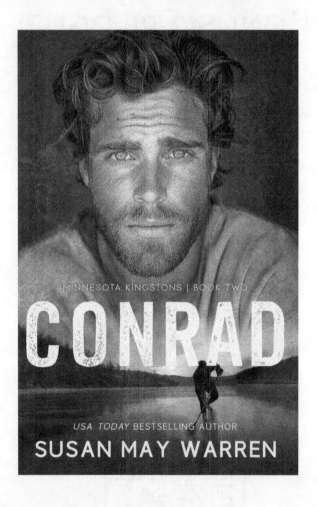

He's an unlikely bodyguard, but some-one has to keep this woman alive...

Meet Penelope Pepper: billionaire heiress, mystery podcaster, and magnet for trouble. If only she wasn't so determined to unravel the mystery of "who killed her sister's fiancé." Because clearly, given her recent kidnapping, with each episode, she's closer to the truth.

And someone wants to silence her.

Probably she needs a protector, right?

Enter Conrad Kingston, power Center for the Minnesota Blue Ox hockey team and a Guy with a Secret. Namely, the panic attacks that haunt him every time he steps into the limelight. Hanging out with Celebrity Penny is exactly NOT what he needs...

Except, Blue Ox need ticket sales and when a mix-up ropes him into playing Penelope's fake boyfriend, he's suddenly the social media darling, driving in fans to the home ice. Only problem...one of them doesn't know the dating is fake.

As Penelope's stalker draws nearer with every juicy episode, Conrad finds himself sliding from fake kisses to real protective instincts, and on thin ice with his heart. But can he find his footing before the killer catches up to Penelope?

Fake dating meets real danger, in this clean, sweet but suspenseful romance in book 2 of the Minnesota Kingstons series.

ONE

LIFE - FRIDAY NIGHT

IF THEY'D BEEN ON THE ICE, CONRAD KINGSTON, center for the Blue Ox hockey team, would have done time in the penalty box.

And pretty boy, television talk-show host Ian Fletcher would have a broken nose, maybe a few gaps where teeth used to be.

Instead, the pretty man sat across from Conrad on the set of *The Morning Brew,* the "In the Locker Room with Fletch" segment, sporting a perfectly groomed fade-style haircut, blue eyes, and a too-wide smile, prying into Conrad's life.

This was not a locker room Conrad had ever seen, with the Chesterfield sofas, a backdrop of fake lockers, and most important, bright lights that burned into his eyes so that the cameras could capture every expression in slow motion as he went over the glass coffee table and neatly put a fist into Ian's prying piehole.

Or at least wished it.

But Conrad was working on his impulse control, at least off the ice, and using his words instead, and so far so good.

See, he could play nicely.

"So, do you have a date for tonight's event?" Ian asked, waggling his eyebrows. "Seems to me that you might have a lineup after your centerfold."

"It's not the centerfold," Conrad growled.

"Sorry. Mr. *June.*"

He should have expected the too-personal, off-script questions, what with his half-naked picture on the screen behind him. He couldn't look at the photo.

One more of his many, *many*, bad yeses.

Instead, of course, he smiled. "Maybe we talk about the charity event tonight."

"Of course." Fletch leaned back, crossed his legs, his grin a sort of victory pump.

Please. Just thirty seconds without the cameras—

No, no. No. The last thing he needed was a splash on social media about King Con being unhinged. Not with the trade season still alive.

Conrad flicked his wrist and managed a glance at his Rolex Daytona. Four more minutes, and then he could flee—

"I've heard tonight's auction already has bids in the triple digits. Everyone wants a piece of Mr.—"

"It's really about raising money for the kids who've been affected by crime."

Something of challenge flashed in Ian's eyes, but Conrad didn't flinch.

"EmPowerPlay. Play strong, heal stronger, right?"

"Exactly." Conrad kept his smile, tried to recall what Felicity had told him to say. "EmPowerPlay is dedicated to empowering young victims of crime by facilitating their involvement in sports. We fund local sports teams, helping children build confidence and resilience, and are designed to foster emotional healing and personal growth, offering kids a constructive outlet to channel their energies and reclaim their strength after facing adversity."

Bam. Just like he'd rehearsed.

"And it was founded by the Pepper family, who are shareholders with the Blue Ox hockey team, right?"

"Apparently." He refused to let Penelope Pepper flash into his brain, although the memory of her in his arms a month ago, after the craziness at his sister Boo's wedding, had done a little number on him. Occupied his brain for far too long.

She'd texted him once, asking to meet for dinner. He'd promptly gone on the road for nearly two weeks with the Ox, and when he'd returned, she hadn't answered his reply text.

So, whatever.

Still.

Nope. Not going back there.

"And you've *met* the Peppers, or at least Penelope." Ian grinned and glanced at the screen behind him, and Conrad tightened his jaw at a bootleg paparazzi picture of exactly his memory—him carrying Penelope up the stairs into the wedding reception after she'd been attacked in the parking lot.

Great. He kept his gaze even, smiled. "She needed a lift."

Ian laughed. "Ah, that's a good one, King Con." He turned to the cameras, somewhere out in the darkness and finger quoted the words. "Just like the lift you gave to Roxie Hartwell."

Aw, shoot. That's what he got for trying to be clever.

His mouth tightened. "That was different."

"Right. That was Tyler Anderson's girlfriend. Bit of a messy dustup there, if I remember right." He winked at Conrad.

Conrad just needed ten seconds. *Less.*

He lifted a shoulder. "Just a misunderstanding. Torch and I figured it out."

"Didn't you take a restraining order out on Roxie?"

He said nothing.

"And then there was that fight on the ice—"

"That's in the past."

"Maybe not"—Ian leaned forward—"given last night's game. You deliberately kept the puck three times when Torch was open, and took failed shots on goal." His smile dimmed. "Are you at all worried about the fact that your contract expires after this season?"

"Listen, it's a fast game, and Torch wasn't as open as you'd think." Conrad's smile had also vanished. "And no, I'm not worried."

Really. He and Torch had ironed out the misunderstanding long before social media made it a deal. Bros over—well, ice bunnies.

Ian held up his hands, as if surrendering. "Just wondering, given the fact that rookie Justin Blake scored for the win."

"Blade is a solid young player, great potential." Oh, Felicity would be so proud of him.

"And a center, ready to take your spot."

Maybe those were veneers. Conrad had a couple of his own veneers, for different reasons.

"It's Coach Jacobsen's call. I'm just there to play hockey." He looked at the camera, gave them a photoshoot smile. "The calendars are available at the Minnesota Blue Ox website—"

"Right," Ian said, following Conrad's lead. "Visit the website to donate or volunteer." He turned back to Conrad. "Thanks for being here today." He stretched out his hand.

Conrad took it. Gave him a firm hold. Added a squeeze.

Ian's eyes flashed and Conrad let go, then waved to the camera.

"And we're out," said a voice in the shadows, and Conrad stood up, ripped off the mic, turned to Ian.

Ian stood also, his smile gone.

And oh, the urge—

No. Impulses always turned to regrets.

Conrad shook his head, headed off the set.

"All press is good press," Ian shouted after him.

A PA met him. "Mic?"

He dropped the mess into her hands and stormed out into the hallway. Ian stayed on set, probably saving his life.

"I thought that went great." Felicity Grant stood in the hallway, holding two cups of coffee, wearing an earpod, her blond hair cut short, an athletic build. She'd played women's hockey at the U of M, and of course knew the sport well enough to talk shop with the players. Now, she shoved a coffee into his hand. "Just breathe."

Conrad headed down the hallway toward the greenroom. "None of those questions were in the pre-interview chat."

"He does that." She followed him inside and stood at the open door as he grabbed a couple wet wipes and ran them over his face. Makeup coated the cloths, and he scrubbed under his chin, hating how it stained his dress shirt.

"I'm never doing this again." He threw down the cloths and grabbed his coat, headed for the door.

Felicity put out her hand and even stepped in front of him. "Yes, you will." She arched a brow. "Attendance is down, and a little good will from our starting center doesn't hurt. You were handsome and fabulous, and who cares what Ian says—you got our message out. Live above it."

"I hate the press. Torch wasn't even dating Roxie—"

"I know. But drama sells." She lifted a shoulder.

His gut tightened. "Wait—you didn't . . . I mean . . ." He met her eyes. "You weren't the one who called the cops that night, right?"

Her mouth opened. "And possibly get you pulled over for DUI?"

"I don't drink."

She smiled. "I know."

He frowned, narrowed his eyes. "That photo with her made me shut down my Instagram account."

"I know. I set up the new one, remember?"

He did know. "Just—no drama tonight, okay? I don't even want to be there."

"You have to be there. It's required in your contract."

"I know. I just . . . Are they really auctioning off *dates*? C'mon—the 1990s called and they want their charity gimmicks back."

She laughed. "It's not a date. It's a seat at the table. Calm down."

"It's hard to stay calm about being property." He stepped past her, headed down the hall.

"You're a professional athlete," she called after him. "Of course you're property!"

He took a sip of the coffee, made a face, and dumped it into the garbage on his way out of the building. The Charger sat in the lot under a dour gray mid-February sky, the air brisk, the snow piles grimy. Winter refused to surrender, a forecast of snow and ice over the next week, which made it uberfun to live in Minnesota.

He got in, turned the car on, and let the motor rumble a moment, the heat turning from ice-cold to warm.

Maybe he should visit his sister Austen down in the Keys during his next game bye week.

The sun hung low, casting late afternoon shadows over the river as he drove out of the city, into uptown, and to his remodeled mid-century-modern home on W 24th, near Triangle Park in south Minneapolis.

Black exterior, angled roofline, too many floor-to-ceiling windows, and inside, despite the hardwood flooring and beamed ceiling, the place felt too austere, too modern.

Another yes he should have thought through.

He pulled into the underground garage, got out, and took the elevator up to the main floor. Amber sunlight streaked the white wooden floor, the bouclé sofa, the concrete countertops. He picked up a remote and shut the shades to the street, then voice activated his audio system.

He had his shirt unbuttoned and off, spraying on stain remover as Tommy Emmanuel came on, plucking out a rendition of "How Deep Is Your Love" on his acoustic guitar.

Breathe.

The sunlight had found Conrad's master bedroom through the transom windows, but the picture window (covered in a one-way film that his brother Doyle had helped him install) overlooked the back of his property and Cedar Lake, still snow covered.

Any day the cold would break, and the thaw could turn the ice on a lake deceptively lethal, cracking and snapping as the currents beneath awoke. But for now it was a glistening, brittle beauty under the twilight hues.

He threw the shirt in a hamper, jumped in the shower, and felt recovered by the time he emerged, donned a towel, and leaned over the sink for a beard trim. His cell buzzed from the bedroom, and he recognized Jack's assigned ringtone—"Go Your Own Way," Fleetwood Mac.

Although recently Jack had decided to put down roots at the family homestead some sixty miles west, at least until he sorted out his relationship with reporter Harper Malone. So maybe Conrad needed to change up songs.

Maybe "Home," by Daughtry.

Video call. He thumbed it open. "'Sup, bro?" He turned his video off, left the call on speaker.

Jack sat in the kitchen of The Norbert, one of the heritage homes their parents rented out on the King's Inn property.

Jack's dark hair lived below his ears and had its own mind, just like Jack. He wore a flannel shirt and a dark grizzle of beard, the perfect look for a handyman, despite his real job as a finder of all things lost.

His most recent finds had been himself, forgiveness, and a second chance with the girl next door he'd never forgotten. And a job, taking over for little bro Doyle, who took care of the grounds and lived in The Norbert. For now.

Apparently, Doyle had decided it was time to escape his grief and the broken dreams of the past, and start new. He hadn't yet left for the Caribbean, but his mother planned a sendoff party next weekend.

About time, really.

"So, just a heads-up," Jack said in greeting. "Penelope is going to be at tonight's gig."

Conrad had been filing through his suits—not the Armani, of course, but maybe the cashmere-wool charcoal Canali Kei. He pulled out the jacket. Slim fit.

He'd put on some muscle since he'd purchased this a couple years ago.

"I figured, since it's her family's gig." He put the suit back, pulled out the HUGO BOSS. "The Pepper Foundation started EmPowerPlay, and they're sponsoring the event."

"You two ever connect?"

Again wool, slim fit. And boring. He put the suit coat back. "No. I texted her after I got back from Nashville. She never answered."

"Probably because she's still working on her murder podcast."

He pulled out the Tom Ford windowpane. He'd worn it for the Blue Ox Man of the Year awards ceremony last year. Understated. Elegant.

"Her only lead in the Sarah Livingston case—Kyle Brunley was killed the night he posted bail," Jack said.

Conrad stilled, his hand on the midnight blue velvet and silk Brioni smoking jacket. "Wait. Kyle Brunley is dead? The guy who tried to kidnap her and Harper?"

Penelope had vanished from his sister's wedding event last month in a move many pegged as a PR gimmick for her show. *Nope.* Conrad might never forget her worn but tough-edged expression when she'd been found . . . having escaped on her own and hidden out.

"Yep. He was arraigned, posted bail, and the next day, vanished. They found him in his car about a week ago in a ditch off Marsh Lake Road. Harper told me about it last night at dinner."

Conrad carried the smoking jacket out to the bedroom. "That's the third person murdered in the Sarah Livingston case."

"If you don't include Sarah."

"Right."

"Harper's worried about Penelope. Penelope hasn't answered her texts either, so . . . track her down, and find out how she's doing."

Conrad found a light blue shirt, matching trousers. "My bet is that she's just fine. She's smart, resourceful, and tough. After all, she did survive four days in a freezing ice house—"

"For *ratings.*"

Well, not quite, but Conrad could see why Jack, who'd found her, might think that.

"Which makes a guy wonder just what else she'd do for her story," Jack continued.

Conrad pulled on a T-shirt shirt, then the dress shirt. "I'm not sure what I can do. She's got her own mind."

"Just . . . I don't know. Harper asked me to call you. She seems to think that Penelope likes you."

He pulled on the trousers. Still a good fit. Then he returned to his wardrobe and opened his tie drawer. Pulled out a black satin bow tie and flipped up his collar. "Fine. Sure. But let's not overthink this. I have a full roster of games, and I need to be on point if I hope to be in a position to renegotiate this summer. And frankly, Penelope is . . . She's all over social media. I'm not going there again, bro." He flipped down his collar. Smoothed it out. "Besides, I doubt she has any bandwidth in her life for anyone extra."

"Even Mr. June?"

He stilled, walked out to the bed and picked up the phone. Jack was grinning.

Conrad turned on his own video.

Jack raised an eyebrow as Conrad's mug showed up. "Wow. Seriously?"

"I swear to you, if I see one calendar at the King's Inn—"

"Dude. I caught your "In the Locker Room with Fletch." You're going to sell truckloads. Did you wax before you—"

Conrad hung up. Threw the phone on the bed. Clenched his fists for a second, staring into the mirror.

The sweat broke out along his spine, his heart slamming against his chest.

And just for a second, the world narrowed.

Breathe. He sank down on the bed. Put his hands on the cool comforter. *In. Out.*

Visualize. His eyes opened, his gaze finding the picture of the sailboat, the one pitched at an angle, the splash of the deep blue lake catching the sun. He sat holding the tiller, hair wild, no beard, barefoot.

He could smell it. Lake water. Wind. Spray.

His heartbeat softened. More breaths.

Getting up, he went to the bathroom, downed a glass of water. It sat in his gut without returning. *So far so good.*

He just might live through this night without being the center of paparazzi attention. *Please.*

The Daytona Rolex said he had thirty minutes before the event—so great, he'd be late. Maybe he could slip in the back.

Except, as he drove up to the event—at the historic Frederick mansion in Minneapolis—the coned entry directed him to the valet entrance.

He surrendered his keys to some youngster in a suit. "Don't dent anything."

The kid—okay, probably a college student—nodded and Conrad got in line to enter the building. He recognized a few of the other Blue Ox players—rookie Justin, of course, grinning for the press, and Wyatt Marshall, their goalie, with his pretty, petite wife, and player Kalen Boomer, and even Coach Jace with his wife, Eden.

A heater blasted the portico, so he wasn't cold as he stood at the bottom of the grand staircase.

A plaque near the walk said the place had been built in the late 1800s. It bore an Italian Renaissance aura, with pillars flanking the doorway of the covered entrance.

Massive floral arrangements in the blue and white of the Blue Ox stood in urns on either side of the door. And from the terrace over the entrance hung a banner with the EmPowerPlay logo.

Music spilled out—Pharrell Williams's "Happy."

This might not be a disaster. He'd get inside, glad-hand a few donors, eat some shrimp cocktail, give Coach Jace a thumbs-up, endure dinner small talk, and then skedaddle.

No harm, no foul, and he'd escape the media chaos.

Except as he neared the door—*no. Oh no.*

Inside the foyer, larger-than-life posters of the calendar models flanked the stairway leading up to the ballroom, and even from here . . .

He looked like he might belong in a *Magic Mike* movie. Shirtless, his body photoshopped into a tan. What hockey player sported a tan in April (when they'd taken the shots)? His beard was tangled, the red hues accented, his hair mussed, and *good grief,* they'd added blue to his eyes.

Forget Magic Mike—he could be on some sordid magazine cover, or worse a romance novel.

No, he couldn't do this—

He turned, and nearly plowed over—

"Conrad!"

Penelope Pepper. She held her hands up, catching his wrists, balancing herself a little.

If he thought he'd lost his breath before . . . He just stared at her, not sure if his thundering heartbeat was panic or . . . awe.

He'd forgotten—or maybe simply tried to—the effect she had on him. The high cheekbones that framed the curve of her face, those golden brown eyes, dark on the outside, radiating to a glimmer of light around the irises, her full, shaped lips, now smiling.

She wore her dark hair swept back and up, trickling in chocolate waves around her slender neck. A white faux-fur shawl wrapped over a white V-necked silk top with puffy sleeves, and a belted long teal skirt. And she smelled—well, not quite exotic, but exciting and fresh and tempting.

And right then, something he'd dismissed awoke inside him.

"Penelope," he managed, aware of her hands on his wrists. He turned them and grabbed hers back. "I'm sorry—I didn't mean to plow you over."

"I missed you too, Con." She laughed, pushed out of his grasp and smoothed her hands on his chest. "And I should know better than to stand too close to a Blue Ox." Then she winked, and *yes, Jack,* Penelope seemed *Just. Fine.* "A gal can get knocked over way too easily."

He had no words for that.

She peered past him toward the foyer, and her eyes widened, her mouth opening to a perfect O. "I see the problem."

"A poster-sized problem."

Then, just like that, she turned him around, stepped up beside him and slipped her hand around his arm. "Steady on, soldier. This is for the kids." Then she looked up and winked. "Don't worry, I got you."

Cameras flashed as she walked him into the event.

And he didn't know whether to hold on, or run.

Note to Reader

Thank you again for reading Jack! I hope you enjoyed his homecoming and meeting the amazing, fun Minnesota Kingstons!

Stay tuned for more Kingston family adventures! There are 4 more books in this series...so much fun. So much *trouble* (and all the beautiful romances!)

If you enjoyed Jack, would you be willing to do me a favor? **Head over to the product page and leave a review.** It doesn't have to be lengthy—just a few words to let other readers know what to expect. (But please, no spoilers! We don't want to spoil the fun for others!)

I am so grateful for the incredible team that surrounds me. A sincere thank you to my editors, Anne Horch and Rel Mollet, for their impeccable and invaluable feedback. Your unique touch truly enhances these stories, and I am deeply appreciative of your efforts.

A warm embrace to my writing partner, Rachel Hauck, and to the brilliant Sarah Erredge, who are always ready to explore new ideas with me, no matter how many questions I may have. Your support is priceless.

A heartfelt acknowledgment to my husband, Andrew, for all the technical questions. I come to him with...I have this problem... and he solves it. Brilliant man.

Cheers to Emilie Haney for her stunning cover designs that create the perfect initial impact for my books, and to Tari Faris, who makes the interiors just as captivating.

Thank you, Katie Donovan, for your meticulous proofreading skills, especially when we're up against tight deadlines.

I am deeply thankful to each of you for your contributions. You're the dream team!

To my amazing reader friends— thank you for embracing my books. It's my sincere hope that the time you spend with my characters enriches your life in some way. I'd love to hear your thoughts—not just about this book, but about any characters or adventures you'd like to explore in future stories. Feel free to reach out at susan@susanmaywarren.com.

If you're interested in news about what's next, upcoming releases, exclusive freebies, and sneak peeks, I invite you to sign up for my weekly newsletter at susanmaywarren.com, or simply scan the QR code provided.

Onto Conrad...!

XO!

Susie May

More Books by Susan May Warren

Most recent to the beginning of the epic lineup, in reading order.

ALASKA AIR ONE RESCUE
One Last Shot
One Last Chance
One Last Promise
One Last Stand

THE MINNESOTA MARSHALLS
Fraser
Jonas
Ned
Iris
Creed

THE EPIC STORY OF RJ AND YORK
Out of the Night
I Will Find You
No Matter the Cost

SKY KING RANCH
Sunrise
Sunburst
Sundown

GLOBAL SEARCH AND RESCUE
The Way of the Brave
The Heart of a Hero
The Price of Valor

THE MONTANA MARSHALLS
Knox
Tate
Ford
Wyatt
Ruby Jane

Montana Rescue

If Ever I Would Leave You (novella prequel)
Wild Montana Skies
Rescue Me
A Matter of Trust
Crossfire (novella)
Troubled Waters
Storm Front
Wait for Me

Montana Fire

Where There's Smoke (Summer of Fire)
Playing with Fire (Summer of Fire)
Burnin' For You (Summer of Fire)
Oh, The Weather Outside is Frightful (Christmas novella)
I'll be There (Montana Fire/Deep Haven crossover)
Light My Fire (Summer of the Burning Sky)
The Heat is On (Summer of the Burning Sky)
Some Like it Hot (Summer of the Burning Sky)
You Don't Have to Be a Star (Montana Fire spin-off)

The True Lies of Rembrandt Stone

Cast the First Stone
No Unturned Stone
Sticks and Stone
Set in Stone
Blood from a Stone
Heart of Stone

A complete list of Susan's novels can be found at
susanmaywarren.com/novels/bibliography/.

About the Author

Susan May Warren is the USA Today bestselling author of over 90 novels with more than 1.5 million books sold, including the Global Search and Rescue and the Montana Rescue series. Winner of a RITA Award and multiple Christy and Carol Awards, as well as the HOLT Medallion and numerous Readers' Choice Awards, Susan makes her home in Minnesota.

Visit her at www.susanmaywarren.com.